MW00613639

PRAISE FOR *THE CREST*

The Crest is a well-researched page-turner set in Prussia, Germany in 1917. It follows the career of an idealistic, patriotic young man, Gerhard, as he leaves home to fight for Kaiser Wilhelm and the Fatherland. The story that unfolds is rich in historical detail and suspense. It was a pleasure to read Jerena Tobiasen's novel both for its vivid imagery, vibrant prose and well developed characters.

~ **Roberta Rich,**
author of *The Midwife of Venice*, *The Harem Midwife*, and *A Trial in Venice*

We find in *The Crest* by Jerena Tobiasen a well written novel spanning the many years of that troubled era that included the 20th century's two great world wars. It touches you deeply in its illustrations of the hardships soldiers endured in their innocent belief that they were serving their countries and the families who were waiting for their return.

In communities away from the killing fields, life moves on and people work together: celebrating different occasions, getting married, having children. Yet at the same time they anxiously fear for their future as warmongering leaders fight among themselves over territory and resources, sacrificing misled civilians caught in the middle.

Jerena skillfully crafts representations of two such different settings to perfection: the painful and visceral realities of war, and beautiful portrayals of love, life and nurturing. Let's all encourage the latter for all of Earth.

Well done and worth the read.

~ **Nasreen Pejvack,**
author of *Amity, Paradise of the Downcasts* and *Waiting.*

The Crest is an exceptionally well-written and detailed book. It follows the life of a German family through World War I and World War II-- not something you read every day. The details are exquisite. I imagine that the author did a fair amount of research to get them right. If you like war stories with a human angle or sprawling family sagas, you will love this first book in the Lange family story.

~ **Malcolm van Delst,**
author of *Do the Wrong Thing*

ALSO BY JERENA TOBIASEN

THE PROPHECY SAGA
The Crest
The Emerald

THE
DESTINY
THE PROPHECY BOOK III

JERENA TOBIASEN

The Destiny
Copyright © 2019 by Jerena Tobiasen

Cover Design: Ana Chabrand,
Chabrand Design House
www.anachabrand.com
Author Photo: Robert M. Douglas,
Copyright © 2018
Interior Formatting: Iryna Spica, Spica Book Design
www.spicabookdesign.com

ISBNs:
978-1-77374-037-9 (Print)
978-1-77374-038-6 (E-book)

For Gerd.

ACKNOWLEDGEMENTS

While the seed of my saga began with the kidnapping of a friend's son some thirty years ago, this story is my own. Along the way, I have been inspired by others and wish to acknowledge their contributions, including:

- Ilse-Renata Schickor, who told me how, as a young woman, she put her trust in her employer so that he could lead her to safety in the spring of 1945, barely escaping the Russian invasion.
- Gerd, Ilse-Renata's son, who shared tales of life in post-World War II, Germany, and the shenanigans that can occur in an all-boys private school. Together, Gerd and Ilse-Renata told me the story of his father's escape from a prisoner of war camp.

- My parents, from whom I learned the art of storytelling.
- Henry Fast, who edited my use of the German language.
- Ben Coles of Cascadia Author Services, who read my manuscripts and gave me hope, and his gang of talent, who helped turn my manuscripts into novels.
- And last, but certainly not least, my wonderful husband, Robert McKellar Douglas, an artist with vision. He not only encouraged me while I wrote, but helped me with research, travelled with me, listened as I bounced ideas around, read my scenes when requested, and provided feedback when I needed it; he is the one who inspired me to keep writing better. "Good photographs are images of the exceptional," he says. "A great painting highlights the universal." I sincerely hope that my readers feel *The Prophecy* delivers an exceptional image that highlights the universal.

TABLE OF CONTENTS

PART I

AGE
OF INNOCENCE

MIRIAM

CHAPTER ONE

Living with a mother who had chosen prostitution as a career was the norm for Mina Kota and, when her mother suggested that she be trained to follow in her footsteps, Mina objected only because she was still in school.

"I'll just teach you about the process," her mother Punita assured her, "and set you up with a patron. By the time you graduate, you will have experience enough to start working in the window. You've already told me about things that are happening in your school. I want you to be introduced to sexual intercourse with kindness and respect, as I was."

Mina contemplated her mother's suggestion and finally agreed. *Perhaps Mama is right. I certainly don't want to end up like other girls.*

At school, Mina had heard rumours of invasive fondling on a trolley late at night, while a boy's dirty, unkempt fingers forced their way into a warm slick goal, his other hand working briskly in his own trousers. Another encounter ended in a garden shed with the girl bent over a work table and rhythmically rammed from behind. Yet another classmate had been braced against a tree in a secluded spot at the park, raked in rhythm with false terms of endearment, tree bark digging into her bared backside. And these rumours were merely a selection.

Those girls, Mina observed, were subjected to sneers from the boys at school. They realized too late that the boy—or boys—wanted nothing more than another story to tell, another conquest. Most of the girls, sullied by their experiences, claimed they would never speak to a boy again. A few said they had enjoyed the experience and arranged further encounters.

⚜

"Dr. Hendrik has recommended a young man who says he's interested in a patronage," Punita announced a few days later. "His name is Willem van Bosch. He's an unmarried gentleman, whose family business requires him to travel frequently. He is from a long line of merchants who buy and sell goods internationally."

"Mama, does he have to be old?"

"Why do you think he's old?"

"If he's a friend of Dr. Hendrik—"

"He's not. He is the son of an acquaintance, and he's only twenty-three."

"Oh." Mina hung her head, abashed at her outburst.

"The doctor says the young man has no interest in marriage at the moment, and he is intrigued at the idea of a patronage. Remember, Mina, the window work will only be temporary. I want better for us. My hope is that, if we work together and save our money, we'll be able to move away from De Wallen. That's the dream that dear

Mathilde and I had. Her untimely death has delayed it, but it's not forgotten. In the meantime, remember that the income is better than any other employment, and it has put food on our table and a roof over our heads for more than sixteen years. We survived better than most during the war, remember that too." Punita waited while her memories settled around her. "I will teach you everything you need to know, as Mathilde taught me."

"Fine," Mina huffed, "but, if I'm to be the one spreading my legs, I want a say in who's to be my patron."

"I'll arrange a meeting," Punita agreed. "But, keep in mind that finding a suitable patron is not an easy task. I believe the gentleman recommended by Dr. Hendrik to be acceptable."

"We'll see," Mina retorted.

⚘

To her surprise, Mina found Willem van Bosch both charming and handsome. He was tall and strong, with a pleasing countenance, and she found his conversation mentally stimulating. When Punita explained to both of them that there need not be love between them, Mina relaxed.

"In fact, I recommend against it," Punita stated. "Trust and respect are the important ingredients in this type of relationship. Without them, a patronage cannot be successful. By example, I can speak of my relationship with my patron—fifteen years, and never a dispute!" She paused for emphasis. "I will review my expectations with each of you. On your first engagement, you will be prepared. As Mina's dear father and I were prepared."

As promised, Punita's instructions were exemplary. The condom was flawed.

On the evening that Punita invited Willem for coffee so Mina could announce her pregnancy, Willem shared his own news first.

"M-my father announced at breakfast this morning that I am to be married in the fall!" he blurted. "I have no say in the matter, you see. He and a long-time business colleague have determined that the marriage would be beneficial to their business." He slouched forward, hanging his head in despair. "I've met her at business functions a few times, but nothing has ever transpired that would suggest a relationship, let alone a marriage! I am so sorry, I feel as if I've let you all down."

"You haven't let anyone down, Willem," Punita assured him. "Your relationship with Mina is a patronage, not a marriage. You are free to do as you please. Will you continue your patronage, or are you suggesting an end to it?"

"I definitely want to continue it!" he replied.

During the discussion that followed, Punita suggested a compromise that appeared agreeable to all but the doctor, who had protested against the patronage in the first place, and now believed that Willem and Mina should be married.

"Why don't you continue the patronage for now," Punita said. "By the time your wedding rolls around, Willem, Mina's pregnancy will have advanced and she will need rest. Perhaps you could take a break until after the child is born and she has healed. During the break, you can take time to get to know your wife. If you wish to resume the patronage in the spring, that will be arranged. Otherwise, we'll find another patron for Mina."

While Mina and the two men came to terms with the proposal, Punita added one last condition, and extracted a promise from the three of them.

"The identity of the child's father must never be disclosed," she said. "It would complicate Willem's life unnecessarily, to say the least."

"I am so glad that I decided to keep my baby," Mina told her mother several months later. "I could never live with myself if I'd had an abortion." As she turned from the Aga Cooker with a pot of coffee in her hand, her free hand snapped to the side of her belly. "Oh! She kicked again!"

"Let me do that," Punita said, jumping up from her chair to take the coffee pot. "You sit. What makes you think it's a girl?"

"She's determined and strong, just as a girl should be," Mina smiled. "She kicks like a horse. Besides, the others keep saying so, Astrid particularly. She put a silver ring on a string and held it in front of my belly. She said the way the ring swung indicated the baby's sex." Mina lowered herself into a chair and took a sip of her milk. "Ugh! I wish I could drink coffee, but Dr. Hendrik says this is better for the baby."

"It is. You keep drinking it," Punita said. "Strong bones and teeth."

With a quiet snick, the outer door of the apartment opened inward.

"Good morning!" Astrid Hansen greeted them. "I've brought fresh bread and cheese for our breakfast." Astrid set her basket on the counter. "How lovely to see you, again—*Mevrouw* Hendrik! Married life certainly agrees with you! Will you eat bread with us?"

10

"No, thank you," Punita replied, "I ate with the doctor. Besides, I'm not staying. Eamon is with a patient. I must be off shortly to help with the delivery." She sipped her coffee, watching the petite young woman put away her purchases and prepare food for the table. Her white blonde hair curled around her face like a feathery cap. "How's the window business?"

"It's brisk," Astrid replied. "I miss Mina's help, but she'll be back to work soon from the looks of it." She sized up Mina's belly and grinned. "Then we will have a lively apartment for sure!"

"Indeed," Punita agreed. "Mina, you should rest all you can now that Willem is no longer visiting. With him away and married, you need only take care of yourself and build up your strength for the baby's arrival."

"Oddly enough," Mina said, "I miss Willem's visits. It's never just about sex with him."

"Mina, take care that you don't fall in love," Punita cautioned her daughter. "That can only lead to heartbreak."

11

"I know, Mama, but I think I can miss his company without being madly in love with him."

In response to her scrunched face, the others laughed.

"Fair enough," Punita said, rising from her chair. "It's time for me to leave you two roommates. Another child is waiting to be welcomed into this world."

CHAPTER TWO

Repairing a woman's torn flesh was Dr. Eamon Hendrik's specialty. In the De Wallen community of Amsterdam, he was renowned for stitching up a young woman in such a way that her future lovers would not suspect that the coveted nest tucked at the juncture of her legs had been torn and stretched by another man's child.

"Right then, Mina," he encouraged his patient, "one last hard push and you'll be done."

Mina summoned the last of her strength and did as she was bid. Dr. Hendrik captured the infant in his capable hands when she finally slipped free. Mina collapsed into her bed, eyes shut tight and breathing deeply.

The baby girl emerged into the world on a stormy afternoon, January 23, 1952, squalling loudly.

"Sounds like neither of us enjoyed that ordeal," Mina muttered. When her mother approached with a towel to mop Mina's brow, she pushed the hand away. "Give me a minute, Mama. I feel as though every inch of me hurts. Eighteen hours of labour was a bit much."

"I'll take it," the doctor said. Still positioned between Mina's bent legs, he reached for the towel Punita offered.

"I'll get more candles," Punita said. "Of all the nights for the power to go out!" Only two of the several candles she had lit earlier continued to burn, and less than three finger-widths of them remained, shedding meagre light.

"I'm glad we have the fire in the hearth to provide extra light and heat," she said, setting a match to more candles and placing them on the table near the doctor. Light from the candle flames danced off the green gem that hung above her breast.

In a business-like manner, the doctor tied and snipped the umbilical cord despite the dim light, wrapped the child in the towel and passed the bundle to Punita.

"Here's your granddaughter, my dear. Clean her up."

Punita had been assisting Dr. Hendrik as a birthing companion ever since their marriage the previous summer. The week before they married, she retired from her career as a prostitute and passed the window on to Mina and her roommate Astrid.

She carried the baby toward the fire, over which hung a pot of simmering water. Near it sat two baskets, one holding items needed for cleaning the child, and the other to be used as a first bed.

Wisps of steam escaped from the pot and faded up the chimney, commingling with smoke from the fire. Three adult bodies and the few candles boosted the warmth from the fire, but with only one small window, which was closed to the winter chill, the room was stuffy. Sweat pearled at Punita's temples and trickled between her small breasts. She swiped a hand across her brow to keep her vision clear.

"As soon as I've cleaned up the child and wrapped her, I'll air the room a bit. Are you all right to continue, Doctor?"

Dr. Hendrick nodded and turned back to Mina. He gently kneaded her swollen belly to encourage delivery of the afterbirth, then used a coarse rag and a bowl of water to rinse his hands.

"Thanks for the candles," he said to Punita. "I'll need them now. Mina, I apologize in advance, but I need you to be brave for a few more minutes. Almost finished."

Returning to his work between his step-daughter's knees, he tugged the table and candles closer. Next, he prepared a thread and needle and began to repair the damage caused by the birth of the mewling child.

"Do what you must, Doctor," Mina said, groaning. A moment later, she hissed as the doctor inserted the needle to make the first stitch. Although she never muttered another sound, tears flowed freely from her tightly-closed eyes.

Punita bent to place the tiny girl in the woven basket, then knelt beside it. As the doctor had taught her, she checked to ensure the baby's mouth and throat were cleared of debris, then dipped a clean rag into the pot. She used the rag to clean the baby's eyes and ears, and gently wiped her face. Taking a clean, coarser rag, she gave the slimy little body a brisk rub to remove vernix, then took another rag, warmed it in the pot of water and gently cleaned the child a second time. The baby closed her tiny fists and wailed in protest.

"Finished!" the doctor said, snipping the thread. "How are you, Mina dear?"

Mina groaned again and rolled onto her side, clutching her belly.

"I'll live, I suppose," she replied. "Mama, is she ready? Can I see her?"

"Give me two minutes," Punita replied.

JERENA TOBIASEN

Punita examined the baby carefully. All of her necessary body parts were present: ten fingers, ten toes, a cap of auburn hair, and a face of promising beauty. Punita grasped the baby's ankles in one hand and bent her knees to her belly, exposing her newborn genitals. The baby grunted and squirmed in protest, but Punita had a firm grip and continued her examination. With satisfaction, the grandmother noted the swollen labia and whitish vaginal discharge that evidenced a functioning female child.

"Shush, sweet thing," she whispered. "All is well."

Punita wrapped her granddaughter in a diaper and covered her with a new yellow blanket, then placed her back in the basket. In one efficient movement, she stood and turned back to face her daughter and the doctor. She stretched her arms to the ceiling and arched her back, moaning with the pleasure of it.

"I'll give them a thorough cleaning later," the doctor mumbled, giving his medical instruments a quick wipe. Then he placed them in his well-worn medical bag, which he had set on a nearby chair the day before.

"Well, Eamon," Punita said, nodding toward her daughter, "that was a bit of effort, but I'm certain Mina is grateful for your handiwork. When will she be able to resume work in the window?"

"Humph," he grunted in contemplation, surveying his patient. He scratched his chin, rasping the two-day growth of beard. "Mina, you'll need at least six weeks to heal. If you must work, use some of your mother's less creative techniques for a while."

"I will," Mina said with a chuckle.

"I, for one, fancy the service of one a little more ... mature." He winked at Punita with familiarity and open appreciation. "By the way, my lovely wife, you did fine work cleaning the child."

Punita reached to open the window. Feeling her nipples harden under her thin blouse as icy freshness fingered its way into the stale room, she gave her husband a flirtatious half grin. The doctor smiled in return and twitched his head toward the door that led into the adjoining room.

"I need to be away. I have to clean my instruments and restock my bag. I have two more young women awaiting their turn and I must be ready. If I'm not home when you get there, you'll know where I am." Mina's stepfather collected his coat and medical bag from the chair, and tipped his forelock to Mina, who was slowly starting to stir. Punita gazed once more at her husband as he closed the door quietly behind him.

"Now, my sweet daughter, you must sit up and prepare yourself. It's time to meet your daughter and put her to your breast." Punita approached the bed, clucking at her daughter like a mother hen. Hooking her arm through Mina's, Punita lifted her daughter to an inclined position, propping pillows around her.

"Ready yourself. I'll get the baby. She'll want to suckle."

Mina obeyed, straightening her night-gown and pushing her shoulder-length auburn hair from her face. She unbuttoned the top of her gown and sighed deeply, while her mother retrieved the dozing infant.

"Ah, poor thing. I'm sorry to wake you, but you must take your mama's breast. Doctor says so. Besides, it'll be good medicine for both of you."

The baby's eyes popped open, then quickly squeezed shut. She fussed, as if readying herself for another wail, but her grandmother was quick and, knocking the edge of the nightgown out of the way with her free hand, had a nipple in the baby's mouth before either mother or child could protest.

Punita looked at them with satisfaction. It was evident that the baby was not going to be one to refuse a meal. Tiny lips wrapped around her mother's areola and the sucking began in earnest. The first squirt of warm colostrum appeared to catch in the back of her throat, causing a momentary gag reflex—a tiny cough of surprise—but she continued, showing determination to consume every drop.

"Here, Mina, put your hand around her head for support, like this, and your other hand just there. When she releases this side, switch her to the other if she's still hungry. It's good to use both breasts so they stay even. Your uterus will recover quicker too." Punita stood, hands on hips, and stretched her back again. "Get to know your child while I tidy up."

Punita deftly replaced puddles of wax with fresh candles and lit them, then returned the room to the orderliness it had two days prior. Mina nodded, tears of joy trickling down her cheeks, ending in small splashes on the baby's forehead,

"I'll put the kettle on," Punita said, disappearing into the kitchen. "I bet you could use a cup of tea and something to eat."

⚜

In the kitchen, Punita retrieved her well-used tarot cards from her handbag. While she waited for the kettle to boil, she shuffled them and deftly dealt them face-down onto the small dining table. She reached for the first card and flipped it face up. Frowning, she quickly turned the other cards.

Punita glanced at her wristwatch and realized that she had been away from Mina and the baby too long. *The predictions of the cards are disturbing.* She gathered the cards and hurriedly stuffed them into her handbag. *They would have me believe that Mina's sweet child will cause us trouble. I must keep an eye on her. Perhaps I'll discover a way to change her course—a hard thing to do, considering the cards don't lie, but there is still plenty of time before the trouble is supposed to start.*

The baby released the first nipple and started to fuss. As Mina had seen other mothers do, she lifted the child to her shoulder and rubbed her back until a soft belch erupted, then she turned her and proffered the second breast. The baby, still hungry, latched on with a shocking tug.

Watching her daughter suckle, Mina gently slid her finger over the downy cheek, and wondered how such a perfect creature could have grown within her. In that moment, Mina fell in love with her daughter. *I can't believe I'm a mother!*

With a full belly, the child dozed, and the second nipple popped free. Mina lifted her to her shoulder again and rubbed the tiny back. When a burp followed, she lowered the baby and cuddled her, not realizing the passage of time, until she heard her bedroom door creak open.

"I have tea and bread," Punita announced brightly, setting a tray on the small table that had recently been used by the doctor.

"How are you managing, my dear? Has the child suckled well?" Punita smiled lovingly as she bent over them to inspect for herself. "Look at my granddaughter. Is she not lovely? She looks just as you did when you were born."

Punita observed her daughter, her brown

24

eyes glistening like melted chocolate. She straightened the linen and perched on the end of the bed.

"Mina, my dear, have you thought of a name for your daughter?"

"I've thought of many," she answered, "but none of them seem to suit her. How did you choose my name?"

Punita's mind drifted, remembering the day that Mina was born.

"I named you Mina, because I loved you so much. You are the daughter of the man I loved with all of my heart." Punita's feelings shifted like quicksilver as she spoke, changing from affection, to longing, to loss. "In German, Mina means love. It has another meaning in Dutch, though. The Dutch meaning is protector. I suppose one could say that love is a form of protection, but love is the reason I chose it."

Mina heard passion in her mother's voice as she spoke of the naming. It made her proud to be Punita's daughter. She felt cherished.

"What about your name, Mama, what does Punita mean?"

Punita rested her eyes on her daughter's glowing face.

"My mother told me that Punita means sacred or pure. It is a name given to the first-born girl in every third generation, so we do not forget who we are and from where we came. Our roots are in India." She paused as if recalling her mother's words, and chuckled. "I'm not so sure about sacred, but it is abundantly clear to me that purity is not part of my life." She cast her eyes toward the baby. "Unless we take a moment to contemplate this small child here. So innocent, so unsullied by life." She reached to stroke the downy cheek again.

"One day, I heard the name Miriam in the market," Mina whispered, gazing upon her daughter's face. "A wealthy woman was passing. She held a beautiful little girl by the hand. The girl had long, golden hair that hung in shiny curls. The two of them were graceful and stylish. The mother called

26

the little girl Miriam." Mina turned to her mother. "This one will be called Miriam. I want her to be beautiful and wealthy one day, too."

"A very nice choice, my dear," Punita said. "Miriam means *beloved* in the Egyptian language, and this little one will certainly be loved." Punita's eyes moved about the bedroom. "In Hebrew, it also has a darker meaning: rebellious or disobedient. Let's hope she remains beloved."

Punita leaned once again over mother and child, first caressing Mina's cheek, as she had done so many times before, then lowered her hand to the cheek of the sleeping child. Intuitively, her free hand reached for the emerald that no longer hung from her neck. Instead, her eyes fell to where it lay glistening above her daughter's breast.

"Mina, the blessing," she urged. Mina shifted the weight of her child to allow a free hand. She grasped the emerald, glanced at her mother, then lowered her eyes to her baby's countenance.

Punita's finger stroked a miniature version of the necklace that hung from her ear lobe—one of a pair of earrings that her husband had given to her on their wedding day. "Welcome, little Miriam," she cooed, delivering the blessing. "May you have a most remarkable life."

While Mina and Miriam rested from their ordeal, Punita returned to the kitchen and spread her tarot cards again, curious to know more about her granddaughter's future. *A happy childhood*, Punita read, *to be replaced by inner conflict and turmoil. If the Water sign rules her life, she will be susceptible to moodiness, unpredictability, and lack of focus.*

Miriam, the cards warned, will be inclined to allow her mercurial personality to flow around any conflict she encountered, rather than address it. She will obsess over the things that matter most to her and dismiss those things for which she has no patience. Unless she learns discipline, she

28

will become selfish, demanding, insensitive, and rebellious.

This worries me, Punita thought. *Miriam may well fulfill the definition of her name—rebellious and disobedient. I must nurture her and help her embrace the positive influence of the Water sign.* She fingered an emerald earring and closed her eyes. *Mama, help me! Tell me what to do!*

CHAPTER THREE

"I am always amazed at how fortunate I was to meet you last summer," Mina said to Astrid. "The timing was perfect. Mama would never have married the doctor if it meant leaving me alone and pregnant."

"You offered me self-employment and an opportunity to earn far more than I would ever make working in a shop," Astrid smiled, bouncing Miriam on her knee. "Never did I expect when I came to this country that I would be an auntie too." She tickled her god-daughter under the chin and received a loud giggle as her reward. "It helps, I think, that I'm the middle of nine children, and the oldest girl. I have first-hand experience with babies."

"Unlike me," Mina replied. "I was worried about childcare while I worked, but trading shifts with you is working out, isn't it?" Mina looked into the wooden-framed mirror mounted next to the hall door and checked her lipstick, before turning to Astrid with a hopeful look.

Astrid's brilliant smile was all the answer Mina required.

"I'd better leave, or I'll be late opening!" As an afterthought, she raced back to her daughter and planted a bright red kiss on her cheek. A second one followed on Astrid's nearest available cheek.

Mama and Mathilde raised me, she thought as she closed the door. *Astrid and I can raise Miriam the same way. She will have a happy home too, especially since Willem has returned. He's such a devoted father. I'm surprised that his wife isn't pregnant already.*

As she walked smartly down the street and through the red-light district to her window, Mina recalled the day a few months ago, when Willem telephoned asking to see her and Miriam. He was pleased, he had told her, that the child was a girl, and when he met his daughter he glowed with pride.

"She's so beautiful," he said. "She looks just like you!"

"She has lovely features," Mina agreed, "but, Willem, we must never tell her that she's beautiful. She needs to find her way on other merits, not because of her appearance."

❦

In the months following his marriage, Willem realized that his wife was an alter-ego to Mina. Where she was tall, she was also frail. She suffered constantly from asthma attacks, making strenuous activity and breathing difficult. Mina was petite and small boned, but she was strong and healthy. He could no sooner impose his physical lust on his wife than he could enter-tain the idea of never being with Mina. His wife closeted herself in their home, while Mina encouraged walks in a nearby park with his daughter. *I need Mina in my life. She keeps me sane.*

On the day that he met his daughter for the first time, he assured Mina of an ongo-ing patronage.

"I haven't figured out how it's going to work, but I am determined that it will," he told her.

Mina poured a cup of coffee for him and set it on the table that sat between two wing chairs and a settee. While he added sugar to his cup, she poured coffee for herself.

"I'd like to try once a month," he finally said. "I know it's not as often as our visits last summer, but … between travel, reporting to the office, and dutifully showing my face at home on occasion, that may be all that I can manage right now."

"Willem, Miriam and I will be glad for any time you have for us. After all, I'm working in the window now. Astrid looks after Miriam when I'm not here, so our schedule is complicated too. I think one day a month is fine."

"I-I just want to see my daughter grow up," he said. "I want to be part of her life, even if she can't know that I'm her father."

"You will be," Mina assured him. "Each time you visit, you will see change, and I will keep a diary of all of her accomplishments, so you don't miss anything."

"Thank you," he said, embracing her fiercely. "I also want to spend time with you too." He blushed as he gazed into her dark brown eyes.

"You will," Mina said, before kissing him hungrily.

Days and years passed quickly. Willem watched his daughter grow from a clever, comely infant into a pretty girl full of confidence and determination. *She is so clever. She grasps everything I teach her. I will provide her the fuel she needs to expand her mind.*

In early fall, 1956, Willem telephoned to tell Mina that he would not be able to keep his appointments for several months, perhaps even a year.

"My wife is pregnant," he said. "I need to be with her. She's not well. I told her she was too frail, but she insisted that we—"

"Willem, don't fuss about it!" Mina

interrupted. "We're not married. You have no obligation to explain anything." She fought to control the jolt of emotion that knotted in her belly. "You don't have to justify to me that you have a right to have intercourse with your wife." Hearing the meanness in her voice, she realized she was being unfair. She inhaled deeply. "As it turns out, business in De Wallen is brisk. I can always work more hours, and if I need a patron, I can always find another."

"Thank you for being understanding," he said, his voice sounding heavy with regret. "I want to see you and Miriam again. I just don't know when I can manage it. I'll phone when things settle down."

Mina did not expect to hear from Willem for a long time. When the telephone rang a week before Christmas, she was surprised to hear his voice.

"Mina?" His voice was small and hollow.

"Willem, what is it?" she asked, startled by his trembling words.

"My w-wife is dead," he said. "She miscarried and lost so much blood ..." She heard him weeping.

"Willem, I'm so sorry for you. What can I do?"

"I know it sounds rude, but I'm wondering whether you might meet me for coffee. I just need someone—"

"Come here," she said. "Astrid is working tonight, and Miriam is already in bed. Give me half an hour."

By the time Willem arrived, Mina had made a fresh pot of coffee and set out a plate of almond cookies. She welcomed him as she always did, by hanging his coat and hat on the hook inside the door, but before she could invite him to sit, he burst into tears. She led him to the settee and sat with him, holding him until the tears stopped.

"I've made a mess of everything," he said. "I should have been strong and said no to the marriage. I should have married you, not her!" He searched in his pocket and retrieved a handkerchief to mop his face, then blew his nose with a manly honk. He leaned back into the settee and gazed at her with glossy eyes.

"I'm sorry that your wife died, and that your child is lost," she said, and meant it.

"I am too," he said, "but if I had married you, she wouldn't have died. It's my fault she's dead."

"No, it's not," Mina said with certainty. "Mama and the doctor would be the first to agree with me. I know you don't want to hear this right now, but dying is part of living, and women die as a result of pregnancy all the time. Eamon says that one day medicine will advance enough to save all mothers and babies, but that is a long way off." She reached for his hands and held them firmly. "It happens, Willem. It just does."

Mina let him talk for a while, until he seemed to embrace his new reality. He raised his head toward the door to Miriam's room.

"Do you think it's too late to see her?"

"She's sleeping," Mina replied, "but if you want to have a look … certainly." Mina walked with him toward the door and quietly turned the knob, one finger over her lips. "Shhh."

Willem stood at the door for several minutes gazing upon his daughter's comely face, then returned to the settee.

"Her birthday is next month. She'll be five," he said. "May I come for the party?"

For the next while, they talked of Christmas and birthdays, and when he seemed to have control over his emotions, he left.

"We'll look forward to seeing you for Miriam's birthday," Mina said as he started down the stairs to the street. She did not wish him a happy Christmas. She knew it was not his to have.

CHAPTER FOUR

Although Mina and Willem had never said so, Miriam was well aware of her appearance by the time she started school.

"I'm not happy with the way she uses her looks to attract attention," Mina mentioned to Punita one Sunday. "Already, she is using it to manipulate people."

"I agree," Punita said. "I worry for her safety. Her beauty might be beneficial in a window someday, but it's dangerous for someone so young."

"We must find ways to down-play her self-perception," the doctor agreed. "By the way, did your mother tell you that Anika Anker has decided that she no longer wishes to work in the red-light district?" He looked at his wife and stepdaughter, and by a shake of their heads learned that Punita had not shared her news.

"Anika never liked working in De Wallen," Punita said. "She found it distasteful. She has strong opinions about prostitution actually, and any pregnancy that resulted from an act ... well, she found that abhorrent. I don't even want to imagine what she must think of us, or how she tolerates the fact that we're related to her husband, for that matter—"

"And," the doctor interrupted, "she has ultimately decided not to assist doctors who work in De Wallen, including me, and that has left a nice little void to be filled."

"Exactly!" Punita said. "At the moment, there are only two birthing companions who are willing to work with prostitutes, and I'm one of them."

"So, I'm asking again," Eamon said, "whether you ... Mina ... would consider a new job. Astrid too, if she's interested. We could use the help."

"And it's not just to work in De Wallen," Punita added. "It's to work with a group of general practitioners and obstetricians."

"I'm hoping to open a medical office where doctors will provide medical support exclusively to women," Eamon said.

"That sounds wonderful, Eamon!" Mina replied. "I sincerely hope you find success with your plans. I'll speak with Astrid about it, and let you know."

When Mina mentioned her stepfather's offer to train them as birthing companions, Astrid was intrigued. Willem was equally interested and supportive.

"I've received a letter from my youngest brother, Tobias," Astrid said. "He left for the west coast of Canada soon after I came to Amsterdam. He has his own fishing boat now and is planning to marry soon. Tobias invited me to live with him until I find a place of my own ... or a husband." The young woman blushed. "He says he has several single friends who would be happy to meet me!"

"I think you will bring happiness ... and pleasure ... to any fellow you chose!"

Mina's comment was deliberately said with suggestion, leaving the other two giggling.

"I'd rather go to Canada as an experienced birthing companion," Astrid said in reply, "than a professional prostitute!"

Her remark caught Willem off-guard. As his coffee caught in his throat, he involuntarily spewed a mouthful across the table, and the three of them scrambled to contain the mess, while he tried to recover his dignity.

"It sounds as though you have it all worked out." Mina looked at her roommate with affection. "I'll miss you. You're the sister I never had."

"I'll miss all of you too," Astrid said, beaming at the compliment.

"What about you, Mina? What will you do?"

"I have a daughter to support," Mina replied, "and her education to think about. If we move away from De Wallen, the costs will be higher and a birthing companion's income will be less than what I'm earning now. Timing is everything."

"I'm happy to increase my patronage fees if you like," Willem offered, "and I'll pay for Miriam's education. Never worry about that. In fact, if you'd just marry me, you'd never have to worry about guilders again."

"We've had this conversation too many times already, Willem," Mina said firmly. She glared at him. "You know my answer."

"All right, you win for now," Willem conceded, "but I won't stop asking."

"Will you tell Dr. Hendrik that we will train with him?" Astrid asked.

"Yes," Mina said. "They've invited us for dinner next Sunday. We can discuss it further then. In the meantime, my friend, you'd better head off to the window or you'll be late."

"I suppose I should," Astrid replied. "Besides, I expect you two have some visiting to do now that Miriam is asleep!" She added stress to the word visiting and winked at them both as she closed the door to the outer hallway.

⚜

Willem continued his patronage and, when his travels brought him back to the city, Mina's time was for him alone. Sometimes he took her out for dinner and they would stay in a hotel for the night. On other occasions, he would visit at the apartment. He would not, he had told her at the beginning, visit her in the *kamer*.

"I don't like the thought of sharing you with anyone," he had said. "That back-room is evidence that I am not the only man in your life, and it feels clinical to me. Besides, it's always so crowded in De Wallen. Clientele and oglers cram the streets, wandering up and down the canals."

"I understand your concern," Mina agreed. "Mama says that, since the war, the traffic in the red-light district simply increases every year. I look forward to the day that I can give up the window, but, until then ..." She let her words drift away.

When Mina entertained Willem in the apartment, he was always invited for the evening meal, so he could spend time with his daughter. He nurtured her bright mind, bringing gifts from faraway places, and books to stimulate her imagination. He brought her an atlas and helped her plot his travels and told of their historical significance. And, with each visit, he marveled at her beauty and intelligence. *I hope one day, I will be permitted to tell her who I am. I hate that she calls me Meneer van Bosch. I want her to call me papa!*

Miriam enjoyed her monthly visits with Meneer van Bosch and looked forward to the gifts he brought and the stories he told. She was also excited to start school and learn.

"One day Mama and I will go there too," she would insist each time he showed her a new place on the map. "I want to see elephants and kangaroos. And when I go to school, I will learn to read and write. Then I can read the books on my own. One day, I will read to you, Meneer van Bosch!"

The school was a mere block away, but in the opposite direction from De Wallen.

Miriam was excited to have somewhere new to visit each day and quickly made friends with her classmates.

"I'm glad we're living outside De Wallen," Mina said to Willem one evening. "Miriam won't be exposed to the same activities I witnessed. She need never know about the type of work Astrid and I do."

"I too hope that she finds other interests," Willem agreed. "Maybe one day, she'll work with me, or become a doctor, or an engineer! She certainly has the brains for it."

"I have that hope as well." Mina gazed into Willem's eyes. "The books and other things that you bring spark her imagination. After every one of your visits, she is inspired to go somewhere or do something unique. During the war, women were forced to find work outside the home and, since the war ended, women have been pursuing higher levels of education. I believe that education is the catalyst for success. That's why we must encourage Miriam to do well in her studies—so she can make wise choices with her life. In the meantime, she seems happy, and we should be grateful for that."

"Can I do anything else to help," he asked.

"Not yet. One day perhaps. For now, Astrid and I have a system for looking after Miriam and keeping the window working. Mama and Mathilde used the same system, and, in spite of growing up in the red-light district, I think I turned out all right."

Willem quirked his eye at her but held his tongue. *You turned out all right in many ways,* he smiled at her, *but I wouldn't include prostitution as part of the summation.*

"I know I can't sit in a window forever," she responded, as if reading his thoughts. "Few bodies age well, and appearance is a large part of the equation when it comes to attracting business. We can't always be fit and healthy and, when our bodies start to fail through ill health or too many births, we must move on. Violent clients are a concern too: workers can be injured beyond recovery, forced out of their window and onto the streets. I don't want to reach either of those crossroads, but it's hard to give up the income."

"It sounds as if your plan is coming together."

"I'm getting there. Already, Astrid and I are training as birthing companions. We just need to work through the transition, and, of course, timing is everything!"

⚜

Punita developed a reputation as a capable birthing companion. Dr. Hendrik particularly appreciated her assistance when a birth was difficult.

"You have a way of quieting a labouring woman that is quite unique," the doctor complimented her after one trying delivery.

"Thank you for your kind observation, Doctor."

"It's as if you've worked with horses in the past," he teased, knowing full well that she had.

"My father taught me well," she agreed, remembering the time she had spent with her father and his horses, a time before the war, before the caravan was forced to split apart, and he was taken away in one of Hitler's round-ups, before he was placed in a camp where he died a horrible death.

"You must ensure that Mina and Astrid learn that technique too," the doctor said. "It will make them invaluable in our office."

As in all business, window work had busy days and slow days. On the slow days, if Miriam was in school, Mina and Astrid studied with Punita, learning the skills required to become a top-notch birthing companion.

"I'm hoping," Punita said on one occasion, "that you two will receive enough work from Eamon's office soon, so you can give up the window."

"We do too," Mina assured her.

"In the meantime," Astrid said, "I'm happy to be training. Window work can be quite boring."

"Precisely!" Punita said. "And a doctor's time is expensive. A birthing companion's time is more affordable. There is an opportunity here, and it ought to be seized. Now that you two are in training, Eamon is pressing the other doctors to finalize the office arrangements. It's something he's dreamed of for a long time, and he truly believes that, with your help, we'll get there. He wants to ensure that all women have access to medical services, no matter what!"

As the doctor's dream slowly came to fruition, Mina and Astrid began working part-time with those doctors who joined his office immediately. The dream took time to organize, however, and several doctors were slow to commit their time solely to the practice of women's medicine. While they waited for the practice to reach a volume that would support them full-time, Mina and Astrid continued operating the window as a means to supplement their income. They hungrily imagined the day when they would sell the window to someone in greater need.

CHAPTER FIVE

Willem loved his daughter, and, when he finally realized it, he knew too that he had loved Mina since the first day he had met her.

"Mina," he asked one blustery afternoon in 1965, "Will you please reconsider our arrangement? Let's make it permanent?"

"I thought our arrangement was permanent." Her response was aloof.

She was curled next to him in that half hour before Miriam was expected home from school, her skin still pink from their loving. She nestled her head in the curve of his shoulder, and his arm held her close.

"Your hair shines like polished mahogany," he replied, watching strands of her dark, silky hair fall through his fingers. "I'd like to see it so every morning when I awake. Your hair splayed across my pillow."

"Willem," she said, infusing his name with caution. "Don't go there."

In the next moment, she found herself shifted unexpectedly onto her side of the bed, Willem rising above her.

"Marry me?" he asked, gazing into her dark eyes. "We can raise Miriam together. Away from here. You'll never have to work again. Marry me?" His question, as always, was eager and sincere, not quite a plea.

"Willem!" She pushed him away and scrambled into a sitting position. "How can you ask such a thing? You know it's not possible. We have an arrangement, and that is how it must be."

She turned away from him, placing her feet on the floor.

"There will be no marriage and you must never mention it again."

"Mina," Willem pleaded.

Mina retrieved her discarded clothes, strewn about the room in haste earlier.

"Hurry!" Mina had said, glancing at the tableside clock. "Miriam will be home from school in a few minutes."

Willem's briefs sailed across the room on the wave of her annoyance and landed on the bed next to him. She opened the door to the bedroom as she collected her emotions.

"I'm going to make coffee," she said, then closed the door behind her.

One day near Miriam's fourteenth birthday, Willem noticed a display of tarot cards in a shop window. On a whim, he purchased a pack as a birthday gift. Magic and mystery, he knew, piqued her curiosity.

Following a celebratory dinner a few weeks later, Miriam opened her gifts with enthusiasm. When she unwrapped the gifts from him, Willem could not have been more pleased, especially when she saw the tarot cards. She danced around the tiny apartment holding them high in the air.

"When I grow up," she announced, "I want to be a fortune teller!"

In contrast to his daughter's enthusiasm, Willem noticed Punita scowling.

"You know nothing of tarot cards," she snapped. "They can be dangerous, if you don't know what you're doing!"

"You know about tarot cards?" Miriam asked.

"I do. Reading tarot cards was an important part of my family's life when I was a child, and I don't want to be reminded of it. The predictions made by the cards must not be taken lightly."

"Mama, don't be bothered by the cards," Mina said, as she gently extracted them from Miriam's hands. "We'll put them away for now." She gave Miriam a stern look as if to terminate any further discussion. "Perhaps later, if you think it appropriate, you might teach Miriam the proper way to use them." Mina wrapped her arms around her mother's shoulders and gave her a hug. Punita responded with a curt nod.

"I apologize," Willem said. "I didn't think they'd cause such a fuss."

"How could you know, Willem," Punita said. "Think nothing of it."

"*Oma*, you must teach me," Miriam insisted. "I must be a fortune teller. I want to be able to tell Meneer van Bosch where his next travels will take him, and all the wondrous things he will see! Please, Oma. Say you'll teach me?"

"They will only bring trouble," Punita snapped again, but Miriam persisted. When Punita realized that she could not dissuade her granddaughter, she acquiesced. "I will teach you on one condition, then. Your mother must learn too. You are not old enough to use the cards without supervision."

"Please, Mama," Miriam whined, batting her eyes at her mother.

"I will, if it keeps the two of you happy," Mina agreed begrudgingly.

The next day, the family gathered around the table.

"These cards are not for play," Punita stated firmly, as she shuffled the deck. "You must treat them with respect."

Miriam watched her grandmother handle the cards with care, shuffling them, dealing them, placing them in a particular way.

"You must listen to the person for whom you are reading and observe. Observation is critical," Punita warned. "If you don't listen and observe, you will miss the meaning. Understand?"

Miriam nodded eagerly, observing the respect with which her grandmother handled the cards. Mina's nod was a little more cautious. Punita gathered the cards, knocking them against the table to square the pile.

Miriam and Mina listened attentively to Punita's instructions and explanations, and quickly showed an intuitive ability to interpret.

"It seems the family talent will survive, regardless of my denial," Punita muttered. Noting her daughter's raised eyebrow, she added, "I just hope neither of you has any intention of trying to earn an income telling fortunes. It's a lost art in which few have an interest anymore."

Before long, Miriam was entertaining her father with an assortment of tales about his future accomplishments and his influences. She even warned him of disaster and risk.

"I'm sorry to say, sir, that this disaster will leave a deep scar on your heart," she concluded a reading with flourish, one particular afternoon.

Willem listened tentatively, indulging Miriam's telling of yet another fairy tale— at least, that was how he referred to the predictions of the tarot cards. He brushed his hand over her head of wavy hair while she knelt beside him, the cards spread out on the floor before them. She smiled at him prettily and told him that very soon he would find great joy and unexpected challenge. In a serious voice, she warned him that the year ahead could be difficult.

"Miriam, dear," Mina interrupted, "it's time to put the cards away. Meneer van Bosch isn't here to visit you alone. You must share his attentions."

Miriam began to protest, but wisely held her tongue and stacked the cards. Instead, she fluttered her lashes coquettishly and glanced at her father. In response, he rested his hand on the top of her glossy head and smiled at her.

"Will you be my window man, one day?" she asked. "I wouldn't mind if you liked to play with me the way you play with Mama. I think it could be quite fun!"

"I beg your pardon!" Willem choked on his response, stunned by her words. His smile disappeared as he raised an imploring gaze to Mina.

Mina froze. *Did I just hear my daughter offer herself to her father?*

"Miriam, child," she said calmly, "whatever do you mean by 'window man'? Where have you heard such a thing?"

"I heard about window workers at school," Miriam said, her face lighting up. "Fritz de Groot told the class that his papa visits the windows all the time. Meneer de Groot told Fritz that he had seen both Mama and Oma working there, and his papa promised that, when Fritz turns sixteen, he'll take Fritz to the windows." She paused momentarily to take a deep breath. "Fritz thinks Mama is so beautiful and declared that one day he will visit her window, too. His papa says that Mama is the best window girl in the entire red-light district. Fritz says that when I work in the windows, he will play with me regularly. It all sounds so exciting, doesn't it? Where is the red-light district?"

Mina's heart was racing. Despite all her efforts to protect her daughter from the knowledge of window work, she had failed at someone else's hands.

"Well," she said, "that is an interesting notion. And what exactly do you think a window girl and a window man do?"

"It's all a bit of silly fun, Mama. Isn't it? Fritz says you stand in a window and, if a man likes the way you look, he'll ask to be invited into the kamer to play." Miriam looked first to her mother, then to Willem. "Fritz said that sometimes the man might even kiss you and then—and this is the best part, Mama," she confided, "he will give you guilders!" Her lips formed a contemplative pout. "I don't know how many, though. Fritz says it depends, but on what I don't know."

"Hm, yes, well ..." Mina forced herself to remain calm. *Does she even know what a kamer is?* "It is as Fritz said, but, you can imagine, it is not easy to always be happy and to show that you enjoy playing with a man." Her eyes cast sideways for a brief glance at Willem. "Some men are not clean, or they have rotten teeth and smelly breath. Sometimes they are quite ugly, or unhappy, or even angry. It's hard work to play with a man who doesn't enjoy playing. Especially one who is angry."

"I see," Miriam said, as if puzzled by her lack of knowledge. "But, if that's the case, I will only play with clean men who are beautiful and have lovely white teeth and the kindness of Meneer van Bosch!" She smiled brightly at her father and fluttered her eyelashes again.

Mina looked at her child, wishing life could be that simple, praying that her daughter would be spared the experience.

"Perhaps it is best that I leave now," Miriam's father said, clearing his throat with a small cough. He rose from his chair and turned toward the door.

"Oh, please, sir, don't leave now! I have more cards to read for you," Miriam pleaded.

"Perhaps another day, hm? I have business matters to attend."

Turning to Mina, he nodded and made a hasty departure.

"Willem?" Mina called after him, running to the door. It closed before she reached it. When she opened it, he was gone, his footsteps fading down the stairwell to the street.

"Mama, did I say something to upset Meneer van Bosch?"

"No child, you did not," Mina said, before changing the topic like quicksilver. "Why don't you put the cards away, now. We should be off to the market to buy food for the evening meal. Come along."

CHAPTER SIX

Once Miriam was settled in bed for the night, and deep in slumber, Mina telephoned her mother and described the afternoon events.

"… and then he just left!" she cried into her apron, eyes red and swollen. She wiped the moisture trickling from her nose. "Mama, what am I going to do?"

"Well, daughter, I'm as surprised as you are. These revelations are not something we expected. Setting aside the marriage proposal for now, I think the time has come for you to leave De Wallen altogether. You need to find a new apartment and change Miriam's school. Let me discuss this with Eamon. We can talk more about it tomorrow."

A while later, Astrid returned from her shift in the window, and Mina repeated her dilemma to her friend.

"Well, that's it!" Astrid said in her sing-song accent. "It's the sign we've been looking for." She sat across the small dining table and reached for Mina's hands. "Dr. Hendrik and your mother have trained us well. We know that because the obstetricians prefer working with us. And, after all this time, the work is finally good. We rarely work the window anymore." Her eyes met Mina's with excitement. "And, if I leave now, you will inherit my share of the work with the doctors! Mina ... it's time!"

"You're right, of course," Mina agreed. A smile spread across her face. "It's exhilarating, to be sure, but there is one downside. You're going to Canada." She saw the sadness in Astrid's eyes.

"Yes," Astrid replied, "but I need to go, and you need to marry Willem and move away from here."

"I can't marry Willem," Mina said flatly. "We promised Mama that we'd keep the patronage free of emotional attachment.

Miriam and I must find a place of our own, and a new school."

"I'm sorry to hear that," Astrid replied. "Can you not speak with your mother? Surely—"

"No, we promised."

When Punita telephoned the next day, Mina told her mother of the discussion with Astrid.

"I posted a notice this morning advertising the sale of the window, and Astrid is making arrangements for travel to Canada. I'm going to ask the doctors for more shifts, and I need to find a new home and a school for Miriam."

"Mina, that's wonderful! What can we do to help!"

"Nothing for the moment," Mina replied. "We've already put things in motion. I was just looking through want ads when you called, looking for apartments." She gazed at the newspaper spread out on the table and straightened a wrinkle as she contemplated a niggling concern. "Mama, what do I do about Willem? He left in such a hurry and hasn't called."

"Hmm, perhaps he was just flustered and felt trapped not knowing what to say—"

"Or perhaps he's ended the patronage, after Miriam's enlightening comments," Mina replied with a hint of sarcasm.

"I doubt it," her mother said. "He is her father, after all."

⚜

Mina busied herself with the tasks required to change their living circumstance. The first was helping Astrid prepare for her journey, and the second was preparing for the move to a new home.

"I can hardly wait to see my brother again," Astrid mused. "I wonder what Vancouver is like. It must be like Amsterdam. It's named after a Dutch explorer after all!"

"Your packing is so much more exciting than mine," Mina replied. "I seem to be tossing more than I'm packing. Each time I pull something out of the closet, I'm reminded of another memory—reminders of life with Mathilde and Mama, Mathilde's horrid death, the German occupation." She shook her head, eyes closed to sadness, then she brightened. "And, the liberation! How wonderful that day was … when the Canadians came. You must give my thanks to every Canadian soldier you meet!"

When Astrid's departure date arrived, Mina accompanied her to Schiphol Airport to see her off.

"Be sure to send me your new address when you've found a place," Astrid said, passionately hugging the young woman who had saved her from the streets. "I miss you so much already!" Then, she swiped a tear from her cheek, lifted her two burgeoning suitcases, and disappeared through the boarding gate without a backward glance.

What am I going to do without her? Mina wondered, watching the bobbing white blonde head disappear into a crowd of passengers. "I miss you already too," she whispered.

Alone in her apartment, Mina again checked the want ads for rentals and found nothing suitable. Her mind wandered as she tried to envision a new life away from De Wallen and window work. She had lived her entire life in that community and knew every street and prostitute. It was the only life she had ever known, and all it took was a few innocent remarks from a naive fourteen-year-old to bring it tumbling down. *In one fell swoop—a new home, a new job, a new school, and no man in my life. I welcome the new home and full-time work with the doctors, but a life without Willem is something I never expected.* She watched her tears splash onto the newsprint and bloom as the paper absorbed them. *I wonder that I miss Willem at all! Perhaps I just miss the regularity of his visits and the predictable income. After all, I never had any assurance that his patronage would continue indefinitely. I hope that my work as a birthing companion will be sufficient to support Miriam and me, and the expense of a new apartment.*

CHAPTER SEVEN

Miriam was unaffected by the departure of Willem and Astrid. She was a beautiful young girl who enjoyed spending time with her friends, and recently discovered that she liked the company of boys. She realized that, with one flick of her long wavy hair, they would gather around her. If Miriam wanted something, she need only smile that sweet, promising smile of hers, and flutter her full, dark lashes.

Occasionally, she examined her young body in the long mirror mounted inside the door of her wardrobe. She was well-aware of her creamy white skin that darkened in the sun, her slender body and her small, pert breasts that tingled when she touched them under her covers at night. Some nights, she would wake in the darkness, dreaming of one of the boys at school and what might happen if she were to let him touch her breasts. On those occasions, she discovered moisture on the inside of her thighs and felt an odd sense of yearning deep in her belly. If she stroked the heat emanating just below the dark curls, the yearning would dissipate, like ice on a fire.

Miriam had learned plenty from her mother and Astrid, listening when she should have been studying, imagining when she should have been sleeping. Living in a home of window workers, secrets of the body were not secrets. They were facts.

One day soon, I will learn how to truly satisfy my yearning, she thought, and each time she made that promise, the spectre of Meneer van Bosch formed in her thoughts.

"Mama, must I go to school again?" Miriam lamented to her mother during a day of shopping, the week before the fall term was to start.

"Yes, of course!" Mina replied. "Why would you ask such a thing?"

"I'm bored," she exclaimed, as she twirled through the town square. Her long wavy hair and pleated skirt belled, exaggerating her turns. "I want to experience life! I'm tired of teachers, and books, and studying. What more can I possibly learn? I want to work, and travel, and come and go as I please."

Miriam stopped spinning, took a deep breath, and carefully delivered her next words.

"I want to work in the window, Mama! Will you show me how?"

"What!"

The response was out of Mina's mouth before it could be contained. Miriam's steps faltered, and she gawked at Mina before resuming her twirling along the square. Realizing the distance growing between them, Mina sprinted to catch up with her daughter, burdened by the parcels she carried. Her mind raced to find an appropriate reply.

"Miriam! Stop!" she demanded, a little too loudly. Other shoppers glanced their way, as if wondering about the fuss.

Miriam stopped as ordered, her arms flopping to her sides. She almost tripped as the momentum of her torso caught up with the stillness of her feet.

"What's the matter, Mama?"

Mina seized her daughter's arm, and half dragged her to a small patio table next to a food wagon.

"Sit. I need a coffee."

She dumped their packages on the table, shoved a chair in Miriam's direction, and stomped off to a food wagon.

"What will it be, mistress?" asked a fellow, peering down at her from a service window cut in the side of the wagon.

A sign to the right of the window boasted that Schmidt Bratwurst was a tasty German treat, and the aroma of roasting sausages and warm bread wafted from behind him. The thought of food caused Mina's stomach to curdle.

"Um, just a coffee and a lemon soda, please."

She placed some coins on the counter,

poured cream in the coffee he had left in exchange, and took the beverages to the table, trying to assemble her thoughts in response to Miriam's unexpected question. Mina set the lemon soda in front of Miriam and sat in the chair opposite. She sipped the coffee, wincing as it burned her mouth.

"Please repeat what you just said," she demanded, glancing at the grey clouds gathering overhead. *They look as dismal as I feel.*

"Huh?"

"Did I just hear you say that you don't want to go back to school?"

"Uh-huh." Miriam sipped her soda through a white paper straw.

"Why? You have always loved school and learning."

"School is for babies," Miriam said confidently. "I'm not a baby anymore. Now that I'm bleeding every month, I'm a woman, and a woman should work!" She sipped her soda again and licked her lips.

"And what exactly do you think a fourteen-year-old girl is qualified to do?"

Mina's heart was pounding. *I wish Mama was here.*

"Well," Miriam huffed in youthful arrogance, rotating her shoulders and batting her eyes, "I presume I have the same body parts as you and Astrid. I want to be a window worker, and I know I can do the job—with a little training from you, of course."

Mina inhaled slowly, struggling for calm.

"Besides, it sounds like you've been doing it for years. The boys at school said that Oma also worked in De Wallen! They call it the family business," Miriam insisted. "Is it not better that I earn money, too, now that Astrid is gone?"

"How dare you!" Mina hissed, her mind racing. She could feel red frustration creeping up her neck and needed to get them home before someone overheard. She had hoped the coffee would calm her, but the reverse was happening.

"Drink your soda," she hissed. "This is not the place for such a discussion. We're

74

leaving." She stood abruptly, knocking her chair to the ground. "Now!" Reflexively, she bent to pick up the chair.

Before Miriam could finish the last slurp of lemon soda, Mina jerked her out of the chair, and led her by the arm down the street toward home.

"Mama, what's your problem!" Miriam whined, trying to wriggle out of her mother's grasp.

"We'll discuss this at home, and not until." Mina stepped rapidly down the street, the heels of her pumps click-clicking on the cobblestones, as she dragged Miriam by the arm. The weight of their shopping bags and her purse were held fast in her other hand, pulling on the muscles in her shoulder. "Up those stairs, now!" Mina said pointing when they neared the apartment.

Tromping up the stairs behind Miriam, Mina could not believe the situation she was about to address. She was so angry with Miriam's fixation on window work that her shaking hand had difficulty fitting the key into the doorknob. "In," she said, pointing again.

Miriam flounced through the doorway, kicked off her shoes and continued toward her bedroom.

"Not so fast, you! Come back here. We are going to talk about your ridiculous notion."

Miriam stomped out of her room and plopped herself onto a kitchen chair. Mina filled two glasses with water from the tap and set them on the table.

"From the top," Mina invited, "what is going on? The truth."

Miriam had the sense to look abashed as she lifted her eyes to her mother.

"I'm sorry, Mama. I thought you'd be happy about my idea to work in a window."

"Why would I be happy about that?"

"We need the money, don't we? Meneer van Bosch hasn't returned since the last time I read his tarot cards. And, besides, Astrid is gone, and we don't have her income, either."

"You are correct with two of your observations—Meneer van Bosch has not returned and Astrid lives here no longer. That is all," Mina snapped. "We are not destitute."

"What's destitute?" Miriam's youthful question betrayed her air of confidence.

"The reason you need to stay in school. Astrid and I had little choice. We needed to work to put a roof over our heads and food on the table, and Oma taught us all we needed to know to earn the best income. I have worked hard, so that you could have choices. Good choices that do not involve window work. How many times have we talked about you finishing school, so you can be anything you want? You can be a secretary or a nurse, even a teacher."

"Meneer van Bosch said I could work with him, or be a doctor, or an engineer!"

"Exactly! If you really apply yourself to your studies—and you are clever enough to do it—you could even be a lawyer. Your opportunities are endless. Your life could be so much better than this." Mina swirled her arm indicating the interior of the apartment. "You don't have to work in a window."

"But I want to," Miriam insisted.

"Trust me, Miriam," Mina asserted, "you do not. But, since you seem so determined, I will tell you what it's like."

Miriam leaned toward her mother with anticipation.

"A man visits a window because no woman will have him, or he has no woman in his life. Window workers are asked to do things no man would ask a genteel woman to do. Some men are filthy. They may carry disease. They often smell. Their breath reeks of tobacco, whisky, strong foods, and rotten teeth. They can be rough, mean, sometimes even brutal." Miriam paced through the apartment's common rooms as she ranted. "One of the workers had her nose broken; another, an arm. Many have died or been maimed by sexually transmitted diseases. There is always a risk of pregnancy." Mina paused as she thought of herself, but quickly carried on before Miriam found space to ask a question. "And through it all, we are expected to smile and be ready to welcome the next client. Our work is physical, and we are always vulnerable. We must constantly check our bodies for diseases that are transferred in the filth. We are required to clean our windows and our bodies, thoroughly, after each client to ensure that neither we, nor the next client, is harmed. And on and on it goes." Mina paused again and frowned. "Do you hear what I'm saying, Miriam?" she asked, hoping that Miriam would understand as the disgust rolled off her tongue. "I have tried to protect you, so you'd never know about the work we've done."

"Tell me about the sex, Mama," Miriam asked, as if trying to soften her mother's ire. "Does it hurt?"

"What? You want me to tell you about intercourse?"

Miriam nodded, her eyes alight with expectation.

"Intercourse has little to do with window work. In fact, most workers frown upon it. It is a risky business that can easily result in disease, or pregnancy, or both. Even when proper precautions are used."

"That's not what I mean. What is intercourse? Does it hurt?"

"Ah! You want to know about the mating of a man and a woman, not the job of a window worker."

"Yes, please," Miriam struggled to restrain her enthusiasm.

"Let us leave that topic for another day—perhaps tomorrow." Mina restricted the conversation to focus on her biggest concern. "For now, I want to talk about school and the fact that you will return when the doors open next week."

"Mama, I can't bear the way the boys look at me, the way the girls mock me," Miriam hung her head, "ever since Fritz de Groot told us that his father knows you, things have changed. I can't go back to that school!"

"Then we will find a school where no one knows who we are. We can move to another district. I sold the window business. There's no need to return to De Wallen."

"You did what!" Miriam exclaimed.

"You must finish school, Miriam." Mina struggled to stay on topic. "If not for yourself, then for Oma and for me. We need you to live a life better than the ones we've had." She reached across the table and stroked her daughter's cheek. "Be patient, my child. You will have a life uniquely your own. One far better than ours."

Miriam hung her head again, appearing to defer to her mother's wishes.

In the following moments of quiet, Mina contemplated her daughter's desire to embrace life. She began wondering whether Miriam was plotting a way to stay out of school. Late that evening, long after Miriam had gone to bed, Mina telephoned her mother.

"What am I to do? I have little time to find another apartment and another school."

The line was quiet for a moment.

"Bring Miriam to me, tomorrow," Punita said, when she returned to the telephone. "Eamon will go with you to find an apartment near a suitable school."

CHAPTER EIGHT

The following day, Eamon Hendrik accompanied his stepdaughter in search of a new home, driving around Amsterdam in his weathered 1950 Citroën. He called it his silver wings, in reference to its colour, and also because it was compact and efficiently conveyed him to medical appointments and emergencies.

That morning, Mina had identified a few advertisements for apartments close to trolley lines and schools. Dr. Hendrik had made a few suggestions as well. Late in the afternoon, as they drove to the last viewing of the day, they considered the pros and cons of the various apartments that they had visited.

Mina straightened a little in the seat next to him when he turned onto Koning-slaan Street.

"Oh, I don't think I can afford anything on this street, Doctor. In fact, I can't afford anything in Willemspark."

"Just have a look," Eamon insisted. "The owner is a friend. I only learned of its availability this morning and was asked to stop by this afternoon for tea and a viewing. So, here we are!"

He parked the Citroën at the curb of a neat row of four townhouses built of light brown brick. The windows and doors were trimmed in white, with white flower boxes hanging under the lower windows, each planted with red flowers in full bloom. The only distinguishing feature was the colour of the doors. Each was painted with a different primary colour—red, green, blue, yellow.

Dr. Hendrik opened the passenger-side door with an invitation to Mina to join him on the curb.

"The blue door, I believe." He indicated a flight of stairs directly in front of them. As if by magic, the blue door opened when Dr. Hendrik placed his foot on the first step.

Ascending the stairs, with the doctor's hand firmly at her elbow, Mina looked more thoroughly at the sturdy structure.

"I don't know, Eamon. The cost ..." Mina raised her eyes, following the stairs ascending to the blue door. "Willem!" Her face lit up as he stepped through the blue door and onto the landing. Her heart began beating wildly and she tripped off the last stair. Willem's hands reached to catch her, and the doctor's grip tightened around her elbow.

"Welcome!" Willem said, a warm smile lighting his face, as he turned to push the blue door wider and invite his guests to precede him into the hallway. He placed his hand on Dr. Hendrik's shoulder.

"Eamon, my friend, very good to see you."

"Are you all right?" he asked Mina.

"I am," she answered. "Just a little surprised to see you." She cocked her head to the right and looking questioningly at the doctor. He grinned and shrugged.

"Please, come in," Willem said, gesturing once again that they should precede him into the parlour. "I've arranged for tea. I thought you'd be tired and perhaps a little hungry after your search today."

Mina glanced sideways at Dr. Hendrik, then back to Willem. *Hmm, this whole thing feels a little contrived!*

"Ah, yes," Dr. Hendrik responded to Willem. "We have been very busy, my friend. Mina and I have looked at several apartments. All have some potential, but we've yet to find the one that says 'rent me' to Mina."

They each took a seat.

"I apologize for catching you off guard," Eamon said to Mina. "Willem asked me to bring you here at the end of our tour, but he would rather tell you the rest himself."

While Willem poured the tea and handed around biscuits and cake, Mina gazed about the room in which they sat.

It was a lovely room. She did not know much about furniture or interior design, but

86

she knew the décor to be much better than that of her home. The windows facing the street were framed in snow-white lace. The heads of the red flowers filled the bottoms of the windows.

The chairs and settee were old, but not worn. In fact, although everything in the room looked to be more than ten years old, nothing appeared to be worn. She had the same sense of the furniture in the hallway and the dining room, where she could see ornately carved dark wood—mahogany, perhaps—a buffet, chairs, and a table. A crystal chandelier hung over the table, its teardrops dripping light into the room and sprinkling rainbows on the walls.

Willem handed her a white china cup and saucer with small blue flowers spilling over the edge of the cup and a chain of delicate blue flowers encircling the saucer.

As he poured tea for the doctor and himself, Mina looked again at the window to the view beyond. She was so preoccupied with the neighbourhood itself and the row of townhouses when they had first arrived that she had not noticed the school across the street. She turned her puzzled gaze to Willem, accepting a piece of lemon cake from the plate he held in front of her.

"Th-th-ank you," she stammered.

"Mina," Willem said, once everyone was settled with tea, "I hope you can forgive me the small ruse that got you here today. I have been preoccupied with other matters, until recently. When I left you and Miriam, not so long ago, I realized that I needed structure in my life. Something I haven't had for a while.

"I realized that I can no longer travel as I once did. Since my father died last spring, I've been forced to spend more time in the office. I need someone else to do the travelling, someone equally as interested in the import-export business. At Eamon's suggestion, I met with Captain Konstantin and Captain Zabar to enquire whether it was possible to merge our businesses. I thought that together we'd have more possibilities, more opportunities. And I said as much to them. They liked the idea and I am pleased to tell you both that I am now a partner in *Oyster Pearl Imports*." He leaned back in his chair and took a long drink of his tea. "I have Miriam to thank for spurring me out of my rut. I will thank her myself, when next I see her."

"But what has that to do with us coming here today?" Mina asked.

"Once the merger was finalized, I wanted to speak with you further about your living situation. As luck would have it, I ran into the good doctor this morning and he told me about your desire to relocate."

Mina sat in silence, not knowing how to respond. Her heart began to pound again.

"So, what do you think of this townhouse. Could you live here?" Willem asked, a pleasant grin enhancing his appearance.

"It is a lovely home, but I can't afford to live here. Although you have paid me well over the years, and the window money was good, I could not have afforded this house.

And now that my sole source of income is from the doctors, I earn much less."

"That's not what I asked," Willem said. "I am just curious to know whether this is a place where you could live. As you've likely noticed, there is a good school across the street. The home has three bedrooms upstairs, a well-stocked kitchen, in addition to these rooms ..." He indicated the parlour and dining room with a sweep of his hand. "... two bathrooms—which is not common for this district, and plenty of storage on the lower level."

"Well, given what I've seen, I suppose I could, but I'd have to see the rest to say for certain." Before the words were out of her mouth, Willem rose and extended his hand to her.

"Come, then, let me show you around."

"But Willem, I can't."

"You can. Come. Trust me."

He led her up the stairs to the third floor. Dr. Hendrik stayed behind and poured himself a second cup of tea. Mina shot him a look over her shoulder as they ascended the stairs. *He looks too confident by half.*

At the top of the stairs, Willem led her to the first room, then the second, then the third. Each room was spacious and well appointed. The largest one was decorated to suit a married couple, including a large bed. The other two were smaller, but similar in size and more neutral in décor. A fourth door led to a toilet and a separate room with a bath.

At the far end of the hall, Willem led Mina down the stairs to the second floor again where they appeared in a small kitchen, complete with a modern oven and refrigerator. The kitchen may have been small, but it was still larger than the main rooms of their current apartment.

"You'll find the cupboards and the refrigerator already stocked."

Mina's eyes lit up as she opened first the oven, then the refrigerator.

"So spacious," she marvelled. "Look how much food can fit into the refrigerator!

Compared to our old icebox and Aga Cooker, these appliances are amazing."

"So? What do you think? Can you see yourself living here?"

"I suppose I could. If I had the money, which I don't. So, sadly, the answer is no."

"Mina, I would like to gift this town-house to you. I own the row, and I live in the unit next door, the one with the yellow door. You might think me devious," he continued, holding up his hand before Mina could protest. "That it's a convenient way for me to have access to you. But that wasn't my intent. You and your mother prefer that Miriam doesn't know that I'm her father, and I respect your wishes. I don't understand them, but I do respect them."

"So," he said, "I'm offering you a separate townhouse. At the same time, I'm hoping that you will let me be your neighbour so I can be available to you, and Miriam of course, should I ever be needed." Reaching toward her, Willem took Mina's hand.

"And if you'll allow me," he said in a quiet, sincere voice, "I'd like to continue my relationship with both of you. I only ask that you allow me to help you find a home in a better neighbourhood, near a better school. That is what you are looking for today, is it not?"

"Willem, your offer is kind and generous," Mina responded thoughtfully, "but I don't know how we can possibly accept. To live here would be to live a fairy tale. What would your neighbours think if they discovered that they had a window worker living amongst them?"

"Mina, Eamon told me that you sold the window, and that you've been working solely with the doctors. How can that be disreputable? Besides, I'm asking that you allow me to take care of you and our daughter. Please think about it, at least?" he pleaded, squeezing her hand as he led her back to the parlour.

Mina agreed to think about Willem's offer. She wanted to discuss it with her mother and the doctor. She promised to give him an answer the following day. To the doctor, she suggested that they leave. It was nearly dinner time and Punita would expect them shortly.

"Very well, I'll look forward to hearing from you tomorrow," Willem said.

Dr. Hendrik rose, and Mina led him toward the door. They were quick with their farewells to Willem, then headed back to the townhouse where Punita and the doctor lived.

CHAPTER NINE

When the doctor opened the front door, the aroma of a long-simmering rabbit stew wafted over them.

"What a lovely way to be greeted," Eamon said, the twinkle in his eye matching the lips of his wife, spread wide and loving.

"Eamon, Mina. You've arrived just in time. Miriam and I have been in a cooking frenzy all day, and dinner is ready for the table."

"I made a spice cake from scratch," Miriam added. "Like the one we buy from the bakery."

She continued to struggle with eye contact, especially with her mother, and looked at her hands as she spoke.

"Everything looks and smells wonderful," Mina said, while she hung her coat and hat and reached for the doctor's. "Let us freshen up first."

Chatter over the meal was sporadic as the dish of rabbit stew made its way around the table. Punita spoke with pleasure as she described the considerable expansion of her culinary expertise. Assisting as Eamon's birthing companion was not all-consuming, she explained, and the spare time allowed her an opportunity to explore interests that piqued her curiosity. Cooking was one of them, and the others marvelled over the curious spices and herbs that made the stew outstanding.

"Little things I remember from the times I travelled with the caravan and lived in a hotel," she said.

As the women cleared the dishes from the table and put coffee on to brew, Punita asked Mina about her day's adventures.

"Were you and Eamon able to find any apartments that you might call home?"

"Yes, we looked at several places; some nice, some not so much."

Mina reset the table with coffee cups, sugar and cream, plates and spoons, while

Miriam placed the spice cake and the coffee pot in the centre of the table. As they did so, Mina described each apartment with helpful input from the doctor.

When the women resumed their places at the table, Mina began to tell of their encounter with Willem van Bosch. She could not bring herself to mention him by name, just referring to him as the owner of the last place. Punita and the doctor exchanged a knowing look and said nothing. Punita and Miriam listened as Mina described each room and the modern conveniences.

"I'd feel like a princess if I lived in a home like that," Miriam said, her face taking on a dream-like expression. "Just imagine what it would be like to live in a space where we weren't stacked one upon the other. And a house, not an apartment—a real home. We could live like a family. Like my school mates. And we would live far away from De Wallen, where no one would know where you work, Mama. And no one would tease me."

Miriam delivered the last sentence with effect. She meant for it to injure Mina, not realizing that Punita would feel the jab, too. Punita placed a stilling hand on Mina's in response to her small gasp. The doctor did not miss the quicksilver shift of expression as each mother heard Miriam's remark and brought their emotions under control.

"Miriam," he said, "I think your comments are unfair. Your mother has worked very hard to make a good life for you, to shelter you from the nature of her work, and keep you safe. From what you've just said, you make it sound like you've been wronged in some way."

The doctor's challenge visibly surprised each of them, and before either woman could respond, Miriam snapped back.

"What would you like me to say? That I think my mother is a talented prostitute? She must be. The boys at school remind me every day."

"You mind your tongue!" Mina barked,

shifting her gaze to Punita and noting the sorrow and regret in her expression.

"But what could they possibly know?" Eamon interjected.

"They know what their fathers and older brothers tell them," Miriam hissed. "School hasn't even started, and already they're leering at me. Some even rub themselves to show me how interested they are, saying they hope that I will join the family business." Her eyes pierced Mina like daggers.

"Well, you have certainly changed your tune, young lady," Mina snapped back. "It was merely days ago that you were dreaming about being a window worker. What's happened in the meantime?"

"Everything's changing: my body, my girlfriends, the boys! They've started grabbing at me when I walk by and saying things that I don't understand. And my girlfriends have been avoiding me since one found out that her father visits you."

"Visited me," Mina corrected, interrupting Miriam's rant, while trying to remain calm. "Perhaps he did, but I've sold the window. Remember?"

"I don't know what you do when you go to work, but I can imagine, and I think you're filthy!" Miriam shouted, shoving her chair from the table. Moments later the front door slammed behind her.

There it was again. That smack of words that caught both Mina and Punita off guard. They had done everything they could to ensure that Miriam's childhood was normal. Mina and Astrid had been discrete in their business, but to no good end.

The women sat slumped in their chairs, tears leaking from their eyes. The doctor rose from his and wrapped an arm lovingly around Punita, while he handed her a clean handkerchief from his pocket.

"Come," he said, encouraging Punita to move to the sofa. "Sit with me."

Mina dashed the tears from her eyes and wiped her nose on the sleeve of her sweater.

"Well, I guess that's it, then. I have no choice but to accept Willem's offer. So much for wanting a life of independence," she mumbled, shuffling behind them. "I'm so grateful for the time you spent training us to be birthing companions, Eamon, and I'm particularly glad to be out of that horrid window business."

Inviting Mina to take the chair opposite the sofa, the doctor suggested that they review their current circumstances before making hasty decisions.

"It is," he said, "important to consider all aspects so that decisions can be made with confidence. We want you and Miriam to be happy, Mina, and certain."

CHAPTER TEN

Once Mina's decision was conveyed to Willem, Miriam was enrolled in the school across the street. The four adults agreed that it was important to continue to shelter Miriam from the consequences of window work.

"Keep in mind," the doctor cautioned Mina, "although you will be working full-time as a birthing companion, that work will include assisting compromised window workers from time to time."

Moving arrangements were made the next day, and the following week Mina and Miriam took possession of the townhouse with the blue door. Mina extracted a promise from Willem to keep out of sight during the move, and in the following weeks. Mina did not want anything or anyone from their past to cause Miriam concern. Willem's comings and goings were to be discrete, ensuring no opportunity for an accidental encounter with Miriam.

When Mina informed Miriam that they would move, Miriam was elated, and felt confident that her temper tantrum during the evening meal was the deciding factor. *Good riddance to those stupid boys who harass me. I'm tired of them and the way they leer at me. A new school is a new opportunity, and it will be on my terms.* When she finally viewed her new home, she was overjoyed. It was everything she had imagined. As she awaited the moving date, she fantasized about life in that house and how magical it would be. *None of my friends—former friends—live in a home as lovely as ours. Good things will follow this move. I know it!*

Living on Koningslaan Street required a few adjustments. To Miriam's delight, her mother took her shopping and bought her new clothes for school. If they were to fit in, they needed to dress the part.

Mina told Miriam that she intended to shepherd her to and from school until she was certain that Miriam felt safe and comfortable in the new school. Miriam allowed the escort the first day, but quickly expressed her embarrassment at being seen with her mother near the school ground.

"Watch from the window, if you must!" Miriam snapped. "I don't need you to hold my hand!"

Miriam set off to school each day feeling like a fashion model, head high and back straight, confident that she was being noticed for her beauty and fine clothes. She was a clever girl, which meant that she could keep abreast of her studies with little effort, while assessing the school population at the same time. Very few of the girls interested her. She found most of them either empty-headed or too intellectual for her liking.

Miriam decided that she was ready to share her body, but she would do so when the situation suited her. A fire burned in her belly and she longed for a man's touch. At night, she would lay outstretched on her bed, her fingers rolling the nipples of her still-maturing breasts, the way she imagined window workers would do it. The muscles in her groin would clench and she would move a hand downward, imagining a man like Meneer van Bosch coming to her. *The cards keep telling me that the move to Willemspark is a sign,* Miriam sighed, *that one day I will be welcomed into the arms of Willem van Bosch. It has to be true. Oma always says that the cards don't lie.*

In the meantime, she bided her time and studied the boys in her school. She quickly identified the studious ones and discounted them as necessary evils. Naturally drawn to the taller boys, she focussed on the rugged athletes, especially the handsome ones. Slowly, her list of interesting young men narrowed to those who came from families of wealth.

Regardless of her analysis, Miriam knew that, to pique the interest of those fellows to whom she was drawn, she would need to tolerate and humour anyone who might help her achieve her goal. She made every effort to fit in with those girls who social-ized with the boys on her list.

Mina would have been shocked to learn of Miriam's calculating thoughts. Never could one girl be so different from the people who had raised her. She and Astrid had chosen to live a simple life, but they had raised Miriam with love. Mina had also ensured that Miriam never wanted for anything—within reason. In return, little was asked of Miriam.

On the day that Mina and Miriam had moved from the old apartment, a kindly neighbour appeared at their door to wish them farewell.

"You mind that daughter of yours," she had warned, waggling her finger under Mina's nose when Miriam disappeared into her room for another box. "She will be nothing but trouble. Never have I met a more selfish girl! Nothing like you and Astrid. You two have been goodness itself."

HART

CHAPTER ELEVEN

Ten-year-old Hart Lange sat in his father's study listening to his father and grandfather recall the post-war recovery of Bayreuth, the city in which his family had lived since 1937.

"Soon after the war ended," Hart's grandfather, Gerhard, said, "the American military established a displaced-persons encampment with the intention of aiding those refugees and expellees who filtered into Germany from East Germany, Poland, and Ukraine, as a result of the Potsdam Agreement. They had two priorities: one was to rebuild the damage caused by the 1945 bombings, and the other was to create housing, not only for those citizens whose homes had been damaged or destroyed, but also for the others forced to leave their homes." Gerhard reclined in an old leather armchair, his legs stretched before him.

"The rebuilding started before I returned home," Hart's father, Paul, said, handing Gerhard a glass of apple brandy. "I remember what München looked like when I walked from the train station to the home of Ilse-Renata's aunt. Already, I saw new and repaired structures." He stopped to straighten the old Spanish painting of Mars, before lowering himself into a second leather armchair.

"By the time you returned home," Gerhard said, "the war had already been over for a year."

"Well," Paul chuckled, his hands dangling between his knees, "it was a long walk from that American POW camp outside Rome!" He rolled the brandy around the bowl of his glass, then took a sip.

Hart listened to every word his father and grandfather exchanged. He knew that the Potsdam Agreement had been implemented two years before he was born and, because of its stipulations, the city had been cleared of rubble and bombs by the time he celebrated his tenth birthday last fall. Able-bodied men living in Bayreuth had been conscripted to ensure that residences were rebuilt quickly. His father said that Bayreuth's population had swelled beyond any numbers contemplated when the city was first incorporated, and that it was important to house and feed everyone.

"I'm glad that you were permitted to resume operations of the farm and dairy so soon after the war ended," Paul said, nodding toward his father. "I like to think our products filled many hungry bellies."

"Not without sacrifice," Gerhard replied, eyeing his son. "That American inspector made us pay. He expected healthy rations of meat and a large basket of fresh produce every time he inspected the farm. That man lived well at the expense of starving Germans. He was transferred somewhere else in the spring of '48, and I, for one, was happy to see the last of him. Corruption like that makes me want to vomit!"

"Excuse me, *Vati*," Hart said, interrupting the discussion. "You did say all of the bombs are gone now, didn't you? My friends and I can really walk to school alone? Without our mothers, I mean."

"You can, indeed," Paul replied, "but be mindful. You don't want to get in the way of the construction workers or the American military. They have important jobs to do."

"Yes, Vati," Hart said with a sigh, leaning back in his chair and marvelling at the freedom he and his friends would have in the coming weeks. His thoughts danced on the little rainbows cast on the wall by the crystal glasses from which his elders drank their brandy.

On following weekends, if weather permitted, Hart and his friends hiked to Bindlach, a small town directly north of Bayreuth, an hour's walk from the Lange home. They made a day of it, hiking through the forest, playing games, and enjoying picnic lunches shared beside the river. When temperatures soared, they stripped to nothing and jumped into the cool water. In Bindlach, they pretended to be soldiers and crawled through the brush to watch the activities on the American military base from an advantageous view point that they had discovered on one of their first forays into the area.

When Hart asked his father about the American camp, Paul explained that Christensen Barracks, as it was properly named, was established in Bindlach primarily to secure the borders with the German Democratic Republic and Czechoslovakia.

"It is also used as a hub to disseminate supplies," Paul said. "Regular shipments of foodstuffs and other items are delivered by rail. Then they are transferred to military trucks and conveyed elsewhere."

As time passed, the boys were emboldened and crept closer to the base established at the top of the hills east of Bindlach. On a sunny July afternoon, they watched as two of the men who had been transferring supplies disappeared, while the others took a smoke break. Moments later, they were startled by a demanding voice, immediately behind them.

"Hey! What are you scallywags up to?" one of the soldiers barked.

"We speak little English," Hart said, jumping to his feet. "Have you something special for us?"

"Cheeky little squirt," the other soldier muttered to his companion.

"All right," he said to the boys, "up with ya."

He pointed toward the truck. Confused and a little nervous, the boys raised their hands above their heads, and followed the finger and the privates back to the truck. The other privates ground out the stubs of their cigarettes and continued their work, transferring supplies from the train to the waiting trucks.

"Say, Roy! What ya gonna do with them

brats?" one of the men asked. The others chuckled.

"These cheeky little brats want something special!" Roy answered, imitating Hart's request.

"You keep us?" Hart asked in his limited English.

"Keep you?" Roy asked.

"I think he's asking whether they're to be arrested or detained," a lieutenant said, as he rounded the front of one of the trucks.

"No, squirt," Roy tousled Hart's hair. "You're not under arrest and you can put your hands down." Roy motioned that they could lower their arms.

"Private! Give them some chocolate and send them on their way," the lieutenant ordered.

"Sir!" Roy saluted his superior.

"Wait," he said to the boys, giving them a hand signal to emphasize his command.

Two privates went to the rear of a truck with Roy. The boys watched bug-eyed as the soldiers moved some boxes, identified the one they needed, and opened it. Roy looked at the boys, counting, and returned with Hershey chocolate bars for all of them.

"*Danke, Kapitän*," they each whispered in return for a chocolate bar, agog with appreciation.

"Hey! I'm no captain," Roy said, pointing to his sleeve. "I'm a private."

He tousled Hart's hair again.

"Now skedaddle before we really do arrest you. Shoo! We have work to do." He motioned for them to leave.

The boys ran off down the hill, waving their chocolate bars in gratitude and shouting *danke*, as they hopped over logs and skidded off patches of pebbles.

The boys returned to the Rock—as the Americans affectionately called their base— several times that summer. On each occasion, the soldiers recognized them and shared something special. The boys lost their fear of the Americans and the soldiers welcomed their youthful boldness. Each time the boys planned a trek to Christensen Barracks, they practised their English, so they could better communicate with the soldiers.

"My mother is very proud that I practise my English all the time. Even during our vacation," Hart told his friends, trailing a stick in the packed dirt of an ancient animal trail. "She thinks I'm a good student. I let her think that. I don't tell her where we go. She'd only worry if I did."

As the other boys shared similar experiences, they became boisterous and confident.

"I wonder what special thing we will get today," Reinhard mused.

"We'll find out soon enough," Matthias said.

"There it is!" Reinhard exclaimed, pointing the way. "Come on!"

As one, they ran, shouting and encouraging each other onward.

"Hello, Private," Hart greeted Roy. "Have you something special for my friends and me today?"

"Cheeky squirt," Roy said, tousling Hart's hair. "Always come with your hand out. One day, I might ask for something from you."

"Hey, Roy!" one of the privates hollered from the back of a truck. "I've got something really special!"

The private stepped from the shadow of the vehicle, hopped out, and turned toward the spot he had vacated. Reaching in, he withdrew a great green oblong with darker green stripes. He grinned from ear to ear as he hefted it to his shoulder.

"This should keep them quiet for a few minutes."

The boys agreed that none of them had seen such a gourd before. They poked at its hard sides, knocked on it.

"Hello?" Matthias said, trying to lift it. "What's in there?"

Two of them managed to lift it off the ground, but they could not carry it far.

"Here. Back off, boys," Roy said, raising his Bowie knife high and stabbing it straight through the middle.

He forced the gourd to turn against his knife, cutting it in half and revealing the deep red flesh and black seeds of a watermelon, ripe and juicy for eating. The boys gasped, as one, and gathered near him for a closer look.

"*Was ist das*?" Hart asked.

"It's called a watermelon," Roy answered.

"Wa-der-mel-n?" Hart repeated, using Roy's pronunciation.

"Wa-ter-mel-on," Roy clarified.

"Watermelon! Watermelon!" the boys jumped for joy, repeating their mantra.

"Here, squirts, try some," Roy encouraged, cutting wedges and handing them to the boys.

Juice ran down their faces and arms and dripped into dusty plops at their bare feet. The boys sucked the juice, enjoying each sweet slurp.

"*Das ist gut!*" the boys agreed, smiling from ear to ear.

Having enjoyed their visit with Roy and his comrades, the boys bid the men goodbye and started toward the path that led them down the Rock.

"Wait!" the private working in the back of the truck hollered. "Take one home with ya. There's lots here."

He handed a second, smaller melon to Hart and Reinhard. The boys beamed their thanks and waddled down the path, the melon balanced between them.

At the first landing, Hart and Reinhard gingerly set the watermelon in the soft dirt.

"This will take us a long time to get home," Reinhard observed. "My arms are already getting tired."

"All right," Hart announced. "We'll take turns. That way we will all have long arms when we get home, not just Reinhard and me."

The boys giggled, and two others stepped forward to take a turn. At the next landing, the melon was transferred to the third pair. At the last landing, Hart and

118

Reinhard stepped forward to lift the melon again. As they struggled to find a balanced hold, the melon slipped from their hands and rolled toward the bottom of the hill.

"*Hurra!*" they shouted, watching it wobble out of sight.

As one, the boys raced down the hill hollering at the watermelon to wait for them. Ignoring their collective pleas, the watermelon continued rolling, picking up speed on the hill's decline. It wobbled drunkenly each time it collided with a root or stone protruding from the path. The boys hastened to catch it, but it staggered beyond their grasp. Near the foot of the path, an overlarge root interrupted the melon's escape, and the force of the collision sent it skyward. Its flight thwarted by gravity, the gourd plummeted toward earth and conveniently shattered into six pieces when it smashed on the plateau of an ancient boulder. The boys skidded to a stop at the foot of the stone and goggled at the jagged pile of melon still wobbling on its plateau.

"Hurra!" Hart shouted again, jumping for joy. "Now we can carry this easily."

He whipped out a folded handkerchief from his trousers pocket, shook out the folds and gently wrapped it around one of the pieces. The others did the same, enthusiastically selecting their own juicy portion. With melon pieces preciously embraced, the boys set off toward home, agreeing amongst themselves that dropping the melon was the smartest thing they could have done.

That summer—the summer of the Americans, the boys called it—Hart's leadership and creativity bloomed. Small glimpses of the man he would become were etched deep into his psyche.

URSULA

CHAPTER TWELVE

Ursula Sertic arrived home from school early on Christmas Eve, 1960. She lived with her parents in a run-down cottage located in a small Yugoslavian village not far from the Adriatic coast.

She had no homework to do during the Yuletide break. Instead, she borrowed three books—two from the school library and one from her favourite teacher, Miss Breskve. Seated on a small, worn chair, Miss Breskve's book felt heavy in Ursula's lap.

"This book is an old friend to me," the teacher had told Ursula earlier that day.

Honoured to have won her teacher's trust, Ursula promised to take very good care of all three of books. Her index finger traced the letters on the worn cover as she mouthed the words: *Alice's Adventures in Wonderland*. Her eyes glazed. *Wonderland ... what would that be like?* As often happens when one wonders, Ursula's mind, by a series of connecting thoughts, fell on her father of nine long-suffering years.

"I have great news!" Edin Sertic had proclaimed just two days before. "I've received a bonus, and I've bought us a most remarkable Christmas surprise."

"What is it, *Tata*?" Ursula had asked her father, excited to know that she was to receive a Christmas gift for the first time in her life.

"Oh, I can't tell you. It's a surprise! You will have to wait two more days." He had tugged at her golden braid with a reddened hand, and chuckled.

"But I must know now!" Ursula had insisted with a stamp of her foot, realizing her mistake as the words slipped from her mouth. She had watched her father's eyes darken and felt his pleasant mood snap.

"I said you must wait and wait you will." His voice had been low, edged with warning. Caterpillar eyebrows had connected across a furrowed forehead that reached to the crown of his hairless pate, and his pale, yellow skin had morphed into a rich shade of scarlet. "Go to your room!" he hissed, pointing the way.

Ursula lowered her gaze and tried to read the first page of the first chapter of her teacher's book, but the words seemed to perform a folk dance, jumbling the letters.

Frustrated, she let her mind wander again. In the past year, her father had been diagnosed with alcoholic hepatitis and warned by his doctor that he would be dead by Christmas if he failed to turn his life around. She and her mother were thrilled to hear the news, confident that he had no capacity for change and that his love for strong drink would control him. They were wrong. Instead, Edin Sertic made their home a living hell.

He was suspended by the Union that had employed him for more than a decade while he suffered through withdrawal and recovery. He took to beating his wife, Slava, as a means to work off his frustrations, and constantly threatened Ursula with the same abuse. On several occasions, his beatings rendered Slava incapable of work. When they had no money for food, Slava insisted that he seek charity from the Church.

"Take Ursula with you," she said. "The priest will give you extra food when he sees how small and thin she is."

Rather than beg for food, Ursula's father took her to confession. When it was her turn to speak with the priest, Edin's threatening voice reminded her to say nothing of her mother's injuries, only that she was hungry. Ursula never learned what her father said when it was his turn in the confessional. She knew only that he carried home a basket filled with food. *I bet he never told the Father that he beats Mamica! One day, I'll tell him.*

Ursula slammed closed the cover of her book, struggling to rein in her frustration and anger. Sighing, she carefully placed the book on the floor with the other two and jumped to her feet. She paced ten steps to the other side of the room, and ten steps back to the chair from which she had popped, turned, and repeated the steps. *Tata is a horrid man. When he's near, I can't breathe.* She slammed a fist into an open palm. *Mamica is too afraid of him, so I must be brave for both of us. One day ...*

She stopped pacing and plopped into the chair. With elbows on her knees, she held her face in her hands. The borrowed books remained neatly piled by her feet. Suddenly realizing the time, Ursula jumped to her feet. *Oh, no! I'd better change my clothes before Tata and Mamica come home.*

In her room, Ursula removed the party dress that she had worn to school and hung it on a hook behind her door—a dress her mother had claimed from the charity bin the month before and altered; a dress that had been cast off by the sister of one of her classmates—and stuffed her legs hastily into a tattered pair of yellow pants, altered and patched by her mother many times. *No wonder everyone calls me Patches!* Pulling a blue knit sweater over her head, she shook out her braid and thought about her father's Christmas surprise.

After eight Christmases of not receiving a gift, Ursula could not contain her excitement. *It must be here somewhere. Tata and Mamica won't be home for a while.* She twirled on the spot, her thick braid flaring around her, her movement fed by edgy anticipation. *I'm certain I can find it, but I must just be careful that they never know. I can look surprised this evening when Tata presents it. I know I can.*

Ursula searched the kitchen cupboards for something unusual. She searched under the tattered armchairs where her parents sat in the evening. She took a kitchen chair, climbed upon it, and looked behind the

126

golden icons of Mary and Jesus hanging on the wall above the door to the yard. Then, she stepped off the chair, feeling disappointment seeping into her soul. Replacing the chair carefully back at the table, she dusted the seat on which she had stood.

This may take a while. She spied the pile of borrowed books and bent to retrieve them. *I'd better put these away, or Tata will yell at me when he comes home. He doesn't like books—thinks they're a waste of time.*

Once the books were stowed in her room, Ursula continued to puzzle on what and where the gift might be. She turned around in the small space that served as both kitchen and living room. In contemplation, she heaved a great sigh, inhaling deeply before she exhaled. *What was that?* Her nose twitched as she caught a whiff of something that was foreign to her. *I don't know that smell!* She sniffed again and again, wandering about the room trying to locate the source of the unusual odour. As she neared the door to her parents' bedroom, it intensified. With trepidation, she put her hand on the doorknob and slowly, quietly, turned it until the latch released.

Once, when Ursula was four years old, she had run into her parents' bedroom in the dark of night, frightened by a nightmare, tears spilling down her cheeks.

"If you ever enter this room again, I will whip you within an inch of your life!" her father had hollered from the bed, while her mother had comforted her and gently removed her from the room.

Ursula remembered the stale stench of alcohol that had permeated the room, paired with the reek of old cigarette smoke that clung to her father's clothes, a smell that had refused to leave even when her mother washed them repeatedly.

Ursula had never again stepped over the threshold of her parents' room.

On that Christmas Eve of 1960, Ursula pushed the door, opening a small crack, and was overcome with a tantalizing scent. She took a step back, as a smile formed on her lips. She gawked about the small room to assure herself that her parents had not returned home, then pushed the door again.

The fragrance was heady. *What is that?* Sniff. *I smell ...* Sniff. *I smell something sweet. What can it be? It's so powerful that my mouth waters to taste it.* She gazed about the room a second time. Convinced that it was devoid of parents, she took one hesitant step into the forbidden room and waited. Nothing happened. She took two more tentative steps into the room and looked behind the door. No parents jumped out to rebuke her.

Ursula tiptoed further into the room, worrying that she might leave footprints on the tiled floor. Standing by the bed, she closed her eyes and inhaled. She turned in a slow circle, continuing to inhale until she determined that the odour came from the direction of the bed. The walls were bare. The bed was bare, but for two small pillows and a thin counterpane. *Where can it be?* As she knelt to the floor, she was overwhelmed by the strange, unknown scent.

Leaning on her knees and elbows, Ursula peered under the bed, but saw nothing in the dark shadow. She reached out her arm and waved her hand freely until it collided with something solid. *Aha!*

She stretched out on her side, freeing both arms and reached under the bed. With a firm grip on a rectangular box, she pulled it toward her. Small vents on the sides of the box allowed the concentrated odour to escape. *What's that smell!*

Ursula dragged the box into the middle of the small bedroom and sat cross-legged in front of it. Gently, she wiggled the lid, until it popped free.

Bananas! Bunches of small, perfect bananas!

"Gosh! They're nothing like the pictures I've seen at school," she muttered, tracing her finger along a smooth curve.

She stroked the length of one curved

fruit, noting a brown mark near its neck. Some of the others had tiny brown freckles marring their perfect yellow coats. A single fruit rested alone at the end of the box. She picked it up, wrapping her fingers around its girth, then held it under her nose, inhaling its sweet scent. Her breath quickened. *I have never smelled anything as wonderful!* A grin of appreciation spread on her thin, pink lips.

She examined the yellow fruit further, then tugged at it until the skin split, exposing the creamy flesh within. Gingerly, Ursula pinched off a piece of the meat and bit into it. She closed her eyes and chewed, feeling the firmness collapse into lumpy mush. She swallowed, ran her tongue around her teeth in appreciation, and smiled with satisfaction. *What a wonderful taste!*

Ursula ate the remainder of the banana, promising herself that she would discard the skin in a neighbour's rubbish bin before her parents arrived home. *They will never know one small banana is missing,* she assured herself.

Ursula picked up the lid of the box and set it down again. *Just one more*, she promised herself. *I'll leave the rest for Tat's surprise.*

Each time Ursula picked up the lid to close the box, she made the same promise.

⚜

An hour later, the last sunbeam had crossed the window, leaving little light in her parents' bedroom. Ursula emitted a banana-flavoured belch, a very satisfied belch. At her knees still sat the box, full of deflated, browning skins. A sense of panic struck her when she realized that her parents would be home soon. She hastened to replace the lid and pushed the box under the bed, as far as it would slide. Before she closed the bedroom door, she looked about the room to ensure that nothing else had been disturbed by her invasion, that no footprints on the tiled floor betrayed her entry.

⚜

In her room, the size of a cupboard, a smile of contentment brightened Ursula's plain face. She stretched out on her slab of a bed and licked her sticky fingers, then she crossed her hands over her gurgling belly and fell asleep. Not long after, her mother arrived.

"Ursula, why are you in bed? Have you no school work?" her mother demanded, startling her from a stupor. "Come and help me prepare the Christmas stew."

Ursula cracked open one eye. Her mother's head appeared to be suspended in the doorway.

"No, Mamica. I'm not feeling well," she lied, forcing herself to stifle a giggle. "I don't want food tonight."

"Very well," her mother said, "but don't forget that Tata plans to share his Christmas surprise before we eat. I hope you feel well enough to come out for that at least."

The frizzy-haired head disappeared, and the bedroom door closed quietly behind it.

Ursula grinned in the dark of her room, and rubbed her satisfied belly, relieved that her mother seemed to think nothing was amiss. With a jolt, she sat upright. *Mamica found nothing amiss, but Tata certainly will, and very soon!* Ursula's grin melted. Her belly full of half-digested bananas roiled.

"You stupid, selfish child!" Slava screeched. She held a damp cloth to her cheek, the blue bruising already visible. "Couldn't you wait?"

Ursula's mother grimaced as she watched Edin raise and lower his belt to Ursula's bared backside. Ten times he whipped it high and thrashed the buckled end against tender flesh. Ten bright red welts, marred with bloody gouges, formed across her buttocks. Droplets of blood pooled before dribbling into groves between the welts.

As each lash dragged across her buttocks, Ursula clenched her teeth and stifled a scream. *I won't let this whipping ruin my joy!* Instead, she focussed on the delightful banana taste that continued to seep up the back of her throat and spew through her nostrils, gratified that she alone had eaten the entire Christmas surprise. Her lip quivered as she fought back the urge to grin, dreading that her father might misunderstand and think that she enjoyed the beating.

When Edin's belt fell for the last time, Slava pointed to Ursula's small room and told her not to come out until breakfast.

"You will have no Christmas dinner," her mother's angry voice promised.

"I hate you both!" Ursula declared, as she stomped into her room and slammed the door behind her.

"Why you—come back here this instant!" Edin shouted, moving to follow his daughter, his belt raised above his head.

"Edin, that's enough!" Slava said, grabbing his arm.

Ursula's backside throbbed for hours following the beating, but she refused to think about the pain. *I have nowhere to sit anyway.* Instead, she crawled onto her

135

bed and curled into a ball. *Who cares about missing Christmas dinner. I hate fish stew!*

Moments later, she stretched and rolled gingerly to her other side. *After Christmas mass tomorrow, I will tell the priest what Tata has done. I will even show him the proof!*

Sometime in the night, when the house was still and only the odour of fish remained, Ursula started from a restless slumber. *One day, when I'm old enough, I'll move away from here! I'll have lots of money, and I'll do what I want.* A small burp sent the last of the banana fumes into her mouth, and a dreamy expression seeped over her countenance, as she murmured, "And I'll have all the bananas I can eat!"

PART II

CHARTING
A COURSE

MIRIAM

CHAPTER THIRTEEN

Once a week, while Miriam was at school, Willem visited Mina. It was a convenient arrangement. He used the door at the back of the townhouse to ensure he could not be seen from the street or the school yard.

Late one afternoon, as Willem and Mina chatted over coffee about the promise of Mina's new career and the convenience of being neighbours, Miriam barged through the blue door, excited about a school dance. She stopped mid-sentence, her hand still on the doorknob, one shoe kicked off, her stocking foot suspended.

"Meneer van Bosch!" she exclaimed, a smile of delight spreading across her face.

Mina's cup halted its journey to her lips and hung between her pinching fingers. Willem gasped. Mina set her cup down, as Willem rose from his chair abruptly.

"I must be going," he said to Mina, reaching for the jacket and hat that he had tossed onto a chair hours earlier. He slipped his feet into the loafers he had shed at the foot of the stairwell prior to their hasty diversion upstairs and twisted the door knob.

"Miriam, nice to see you again," Willem said, planting his hat on his head and shutting the door behind him.

Miriam watched Meneer van Bosch trip off each step down to the street, so quickly that he appeared to slide from one to the next. On the walkway, he turned right, away from the yellow door of his home, his brisk stride taking him to the corner and right again, out of Miriam's sight.

"You didn't tell me Meneer van Bosch would be visiting today," she challenged, glowering at her mother, her brows raised in question. "I would have come home early if I'd known he'd be here." She kicked off her other shoe and set the pair neatly at the door, stuffing her feet into house clogs.

"Come home early!" Mina exclaimed, seeming flustered by her daughter's abrupt entry. "What do you mean? You are home early!"

"Oh, yeah. We were let off early today. Teachers had a meeting. So, what's with him?" Miriam ticked her head toward the closed door. "His behaviour was odd. Why did he run away so fast?" She cast an accusatory glance at her mother. "I thought you weren't doing window work anymore?" She struggled to keep her comments casual.

Mina extracted herself from her chair and moved to the sofa, inviting Miriam to take the seat opposite. Miriam plopped into the chair and crossed her feet over her thighs, soles pointed skyward, her face full of expectation.

"Well?" Miriam urged.

"I don't do window work anymore. Meneer van Bosch is a friend, that's all. He visits from time to time."

"What! When I'm not here? Why doesn't he visit me anymore?"

"He will, eventually. It's just that, well, he has a new job and his time isn't his own. He visits when he can, which happens to be during school hours. That's all."

"Oh," Miriam responded with disappointment. "Well, I want to know when he can come to visit me. I must know. I must be here when he comes again."

Miriam's thoughts twirled about, making every sense to her. *If Meneer van Bosch is merely mama's friend, maybe there's a place in his life for me. He's so handsome. I don't care that he's old.* Her mind wandered on with thoughts about his powerful arms wrapped around her, crushing her small breasts to his hard chest. She started to tingle again, and her breath became shallow.

"Miriam? Are you all right?"

"Huh? What did you say?" Miriam blinked a few times, feeling the beat of her heart slowing. "Yes, I'm fine. I just have a small headache. I think I'll go to my room and lie down."

"That's a good idea."

They both rose.

"Would you mind taking the dishes to the kitchen first? I have to run upstairs for a moment."

"Sure," Miriam agreed, watching her mother dart up the stairs. She moved the dirty dishes to the kitchen and went up to her room, stopping at the front door to collect her school books. As she passed the doorway to her mother's room, she saw Mina straightening the bedding.

"What are you doing, Mama?" Miriam asked, realization dawning. "Did you just have sex with him? After you told me you weren't a window worker? You told me you were just friends!" Hysteria tickled Miriam's brain. *If she's still entertaining him, my plans could be ruined.*

Mina stepped through the door frame and wrapped an arm around her daughter's shoulder.

"Come, my dear. You've gone quite pale. Let me tuck you in for a rest. I'll get you a tablet for your headache."

"Leave me alone," Miriam shouted, shrugging her mother's arm off her shoulder and stomping down the hall to her room. "Liar!" Her bedroom door slammed behind her, emphasizing her anger.

⚜

Mina took heavy steps down to the main floor clinging to the handrail for support, stooped in misery.

"What was that about?" she puzzled aloud. "Why would she call me a liar?"

Seated on the sofa again, Mina reflected on the events of the past months, from the time Willem had walked out of the old apartment, until now. She did not understand her daughter. She had done everything she could to raise her well and protect her, and yet the girl seemed to be so angry. Even the move away from De Wallen, switching schools, and changing her own employment did not seem to be enough to alter Miriam's attitude.

Slowly, Mina rose, took her coat and hat from the hook by the door, and slipped out of her house clogs into street shoes. She opened the blue door, descended the steps, turned right on the side walk, and right again at the corner. At the next corner, she turned right again, and repeated her actions once more at the next corner. Instead of heading once again to the next corner that would lead back to her own front door, she turned down the lane and ascended the back stairs of the first townhome. Willem opened the door to her rap and welcomed her inside.

Mina had never been inside Willem's home and, until recently, had never seen the outside. As she looked about it, she was surprised. Compared to the townhome next door, its furnishings were sparse. The kitchen was similar so far as cabinetry and appliances were concerned, with a simple wooden table and two chairs. Through the passageway into the parlour she saw only two large, wing-backed chairs, a small table, and a footstool.

Willem took her coat and hat and hung them next to the rear door, then invited her to precede him into the parlour. Mina had yet to speak, but her furrowed brow and trembling body conveyed clearly to Willem that she was deeply disturbed.

"Go along. I'll make some tea and be right in," he said. "Hot beverages seem to offer comfort in a time of stress."

Overwhelmed by her own concerns, Mina did not have the energy to puzzle through his comment. A short time later, Willem placed a tray of tea things on the table between the chairs and poured tea into a simple heavy mug.

"Tell me what's troubling you, my dear."

A tear traced a line from the corner of her eye to her lip, where the tip of her tongue captured the salty drop. She sobbed and turned her glossy brown eyes to Willem.

"I feel helpless," she said. "Miriam is so angry, and I don't know how to fix what troubles her. She used to be so open and easy to please, but since that episode a few months ago —when you walked out—she's changed."

"Wait! Are you blaming me?" Willem's words sounded defensive.

"No! Of course not. I'm just noting the timing." Miriam contemplated the hot tea, took a tentative sip and lowered the mug to cradle it in her lap.

"Help me?" she pleaded, tracks of her tears still glistening on her face.

"Of course," he comforted her, reaching across to stroke her hand. "Do you think she might talk to me? We have never had a private conversation, so I can't imagine I can do much. On the other hand, she might find it helpful to speak with someone she hopefully perceives as objective. You're certain she doesn't know I'm her father?"

Mina hesitated, contemplating his question.

"No. That's not possible. The only people who know are you, me, Mama, and the doctor. Astrid doesn't count. She's not here."

"Fine, then. I'll send Miriam a note and ask her to meet me for tea next week, after school."

"Not here, Willem," Mina said, reaching her hand to rest on his arm. "She doesn't know."

"Don't worry. I'll suggest the tea shop on Kastel Street. It's not far. She'll be safe walking there. I'll bring her home afterward."

Mina recovered from her sense of despair once the plan was set and took her leave.

The aroma of a simmering dinner finally brought Miriam down the back stairs.

"Hungry?" Mina asked.

Miriam kept her eyes on the floor but nodded. Zombie-like, she moved about the kitchen, avoiding any possible collision with Mina, and set the table. They ate in silence and, as soon as the dishes were cleared away, Miriam stomped up the back stairs to her room.

The following day was the same. Mina often caught Miriam scowling when she thought her mother was out of sight. *If looks could kill.* Mina's only solace was the time Miriam spent at school.

On the third day, Willem's invitation arrived with the post. Mina set it on the hall table, in clear sight so that Miriam would see it when she returned from school. She did. Without removing coat and shoes, she snatched it up and tore it open.

Miriam read the note and hugged it to her chest, her expression dreamy. She kicked off her shoes, flung her coat onto the hook, grabbed her school books, and ran up the stairs to her room.

Odd, thought Mina, who was seated on the sofa sipping a cup of coffee, *she did not even notice me sitting here.* The bang of Miriam's bedroom door startled her from her reverie. The Hermle mantle clock, its moon phase rising, started to chime five o'clock.

Time to prepare dinner. Lately, dinner is one of the few occasions when Miriam spends time with me. Better than nothing, I suppose.

Mina sensed a slight shift in Miriam's attitude when her daughter came down for dinner. She hoped that was a sign of better days to come.

"I saw you had a letter today," she said in a forced, but cheery voice. "You don't usually get letters. Is it from one of your old school mates?"

For the first time in three days, Miriam raised her head and glared at her mother, then returned her eyes to her meal.

If looks could kill.

Miriam continued her silence for the next week, responding to Mina's attempts at conversation with an occasional scowl. On Tuesday morning, she left for school with the usual banging of the blue door and tromped down the steps.

A while later, when Mina descended the steps with an armful of laundry, she found a folded paper on the hall table with her name printed neatly in Miriam's hand. *Why my name? Why not Mama?* She set the laundry on a stair and reached for the paper, her hand trembling. The message was short and terse:

Mina,

You're a liar. My whole life you have pretended to work in a shop when all you are is a cheap prostitute. You pretend to play house and that we are a happy family, while you dare to have sex with Meneer van Bosch. You don't deserve him. He is too good for you. He will be mine, now. I won't be back. I'm going to him. I hate you!

CHAPTER FOURTEEN

The note was unsigned, but it was clear that Miriam had written it. Mina kicked off her clogs, jammed her feet into her shoes, and grabbed the note. This time a coat was not needed. She went out the back door that fed into the lane, downstairs and upstairs, and pounded on Willem's door.

"Mina. What is it?" Willem asked when he opened the door.

In response, she jabbed the note at his chest. He took it without moving his eyes from her face.

"Read it!" she demanded, and he did.

"She thinks—oh my!—she thinks ..." she covered her mouth, gasping, bending forward as if she expected to vomit.

Willem wrapped his arms around her and held her until the trembling stopped. He guided her into the kitchen, shutting the door behind them. An odour of break-fast-past lingered in the room.

"She th-thinks you've turned from m-me. That you want h-her instead!" Mina stammered.

Willem released Mina long enough to put the kettle on the fire, then led her through to the parlour, his mind rapidly reviewing their prior discussions and decisions.

"How could our good intentions have turned on us?" he asked the steaming kettle.

Mina calmed herself while Willem organized a tea tray and brought it into the parlour. He poured tea into a mug and handed it to her.

"What exactly did you write in your note?"

"Are you suggesting that this is my fault?" he exclaimed.

"No, not at all. I am the one who is at fault. Everything I have done to ensure that her life was better than mine has failed. If only we could see the consequences of our actions before we take them. I keep asking myself, what could I have done better or differently?"

"I understand. It's my fault, too," he assured her. "I should have been more assertive about being involved in her upbringing, but I respected your mother's decision, and yours. I have failed you, all of you." His clasped hands hung between his knees, while he silently reviewed their predicament. "As to the note," he said, "I simply asked if she was available to have tea with me next Tuesday—that's today, of course—at 4:00 p.m., and gave the name and address of the tea shop. I wrote nothing to suggest more than tea and a chat. I don't understand how she can think anything else."

"Ha! I can. She's a child becoming a woman. She's struggling with her identity and what will become of her. She has needs and doesn't know what to do about them."

"Well, she must be told that those plans don't include me! This is preposterous."

He jumped from his chair and began to pace.

"Willem," Mina looked up at him, "I think we must tell her who you are. Meet her for tea this afternoon and bring her home afterward. We can tell her together."

"You're certain?" he asked, a glimmer of hope kindling in his eyes.

"I'll tell Mama," Mina said, nodding with a determined expression.

By the time the mugs were empty, Willem and Mina had devised a way to tell Miriam the truth.

"I'm relieved to know that the fuel for lies between us will end," Mina said.

"And I'm excited to finally be able to tell my daughter of our relationship," Willem replied.

At 4:00 p.m., Willem watched his daughter appear in the doorway of the teashop and take slow steps toward the table where he sat. Normally a confident child, she appeared apprehensive and timid.

"Welcome, child. Have a seat."

He placed a slight emphasis on the word child as he indicated the chair opposite, gallantly rising to pull it out for her. Miriam sat as directed, perching on the edge of the chair, hugging her school bag to her chest.

"I've ordered tea and biscuits for us. Shall I pour?" he asked.

Miriam nodded.

For several minutes, no words were exchanged as they sipped their tea. Finally, Willem broke the silence, asking Miriam how she was faring in school.

"It's difficult," she told him. "I don't know many students, and they all have their own groups of friends. I've met a few nice boys, but the girls aren't so friendly. There is one girl. She's in the next level. Her name is Kristina. I like her. She seems nice."

"How long have you been at the school, now? Four, six weeks?"

Miriam nodded again.

"These things take time, especially as you get older," her father advised. "When children are young, they think everyone is their friend, but as they get older, they develop opinions and suspicions. You will overcome those obstacles."

"I hate it. I feel like everyone is looking at me, wondering whether I'm a prostitute, too." Her words seemed forced and low. Anger flared in her eyes, as she cast about the café to ensure that no one was listening.

"Miriam, that's not fair. I think you need more information. Why don't I take you home and we can talk with your mother about this?"

"Take me home?" she said, recoiling into her chair. "I'm never going back there. I hate her. I want to be with you." Her eyes pleaded with him. Willem heard her desperation and searched for the appropriate words.

"I've an idea," he said without certainty. "Let me take you home. If your mother agrees, I will take you with me, but not until you've heard what needs to be said."

⚜

Miriam was surprised. The cunning in her eyes shifted for a moment, then returned. She almost had what she wanted. He would take her away. He was willing to be her lover. She could see affection in his eyes.

"All right, if you promise to take me with you."

"I promise that if your mother is unable to change your mind, you may come with me."

The uncertainty that appeared on Miriam's face when she entered the café disappeared into a toothy grin. *I've won!*

Willem paid for the tea and escorted Miriam to his car, then drove the few blocks to the townhouse with the blue door. As Willem and Mina revealed their relationship and Miriam's parentage, Miriam's anger swirled in her gut. Her hands trembled, and her knees jumped.

The two of them sit there holding hands, trying to convince me of their love. They want us to be a family! They've ruined everything. This is not what I planned! Miriam's mind raced.

"I've heard enough!" she screamed, jumping from her chair. "You two are disgusting! I hate you both!" Tears of frustration and anger poured down her cheeks as she ran up the stairs to her room and slammed the door behind her.

Willem and Mina sat quietly, cocooned in frustration.

"Whatever are we to do?" Mina asked into Willem's shirt, her tears melting its crispness.

"There's nothing to be done in the moment. Let's give her time to think about what we've said and we'll try again."

As the week progressed, Miriam's silent resentment increased. The routine continued as it had before she met Willem for tea. She said nothing to Mina and spent her time in her room unless it was to eat or go to school. She refused to even look at Mina. The townhouse was electric with Miriam's anger and hatred.

Although Willem ate dinner with them every evening, Miriam's reception of him was just as icy. At the end of the weekend, however, Miriam's attitude changed. She was not happy, but she was friendly enough. She spoke to Mina about general day-to-day things but revealed nothing of her true feelings.

Miriam had worked out her own dilemma. She realized that being angry all the time would not help her reach her goals any faster. *It's better to take advantage of the situation. I need to get away, but to do that, I need money.*

She had not decided where she would go, but it would be far away. Every day since Tuesday, she had spread the tarot cards over the desk in her room and contemplated her destiny. Every day, the answer had been the same. Travel and rich men were her future. Opportunity would present itself soon. She knew it. *The cards didn't lie. Oma taught me that.*

CHAPTER FIFTEEN

Life behind the blue door eventually returned to a new normal. Miriam's naiveté morphed into a determination to see her plan fulfilled. She closed herself to emotion, focussing instead on her escape and realizing her own desires.

She watched people and identified their vulnerabilities. She kept a book of weaknesses and hid it in the pocket of an old green coat, hanging at the back of her closet. In her book of weaknesses, she noted how defenseless Willem and Mina were. *Now they're married, and I finally have the name I should have had from birth! They think that life is so wonderful*, she mused, resentment gnawing away her logic.

She recalled how, on the wedding day, her grandmother had handed her mother a box of emerald earrings that matched the necklace that her mother always wore.

She had been stunned by the gesture. Her grandmother, she knew, always wore the earrings.

"Just for today, right Mama," Mina had said. "Eamon gave you these. You can't give them away."

"Just for today," Punita agreed, embracing her daughter fiercely.

Why so much emotion over a pair of earrings, Miriam thought with a shudder. *You'd think they were never going to see each other again. I'll never understand those two. If I ever inherit that stupid necklace, I'll sell it and put the money to good use!*

As Christmas approached, Mina invited her mother to join her in a day of holiday shopping followed by afternoon coffee in the townhouse. While Mina arranged a coffee tray, Punita contemplated the results of the chaos that Miriam had wreaked since early spring.

"I sincerely hope that your marriage will ground Miriam and settle her," Punita said, spreading her tattered tarot cards over the end of the dining room table. She sighed deeply as she read and reread their meaning.

"The cards tell of the challenges that Miriam will encounter as she matures—the same message as always. I had hoped to change her course, but it seems I've failed." She flipped a few more cards. "The cards are full of foreboding. Always speaking of dark brown eyes, the colour of melted chocolate. The prophecy Mama warned me about years ago still haunts us. We three have eyes that colour, and Mama did too. And now the cards tell of German men who appear as soldiers! Mama, help us understand!" she prayed to the soul who had always guided her, quivering at the thought of more German soldiers.

Following the wedding, Willem moved into the townhouse, and openly shared a bedroom with Mina. *I don't want to imagine what they do at night when the door is closed,* Miriam contemplated with resentment. *That should be me in his arms. Why does he have to be my father!*

She let her parents think she was happy and bided her time. Instead, she used her charm to cajole them into buying new outfits for her, and anything else she needed to be part of the elite school clique.

At school, Miriam charmed the teachers until they favoured her; she charmed the popular girls into thinking she was one of them; and she charmed one of the studious boys, so he would help her with her homework. If the boy only explained an answer, she kissed him on the cheek. If he did the work, she let him kiss her mouth. If she was particularly pleased with his work, she might let him run his tongue along her lips.

Miriam particularly charmed the boys that she had named on her exclusive list of possibilities—the ones she thought suitable for her ultimate purpose. She learned that using charm to achieve goals took time. She also learned to be patient.

Willem and Mina seemed delighted that their daughter fit into the school's society. They often expressed pride in her accomplishments and rewarded her for her high marks. They opened a bank account in her name and made generous deposits each time she achieved a perfect score on an exam.

When Miriam achieved a goal, she recorded her success in the book of weaknesses: what was required to stroke an ego; whether it was worth the effort; how long it took to reach success.

By the time her seventeenth birthday arrived, she felt ready. *I've reached every goal I've set so far, and I have money in my bank account to fund my ultimate escape.*

HART

CHAPTER SIXTEEN

In mid-August of 1964, Hart's parents informed him that his father had been diagnosed with throat cancer and that he was being sent to München for surgery.

"The doctor says that the recovery process will be slow and that I should expect to be in München for some time," Paul told his son. "We have made arrangements for your mother to stay at your aunt's house, which is close to the hospital, and because Emma isn't in school yet, she'll come with us."

"What about me?" Hart asked, wringing his hands.

"I've made arrangements for you to attend a private boys' school in Marburg,"

Paul replied. "It's a very good school, and I think you'll thrive there."

"How long do I have to stay there?" Hart asked, looking first to his father, then his mother.

"You will have to consider this as an adventure, son," Paul said. "Once you start at the school, you will be expected to complete your studies and graduate from there. You can come home on school breaks, but during study time, you will reside at the school."

"Do I have any say in this?" Hart asked, already beginning to feel a sense of isolation.

"I'm afraid not, son," Paul said kindly, as he placed a reassuring hand over his wife's. She had been sitting next to her husband with her head down, but raised it when he touched her, blinking to clear tears pooling in her eyes.

"Hart, you must take this opportunity for yourself and grow from it," Ilse-Renata said. "Your father's illness is serious and he will need me by his side while he recovers. You, on the other hand, are a clever student and the challenges set by the new school will help you grow in knowledge and character. You must do this not only for yourself, but for your family too. This is how you will help us. Do you understand?"

"Yes, *Mutti*, I understand," Hart replied, disheartened at the thought of being separated from his family. "I would rather be with you and Vati though."

"We will talk on the telephone," Ilse-Renata said. "You can call us anytime you feel the need, and we will call you with updates."

"All right," Hart replied, already feeling more confident.

At the end of August, Hart travelled with his mother and father to the school in Marburg. They were greeted by a school director who had arranged for Hart's luggage to be delivered to a room in the dormitory, his home for the next three years. Senior students escorted them into the school dining hall where other parents mingled and enjoyed refreshments, while their sons introduced themselves.

After a short welcome by the Chair of the school, each new student received a card on which their room number was noted, together with instructions for unpacking, and an agenda for the remainder of the day. The Chair thanked the parents for accompanying their sons, then concluded the visit.

Hart hugged good-bye with his parents, wishing his father success with the medical treatment, and waved until their vehicle turned the corner at the end of the block. When he could no longer see them, he withdrew the card from his pocket and noted the Chair's instructions. Tucking it back into his pocket, he went in search of his new accommodation.

Within the first week of school, Hart had singled out new friends with whom he would navigate the high school years, in particular Manfred Bartz, Konrad Schneider, and Penn Tresler. Each boy was clever, creative, and athletic in his own way. Other than Penn, they qualified for the school's soccer team, the swimming team, and the rowing team.

"Before my second birthday," Penn told them, "I contracted poliomyelitis. I can use my legs to stand and to shuffle a few feet, but I'm told that I will never walk again." In response to the pained look on the faces of his new friends, Penn replied, "Don't look sad on my account. I'm a very strong swimmer and can easily challenge anyone with perfectly-functioning legs. Besides, if you three take turns pushing me in my wheelchair on the jogs around the grounds, you'll build up greater strength than any other competitors!"

Together, they established a study routine, so they would excel in their schoolwork, and have free time for sports and other activities that might inspire them. While each had his own inner confidence, it was Hart's leadership and forward-thinking that kept them organized and together.

⚜

Manfred took a long draw from his cigarette, inhaling deeply and releasing puffy clouds of smoke from his nose. Penn waved his hand in disgust and wrinkled his nose.

"Manfred, you know you're going to have to give up smoking, don't you?" he said. "My father says that smoking damages your lungs. If you're going to be an athlete, you need to have a pure body. Am I right?" Hart and Konrad nodded in agreement.

"*Ja*," Konrad said, "and we want to win the first-year competitions."

It was during the first term of their first year together, and the four boys had been out for a Saturday morning jog before they returned to the library to study. Their still-developing weekend routine involved an early jog, studying until noon, and training after lunch.

"Well, it won't be hard," Manfred said, in self-defense. "I'm only getting one smoke a day now, anyway."

"What does 'only getting' mean?" Konrad asked.

"There's nowhere to smoke around here. Unless we're off the school grounds, like now, or in the communal toilets." Manfred dropped his half-smoked cigarette and ground it with his toe.

"And so ..." Konrad encouraged him, as the boys started walking toward the main building.

"Well, jeez. If we go into the toilet to smoke, we barely have a chance for one drag, and some senior's there snatching it away, telling us to get lost!"

"So, on the up side," Hart summarized, "you're being forced to quit smoking by an extenuating circumstance. And, at the same time, the thieves are damaging their own health and therefore possibly their ability to compete successfully."

"Probably," Manfred agreed, his voice sullen. He rolled his shoulders and crooked his neck.

"Who steals your cigarettes?" Hart asked.

"Seniors, of course! They're bigger than we are and throw their weight around."

"Exactly!" Hart stopped walking and looked each boy in the eye. "If the seniors keep smoking, they'll be winded faster. We'll be able to beat them in sports competitions!"

The boys contemplated Hart's argument.

"Of course, we want to win," Konrad added, "but I don't think we want to condone what the seniors are doing. It's not right that anyone should steal, even cigarettes."

"Let's think on this," Hart agreed. "I bet we can come up with a way to handle the problem." His eyes twinkled with mischief.

The first weekend in November, the four friends wandered into Marburg to enjoy some of the Carnival festivities. They purchased *Bratwurst* and *Brötchen* from a food wagon and watched the parade of musical bands and street entertainers.

As he ordered a sausage and bun, Hart pointed to an advertisement on the side of the wagon.

"Hey! Schmidt Sausages is one of my family's businesses," he boasted.

"Then I'm going to buy one too," Manfred said, placing his coins on the counter. "I want to taste this fabulous sausage that you rave about!"

Hart watched young boys ranging in age from ten to twelve years scoot throughout the throngs of townsfolk, lighting bangers and tossing them near the show wagons, laughing with glee as a pair of horses standing nearby began snorting and bucking. As quickly as the young boys appeared, they were gone.

At the end of the afternoon, Hart and his friends started to retrace their steps back to the school. A string of unexploded bangers bounced off the tip of his shoe and skidded ahead of him. He bent to retrieve them, a sudden realization solving a problem he had been puzzling on for weeks.

"Look!" he said, holding up the unexploded string. "There are ten bangers here. Some kid's going to be disappointed that he's lost them."

The tiny red explosives, imported from

China, were appreciated mostly for the loud bangs they made when their fuses were lit.

"He may be disappointed, but I bet his parents are happy," Konrad replied. "Do you know how many children lose their fingers every year because they mishandle fireworks?"

"But these ones only make a noise," Hart countered. "It's when they are together in a bunch that they can cause serious harm. Besides, there's something more here." He stopped and turned to the others, eyes bright as his mischievous smile began to grow. "I think we have a solution to Manfred's problem!"

Hart explained his idea to the others and together they devised a plan. At the next street corner, Manfred jogged into a smoke shop and purchased a package of cigarettes, then they raced back to the school, eager to put their plan into action before the dinner bell rang.

During the first break on Monday morning, Manfred and some of the other first-year students headed for a quick smoke in the toilets nearest their next class. As expected, seniors followed them and stole the cigarettes before they could be lit. While the seniors lit their matches, the first-year students backed toward the hallway doors and quickly exited. They waited outside the toilets until they heard the first pop. Almost in unison, loud pops echoed throughout the campus. Laughing hysterically at the imagined scenes inside the toilets, the first-year students hastened toward their next class.

Each of the high-handed seniors, on the other hand, stood in stunned silence, staring at one another, mouths gaping—an extinguished match in one hand, a frayed cigarette stuffed with a tiny banger in the other. A few careless seniors sported singed eyebrows from flaring matches. Sooty lines streaked their faces, while red rage grew beneath. The smell of burned hair and fired black powder followed them along the corridors as they made their way to their next class, seething.

"That was a brilliant plan!" Penn praised Hart, as the boys reminisced the escapade a few weeks later. "Not only have the seniors stopped stealing cigarettes, but the school has designated a smoking area for anyone over sixteen."

"You've forgotten the most important part," Hart responded, his eyes alight. "Manfred quit smoking!"

CHAPTER SEVENTEEN

Near the end of the first term, as the four friends studied for their final exams, Penn pushed his chair away from the library table, and stretched. "God, I'm tired of studying."

"Ja, I feel like I'm seizing up," Hart agreed.

"Me too," Konrad said. "I'm looking forward to some winter sports during the school break."

"That doesn't help us now," Manfred replied. "We need to do something. Come on."

"Where're we going?" Penn asked.

"I don't know," Manfred answered, "somewhere."

"Wait!" Hart exclaimed with a victorious grin. "Get your coats and stuff, and meet me behind the old barn. I have an idea!"

"Now what?" Manfred asked, once they were re-assembled outside the barn. His breath carried his words on a misty cloud that dissipated into the frosty air.

Manfred and Konrad stamped their feet and flapped their arms, warming themselves against the winter chill. Ice crystals floated around them, sparkling in the autumn sunlight.

"Grab eight of those bricks," Hart said, "and follow me. Quietly." Another cloud of words dissipated into their circle.

The boys gave him a quizzical look before retrieving red bricks from a discarded pile near the garage. Hart skulked along the side of the building, then opened the side door typically used by instructors as a quick access to the adjacent science building.

"I could use assistance getting over the threshold?" Penn said. Hart tipped the chair and gave it a shove.

The boys followed Hart into the dim interior of the garage, toward the darkest corner and a small, blue '62 Fiat 500. Hart took two bricks from Penn and set them next to one of the Fiat's tires.

"Set a pair of bricks to the left of each tire," Hart instructed. "Make certain they're lined up precisely."

"You two," he said to Konrad and Manfred, "prepare to lift the mid-section of the car when I tell you. Penn, you watch the door. If you see any teachers, whistle and we'll duck out of sight."

"What are you going to do with the bricks?" Penn asked.

"Have a little fun," Hart said, winking at him.

"Okay, on my count of three, lift the vehicle and shift it to the left so that each tire settles on a stack of bricks. Ready?"

Konrad and Manfred nodded.

"One, two, three!" Each boy dug deep for strength, bending his knees and lifting. Their sinewy bodies held the little car easily, as they crab-walked left, hovering the tires above the bricks, while Hart scurried around them to ensure the landing would be accurate.

"Easy now," Hart instructed. "When you put the car down, each tire must sit centred on the bricks. Don't let go until I tell you." Hart looked toward the dirty window through which Penn peered. "Penn? What's happening?"

"Nothing now," Penn answered. "A grounds keeper was headed this way, but he veered off at the last minute."

"Why didn't you whistle?" Hart demanded.

"I can't," Penn said abashed, "never learned."

"Well, you'd better learn before next time," Hart teased. "We have to be able to rely on each other, if we're going to be a team." Hart turned his attention back to the Fiat. "Manfred, take your hands away." Manfred slowly stood and stretched, watching the weight of the tires settle. "Konrad, now you." Hart allowed them a moment to appreciate their efforts. "This car isn't going anywhere anytime soon. Let's go." He waved his hand in the direction of the side. Using the same stealth that they had employed when they had first entered, they filed out of the garage.

Outside again, the boys breathed deeply, welcoming the fresh air, visibly relieved that the prank was over. Penn sulked in his chair. Sensing his discomfort, Konrad wrapped an arm around Penn's neck and punched him in the shoulder.

"Hey, Penn, don't worry," he said. "I'll teach you to whistle. You have to be able to whistle if you're going to catch a girl's eye," he said.

"Or call your dog," Manfred replied, his mouth pinched to suppress his mirth.

"Enough, you guys," Hart said, putting an end to the teasing. "Come on. We have studying to do." While Hart pushed Penn's wheelchair, the three boys jogged back to the main building and returned to the library.

"Hart, why did we put the car so close to the wall? Why not leave it in the centre of the stall?" Konrad asked, as the boys doffed their coats.

"Shhh. Keep your voice down," Hart hissed in a loud whisper. "That car only locks by the left door."

Refreshed, the young men returned to their studies and gave no more thought to their adventure. Close to 17:00, Konrad's belly let out a loud growl. He looked up from the book he was reading, a shock of sandy hair covering his blue eyes.

"It must be near dinner time, I'm done for the day."

As they finished their work, they closed their books and piled them in the centre of the table.

"One of the things I like about being a resident student is not having to cart our books around," Penn said.

"Ja, certainly makes life easier," Konrad agreed.

Down the hall, the front door of the main building banged shut. The four friends looked up in surprise.

"Someone's in for it," Manfred whispered. "They let the door slam. The Chair won't be happy about that!"

The sound of heavy, clacking footsteps echoed in the hallway, coming toward the library. *Herr* Grunn rose from his desk, preparing to scold the errant student. Moments later *Frau* Kertz burst into the library.

"Oh! Herr Grunn! Oh my! A most egregious thing has happened!"

Herr Grunn wrapped an arm around the shoulder of the flustered instructor, guiding her into the room.

"Here, Frau Kertz. Have a seat and tell us what's wrong."

"One of you boys, fetch a glass of water from the dining hall for Frau Kertz," Herr Grunn commanded.

Manfred jumped at the command and ran from the library.

"Now, tell me what's troubling you. Are you unwell?" Herr Grunn asked, squatting before her, rubbing her hands in earnest.

"No, no," Frau Kertz said, coming to her senses. Her face was flushed and her breathing heavy. The trot down the hall had challenged her stout, middle-aged body. "A terrible thing has happened!"

She tugged her hands from Herr Grunn's grasp and flapped them freely.

"Some scallywags have mounted my dear Fiat on a pile of bricks!" she exclaimed.

"Can you not just reverse your vehicle off the bricks," Herr Grunn asked.

"No, no," Frau Kertz fussed, ringing her hands anxiously. "That would be impossible. My little Fiat would be destroyed! Besides, it's so close to the wall that I can't open the door. Oh, dear me, what am I to do!"

The three culprits busied themselves with the collection of their coats, turning away from the scene to hide their humour, coughing to avoid giggling. They looked everywhere but at each other, knowing

185

full well that, if they did, they would lose control. Manfred returned to the room carrying a glass of water. He handed it to Herr Grunn and looked to his friends for information. None came.

"Drink a little water, Frau Kertz," Herr Grunn suggested, "then we'll go have a look at your car."

The boys moved as a group to exit the library.

"Where do you boys think you're going?" he demanded. "Did you not hear that Frau Kertz has a dilemma? We must go with her and see what we can do to help! Wait for me at the front door. Tresler, you can wait here."

The frosty walk to the parking garage was a long, foreboding walk for the three friends who followed the lanky Herr Grunn and the waddling Frau Kertz. They had not expected to have to undo their handiwork.

"Just look what they've done!" Frau Kertz exclaimed, pointing to her beloved Fiat, each wheel sitting on bricks, its roof floating above the other staff vehicles. "They should be woefully punished!"

"I think we can help, Frau Kertz!" Hart offered with enthusiasm. "Two of us can lift the car by the mid-section," Hart said, "while the other removes the bricks. Konrad, will you remove the bricks?"

Manfred and Konrad glared at Hart, seeming to ask: *Are you crazy?* Hart smiled reassurance at them.

"On my count of three, lift—one, two, three!" Hart commanded.

The Fiat floated on air while Konrad quickly removed the bricks.

"On my count of three, set the car down," Hart commanded again. "One, two, three."

The Fiat floated safely to the floor of the garage, the two boys lowering it.

"Wait!" Hart shouted.

"It's too close to the wall. We must move it farther so Frau Kertz can open the door!"

Once again, the Fiat took wing and floated to the centre of the parking stall before it landed gracefully on the spot it had occupied earlier in the day. Clapping her hands with delight, Frau Kertz's chubby body wobbled as she praised the careful, thoughtful actions of the three first-year students.

"I don't know how to thank you," she said. "You deserve a reward and I will see to it that you have one. The scallywags who did this to my dear Fiat will be severely punished ... if I ever find out who's responsible!"

In response to her praise, the boys doffed their hats. Each picked up a set of bricks and bid a good evening to the two teachers. They returned the bricks to the brick pile and jogged back to the main building for dinner. By the time they reached the main building, they were laughing so hard that they could not speak. Steamy tears carved paths down their chilled cheeks.

"Let's take our coats to our rooms and try to calm down," Hart said, catching his breath. "We can't go into the dining hall laughing like this."

Ten minutes later, they appeared in the dining hall for their evening meal, and calmly took their seats next to Penn just as the first course was served. Sporadically, during dinner, one or the other of them received a good backslapping to interrupt a spontaneous fit of laughter. The Chair would not approve of their disturbance. Meals were a time for reflection, he insisted.

CHAPTER EIGHTEEN

Hart, Manfred, Konrad, and Penn had become trusted and loyal friends. They also became part of an elite group of boys who resided full-time at the school during the academic year. Those students were permitted, but were not required, to return home during school breaks. Many of them preferred to stay at the school with their friends during the short breaks, the four friends included.

"Anyone interested in joining a science club?" Manfred asked when classes resumed after the Christmas break. "I feel a need to be creative."

"I'll pass," Konrad and Penn spoke as one.

"I'm curious," Hart said. "I'll go with you."

As the weeks passed, Manfred and Hart realized a new way to express their creativity when they began building electronic gadgets.

"I have an idea," Manfred said, as the warm weather tickled new growth from trees around the school property. "Want to help me build a ham radio?"

"Of course!" Hart replied, grinning mischievously. "That sounds like fun."

The radio was assembled without fuss, and soon the boys were testing the transmitting capacity.

Manfred proved to have a talent for transmitting and broadcasting. He discovered that the frequency assigned exclusively to the American Armed Forces was not always in use, and he was able to pirate some of the unused air time. Soon, word spread amongst the students that they could tune into the AFN station to listen to Manfred's rogue broadcasts—even from home if they lived near the school—with one small difficulty. The air time could not be predicted. Listeners had to scan the frequency until they picked up his random signal.

Everyone knew that, if Manfred was caught, not only would his radio station be disbanded, but he would lose his seat at the school. They listened to his broadcasts, and not one student betrayed him.

"Aren't you worried about being caught by the German mobile station?" Konrad asked.

"Sure," Manfred responded, with obvious confidence. "That's one of the reasons why I broadcast randomly."

"Ja, but the school is only two hundred metres off the road; the mobile direction finding station could pick up your broadcast and nab you," Hart noted. "You need to have a mobile unit, too."

Hart and Manfred assembled a group of students interested in the benefits of ongoing broadcasts and, together, they designed a bicycle that could transport both the portable radio station and strong, durable batteries. Further, Hart organized a team of resident first-year students to monitor the presence of the mobile DF station whenever Manfred broadcast.

On any sighting of the DF vehicle, the first-year monitor reported to Manfred immediately, and together they loaded the radio and the batteries into a sturdy luggage rack rigged on the bicycle. Manfred then pedalled hastily in the opposite direction, sticking to paths too narrow for heavy DF trucks. As soon as the clever broadcaster found a safe location from which to transmit again, his program resumed.

From time to time, Manfred embellished his programs. On one occasion, he lowered a microphone from his second-floor dorm room and allowed it to rest on the ledge of an open window. On wisps of steam escaping from the senior boys' shower room, listeners overheard the inside scoop of the day's athletic competitions, blended with bawdy jokes and the players' latest conquests. Manfred was not one for censorship.

Those who knew Manfred delivered words of praise and encouragement personally, sometimes accompanied by a congratulatory back slap. Others used discretion and passed him notes in the hallway. If asked, any student would claim Manfred as their best friend. His broadcasts kept them united, entertained, and always wanting more.

In the City of Marburg, rumours began to circulate about a rogue radio station, broadcasting via the American Forces Network. The American military base had searched for, but had been unable to locate, the wireless bandit. AFN broadcasted solely to the American base—they believed—and, since the Americans had no interest in listening to a German broadcast, they chose to ignore the pirated usage, unaware of Manfred Bartz's uncensored programs.

CHAPTER NINETEEN

In 1965, Hart and his friends organized themselves for another term. During the week before commencement, they trickled into the school slowly, with a plan to meet every evening after dinner in the library. There, they would decide what activity they would undertake for the remainder of the evening.

Three days before commencement, the list of classes was posted. After dinner, the friends met at the bulletin board outside of the library and scanned through the lists, looking for their names and the classes that they would take, some together, some not.

"Oh, look," Manfred said, pointing to a page. "We four will be in the same economics class!"

"Yes," Konrad said, "but look who is to teach us ... Dietrich Neumann!"

The boys groaned as one, making faces of dislike.

"He's unbearable," Penn remarked. "He was my instructor for class last term. He can be nasty."

"I had him, too," Konrad said, curling his upper lip. "He went on and on about some special chalk boards that he had ordered for this term—how fantastic they are, how privileged he would be to have them. And so on, and so on." He rolled his eyes.

"Well, then," Hart said. "I think we will have an entertaining term!"

"Hart, why do you always have to be so happy about stuff like that?" Konrad chuckled, striking a boxing pose. "I'm going to wipe that grin off your face!"

"Aw, come on!" Hart assumed a boxing response.

The boys air-boxed, until Hart was able to crook his arm around Konrad's neck and knuckle his head, before releasing him. Hart threw up his hands.

"It's a challenge, guys! We love a challenge. Remember? It builds character!"

"You're the character," Konrad grumbled, punching Hart's arm playfully.

"We just have to bide our time," Hart assured them. "Neumann will soon provide us with an opportunity to have a little fun. You'll see." Hart's eyes twinkled with anticipation, infecting the others with the same mischief.

As predicted, an opportunity soon arose.

On the first day of classes, Dietrich Neumann boasted to each of his classes how privileged he was to have the first reloadable chalk boards.

"Look how wonderful they are!" he exclaimed, sliding one board out of the way to reveal another behind it. "I can write twice as many notes as I have in the past, before having to erase anything!"

With his back turned to the class, fists on hips, he admired the new boards with pride. Behind him, twenty boys sat, two to a table, two tables across, and five tables back. There were several rolled eyes on assorted impatient faces. Some threw up their hands, aping the teacher's enthusiasm.

"Oh, yes," Hart muttered at the back of the class. "This is going to be a great term!"

"Herr Lange!" Herr Neumann barked, returning his attention to the class. "Did you have something to say?"

"Sir!" Hart responded. *This guy has good hearing! I'll have to take care.* "I merely ..."

"You will stand in this class when you have something to say," Herr Neumann barked, turning to each student as if planting a seed of orderliness.

Hart arose from his chair.

"Sir, I merely said this will be a great term. Your new board is a marvel, indeed!"

Several of Hart's classmates suddenly developed coughing fits, their hands clamped against their mouths to cover grins.

"Welcome praise, Herr Lange," Herr Neumann said, fluttering his eyes at Hart's flattery. "But in future ..." Herr Neumann's glare was stern as he looked each student in the eye. "In the future, we will not speak unless spoken to. Is that clear, Herr Lange?"

"Yes, sir, Herr Neumann!" he said, feigning abashment, dropping his head for a moment and letting a shock of blue-black hair cover his face. With his emotions under control, he raised his head again, biting the inside of his cheeks to still his mirth.

"You may be seated, Herr Lange," Herr Neumann said, dismissing the interruption, and continuing with the lesson.

A few weeks into the term, Herr Neumann announced that they were to be quizzed on their lessons in two days and warned his students to study their notes diligently. The scores from the test would count heavily toward their final marks. Hart and his three friends spent a considerable amount of their study time reviewing their economics notes and speculating on the test questions. Two days later, they felt prepared.

Herr Neumann walked up and down the aisles, placing three sheets of stapled papers face down on the table, in front of each student.

"Do not turn the pages until I tell you to do so," he barked.

The students sat with their hands in their laps and eyes forward, their writing tools neatly placed on the table before them.

"You will have one hour to complete the test," Herr Neumann said, retrieving a stopwatch from his desk. "On my say so, you may turn over the pages and start writing. Remember! No cheating! Anyone caught cheating will relinquish their paper and leave the room immediately. Is that clear?"

"Yes, sir, Herr Neumann, sir!" the students shouted together.

Herr Neumann's stern glare held their attention for a heartbeat, then he raised the stopwatch for all to see.

"You may begin," he said, depressing the switch with a flourish.

Each boy flipped his pages over and began scribbling. After half an hour, Herr Neumann wrote '30 minutes' on the chalk board to start the countdown for the remainder of the hour. The scribbling continued. As Herr Neumann wrote '10 minutes' on the board, Hart and his three friends began replacing their pencils on the table and reviewing their answers. Others followed. By the time Herr Neumann announced the end of the test, each boy had finished his test. The end-of-class bell rang.

"Leave your papers face down on my desk as you leave," Herr Neumann shouted over the din of departing students.

Hart collected his books and followed the line of boys who passed by the desk. Penn remained in his wheel chair at the table near the door.

"Would you like me to hand in your test?" Hart asked as he approached.

"If you wouldn't mind." Penn passed the test to Hart.

While Hart retraced his steps to Herr Neumann's desk, Penn navigated his wheelchair and preceded Hart out the door. Hart walked beside Penn, moving toward their next class.

"Thanks, Hart. I appreciate that," Penn said, with a head nod. "Sometimes, steering this chair in tight spaces can be a challenge."

At the end of the corridor, the boys separated, heading in different directions for their next class.

The following week, the economics students sat in their classroom, waiting for Herr Neumann to distribute the tests from the previous week. As he handed each paper to its owner, he announced to the class the test mark. Out of one hundred points, most of the boys scored above eighty-five. Hart's group received scores of ninety-one and greater. Herr Neumann wandered up and down the aisles, finally stopping at the desk where Penn Tresler sat.

"I must tell you, class, that I am very pleased with your study efforts," he said, before handing the last test to Penn. "This test, I know, was a very difficult one and many before you have failed." His eyes scanned the room. "You are to be commended, but, you are none so clever as Herr Tresler, who today has scored one hundred percent!"

He motioned as if to hand the last paper to Penn, then pulled it back, close to his chest. Penn dropped his hand looking with confusion at the teacher's movement.

"Truly a genius, Herr Penn," Herr Neumann said. "I can't imagine how you were able to answer each question so precisely." Herr Neumann's humour had vanished. His voice sounded threatening. "I wonder, Herr Tresler, if I ask you the questions again, whether you can answer with such precision. Shall we try again to see whether you are truly the genius of the class? Or a cheater! Hm?" Herr Neumann let his words dangle accusingly.

Penn frowned. He rolled his chair away from the table, set the brake, and wobbled upright, leaning on the table for support.

"Sir, I ..."

"Silence!" Herr Neumann bellowed. "You will speak when I ask you to!"

Penn hung his head, appearing intimidated by the teacher's shout.

"Herr Schneider!" Herr Neumann snapped.

"Yes, sir?" Konrad responded, rising to his feet.

"Herr Schneider, read for the class question number one of the test," Herr Neumann demanded in a silky voice.

Konrad read the question aloud.

"Now, Herr Tresler," Herr Neuman turned from Konrad toward Penn, "please share with the class your most precise answer from last week."

"Sir, I ..."

"Come, come, Herr Tresler. What is the answer?"

Penn, embarrassed by the class' attention, focused solely on the teacher, stuttered through an answer to the question, and waited for Herr Neumann to respond.

"Not good enough!" Herr Neumann screeched, turning to the other students. "Herr Bartz! Read the second question. Let's see if Herr Tresler can provide a better answer."

Manfred reluctantly rose and read the second question aloud.

"Herr Tresler, what is the answer?"

Uncomfortable that they were forced to witness their teacher's abuse, Penn's classmates began to squirm in their seats. Beads of perspiration erupted on Penn's forehead, as he struggled to stand and stuttered through another answer.

"Incorrect again!" screeched Herr Neumann. "It seems to me, Herr Tresler, that perhaps you are not the genius that you would have us think!"

Herr Neumann turned to the class.

"You two," he barked at Manfred and Penn, "sit!"

The boys dropped to their seats. Over his shoulder, he directed his words toward Penn.

"One week, Herr Tresler. You will have one week to review your notes. Next week, we will ask the questions again, and you will provide the precise answers, or you will receive a failing grade."

Herr Neumann spun around to face Penn. The shock of the situation fell fully on the student, his eyes narrowed, and he clenched his jaw, appearing to struggle with control of his emotions.

"Yes, s-sir," Penn stammered in a quiet voice, carefully lowering himself to his wheelchair.

"Now to our lesson," the arrogant teacher declared, ending his tirade.

For the remainder of the class, Penn sat quietly taking notes, instead of participating in class discussions, as was his usual custom.

✧

Later that evening, the four friends gathered around the library table where they conducted their studies. Far in the back of the vast room of books, magazines, catalogues, and maps, they considered the episode that had occurred in their economics class earlier that day.

"He can't get away with it!" Manfred exclaimed.

"Neumann was totally out of line!" Penn hissed.

"What can we do?" Manfred asked. "Should we speak with the Chair, do you think?"

During the discussion, Hart said little, leaning back in his chair with arms crossed. He raised a hand to his lips and tapped his teeth with the nail of his right index finger. Then he leaned forward, resting his elbows and forearms on the table. He clasped his hands, while he waited for quiet to settle on the group.

"Oh, oh!" Konrad said, "I think Hart has an idea."

"I do," Hart said, leaning back in his chair and cracking his knuckles.

Keen to hear, the others leaned toward him. By the time the study hour ended, the four friends had a plan.

Herr Neumann began the next economics class with a further attack on Penn.

"Herr Tresler, are you prepared today to provide us with the precise answers to the last test?" He glared at Penn from the front of the classroom, as if daring him to make a mistake.

Penn pushed his chair from the table, locked the brake, rose on wobbly legs, then cleared his throat.

"No, sir, I am not."

Redness crept up Herr Neumann's neck.

"I studied for the test two weeks ago," Penn continued, "and I wrote the answers as I studied them. In the meantime, I have studied for other tests, and continued to do my homework, for all of my classes, sir."

Herr Neumann inhaled deeply, the red

208

hue of his face deepening. Absentmindedly, he converted the sheaf of papers he held in his hand into a tightly rolled tube, his narrowed eyes fixed on Penn.

"While I can retain the information when I study for a test," Penn said, taking a deep breath, "I cannot retain all of the information, indefinitely. With respect, sir, I think your questioning is unfair and out of line." Penn pressed his knuckles into the table as if to alleviate some of the weight on his legs.

"That is enough!" bellowed Herr Neumann, outraged at Penn's defiance. He advanced toward Penn's table. "Herr Tresler, you will leave this class at once!"

"But, sir!" Penn protested.

Herr Neumann hunched threateningly over Penn, raised his arm, and struck Penn on the side of his head with the rolled papers. Penn teetered under the impact of the blow. His legs gave way and he fell sideways. The class of boys gasped as one.

Hart was out of his seat and running to Penn's aid, before Herr Neumann could open the door and shout 'Out!' He and two of his classmates helped Penn to his wheelchair, while Herr Neumann pointed into the hallway from the now-opened door.

"You will report to the Chair, immediately, and explain your outrageous behaviour!"

"It's all right," Penn motioned quietly to his rescuers. "I can manage."

Hart collected Penn's books and pencils and put them into Penn's satchel. Penn nodded his thanks, plopped the satchel in his lap, and wheeled his chair out of the room.

In the commotion that followed Penn's departure, Hart caught the eye of Manfred and Konrad. Each tipped their head slightly. They were ready.

"Right then," Herr Neumann huffed, shutting the door behind Penn. "Let us continue with our lesson for today." He placed the rolled papers on his desk and took a fresh stick of chalk from the ledge under the first chalk board. "Today, we are going to consider ..."

The students diligently copied the notes written by Herr Neumann on the new green chalk board. The teacher filled the first board, set down the chalk, dusted his hands, and pushed the board aside to reveal the second clean board. Before he took up the fresh piece of chalk, he signalled to Manfred—the designated board cleaner for the week—to clean the first board and ready it for the next set of notes.

Covertly, Manfred slipped a damp sponge from the inside pocket of his school jacket as he approached the board, used it to clear the board, then slid the board behind the second, yet-to-be used one. Turning toward his desk, he slid the sponge up his sleeve, then deposited it into his satchel as he sat down.

Manfred picked up his pencil and began scribbling the notes from the second board before he was called to erase it. Herr Neumann ended his writing at the foot of the second board and turned to the class. He spoke at length on the day's topic, never referring to the boards again.

The bell rang, and the boys bounced from their chairs, moving toward the door as quickly as possible. Manfred retrieved the sponge from his satchel, hastily scrubbed the second board, and joined the last few boys leaving the room.

Walking down the hallway, the three boys burst into suppressed fits of laughter, as they headed off to their next class, wondering what Herr Neumann would do when he observed their handiwork.

"I never would have guessed that hydrochloric acid could do that!" Konrad chuckled.

"Let's hope we've made a difference," Hart said.

"First, let's find Penn before the next class starts!"

⚜

Herr Neumann turned to his treasured chalk boards, preparing to record notes for the next class. He stood anchored where he was, his mouth gaping fish-like in disbelief. All of the words that he had written on his precious boards had turned bright blue. He snatched an eraser and began scrubbing with short, brisk strokes. Nothing happened. The bright blue lettering remained. Stunned, he collapsed into his chair, a hand braced against his pounding heart.

The boys found Penn sitting in his wheelchair outside the administration office.

"Did you speak with the Chair?" Hart asked.

"No, I couldn't," Penn replied. "It could cost Herr Neumann his career, if I were to complain, and I don't want that responsibility."

"But he could fail you!" Konrad declared.

"I don't think he will. My responses today may not have been identical to my exam answers, but they were correct."

"I'd certainly report him," Hart said. "But I'm not you, and I respect your decision."

"How did it go after I left," Penn asked.

"Brilliant, as expected," Manfred replied.

"We'll share the details with you later," Hart said, turning Penn's wheelchair into the hallway. "We need to hurry or we'll be late for the next class. Penn, I'll push."

"I don't know what happened," Herr Neumann lamented when he appeared before the school's board of directors. "There must be a fault in the chalk board, or with the chalk."

"It is clear to the Board that this work is the result of a prank, Herr Neumann," the Chair said. We have interviewed all of the students in your class. Not one of them will speak of the matter. One or two of them did, however, mention the mistreatment of your student, Penn Tresler. Perhaps the two incidents are related?"

"Herr Chair. That is a lie! I would never mistreat my students." Herr Neumann spread his hands in innocence. "Why, that would be reprehensible!"

"Reprehensible or not, I can't imagine any of our students creating such damaging mischief without provocation. Unless you can prove otherwise, you will be held personally responsible for the expense of replacing the chalk boards."

"But, sir! The cost!"

"We know full well the cost of the boards, Herr Neumann. We approved their acquisition in the first place!"

When the boys heard that Herr Neumann was to bear the cost of replacing the boards, they shared a gleeful round of back slapping.

CHAPTER TWENTY

Following the 1966 summer break, school resumed under a heavy pall. Hart and Konrad sat at their preferred study table in the library, days before the commencement date. Manfred was dead, and his death hung like a heavy curtain encasing them in darkness.

"It must have been awful," Hart lamented, shaking his head, his hands hanging between his jumping knees. "I can't get the image out of my head!"

"Poor Manfred." Konrad swiped a tear from his cheek before the others saw it. "What a loss!"

"What's a loss?" Penn asked, rolling his wheelchair into the vacant space next to Konrad. "You two look like you've lost your best friend!"

"We have!" Hart exclaimed, watching the smile slide from Penn's face. "Manfred was killed during the summer break. It was a freak accident. Apparently, he was home alone and decided to convert one of his father's televisions into an oscilloscope, as an experiment. It imploded. When his parents arrived home, they found him dead on the living room floor. A glass shard pierced through his eye and into his brain."

"Truly a loss of a brilliant mind," Penn agreed, pooling his grief with the others.

"The whole thing is so stupid!" Hart smashed his fist into the table, pushed back his chair and began pacing the length of their quiet space. "What was he thinking?"

"Hart, why are you getting angry?" Konrad asked.

"We have a remarkable future ahead of us," Hart lamented. "Manfred was the best of us, and he's wasted his chance."

Konrad rose from the table, and intercepted Hart.

"I'm angry too," he said, grabbing Hart's arm, "but anger won't bring him back. We should use this energy constructively."

217

"My mom says that, even when someone dies, their soul remains," Penn said. "I like to think that he is with us now."

"I have my doubts," Hart replied. "I want to know where God was. He should have protected Manfred. Kept him safe!" Hart collapsed into his chair and hid his face in his hands, sobbing. When he lifted his head several minutes later, his face glistened with tears. Spikes of blue-black hair stood where he had run his fingers. "I can't just sit here. I need to move."

"Let's go for a jog," Konrad said, withdrawing a handkerchief from his pocket and mopping his own face.

Contrary to past term commencements, the year began without energy and enthusiasm, each student carrying the burden of Manfred's death. In their collective opinion, Manfred Bartz had been a great friend, and they all grieved for him.

While the school's board of directors was unable to understand the impact that the young man's death had on the students, they could not deny his popularity. At the Board's September meeting, the directors decided that the school would host a memorial service to allow the students an opportunity to mourn him so their focus could shift back to their studies. Before their plans could be announced, though, an unexpected event occurred.

"We'll never get through the year if we live every day carrying the grief of Manfred's death," Hart complained, pushing away from the library table one Sunday afternoon in early October. "Come on. I have an idea."

The friends grabbed their jackets and followed Hart out into the still, autumn afternoon. Leaves of deciduous trees had started to change colour. Some of the first to fall crunched under their footsteps, releasing a pungent smell of decay into the frosty air. Puffs of steam escaped like smoke from their nostrils and mouths as they spoke.

"Where're we going?" Penn asked, his words dissipating in the hazy light.

"Science building, first," Hart said, setting off in a jog.

"We're not supposed to be in there except for a class," Konrad reminded them.

"Ja, but it's the only place we'll find a human skeleton," Hart answered.

"A skel—Never mind," Konrad muttered.

"Are you going to share your plan?" Penn asked.

"Not yet," Hart replied. "If we get caught, you won't get into any more trouble than what you know."

They followed Hart to the only part of the building where they could find a human skeleton—the biology department. Never had the skeleton left the biology department, although it had passed from class to class within the department. Hart looked around the outside of the building to ensure that no one saw them, then slipped through the unlocked door. The others followed.

"Keep away from the windows," Hart warned. "Penn, take the elevator. We'll meet you up there." Penn rolled his wheelchair into the elevator.

As the doors closed, Hart and Konrad scooted along the corridor, staying in the shadows, and sprinted easily up the stairs to the second floor. Penn exited the elevator and rolled his chair toward the biology department at the end of the hall, quickly catching up with Hart and Konrad.

"Search the rooms, find the skeleton," Hart said, indicating that the others should look through the glass windows of the locked classroom doors. "I'll be right back." Hart then raced down the stairs to a lower floor, and returned moments later burdened with paraphernalia.

"Here it is," Konrad said, peering through the window of a door further along the corridor. "But the door's locked."

"Step aside," Penn whispered. "I've got this." Penn removed a small case from the inside pocket of his school jacket, removed a pin and began jiggling the knob. Snick. He turned the knob and pushed the door.

"Voila!" He raised his arms like a magician showing off with his latest trick to curious onlookers.

"Where'd you learn that?" Konrad asked.

"I studied magic during summer vacation," Penn answered. "I never thought this pin would come in handy, though."

"It's illegal," Konrad objected.

"Konrad," Hart said, pushing open the door, "we're just having fun. Keep it in perspective."

Konrad frowned, but followed the others into the room.

"Let's be quick," Hart said, searching the room. "Penn, put the skeleton into this bag."

Hart held up a black bag made of soft fabric with a gold drawstring that he had found in a storage room in the basement.

"Konrad, grab that chair." Hart indicated a wooden school chair near the doorway. "Lock the door and follow me."

Hart gave Penn the other items that he had brought from the storage room, and pushed the wheelchair quickly down the hall, back to the elevator. The three boys rode the elevator to the basement and exited the science building through another door, and out into the shadows of shedding trees. Eight minutes later, they stopped beneath the overhang of an old administrative building that had been abandoned by the school five years prior. The windows were boarded over.

"This looks ominous," Konrad said.

"Ja," Hart responded, turning the wheelchair and hitching it up four stairs to a veranda-like landing. "It does, doesn't it? Can you open this door?"

Penn applied his magic to the front door of the building and, once again, the boys slipped inside.

"Where to now?" Penn asked.

"We have to part company for a while," Hart said. "We need you to keep a look out, Penn."

"Don't worry," Penn replied. "I can whistle now!"

"I don't think a whistle will work this time," Hart said. "We're going up to the roof, from the fourth floor." Hart wandered into the musty foyer and looked skyward. "I think that's a glass ceiling up there." He pointed to the top of the second floor. "If you spot trouble, try whistling. We'll leave the doors open too. Hopefully, we'll hear you, but if we don't, you'll need to hide till we get back."

"I'll have a look around for a spot where I can be invisible," Penn grinned.

Hart led Konrad along the corridor to the main stairwell, up four flights of stairs to a door under the roof.

"Rats!" Hart hissed. "I should have borrowed Penn's magic key, this is probably locked too." He grasped the knob and twisted it hard. To his surprise, the knob fell easily away from the rotting door.

"That was easy!" Konrad giggled. "Won't this take us up to the clock tower?"

"Ja," Hart answered, stepping through the door and brushing cobwebs out of his path. "This way."

At the top of the stairs, they encountered one more door. Hart gave the knob a tentative twist and the unlocked door opened onto a small landing.

"Watch your step," he cautioned, "the boards may be rotten."

Konrad followed, stepping gingerly onto the landing and grabbing the railing for support, realizing almost too late that it was rotten too. He promptly released it, hissing relief through his teeth, then held his hand aloft and watched flecks of old paint fall away.

Hart's next step reverberated under their feet when a loose board cracked.

"Careful!" Hart said. "And, stay low so we can't be seen."

As if on command, dark storm clouds gathered above them, greying the light. Tick. Tick. The tower's clock marched on, its cogs vibrating below them.

"Twist this wire into a firm hook," Hart said, handing a coil of thin wire to Konrad. "I'll take care of the skeleton." Hart removed the skeleton and a fine rope from the velvet bag and began tying it to the chair.

The boys worked quickly and thirty minutes later, after much huffing and puffing, their task was complete. They retraced their steps to the main floor and found Penn. On their return to the library, Hart and Konrad explained what they had done, barely able to contain their excitement about the latest prank.

⚜

The following morning, just before eight o'clock, students, teachers, and administrative staff crisscrossed the campus in the dim morning light, heading to their first destinations of the day. It was a hive of activity, as all sought to be in place by 8:30. At that hour, the light rapidly increased, welcoming a new fall day. With the light came gusty winds from the north that danced fallen leaves crisply across the school yard and forced scarves to be tightened securely around exposed necks.

Bong! Bong! Bong! The clock in the tower of the old administrative building chimed. Bong! Bong! Bong! As the seventh chime sounded, the scurrying people simultaneously raised their arms to reveal wristwatches, or pocket watches pulled from their vests. The Monday morning habit of everyone on campus was to set their clocks by the eighth chime. Raising their eyes to the clock tower, their mouths dropped. A wooden school chair stood atop the clock tower. The human skeleton from the biology department sat on the chair with hands resting on its hips. Its skull looked downward, appearing equally amazed to see the audience below.

A one-metre noose hung ominously from the chair's rung below the skeleton's feet, dangling at the 12:00 mark of the old clock. As the morning light brightened, it reflected off the wire fastened to the clock's minute hand. Only a few saw the hook reaching upward. A murmur spread through the crowd, as fingers pointed skyward, drawing the hook to the attention of others. The minute hand inched toward the 12:00 mark, and the wire hook lined up with the open neck of the noose. When the eighth chime sounded, the minute hand caught the loop of the noose. With the next tick, the rope was snagged by the wire and pulled taught. The crowd below stood motionless, waiting. Tick. Tick. A grating noise complained from the roof of the tower, echoing in the yard below. The chair supporting the skeleton shifted. Tick. Tick.

In stunned disbelief, the onlookers watched the chair begin to sway from side to side. Abruptly, the rocking stopped. The rope securing the skeleton to the chair snapped and the pop-eyed, wide-mouthed crowd watched as the skeleton fell, bony arms stretched forward, diving to its second death. Those of fainter heart shrieked and ran for cover. Others continued to watch as the wind wrapped its chilly fingers around the skeleton, slowing its descent. A strong current caught the cavernous skull, leading the skeleton into a somersault. Another draft held it aloft, its arms and legs flailing. One lone screech filled the yard, seeming to come from the skeleton itself as it folded inward and plummeted to the stone steps below.

The screaming teacher fainted, her fall cushioned by grabbing hands. Smashed pieces of bone scattered in every direction. The detached skull bounced once, spring-boarding to land in the limp hands of the fallen teacher, just as she opened her eyes. She screamed again, then collapsed into the hands of her rescuers. The skull rolled free and stopped, upright, in a puddle of dried leaves, grinning as if pleased with its successful landing.

A moment devoid of sound followed, only to be shattered by a loud groan issuing from the roof. All eyes turned skyward, looking for the source. The wooden chair perched on the roof above the clock was no longer secure and teetered drunkenly on the roof's peak, its feet grating against the old tiles. Storming winds whipped through the yard, increasing in strength, ushering in roiling, dark clouds, and changing the light to dark. Icy fingers lifted the chair, twirled it, and dashed it on the stone steps. Splinters of wood flew in every direction.

Seconds later, the threatening clouds released their wrath. Heavy half-frozen raindrops pelted down, sending the remainder of the crowd racing indoors for their 8:30 appointments.

Penn's chair sat backed against the teachers' parking garage. Hart and Konrad stood next to it, their backs pressed against the wall. A look of satisfaction stained their faces.

"We couldn't have asked for better," Hart said, standing upright and looking skyward. "That was for you, Manfred."

"Hope you enjoyed our bit of mischief!" Penn sighed, wiping a tear from his eye.

"Come on!" Konrad said. "We'll be late for class if we don't hurry."

⚜

The storm raged throughout the day. Between classes, boys and teachers scurried through sheets of frozen rain, jumping small puddles or sidestepping larger ones. Not all of the school's buildings were connected by covered passageways.

At the end of the day, students, teachers, and administrative staff gathered in the school's main auditorium to hear the Chair deliver his opening remarks for the new school month. The room was humid with moisture evaporating from the heated bodies of those who had dashed the farthest.

"I have one last item on the agenda," the Chair told his audience. "On Friday morning, we will gather here once more at 8:00." A humid moan filled the auditorium under the boys' collective protest. The Chair continued. "We wish to acknowledge the sudden and unfortunate passing of one of our valued students, Herr Manfred

Bartz." The groaning changed to cheers, and the Chair was forced to wave his arms to quiet the din. "Anyone wishing to say a few words about Herr Bartz is encouraged to do so on Friday. That is all. Dismissed."

An enlivened group of students exited the hall, grateful to know that Manfred would be remembered well.

"I think we've already done our bit," Hart said. "Somehow, I don't feel any better, though."

"I miss him too," Konrad said.

"And I," Penn agreed.

CHAPTER TWENTY-ONE

Hart's loyalty to his friends remained steadfast and true. The boys had done everything—well, almost everything—together. They had formed a successful study group and had maintained high marks through each term. Their participation in school sporting events was also notable. Individually, they were competitive; as a group, they were a force with which to be reckoned.

It was not until the end of their last year of school, however, that they paid any particular attention to girls. Konrad was the first to fall prey to female allure. Following the Easter break, his behaviour changed. He started arriving late for weekend study groups and sports practices.

"What's going on?" Penn asked on the third occasion of his late arrival.

"Found a girl?" Hart jibed.

"Leave off, guys." Konrad shrugged at their comments and ducked their questions, a red flush creeping up his neck. "Are we here to study, or what?"

"He really has found a girl," Penn commented the first time Konrad missed a study group entirely.

The next day, Hart took his friend aside as they headed toward their first class.

"What's going on, Konrad? I thought we had a pact to graduate as one, all at the top of our class. You seem to have lost your focus. Is something wrong at home?"

Konrad looked abashed. He hung his head and hugged his school books to his chest. Sandy blond hair fell forward and covered his pimpled complexion. When he raised his eyes to meet Hart's, they pleaded for understanding.

"I met someone during the summer break," he said, his voice so quiet that Hart almost missed his words. "She lives here, in Marburg."

"Y-you—met someone," Hart repeated in disbelief.

"Yes."

"Why haven't you told this to us?" Hart asked, his lips curving upward.

"Because I knew you'd laugh and tease me, and I didn't want that," Konrad finished firmly, a blush blanketing his face.

"Hey, we might tease you a bit," Hart said. "That's what guys do to other guys who stray from the fold, but don't worry about it. It'll pass. You'll see." Hart turned toward the science building.

"There's more," Konrad said, grabbing Hart's arm. Hart stopped and waited. "W—we ..." Konrad's blush deepened and he seemed to find difficulty finishing his sentence.

"You what?"

"Well ..." Konrad's eyes again pleaded for understanding before he dropped his head and kicked at the grass underfoot. "We ... did it!" he hissed, anxious for Hart to understand and not press him for details.

Initially, Hart failed him. Then he realized what his friend was trying to say.

"You did it!" Hart looked incredulous, grabbing Konrad's arm with his free hand. "You did it, man?" He smacked Konrad on the back, laughing his excitement. "What was it like? Was it as good as we hear? Who is she, by the way."

"You don't know her. I met her at a family wedding during the summer. We've been seeing each other ..." Konrad looked at his watch and turned toward the science building. "Come on, we're going to be late for class."

Nothing more was said until they spied Penn waiting near the door to the science building. Konrad looked sideways at Hart.

"Promise me, you won't tell," he begged. "Promise!"

Hart raised his hand to his lips and discreetly drew a zipper, confirming that his friend's secret was his own.

URSULA

CHAPTER TWENTY-TWO

Following Christmas of 1960, Ursula devoted herself to her studies with a competitive spirit. *I have to be the best student, if I'm ever going to escape this horrid existence! I'm glad Mamica taught me the importance of education.*

Although her father stopped drinking alcohol in 1960, his wrath never waned. When Ursula was sixteen, he killed her mother with a blow to the back of her head that knocked his unsuspecting victim off balance. She fell into the corner of the kitchen table, spun, and landed face down on the tile floor. Ursula knelt next to her mother's still form and twisted her lifeless face upward, smearing the blood pooling beneath. The paring knife that Slava had been using to peel the evening's potatoes was still gripped in her hand, the blade embedded in her chest to the hilt. *Good-bye, Mamica. At last you are free!* Ursula thought, grabbing a dish towel to cover the look of surprise on her mother's face. She left her father to his own distress and ran next door to ask a neighbour to telephone the police.

During subsequent interviews, Ursula omitted any disclosure to the police officers that her mother's fall had commenced with her father's blow. She told only what happened when her mother fell. Her father was docile throughout the entire process and kept his anger in check.

The coroner concluded that Slava's death was accidental, and Edin repeatedly expressed his gratitude to Ursula for her small omission. As soon as the accidental death verdict was released, however, Ursula watched her father hasten to the nearest pub where he apparently drank until closing time. In the small hours of the morning, she heard him stagger through the front door and drop onto his bed.

Ursula was careful not to disturb her snoring father the following morning. She dressed quickly, ate some black bread and cheese, and tiptoed out of the house. Arriving early at the high school, she sat on the doorstep and contemplated what she would do next.

Without her mother to shelter her from her father's anger, she would be in constant danger. After her feast of bananas years before, Ursula had shown the fresh welts of her beating to the priest. The priest had agreed that her father was justified in the beating and saw no need to help her. She had no faith that the same priest could save her now and believed the police would be useless too. *They'd twist the truth against me, if I tried to tell it. I must get away!*

The following spring, Ursula found a part-time job in a restaurant, located halfway between the school and her home. It was on a hill overlooking the Adriatic Sea.

In fine weather, the restaurant was popular with tourists. By her eighteenth birthday, she had saved sufficient funds to get herself out of town. She observed that, if she provided customers with stellar service, they would tip very well, especially the tourists.

By her nineteenth birthday, Ursula had earned enough to pay her college tuition. She had also managed to keep her father's behaviour stable by threatening him that, if he touched her or her money, she would go to the police with the full disclosure of her mother's death.

PART III

DEFINING ONE'S SELF

MIRIAM

CHAPTER TWENTY-THREE

Of all her accomplishments, the one Miriam intended to savour was her first sexual experience. Rask Penner was the captain of the school football team. He lived in a big house, not a townhouse, two blocks from the school. His father, a lawyer, was very wealthy. Rask was tall, blonde and fair skinned. He was not the smartest boy in her classes, but he never failed his grades.

"My father," Rask boasted during lunch one day, "hired a private tutor to ensure that I complete every grade. He expects me to join his law firm once I graduate from university."

Following Christmas of their last school year together, he intercepted Miriam when she exited the main doors of the school. They walked side by side, chatting about the football game scheduled the next day, their frosted conversation disappearing above them.

"Will you be there?" he asked.

"Yes, I'm going with Kristina."

As they reached the two old elms that marked the entrance to the school property, he grabbed her arm and backed her against the trunk of one of the trees.

"You're beautiful," he said, fingering a strand of her auburn hair. "You make me think of exotic things and dark secrets waiting to be explored."

She could feel the warmth of his breath on her chilled cheek. Heat pulsed through her.

"Why have we never gone out on a date?" he asked.

"Perhaps because you've never asked," she said flatly.

"Never?"

"Uh-uh."

"That's negligent on my part," he said, unabashed. "Want to? Go out with me, I mean."

"All right."

"Where do you want to go?"

"Can we go to a movie?" Miriam asked, feeling a thrill run through her body. "I've never been to one."

"Of course!" he agreed eagerly.

When Miriam announced to her parents that she had a date to go to a film with the captain of the football team, they were not as pleased as she expected them to be. They questioned what she planned to wear, and insisted that if she must use make-up, it be minimal. And they wanted to meet him first.

Rask knocked on the blue door an hour before the film was to start. Mina and Willem invited him in and offered him tea and biscuits.

"No, thank you," he told them politely, "I've just eaten my midday meal. Besides, I'd like to buy chocolate to share with Miriam during the film."

Miriam's parents visited with Rask for twenty minutes, while they waited for her to dress. When she descended the stairs, he rose to greet her. Seemingly smitten by her beauty, he blushed and coughed to clear his throat, before complimenting her appearance. Miriam grabbed her coat and hat and beckoned for Rask to follow her out. She was careful to remain cool and aloof until the door closed behind them. She knew her parents would watch as they bounded down the stairs, mounted their bicycles, and pedalled down the street.

"She has that boy wrapped around her finger," Willem said, chuckling.

"I know. That's what worries me," Mina added, releasing the lace curtain. "She's wearing more make-up than we agreed and her dress is far more provocative than it should be. Unfortunately, neither is enough to cause a fuss. And she's done it deliberately! The only saving grace is that it's drizzling. She's had to wear a coat. At least one of her transgressions is covered."

✢

Miriam had never been to the cinema before. Her parents preferred that she focus on her studies and encouraged her to be involved in constructive activities, but she had heard stories from her friends.

"Saturday matinees are always quiet," Kristina had told her. "And the theatre is dark. If you sit at the back, you can hold hands and kiss a little if you want to."

Earlier in the week, Miriam and Rask agreed on an action film. When they arrived at the cinema, they racked their bicycles and Rask bought the tickets. Inside the foyer, Rask bought a chocolate bar and a soda with two straws. He took Miriam's hand and led her into the theatre. Her pulse raced at his touch.

"I thought it would be dark in here," she whispered, surprised that the theatre was not as dark as Kristina had suggested.

"It will be," he answered. "When the curtain opens, the lights will go down. Where do you want to sit?"

Miriam surveyed the theatre. Two young men sat in the middle of the middle row. Avoiding them, she suggested the back-row seats, farthest from the door. As she spoke, she thought she saw movement in Rask's eyes. A small grin hinted at the corner of his mouth and disappeared.

"The movie will start in ten minutes," he said, looking at his watch. "You go ahead, I'm going to the toilet."

Rask washed his hands and straightened his mop of golden hair. Checking his profile, he decided that he would look more like the lead singer of his favourite British pop group if he dyed his hair darker. He wiggled his billfold out of the pocket of his skin-tight pants and removed a condom packet. He tore the top of the packet, tucked it into his shirt pocket, and strutted back into the theatre. *Always be prepared. That's my motto! And I've never wasted one of these little treasures.* He gave his shirt pocket a little pat while he allowed a

248

moment for his eyes to adjust to the dimness in the theatre.

Miriam had removed her hat and coat and carefully set them over the seat ahead of hers. From the doorway, Rask watched her fidget in the seat by the wall, pulling the neckline of her sweater lower and crossing her legs to reveal more of her thigh. The lights dimmed, and the curtains drew back to reveal the screen. The dimming lights caught her attention and she looked up, noticing that Rask was watching her. She flicked her long, lustrous hair over her shoulder, dipped her chin and looked up at him, causing her hair to cascade forward again. She smiled sweetly as he sidled along the row and sat next to her.

"Chocolate?" he asked, raising the bar as evidence.

They shared a few pieces as the film began and sipped the soda. Then he took her hand and held it on his thigh. They sat motionless for some time. Rask heard the rhythm of Miriam's breathing change. With patience, he observed her cues, confident that he would know exactly what to do when the time came. He paced his progress in time with the film, remembering how successful he had been with Kristina, the previous Saturday. First an arm around her shoulder. She smiled sweetly again. He pulled her to him and kissed her, tasting her chocolaty invitation. He waited and kissed her again, deeper. On his third attempt, he used his tongue. She hesitated at first, then allowed the experience. *Way easier than Kristina. Maybe I'll get further with this one.*

Miriam was elated. She had thought that she would have to initiate the process, but Rask was taking the lead. *If I'd known it would be this easy, I'd have done something long ago.*

Rask twisted in his seat, turning toward her, placing his free hand on her knee. Several minutes later, his hand had found its way up her leg, under her skirt. A finger caught the elastic leg of her panties and stroked the coarse dark hairs it found. Miriam gasped. The finger stilled. In the light shed by the film, she cast Rask a small grin and her eyelids fluttered.

On this cue, he leaned toward her, shifting his wandering fingers. He kissed her deeply and, in response, her lips parted to meet his. As they did so, her legs opened involuntarily, and his fingers tickled their way to his ultimate target. Miriam wrapped her arms around his neck and pressed her pelvis into his hand.

With the next flash of light, she noticed Rask scanning the theatre; there were six people, all near the middle.

"Miriam," he whispered. "Are you enjoying the film?"

"Oh, yes," she panted.

"Want more?" he asked, his voice husky and intimate.

"Oh, yes!" she searched his lips, shifting her pelvis.

He manoeuvred her, first to his lap guiding her hand so she could feel his readiness.

When they were both sufficiently stimulated, Rask invited her to stand in front of him, turning her toward the screen. He continued to massage her until he had the condom free. She heard rather than saw what he was doing but knew what he did. Her friends had told her about condoms and what to expect.

In the next moment, she felt the tug of her panties to her knees, and his firm hand on her back, bending her forward into the seat ahead. In response, she braced herself, feeling him loom behind her.

Rask's penetration was quick and hard. A ready hand—fingers smelling of her intimacy—stifled her cry of pain. He muffled his grunts and climactic groan into her back, then he pulled away and collapsed into his seat, rolling the used condom into a tissue, and zipping his trousers.

Miriam remained as he had left her, leaning into the seat. When she realized that his efforts had ended, her anger flared. *That's it?* She leaned down and pulled up her panties. Smoothing her skirt, she turned to him.

"Excuse me," she said, grabbing her handbag and sidling along the empty seats.

In the toilet cubicle, she finished the job that Rask had started, finding her own satisfaction, and used a paper towel to wipe the blood from her inner thigh. Once more, she straightened her clothes, then washed her hands and fixed her make-up. By the time she collected herself, she found Rask waiting in the foyer. He handed Miriam her hat and coat. The film was over.

"So, did you enjoy the film?" Rask asked as they pedalled back to the blue door.

"Not really," Miriam replied, sitting awkwardly on her bicycle seat. "There wasn't as much action as I had hoped for."

Rask accompanied Miriam to the door. She thanked him politely for the outing. When he leaned toward her, as if expecting a kiss, she turned her head and stepped back.

"Goodbye," she said, opening the door wide enough to allow her entry, then closing it quickly before he could say more.

253

✧

Mina and Willem were in the parlour, reading.

"How was your date?" Mina asked, watching Miriam kick off her shoes and hang her damp hat and coat.

"Fine," she answered curtly.

"Did you enjoy the film?" Willem asked, smiling at her.

"Not really," she said, already heading up the stairs. "There was so much distraction that I couldn't concentrate. Hopefully, next time I'll get more out of it."

CHAPTER TWENTY-FOUR

The more Miriam thought about her first sexual encounter, the angrier she became—with herself. *I lost control of the situation. I trusted that Rask would know what to do. All he cared about was himself.*

Whenever she saw Rask at school in the following weeks, she endeavoured to avoid him. If he managed to trap her and ask for another date, she found a reason to refuse. After a month of him asking and her deflecting, his invitations became terse and demanding.

Miriam heard rumours that Rask was furious because she dared to defy him—him, the captain of the football team! She overheard his ire and frustration when he spoke with his friends and found satisfaction in his suffering.

One morning, as the bell rang for class commencement, Rask noticed Miriam enter the school office and realized that, no matter what her reason for doing so, she would be late for class. He sauntered down the hall toward the classroom for his first subject, but instead of entering the room, he walked on, toward the stairwell at the end of the hall. Ducking, he stepped into the shadow below the stairwell and waited.

Rask knew that Miriam's class was on the upper floor, and that she would have to pass by him to ascend the staircase. Fifteen minutes later, he watched her silhouette walk smartly toward him. At the foot of the stairwell, she raised her foot, but instead of connecting with the first step, she responded in fear to a hand being clamped over her mouth and an arm securing her waist.

"Make a sound and I'll hurt you," Rask hissed. "Understand?"

She nodded, eyes bulging. He half dragged, half guided her down the stairwell to the floor below.

Her eyes searched for help, but she knew

there would be none on the lower floor. No one went down to the lower floor except the janitor. It was a floor of storage closets full of chemicals, mops, brooms, and mechanical things.

"What do you want, Rask?" she demanded, twirling out of his grasp at the foot of the stairs—panting with anger, and desire.

"You've been avoiding me," he spat, standing tall and menacing before her. "I'm tired of chasing after you. I don't chase girls!"

"I'm not avoiding you," Miriam snapped. "I just want nothing to do with you, y-you self-centred, egotistical jerk!"

"What? I am not!" Rask snapped back, reaching for her again. "You're a tease, and I don't like to be teased."

"I don't care about you, or what you like and don't like," she hissed back, shoving him. "No more than you cared about me in that damn theatre. You're a selfish brute! Now let me pass. I'm late for class."

"Not so quick, my little window worker," he said, grabbing her arm.

"Don't call me that!" she shot back defensively, trying to shake her arm free of his grasp.

"Like mother, like daughter, I always say," he replied, arrogantly.

Miriam panicked. *How does he know! We've been very careful to hide the past.* She backed away from him, assessing her probability of escape.

Rask lunged, grabbing both arms and pinning her wrists behind her. He pushed her ahead of him, under the stairwell and out of sight, and braced her against the cold concrete wall. She struggled to free herself, but his weight held her. She felt jerky motions, as he unfastened his belt and zipper, and heard the buckle clank on the linoleum floor.

Rask released her wrists and, with one hand, pressed her face into the painted blocks that formed the basement wall. She tried to break free of his grip, but the captain of the football team held her head firmly in position. With the other hand, he reached under her skirt and ripped her panties free. She panted heavily into the wall, saliva flowing unchecked from her gaping mouth. Adrenaline coursed through her veins, arousing her to the danger as she struggled to be free.

"Make a sound, and I'll hurt you," he said again, hitching her skirt above her waist and pulling her bottom toward him.

Miriam inhaled deeply. Rask slammed her head with the back of his hand, temporarily stunning her. Her breathing came quick and hard, her mind spinning from the concussion. She braced her hands on the wall, as if to clear her thoughts.

When her resistance shifted, Rask seized her hips and rammed her with relentless thrusts. Excitement seemed to overcome him, and he moaned through his orgasm. Once his final shudder passed, he released his hold on Miriam. Without his anchoring support, she slumped to the brown patterned linoleum, gasping.

Through the veil of her hair, Miriam watched as Rask refastened his trousers and belt. He straightened his clothes and ran his fingers under his nose and through his hair, then disappeared up the staircase, whistling.

✥

Miriam's shock had quickly changed to excitement when she realized Rask's intention. As he groaned through his release, she silenced hers, refusing to give him any power over her. She sat crumpled on the floor for several minutes, allowing her breathing to slow.

Now she had the thrill of an orgasm to add to her list of experiences, and Rask was unaware of the pleasure he had delivered. She would take time to consider how this incident could play to her advantage. Subconsciously, she rubbed her face where he had pressed it into the wall. She enjoyed the threat of danger, and the ramming. A smile played across her lips. *How interesting—I could cry rape and destroy him, or I could use him for something more worthwhile. I'll write in my book of weaknesses tonight. Ideas will come to me.*

As Miriam stood, she retrieved her torn panties from the floor. She used them to wipe the slime from between her thighs and tossed them into the garbage bin in the girls' toilet. She missed her class but was ready for the next one when the bell rang.

The adrenalin release she experienced under the stairwell carried her through the day. She was pleased to realize that her second sexual encounter brought her a satisfaction that she had failed to experience with the first.

CHAPTER TWENTY-FIVE

By the time school closed for the year, Miriam knew she was pregnant. She was not surprised. She had had several more unexpected, and stimulating, encounters with Rask. Neither of them bothered with condoms. That would have ruined the spontaneity.

Miriam knew about abortion and the importance of engaging someone capable. Having overheard many hushed discussions between her mother and grandmother, she also knew whom to ask. And, thanks to her parents, she had a savings account from which she could draw the necessary funds. *But a withdrawal won't be necessary. Rask will pay, when I explain our predicament.*

Abortion was illegal in the Netherlands, but the pitch to legalize it was increasing. Fortunately, window workers had helpful connections. Miriam made an appointment, arranged the procedure, and took to her bed with "a bout of influenza".

✤

During morning rounds with her husband, Punita visited women who were early in their pregnancies, while the doctor spent time with those whose pregnancies were more advanced. In the summer of 1967, not long after Miriam had graduated, Punita was visiting Dunya Horen, the young woman who had bought the window from Mina. Dunya was five months pregnant and did not know who had fathered her child.

"Mina warned me," she told Punita, "not to allow full intercourse. But two of my clients were very persistent and … well … once I allowed one, I couldn't stop the other. Neither of them wants anything to do with me now!" She rubbed the roundness of her belly absentmindedly.

"That may be," Punita replied, "but you made the decision to keep the child."

"Yes. I decided that, if Mina could raise a child in this business, so could I. I couldn't bear the thought of killing my child," she said. "Not like Miriam. I don't know how she could do that!"

"Miriam? Miriam who?" Punita asked, afraid to know the answer.

"Why, your Miriam, of course!"

"Are you suggesting that my grand-daughter is pregnant?"

"Oh no. Not now," Dunya said, her blonde curls bobbing with effect. "She had an abortion last week, so far as I know."

Punita heard the click in her brain. *So, it wasn't influenza after all.* She patted Dunya's shoulder.

"I must be off. I'll see you next month. Remember … no intercourse. It isn't good for you or the baby."

"I will," Dunya said, escorting Punita to the door.

Punita made a mental note to discuss the possibility of Miriam's abortion with her husband later, and whether it was worthwhile to tell Mina and Willem. *I'll need to monitor Miriam's behaviour more closely. Not that I can do anything about it. The child is wild, despite my attempts to guide her otherwise. I have no idea how to deal with such selfish and irresponsible behaviour.*

Miriam was frustrated by her parents' constant nattering about studies at the University of Amsterdam. In spite of Willem's recommendation that she study business, so she could work with him at *Oyster Pearl Imports*, she resisted and enrolled in liberal arts and sciences. By the end of the first year, she was bored and refused to continue.

"I want to travel. I want adventure!" Miriam insisted. "Every day, it's the same thing. Go to school, come home, and study. Next day, repeat."

"That would be a mistake," Willem cautioned. "Have you given serious thought to this?"

"Only every day!" Miriam snapped back.

She was recovering from another "bout of influenza". During her most recent appointment, the abortionist had warned her that further procedures could cause her irreparable harm, if not death. *I need to get away from Rask and make myself pure again.*

"Where would you go?" Mina asked, feeling exasperated by her daughter's behaviour.

"Oh, I don't know," she mused, "Paris, New York, Canada—Kristina's family moved to Canada at the end of school and she's always inviting me to visit. They ski in the mountains!"

The following month, once Miriam had regained her strength, Willem took Mina and Miriam to Paris for a week. Her parents knew that once Miriam set her mind to an idea, she was almost impossible to shift. Her return to university was cemented in resistance.

From Paris, they flew to New York City and stayed for two weeks, touring the city and the state. Willem and Mina agreed to allow Miriam to travel alone from New York to Calgary, where she planned to visit with Kristina for a month before returning to Amsterdam. Near the end of the month-long visit with Kristina, Miriam telephoned her parents.

"I'm not returning any time soon," she told them, "I've cashed in my plane ticket. Kristina and I are going to the mountains for the winter, to work and ski."

HART

CHAPTER TWENTY-SIX

While Konrad and Penn made plans to attend university the following September, Hart made no such commitment. Manfred Bartz's death continued to haunt him, causing him to rethink his ability to focus on advanced studies without first addressing what troubled him.

Home for the last school break before graduation, he sat alone in his room, pondering how to overcome his haunting thoughts, and what he might do instead. He took a swig of ale from the bottle that dangled between his knees and resolved to speak with his father the following morning. He slept soundly until the early hours when he awoke from a nightmare. Sitting upright in his bed, Hart rubbed his eyes and scrubbed his head, still hearing the skeleton call his name.

"Vati," Hart said, catching Paul in his study the following morning. It was Easter Sunday and a March storm raged outside the window. Sheets of rain pelted against the panes, casting a grey gloom into the room. "Do you have a few minutes?"

Paul welcomed his son into the study and poured coffee for both of them.

"I was expecting your mother," he said, explaining the two cups, "but Cook can bring another, if necessary."

He handed a cup to Hart.

"What's on your mind?" he asked, switching on more lamps to brighten the room.

"I'd like to take a year off," Hart said.

"A year off?"

"Yes. Before I go to university, I'd like to take a break. Something's bothering me, and I need to address it before I continue."

269

"Of course," Paul agreed easily. He had often told Hart of how his plans for the priesthood were waylaid when World War II erupted. "Why don't you begin by telling me what's troubling you, then we can talk about how to help you move on."

"What's troubling you, *mein Herz*?" Ilse-Renata asked from the doorway.

"Ah! Ilse, we'll need another cup," Paul apologized.

His wife disappeared, momentarily, and returned with a third one. As Paul poured coffee for her, Hart spoke of his friendship with Manfred Bartz, and of his friend's unusual death, omitting any mischief involving the skeleton.

"Sometimes, I awake from nightmares, not of his death specifically—I wasn't there, nor responsible, after all—but, when I awake, it is Manfred who fills my thoughts," Hart said. "I think I should speak to someone about it, but I don't want to interrupt my studies. Perhaps I'll get counseling after I graduate. Here, not in Marburg. I'd rather my friends didn't know about it."

His parents listened earnestly.

"When your father returned from the war," Ilse-Renata said, "he had many nightmares. Still has the occasional one, as a matter of fact." She reached over toward Paul and took his hand in hers. "Counselling helped him a lot, and I'm certain it will help you, too."

"Whatever support you need from us, son, you will have it," Paul added.

"Thank you both," Hart said, sipping his coffee.

A moment passed before Paul interrupted the companionable quiet.

"You mentioned earlier that you'd like to take a year off before continuing your studies."

"Yes," Hart answered. "I'd like to spend some time with you in the factory. I'd also like to spend time at the summerhouse, boating and swimming. And ... I'd like to spend time in the mountains.

Last winter, I was offered a job as a ski instructor."

"Those are great plans!" Paul said.

"Absolutely!" Ilse-Renata agreed.

Hart returned to Bayreuth at the end of May. By then Ilse-Renata had made arrangements for counselling, and his appointments were scheduled frequently over the next two weeks. By mid-June, he and the counsellor had agreed that Hart should take some time to reflect on their discussions and made a follow-up appointment for the end of August.

The next day, Hart finished loading his Mercedes-Benz sports car—a graduation gift from his parents—with everything he would need for a summer of sun, sea, sand, and fun, and drove to the Lange summerhouse. The weather was warm, allowing him to drive the entire way—a fourteen-hour journey—with the roof down, making only necessary stops for gas and personal relief. He had never felt so free, so alive. Wind whipped through his hair. Sun bounced off his Ray-Ban Aviators and browned his face. If not for the windshield, his toothy smile would have snagged a myriad of insects.

Hart spent the next two weeks puttering around the family compound, exercising his imagination. From time to time, he would laze on the beach watching beautiful young women saunter by in skimpy bikinis or monokinis. He admired their varying shapes, sizes, skin colours, and hair shades. He found them all intriguing. He fantasized about spending time with a few of them but made no effort to do so. He was content with time to think and read.

In July, Hart was joined at the compound by his parents, his eight-year-old sister Emma, and Emma's school friend, Marte. Under the Adriatic sun, it did not take long for their all-over tans to equal his. While their parents relaxed in their hammocks, reading books or chatting, Hart took the girls for drives around the island, walks along the

seawall, or out on the water in the speedboat he had bought when he was sixteen.

Late one morning, he told the girls that
he would take them out in the boat, if they
packed a lunch. The girls scrambled to prepare a picnic lunch and meet him on the
dock. Soon, the boat was skipping over
waves, marring the clear blue water, with
the girls clinging to the dashboard, wind
whipping their long hair behind them like
pennants. Just before noon, Hart slowed
the motor and the speedboat crept into a
secluded cove.

On the bow of his boat, Hart stretched,
inhaled deeply, and plunged head first into
the sea. He swam underwater until his
lungs threatened to burst, then popped to
the surface on the other side of a patch of
reeds. He pushed dripping blue-black hair
out of his eyes and wiped the water from
his face, looking about to find his bearings.

The girls, already in the water, giggled
at his sudden reappearance. Emma bobbed
up and down three times, using the last

and highest bob to propel herself deep into the water, through the reeds and between her brother's knees. She popped up behind Hart, laughing. He turned around, grabbed her by the waist, and threw her high into the air to splash wildly as she re-entered the water.

"Me too!" Marte squealed and followed Emma's example.

They played at their bridge and toss game for a while, until the girls tired and decided to swim for a bit. When they climbed back onto the stern of the boat, Hart's swim suit was already dry.

"Here," he said, tossing a towel to each of them.

"Dry yourselves thoroughly, then wipe down the boat where you've dripped. The salt water will ruin the finish if you don't."

Hart opened the boat's sun visor to provide them a reprieve from the sun and set the cooler in front of them.

"We'll eat now," he said, "before we head back."

"Aww!" the girls whined together, protesting the end of their water fun.

"While I put the visor back," he said, thirty minutes later, "you two pack the cooler, and we'll be underway."

Reluctantly, the girls did so, and Hart started the motor. It fired smoothly, and he throttled forward, crawling the boat out of the cove and back into the main waterway.

Once he had it settled into a course back to the compound, Hart looked over his shoulder at the two girls. Exhausted from their water sports and a day in the sun, the two were curled together like sleepy kittens on the white leather bench behind him. He moved the throttle forward again, slowly increasing the speed. The wind whipped his hair, as he kept an eye on the sea ahead, watching for logs or any other debris that might mar his precious speedboat.

⚜

When the Bora wind won its battle with the Mistral wind at the end of July, the hot temperatures dropped, and Hart's father gave instructions to pack up. It was time to head home. Two days later, in the dark of early morning, Hart stood by his father's loaded Mercedes sedan.

"Have a safe journey home," he bade the four of them. "I'll see you in September."

Hart waved goodbye until they disappeared at the end of the lane, then returned to the house. It was still early. He crawled back into bed and enjoyed the solitude.

During August, Hart passed the time with boating, reading, and designing. On occasion, he drove into town and passed the evening at one of the pubs or garden patios. He found the patio nightlife invigorating and met several young women who wanted to spend more time with him. Sometimes, he invited one of them to the compound and took her boating. If any expressed a desire to stay longer, or through the night, Hart never objected. He embraced each experience and welcomed any enlightenment.

✤

In late August, Hart repacked his convertible and headed back to Bayreuth so as not to miss the next appointment with his counsellor. He spent the fall in the factory with his father, discussing his designs and learning more about his father's business. Paul encouraged him to spend time with the fabricators, to understand the process required to convert paper drawings into something tangible. He worked with molten iron, packed sand moulds, and operated the grinding machines. He listened to the men who handled each stage, asking questions and absorbing answers.

"Be careful when you work with the iron," the shop foreman told him. "Wear the gear. You may find it cumbersome, but it's there to protect you. One of the men tends to forget his heavy boots when he's hung over. A year ago, he spilled molten iron on his running shoe. He spent weeks in hospital and lost three of his toes!"

In early November, when the weather turned cold and snow began to fall, Hart once again packed his sports car—with winter gear—and headed to the Harz Mountains. As promised the previous winter, he was engaged by one of the resorts and trained as a ski instructor. The winter passed quickly, his days filled with individuals hoping to either learn to ski or to improve their alpine style. Initially, he was assigned to bunny hills and beginners, but he soon proved his prowess on the slopes and advanced to more challenging positions.

Several weeks into the ski season, one of the senior instructors was broadsided by an out-of-control novice, the impact forcing both beyond the forested boundaries. The novice received a serious head injury when he collided with one of the ancient fir trees. The instructor's leg was bent awkwardly around the same tree. Both had to be removed from the mountain by medic sled. The instructor later learned that his injuries would not heal before the end of the ski season. As a result, the resort offered the vacant position to Hart. He accepted and relished the opportunity given to him.

In early December, Hart telephoned Konrad and invited him for a visit before Christmas.

"I have exams this week and next," Konrad replied. "I'll come the week before Christmas."

"How are your law classes going?" Hart asked.

"Very well," Konrad responded. "Penn and I have kept the same study routine that we used in Marburg, and we're seeing the same results."

"How is Penn?" Hart asked.

"He's fine now," Konrad replied, "but you know how his immune system was compromised by the poliomyelitis. He still misses classes, but, with our system and his brain, he stays on top."

"If he's up to the trip," Hart suggested, "bring him along."

"Will do! See you soon."

A day before they were to leave for the mountains, Penn developed a seasonal cold and was forced to decline.

Konrad and Hart enjoyed skiing during the day, and clubbing in the evenings. When Konrad left for home, Hart once again found himself spending some of his off evenings in bars, on and around the mountain. He honed his connections and enjoyed the companionship of the occasional woman who welcomed him into a warm bed.

By the time Hart returned to Bayreuth mid-spring, he was confident, strong, and determined to see his designs manifested into usefulness. He returned to the factory for several months, then joined his family for their annual vacation at the seaside. At the end of July, instead of lingering, he returned to Bayreuth with his family, ready to commence studies in September at the Technical University of Clausthal-Zellerfeld.

"Your school break seems to have paid off," Paul said, handing Hart a glass of French brandy.

He straightened the Spanish Master hanging above the brandy tray and seated himself opposite Hart. They were reclining in the study following a weighty Sunday lunch.

Hart's free hand mindlessly roamed the cracked leather of his chair's arm. The other rolled the brandy around the bowl of the crystal glass. He watched the light cast rainbows on the wall as it ricocheted through the cuts in the glass, while he inhaled the aerated fumes.

Hart raised the glass to his lips, allowing the golden drops to flow into his mouth and onto his waiting tongue. The crisp apple taste bloomed on its descent into his belly, and he coughed to reduce the burn. Charcoal eyes watered over flushed cheeks.

"I believe it has, sir," he said, focussing his eyes on his father. "I am ready for school. I have some great ideas that I plan to explore over the few next years, and I'm keen to join you full-time at the factory in a few years."

"A toast, then," Paul said, raising his glass, "to your successful studies and your speedy return to the factory!"

Hart lifted his glass in answer to his father's toast, and sipped again, filled with anticipation.

A year later, he transferred to Essen to study Industrial Design.

URSULA

CHAPTER TWENTY-SEVEN

A week after her nineteenth birthday, Ursula completed an application for the Essen School of Industrial Design, located in north west Germany. She had determined some months earlier that that School was the best at which to complete her studies. She submitted her application and registration fee, then waited for receipt of a positive response. While she waited, she cast about for accommodation, and found a suitable location near the school.

Excited about her accomplishments, she purchased a bottle of cheap wine and asked her co-worker, Dragan, if he would like to take a walk with her after work. He accepted enthusiastically, and later that evening, they walked along the seawall, sharing the wine and talking of the future—how it would be for each of them.

"Have you ever had sex?" Dragan asked, as he tossed back the dregs of the bottle.

"No." She watched his face for mockery. "Have you?"

"Uh-huh."

"Was it good?" Her face brightened with curiosity.

"Oh, yes. Very good." Dragan paused. "Want to try?"

Ursula nodded her agreement. She had been exploring her own sexuality for several years, in anticipation of such an invitation, and had learned how to stimulate herself—the lightness of a touch, the pressure of a caress. Each experience had surpassed the previous. She was confident that an experience with a boy would be the most fulfilling. The mere thought of it made her tingle deep inside.

Dragan took her hand and led her to a secluded spot in the centre of some nearby trees. He pulled her close and kissed her hard, forcing his tongue into her mouth and grabbing at her breasts, his breathing escalating rapidly. Ursula was shocked by his urgency and assertiveness, and pushed him away, gagging. *Well, that was unexpected, but interesting. My body seems to be responding to his touches.*

Dragan reached for her again, snagging her shirt and pulling her toward him.

"Hey!" she snapped when she heard a seam give in her blouse. "Not so rough."

"Sorry," Dragan said. "I'm a little excited. This is only my second time."

He snatched at her skirt, trying to push it down. Ursula slapped his impatient hands out of the way, unzipped the skirt and let it fall to the grass. Dragan's next grab resulted in the two of them tumbling onto the dewy lawn. He rose to his knees and pulled at her panties until she shimmied out of them and lay naked from the waist down.

"Gosh!" Dragan exclaimed in awe. "You're so blonde down there!"

Ursula raised herself on her elbows and followed his gaze, the source of his comment reflected in the moonlight.

"So—" she snapped, panting slightly. "What colour is yours?"

Dragan looked abashed at her question and her state of undress.

"Oh yeah!" he said, scratching his crotch. He unzipped his jeans and pushed them and his underwear to his knees revealing an eager penis, nestled in a tuft of brown pubic hair.

"Want to touch it?" he asked, seeing her ogle his proud standing cock.

"Sure."

Ursula pushed herself to a sitting position, feeling blades of grass prickle at her bare bottom. She reached for the exposed flesh and grasped it firmly, wiggling it from side to side. A sudden vision of bright yellow bananas flashed in her mind.

"Ouch! Careful! It's attached you know."

"Sorry," she said, releasing the enthusiastic member.

287

"Have you ever seen anything so impressive?" Dragan boasted. Hands resting on his hips, he thrust them toward her face.

"No, I can't say that I have," she replied, leaning backward, "but I've never really seen a penis up close, so I don't think I'm qualified to compare."

"Oh, right!" he said, rummaging hastily in a trousers pocket.

"What's that?" she asked as he withdrew a small, dog-eared package.

"A condom." His words were muffled as he tore the package open with his teeth.

"What's it for?"

"What's it for?" he asked, appearing surprised at her naiveté. "You don't know about condoms?"

Ursula shook her head. He explained the need for a condom, as he rolled it over his still-standing member.

"Want to touch it?" he invited again.

Ursula extended her index finger and slowly slid it up and down the encasement,

288

once again distracted by thoughts of small, perfect bananas.

"The next part might hurt," he warned.

"What?"

"This might hurt," Dragan repeated, while he pushed her back onto the grass.

"My girlfriend screamed. Try not to scream," he encouraged, gazing over his shoulder, as if worried that someone might be watching.

Ursula nodded, her brow furrowed in anticipation of the pain.

"Why should it hurt?" she asked, taking hold of the threatening penis, and fighting to sit up. "I've never felt pain before."

"I thought you said you'd never had sex," he exclaimed.

"I haven't. Not with a boy."

"You like girls?" he asked.

"No." Her answer was uncertain. "It's just … I mean, I-I do it myself."

"Oh!" Dragan giggled nervously. "You like to please yourself! Ha! I thought only boys did that sort of thing." His amusement made his voice sound a little higher than normal.

"You didn't answer my question," she insisted. "And don't laugh at me or this won't happen."

"I'm sorry," Dragan said. "I'm not sure why it hurts. I only know it does ... but it only hurts once, and it's quick."

"All right," Ursula said, relaxing into the grass again.

She had no desire to have Dragan hurt her, but neither was she about to interrupt the very thing for which she had been yearning for years. Her body craved whatever he was about to do.

Dragan nudged her legs apart, knelt between them, grasped her hips, and rammed his stoic fellow home. She felt pressure and a little pain—like a nasty pinch—when he entered her, but it was not enough to make her want to stop. When the pressure eased, and Dragan began pumping, Ursula found his rhythm and met each thrust with her own. The thrusts ended

abruptly when the boy cried out, collaps-
ing onto her chest and crushing her with an
unexpected weight.

Annoyed, Ursula pushed Dragan off her
chest, and they lay side by side, listening to
their panting subside.

"How was it?" he asked.

"Well, it wasn't like I thought it would
be, that's for sure. I don't feel as satisfied as
I do when I take care of myself."

"Gosh! Let me help," Dragan said,
reaching for the slimy cave his deflated cock
had abandoned. Using his fingers, he began
to rub vigorously.

"Oooww!" Ursula exclaimed, pushing
his hand away. "Let me do it!"

A while later, they donned their clothing, and lay side by side, staring at the stars.

"So," her companion asked with uncertainty. "Would you like to try that again?"

Ursula considered his question for a long
moment.

"I suppose so," she said. "I'm going to
guess that we'll get better with practice.

I don't need a boy to please myself, but if we could learn to please each other, it has potential."

"That sounds great," he responded, with enthusiasm. "When would you like to try again?"

"How about tomorrow night?"

HART AND URSULA

CHAPTER TWENTY-EIGHT

Ursula Sertic strutted into her first class at the Essen School of Industrial Design and plunked her books on the centre table of the first row of desks. Before sitting on the adjoining student chair, she turned to survey the room, eyeing the other students. She slinked her arm around her pale neck, deftly collecting golden waves of hair and drawing them forward, to cover one breast. With a coy smile, she slowly turned toward the front of the room, allowing the other students an opportunity to observe and appreciate her shapely figure, then she lowered enticingly into the chair.

While she worked as a waitress in the seaside restaurant, Ursula had discovered that holding a man's interest could be beneficial to her advancement. She was especially fond of handsome men with money. As a result, she had chosen courses that tended to draw more men than women. She enjoyed sex and money, and if the two came together in one tidy package, she would consider herself most fortunate. Her survey revealed a few possibilities, especially the dark-haired fellow at the back of the room. She would know after one date whether he had money. If not, she would find another.

An instructor flitted into the room with an armload of books, closed the door, and began his lecture. Ursula listened keenly and took copious notes.

Ursula juggled classes, studies, and men easily. She was quick to organize a study group that helped her advance through the school program. She also sought inspiration for a graduation project and hoped that

294

ideas shared by the group would manifest into something concrete.

She dated some of her study partners, but none of them interested her beyond a first date. She fancied Hart but found him aloof.

Hart's participation in her study group differed from the others. He seemed focussed on the school work and not inclined to share ideas that would advance a design project for graduation, hinting instead that he already had a design in mind.

Well into their second year, Ursula concluded that, if she wanted to be alone with Hart, she would have to take the initiative. When she extended a dinner invitation, Hart accepted politely, and without enthusiasm. During dinner, they discussed their school work, but he avoided any discussion regarding his graduation project.

Two weeks before Christmas, Ursula succeeded in her seduction of Hart. As she nestled in the curve of his shoulder, skin

flushed from the pleasure of their love-mak-
ing, she reflected on the minor obstacles he
represented. *Winning him over has been
difficult, sure enough, but nowhere near
as painful as father's beating after I ate the
bananas. That Christmas changed my life
and gave me the strength and determination I've needed to achieve my goals.*

Hart ran his fingers through the golden
tresses draped across his chest. Encircled in
his right arm, Ursula appeared to be dozing.
He felt the weight of her legs entwined with
his, warm and silky.

He had not planned a tryst while he
attended the school. He had planned to
focus on his studies, learning all that he
could to effectively express his design ideas.
He was anxious to return to Bayreuth to
work with his father at the factory. *I'll
have to keep this moment short and sweet.
I can't let sex disturb my concentration.
Sure, it was amazing. She's quite creative!*
The corner of Hart's mouth twitched, but

he silenced a chuckle, not wanting to disturb Ursula's slumber.

Moments later, he forgot the heaviness on his shoulder and began to air-draw the design of the recreation vessel that he planned to submit for his final paper. He intended to use his new knowledge to fabricate the most impressive creation the school had ever seen. *My classmates talk about deferring their designs until the last year of the program. They seem to think it's important to wait until they have all of the knowledge and tools needed. Not I! I will review my work at the end of each term and apply any new knowledge while it's fresh in my thoughts. When the time comes to reveal my project, it will be perfect and complete.*

CHAPTER TWENTY-NINE

During spring break of their second year, Hart invited Ursula to accompany him home.

"You never speak about your parents or any siblings or going home. Would you consider being my guest for the week?"

She thanked him for the invitation.

"In the first place," she said, "my mom is dead, and my father's a nasty drunk, so I have no desire to go home. I ask nothing of the old bastard, and that's exactly what he gives me—nothing!" Her voice became venomous as she described her father. "I will never go home," she spat, carefully eyeing Hart for a reaction. "Plus, I can't afford the expense of travelling to Bayreuth."

"I'm sorry to hear about your parents. I didn't know."

Ursula shrugged away his apology.

"Besides, I'm inviting you to come as my guest. My treat!" he assured her. "I understand that you may be apprehensive about meeting my family but ... they really are good folks, even if I'm the one to say so."

"I don't know ... I should stay and study."

"Aw, come on," Hart encouraged her. "We both know you don't need to study. It will be a toss-up to see which of us graduates at the top of the class, and I wouldn't be surprised if we tie! Plus, we can study together at home. We won't always be involved with my family."

In the end, Ursula agreed to accompany him, curious to see how people with money lived.

Hart left his car in Essen. He and Ursula took the train to Bayreuth, so they could study en route. They travelled light and walked from the train station to his childhood home.

At the entrance he stopped, set his bag on the landing and reached above the door frame, placing his right hand over the Lange family crest.

"I'm home," he murmured. Satisfied with his ritual, he retrieved his bag, opened the door, and entered the dimly lit foyer.

"Mutti! Vati! We're here!" he announced. Turning to Ursula, he invited her to follow and closed the door behind her.

"What was that all about?" Ursula asked, nodding back toward the crest as they removed their shoes.

"Oh! Old family tradition. Every time a soldier goes off to war, he salutes the family crest. When he comes home, he does the same."

"But you're not a soldier," Ursula said.

"No, I'm not." He blushed. "But it's tradition! Besides, my father trained my brother and me to be soldiers when we were young. He wanted us to be prepared should another war start. It's all part of the family ..."

"Tradition!" they said together, laughing.

A moment later, the foyer filled with the noise of welcome and they disappeared into the warmth of a Lange family visit.

⚜

"What a blast!" Ursula remarked excitedly on the train trip back to Essen. "I don't know what I expected, but your parents are amazing. I'm not sure about your brother and his wife. They're a couple of snobs."

Hart nodded his agreement.

"But your sister is very sweet."

"So, they didn't scare you away? You'd come again?" he asked, thrilled that she enjoyed the visit, and that he was able to sneak a few late-night trysts at the same time.

"I had a wonderful time," she assured him. "If I'm asked again, I won't say no." She raised her pale blue eyes to meet his, black as charcoal.

"I liked the family crest thing, too," she said. "You're lucky to have that kind of tradition and history. I know nothing of my

301

family. Not that I really want to know. The whole idea of old soldiers going off to war, blessed in advance by the family crest, and returning to be greeted by it before anyone or anything else," Ursula prattled, bobbing her head up and down, "that's neat, man!"

PART IV

LIFE'S LITTLE CHALLENGES

MIRIAM

CHAPTER THIRTY

At the end of the 1974 ski season, Miriam flew home to Amsterdam, announcing to her parents that she would remain only until ski season began again. Then she expected to return to Canada.

To her surprise, Miriam felt more comfortable with her elders. Her time away and independence had allowed her to release the emotions that had driven her to madness as a teenager. Her demeanour seemed to surprise them too, and they appeared to take great care to ensure nothing triggered a reverse of her good humour. *Let them fuss. It leaves me in control.*

Miriam enjoyed her lengthy vacation. She contacted a few friends from her university days, and they organized social events. Most of her friends had graduated from their university studies and found positions in firms where they could advance in their chosen careers. They had money to spend and enjoyed the nightlife of Amsterdam.

A week had not passed since her return, when Rask telephoned her parents' number. He practised law with his father, he told Miriam, and he wanted to see her. He had an apartment of his own. Not knowing what to expect, Miriam packed a few extra items in her handbag. She told her parents that she would be visiting some friends, and that they should not be surprised if she did not return that night.

On Friday evening, she knocked on the door of Rask's apartment, nervous to see him again, yet anticipating a thrill of intimacy. She was not disappointed. Rask was ready for her. Within minutes of her arrival, clothing was strewn about the living room, creating a trail to the bedroom where they thoroughly indulged in their desires.

"Rask," she said, twisting her red lacquered nail through the coarse golden hairs on his chest, "we need to be more careful. I can't risk another abortion. If I get pregnant again, there could be an expensive consequence." She smiled coyly at him, delivering her threat with sweetness.

"Ah, come on. You know you were as excited as I was. We didn't have time." He pulled a curl of her hair toward him, requiring her to lower her head to avoid any pain. "Kiss me, and this time I promise to use a condom."

Following a marathon of lovemaking that sated both, Rask returned to work on Monday and Miriam returned to the blue door. They continued their trysts through the spring and into the summer.

"We're like rabbits," she said to him one evening, feeling the sweat evaporate from her pulsing skin.

He lowered himself to her side, inhaling her musk and ran the nail of his right index finger from navel to sternum leaving a white line on her pinked flesh. His breathing slowed.

"Ja, we have good sex." He grinned.

"Ja, too good, I think." Her expression was solemn. "I'm pregnant again, Rask, and I can't abort. I was warned last time that another abortion could kill me."

"So, what do you want to do about it?" he asked.

"Well, let's put it this way," she paused. "I have no intention of raising a child on my own. It's not about me anymore. The question is ... what are *we* going to do about it."

"Shit!" Rask spat. Snapping to a sitting position, he looked down at her. "My parents expect me to marry the daughter of one of the partners. We've been dating for the past year."

"Is she any good in the sack?"

"How would I know?" He ran his fingers through his mop. "She won't let me near her. She's a stuck-up prude!"

"Well, then," Miriam was sly with her delivery, "I guess you have some thinking to do." She swung her legs off the bed and padded into the bathroom. "I'm going to take a shower," she said, deliberately leaving the door ajar.

By the time Rask stepped into the shower, the walls were slippery with steam. He took the bar of soap from her and slid it sensuously over her body, lingering on the more sensitive parts, caressing, massaging, licking, sucking, probing. He waited for a few minutes to pass after her final release, then handed the bar to her, allowing her to reciprocate.

"I have to go," she said, closing the taps, five minutes later.

She dried herself and dressed in a white tube top and white short shorts, while he returned, still dripping, to the bed. It was hot. The humidity from their steamy shower permeated the apartment, making it difficult to breathe.

"We'll need to resolve this," she said, patting her belly, "soon. My mother's birthday is next week. Come for dinner."

✿

Miriam and Rask were married within the month, and Miriam undertook the task of locating and furnishing a townhouse in Willemspark. Her dreams of snowy mountains in Canada melted away.

The early months of their marriage were exciting. The worries of conception no longer being an issue gave Miriam and Rask freedom to enjoy their sexual exploits. Every corner of the townhouse was baptized with their activities. As Miriam's girth increased with the advancing child, they were forced to curtail their intimate activities and be more creative.

"Don't worry, darling," Miriam consoled Rask, "as soon as it's out, we can return to normal."

"I've always been normal, Miriam, you're the one who's changed. This guy is finding it more difficult to stand to attention these days." Rask massaged his groin. "If you weren't so good at exercising him, he'd never wake up. You've become such a cow!" He failed to notice the anger that passed behind his wife's eyes.

Rask's parents, who had not forgiven him for the betrayal of his engagement—although it had never been formally announced—were conveniently unable to attend the wedding or the birth.

On an icy day in February of the following year, their daughter was delivered, without consequence, by Dr. Hendrik, assisted by birthing companions Punita and Mina. Willem kept Rask company in the sitting room while they awaited the birth.

"Miriam, your daughter is beautiful!" Mina praised, cradling her granddaughter, wrapped in the same yellow birthing blanket that her mother had wrapped around Miriam. "She looks just as you did when you were born. Hello, little Punita," she cooed, as she leaned over to hand the child to Miriam she stroked the baby's cheek.

"Pu-ni-ta! What makes you think I would give her such an awful name," Miriam retorted, her face contorted in disgust. "Do you have any idea what an outcast she'd be with a name like that?" The venom in her voice blind-sided her elders.

"It's all right, dear," Punita said, recovering quickly from the slight. "Your mother is remembering our family tradition to name the first daughter of every third generation *Punita*, so we always remember our roots." She shuffled toward her granddaughter and admired the baby. "Have you thought of a name, then?"

"No. Maybe," Miriam sputtered. "I've been thinking of Pauline. It has a modern sound to it."

"It does, indeed, sweet girl," Punita said. "Pauline has many good qualities."

Punita's slender finger lifted the blanket where it had fallen on the baby's face, revealing eyes tightly closed, a button nose, and pouting ruby lips.

"Pauline means amazing and kind-hearted. She may be shy and humble, but she will never settle for less than best. She must take care, however, never to carry the

312

burdens of others. She will worry enough for herself." Punita straightened, a hand on her lower back as she stretched tired muscles, then stroked an emerald earring. "Welcome, little Pauline. May your burdens always be light."

"Amen to that!" Mina agreed.

In that moment of naming, Miriam had broken the tradition of generations and moved into unchartered waters, ensuring a future unlike anything her family had known before. Punita felt the pain in her heart but saw in her mind the vast fissure that severed the past and all that she held dear.

As soon as Pauline was born, Miriam reduced her food consumption and refused to nurse the child. She continued to service Rask as she had done in the last trimester of her pregnancy, allowing herself to heal. She was determined to hold his attention until her body regained its former shape.

She planned romantic meals and outings but found the child to be a hindrance to holding Rask's attention. Eventually, his interest in her faded. They both became bored with their sexual relationship and their marriage. Rask had no interest in the child. He allowed the demands of his practice to rule his time. On the rare occasion that he was home, he spent the time in his study, working.

Miriam cycled the neighbourhood with Pauline seated in a bicycle carrier. She sought distraction in shopping, visiting her parents, and touring about the city. Pauline loved the fresh air and chattered unintelligible words of pleasure. Miriam found companionship in like-minded mothers and fathers and whiled away her days.

At the end of 1976, Rask announced that the marriage was over.

"You're too wild for me," he told her. "I'm a lawyer and I need a wife who is respectable, who respects me and my status. I'm filing for a divorce. You can keep the kid. I can make more."

"Make more!" Miriam's mind raced. *Divorce!* "With whom?"

"As soon as the divorce is decreed, I'm going to marry the woman I was engaged to before you came back from Canada."

"If you want a divorce," she told him, worrying about her future, "I'll give it on two conditions: I want the house, and you will support Pauline and me, indefinitely." His parents agreed, with a slight modification: Pauline alone would receive support until she turned eighteen.

CHAPTER THIRTY-ONE

In celebration of her twenty-fifth birth-day, Miriam's university friends took her out to a nightclub. She left Pauline with her parents and enjoyed a night of freedom and fun, dancing to pop music and meet-ing energetic, like-minded, young people. After months of pregnancy, motherhood, and a miserable marriage, Miriam cele-brated her birthday with adults, single and uninhibited.

One by one, her friends left the night-club, claiming a need for sleep before work the next morning. By midnight, she was alone and reluctant to return home. Sit-ting in a booth, she sipped her cocktail and listened to Elvis Presley crooning *Are You Lonesome Tonight*. She closed her eyes and swayed to the soft music.

"Hello," a deep, accented voice said, "care to dance?"

a panther, she realized, mesmerized by the lilt of his voice.

Their conversation touched on many topics, avoiding the obvious, until Miriam sensed his nerve shift. He moved closer and took her hand.

"I should leave soon," he said, "I have packing to do."

Her body thrummed from the physical contact. She waited a heartbeat.

"May I kiss you?" he asked.

Her grin was slow and inviting. He leaned toward her, kissing her once, chastely, then again, more fully. She parted her lips and responded. His tongue found hers. Minutes passed.

"Last call!" The barman's announcement startled them apart.

Some folks called for one last drink, while others took their leave. Some who had arrived alone left arm in arm with another. Miriam snaked her hand through Jarome's arm and smiled as he led her out of the nightclub.

The air was fresh and sharp, but not enough to break the spell that bound them. They walked around the corner to his hotel and into an elevator. He pushed the button for the eleventh floor. The doors closed, and the elevator rose. Jarome put his massive hands on her shoulders and drew her to him, kissing her fervently until the doors opened again.

Breathless, Miriam followed him to his room. He ushered her in, closed the door, ensured that it locked, and tossed the key onto the credenza. She waited, but not for long. As she wandered deeper into the room, she felt his hand on her shoulder and turned to him.

Their passion had begun on the dance floor, and now continued behind the closed door of the hotel room. They stripped each other in haste, strewing their clothes on the floor. Jarome lifted her, naked, onto the bed, and knelt over her, before lowering himself lengthwise, running his fingers lightly around one nipple, then the other. Miriam closed her eyes, feeling them harden to his touch. Possessive and demanding, his ebony hand crawled the length of her pale belly, exploring, until his fingers collided with and caressed the dark springy hair in their path. Miriam opened her eyes, hot desire burning in them.

Jarome chuckled deep in his throat. He took her hand, guiding it.

"I thought you might like this," he said, wrapping her fingers around the shaft protruding from the top of his thighs. She smiled at him, clenching her fingers.

"You're very clever," she purred, rising to better view the rod she held. "I'm glad you left the light on. I want to see what you can do with it!"

"Miriam! Can you not be more responsible with your behaviour?" Mina demanded, when her daughter's pregnancy became obvious.

When the child was born, Mina said nothing more. The baby's coffee-coloured skin confirmed that Rask was not his father. While Dr. Hendrik repaired Miriam's torn flesh, Mina cleaned the vernix from her grandson and examined him carefully. All of his necessary body parts were present: ten fingers, ten toes, a cap of tight black curls, and a sweet face. She wrapped him in the yellow blanket and handed him to his great-grandmother.

Punita tucked the blanket around his tiny face and approached the delivery bed.

"Miriam dear, have you a name in mind for your new son?"

"His name is Jacob. And don't give me any of that nonsense about the meaning of his name. I don't believe in it!"

Punita stepped back at the slight.

"I'm sorry, Mama," Mina whispered, wrapping an arm around Punita. "Miriam has no sense of tradition."

"Indeed," Punita replied. "I worry about the future of her children. Jacob will be kind and loving, with the mind of an athlete. He will also be a fighter and will have to learn to manage his anger issues. I hope that he finds his way, in spite of his mother."

Miriam never saw Jarome again. She sent him a note to tell him that he had a son and that she had named him Jacob. A month later, a cheque arrived in the mail. The amount was significant, the note short:

Use this. Don't contact me again.

Although a second child was inconvenient, Miriam loved her son. His black eyes and tight, curly hair were endearing. He was a miniature of his father, with no evidence of her genes.

"He's like a teddy bear, Mama," his big sister said in her small voice. "I love him!"

Rask threatened to discontinue his child support if she kept Jacob. Miriam refused to give up her son and told Rask that he would regret any interruption to the flow of his support payments. Her threat was sufficient to silence Rask, and, except for Rask's brief protests of her obvious involvement with another man, nothing more was said. Miriam was left to raise her children as she chose.

As Jacob's second birthday approached, Miriam's restlessness grew stronger. *It's too close in this city. I'm bored. I need to get out of here.*

CHAPTER THIRTY-TWO

In the summer of 1980, Miriam announced that she planned to return to Canada, taking Pauline and Jacob with her. She sold the townhouse that Rask had given to her as part of the divorce settlement and assured her parents that she could live a long time in the mountains if she spent her money wisely.

Although they worried for Miriam's children and how she intended to support them, her elders breathed a collective sigh of relief knowing that she would not be turning to them for help so long as she lived abroad. She had been very clear about that when she informed them of her plans.

"I hate to say it of my own daughter," Willem said to his wife, Eamon and Punita, as they watched from a window in Schiphol Airport, waiting for the flight to Canada to back away from the gate, "but I'm glad she's going. And I hope she doesn't come back … at least for a while."

"Willem!" Mina responded appearing shocked by his comment.

"You know I'm not speaking with malice," Willem said, embracing his wife, 'but we must be honest with ourselves." He gently set her from him and directed his comments to both women. "Miriam was a precocious child. She's rebelled against everything we stand for, since she was fourteen. Her presence is taxing. My worry is more for her children and what will become of them." He wrapped an arm around each woman and led them from the airport terminal.

"Sometimes," Mina lamented, "I wonder whether we protected her too much."

"No, I don't think so," Punita answered. "On reflection, the signs were there."

"I have seen this struggle in others," Eamon said, contributing to the conversation as he trailed behind. "It matters not how good a family is, or how well a child is raised. The struggle comes from within and only that person can sort themselves out. First, however, there must be acknowledgement and then change. Unfortunately, I don't see Miriam ever acknowledging that she has a problem. Her attitude worsens every year."

In Canada, Miriam rented a small house in the town, at the foot of the mountain where she liked to ski. She enrolled Pauline in a nearby school and found a part-time job, planning to work full-time once the ski hills opened. She found daycare for Jacob on the days that she worked. She had a nest egg of sorts, thanks to Jarome and to the sale of the townhouse in Amsterdam, and she planned to stretch that, trying to use only the money she earned.

Miriam and Kristina revived their friendship and, when time permitted, Miriam joined Kristina for evenings out. Soon, Kristina met and married a local fellow, and she and her husband bought a house on the same street where Miriam lived. Kristina was the only person Miriam had ever trusted. She neither betrayed nor challenged Miriam, merely accepted her as she was.

Miriam also renewed a relationship with Pete Dense, a fellow she had met during her earlier stay in Canada. Pete was a carpenter and owned a white house, with a green door and a white picket fence encircling its yard. Pete was smitten with Miriam and often asked her to move in with him.

"The children will be safe in the fenced yard and the school is close," he offered. "We'll be a family. I'll take care of all of you. You won't even have to work, if you don't want to."

Miriam valued her independence and declined.

Miriam's frugal intentions evaporated in the first months of life at the foot of the mountain. The money she earned did not meet her monthly expenses: she and the children needed warm clothes; the children had winter maladies, requiring medical treatment and medicine; and daycare was more expensive than she had anticipated. She was forced to supplement her income by withdrawing funds from her nest egg. In addition, partying, skiing, and trips to Calgary—cruising the nightclubs for one-night stands to sate her sexual cravings—all ate into her savings. *Everything costs money*, she worried at the end of each month, while giving it no thought at all in between. *If I'm going to minimize my financial worries, I'm going to have to accept Pete's invitation the next time he offers to house us.* She resented having to give up her independence, but endeavoured to make the best of an undesirable situation. *At least, I won't have to pay rent, she justified. Besides, I'm bored. Pete might be just what I need right now.*

By 1985, little remained of Miriam's nest egg. Although she still received regular support payments from Rask, and Pete provided a home, her excess funds were not sufficient to support the lifestyle to which she felt entitled. She was also frustrated with Pete's violent outbursts. He vehemently objected to her forays into the Calgary nightlife, while he stayed behind and cared for her children. Her return from Calgary usually ended in an argument, followed by rough but fulfilling sex. On a rare occasion, Miriam contemplated the effect her relationship with Pete might have on her children, but such contemplations rarely lasted long.

A year later, Miriam could no longer tolerate Pete's obsessiveness. *I need to get away from him. He's choking me!* Within days, her luck turned.

"I'm divorcing my husband," Kristina announced. "He drinks every penny he earns."

"Why don't we get a place together," Miriam suggested, plying the same charm she used on her male conquests. "I bet we can find something near the elementary school. Our living expenses will be halved, and we can take turns babysitting if we feel like dating. Our kids get along so well, after all."

Kristina agreed, and before her Decree Absolute and Custody Order were even signed, she was living with Miriam in a large three-bedroom apartment, close to the elementary school.

HART AND URSULA

CHAPTER THIRTY-THREE

As they approached graduation—tied for first place—Hart and Ursula were known as the class couple who would succeed no matter what. On the last visit home before graduation, Hart caught his father in the old study and asked his opinion about Ursula, whether Paul thought they would make a good match.

Paul poured two glasses of French brandy into the crystal glasses, neatly placed on a silver tray. He handed one glass to Hart and sniffed his own.

"God, I love this stuff," Paul said, sipping a burst of warm apple liqueur.

Hart watched him hold it in his mouth for a moment, before easing it down his throat. While he awaited his father's thoughts about Ursula, he sipped his own.

"Well, you're certainly compatible," Paul answered. "You could do worse. Do you love her?"

"Yes, sir."

"Let me ask my old friend, Sergeant Albrecht. He's with the Bayreuth police now, and he's very good at conjuring up information," Paul suggested. "Just to be certain ..."

"You're worried that she may be after family assets?"

"That, and the fact that you don't know a lot about her past. We have a family reputation to maintain, and I'd prefer to avoid any controversy if we can. Besides, if she's engaged in any type of espionage, I'd like to know now, before she steals any trade secrets."

"Sure, go ahead," Hart replied. "Is Albrecht able to obtain information from Yugoslavia?"

"I'm sure he can."

They enjoyed the remainder of their brandy in silence, each lost in his own thoughts, until Paul interrupted.

"Since you're off to Essen tomorrow, I'll call you when I have a response from Albrecht."

"Thank you, Vati. I'll await your call."

⚜

A few days later, the telephone in Hart's dorm room rang. His thoughts were deep into his studies as he crammed for the last test, making him slow to pick-up.

"Am I interrupting something?" Paul asked. "You usually answer on the first ring."

"Sorry, Vati," Hart said, scratching his head, leaving black spikes of hair projecting randomly, "I'm cramming for my last exam."

"I won't keep you long, then," Paul said. "I have news about Ursula."

"From the tone of your voice," Hart guessed, "it doesn't sound all bad."

"No, it's not," Paul continued. "Albrecht found an incident some years ago. The death of her mother was a bit suspicious. Ursula was present when her mother fell while preparing dinner. She landed on a paring knife. It pierced her heart. No charges were laid. It was her father, not Ursula, whom the police suspected. Albrecht said that, although there wasn't much money, the family coped. Father has a drinking problem. No siblings."

Hart sat straighter in his chair, relief seeming to unbend him.

"She doesn't speak much of her past, and when she does, she's careful about what she says," Hart acknowledged. "On the train ride back to Essen a while ago, she told me about her mother's death. Apparently, the woman fell because her husband struck her on the head."

"I see," Paul said. "I won't keep you, son. You'll want to get back to your studies. In conclusion, though, if you think she's the one you want to spend the rest of your life with, you have my blessing."

Hart hung up the telephone and returned to his studies, feeling light and struggling with focus.

"It's a good thing I know this stuff," he mused aloud. "otherwise, Ursula might unseat me!"

Prior to graduating, Hart submitted his final project, for which he received top marks: a unique, multi-purpose, recreational water vessel that not only offered sun tanning surfaces, but a vehicle that made fishing, water-skiing, and rescue operations easy. He described the design to his father, explaining that it included an array of advanced safety features that the life-saving society of Germany determined to be superior to other life-saving products on the market at that time. Paul responded with pride saying that he was impressed with his son's forward-thinking. During a subsequent telephone conversation, Paul encouraged Hart to return to the foundry as soon as possible.

"Not yet, Vati," Hart said, taking a sip of his apple brandy. "I still have to complete a six-month internship."

"An internship should not be difficult to find. If you need help, let me know."

"No need, Vati. I'm expecting an offer on Monday." Hart smiled into the handset. "Thanks, by the way, for sending the brandy. I've missed our father-son discussions in the study." He rolled the crystal glass in his hand, catching the late afternoon sunlight, and played with the placement of prisms on the wall.

"Just a small token of congratulations for a job well done," Paul replied. "We'll have plenty of time for father-son conversations when you graduate and return to Bayreuth. See you soon, son."

Hart signed off the weekly call and returned the handset to the cradle. He leaned back in his chair, released a sigh of pleasure, and enjoyed the last drops of the crisp apple nectar.

⚜

Hart accepted an offer of internship made the following Monday. The terms of engagement were more than agreeable. *It helps to be the son of Paul Lange, owner of Mikel & Co., but it can also be a hindrance,* Hart mused, recalling his imminent employer's expectation that his ingenuity should be comparable to, if not better than, his father's.

Fulfilling that expectation, Hart designed a unique pump system that would catapult his employer's business into the future, the first apprentice to ever accomplish such a feat. Hart graduated from the School of Industrial Design with high marks and returned to Bayreuth where he assumed a position in the foundry. Paul expressed his delight with the innovative designs that Hart planned to implement and encouraged his continued creativity.

In June 1976, a month following the completion of their practicums and final graduation, Ursula and Hart were married. Following a simple service in a Catholic church not far from the Lange family home in Bayreuth, the newly-weds, the groom's parents, and his sister returned home for a wedding feast prepared by the cook. Then, the newlyweds took a short honeymoon in Nuremberg before returning to Bayreuth.

They found a small apartment in the centre of the old town, and Hart prepared to start work at the foundry.

On the evening before his work at the foundry was to commence, Hart sat alone in the living room of his new apartment, nursing a glass of brandy. It was late. Traffic outside had subsided. Within, only the ticking of a mantle clock disturbed the silence. Hart felt satisfied with his life, cocooned in the comfort of his new home, his wife asleep in the next room. His mind wandered aimlessly at first, then took a path of its own, reflecting on youthful adventures that had shaped his life.

He remembered the day his father had told him that he would have to attend a private school while his parents and Emma travelled to München where his father's throat cancer would be treated. He had been heartbroken to have to leave his family so early, but his father had encouraged him to take advantage of the situation and to learn from it. On reflection, Hart knew his experiences had brought out some of his best qualities—creativity, leadership, compassion, responsibility, loyalty, and integrity. In addition, he had found life-long friendships with Konrad and Penn.

Ursula was standing at the kitchen counter the next morning, assembling a plate of black bread and cheese for Hart's breakfast, when he appeared at the doorway.

"Is my tie straight?" he asked.

Ursula wiped her hands on her apron before turning toward him.

"It's perfect," she said, standing on tiptoes to kiss him.

"I've packed a lunch for you," she added, waving toward her handiwork, "and I've made your breakfast." She placed the plate of bread and cheese on the table, then reached for the coffee urn.

"What will you do today?" Hart asked.

"Look for a job, as usual," she said. "I don't want to make any rash decisions. I want to choose the perfect position."

"Take all the time you need," Hart encouraged her. "I want you to be as happy as I am."

CHAPTER THIRTY-FOUR

Paul had always been haunted by the last words of his father Gerhard: "You must have a backup plan," and by the vow that he had made in response. He had spent hours puzzling over what could be done to protect his family.

In 1977, Paul shared Gerhard's concern with Hart and together they discussed what the backup plan would entail, and how to implement it. Over the next several months, Paul organized the family businesses to allow liquidity, if necessary. At the same time, Hart and Ursula made and implemented plans to relocate to Canada, a country far removed from instability and the possibility of war or invasion.

Disappointed, Ursula agreed to give up her newly-found employment and her dream of a marketing career in Bayreuth, determined to embrace the Canadian adventure.

The couple established a division of Lange Machinery in southern Alberta, the seat of a large, well-established farming community. Hart made valuable connections within the local farming community and travelled about the countryside introducing Lange Machinery to farmers and ranchers. Lange Machinery debuted as a direct competitor of one of the leaders of farm equipment in North America, with the advantage of having a relationship with Mikel & Co. and its innovative systems for converting barn waste into fertilizer and clean drinking water.

Ursula busied herself with the creation of advertisements for trade journals, as well as brochures and signs for trade shows. Hart hauled his samples and signs to trade shows and exhibitions, reaching out to anyone who would take the time to listen.

Before the end of 1979, Lange's innovative designs were being widely praised in southern Alberta, and elsewhere, but it was the Hutterite colonies who embraced the ideas wholeheartedly, purchasing the systems and putting them to work with great success. The colonies were so impressed with the Lange designs that they often engaged Hart to design additional systems, specifically suited to their farming needs.

As the years passed, Hart became renowned for his innovative ideas. He was approached several times by individuals and groups expressing interest in his insights and designs. He travelled throughout North America, meeting with dignitaries, wealthy individuals, and conglomerates, all with farming interests. He was wooed by the Mexican Department of Agriculture, who promised to buy Lange farm systems on two conditions: they were to be installed at Lange's expense, and Hart was to reside on location for the years it took to prove the system's success. Hart respectfully declined, pointing out that the farmers in Alberta had no such expectations, and their farms were successful nonetheless.

At trade fairs in the United States he

met wealthy businessmen keen to invest in a joint venture for improving American farm systems. Unfortunately, one died on the eve of signing a fortuitous contract, and another lost his fortune when the silver market collapsed.

Hart soon realized that with his success came disappointments.

A third potential investor, whose farming interests waned when an international burger business expressed interest in his potato farm, thought the Lange's systems had significant merit, and expected that the systems would help him rebuild his cattle ranch. His sons did not agree.

"We make more than enough money turning our spuds into fries," one son said. "Why would we compromise our meal-ticket?"

"We don't care about farm systems," the other son said. "We're potato farmers, now."

In the end, the old man admitted that he was too elderly to pursue the dream without the help of his sons.

"If I were even twenty years younger," he lamented to Hart. "Alas, I don't need the money. I'll never be able to spend what I have before I die. My family is financially set for generations, thanks to that burger company and its cheap prices."

The Lange business was not immune to shysters either. In 1982, Hart was approached by two Irish men who proposed to establish an organization using European Simmental cows to create a dual-purpose farm.

"Simmental cows are both milk and meat producers," they told Hart, "and we believe your systems to be invaluable for our venture."

They worked with Hart for almost two years, analyzing and designing their proposal, and together they drafted an application for research and development to submit to the Ministry of Agriculture in Ottawa. The plan was convincing. So convincing, it turned out, that the Canadian government agreed to invest millions of dollars to subsidize it.

Both Hart and the Ministry were blind-sided, however, by the insincerity of the two men, who insisted that the Ministry and Hart front the initial costs. The Ministry wired funds as instructed, but the Lange parent company dragged its heels, which turned out to be a good thing.

Ned Roberts, a reporter from the *Calgary Herald* called Hart early one morning.

"Listen," he said, "I've been following your progress with the Simmental venture. Your ideas are amazing!"

Before Hart could express his thanks, the reporter had cut him off.

"You need to know, though, that the two guys you've been working with are bad news. They're involved in fraudulent deals all over the place."

"How can you say such a thing?" Hart interrupted. "These guys ..."

"Can't be trusted as far as you can spit," the reporter finished. "Listen. I cover white-collar crime. It's unusual for me to follow agricultural news, but the antics of these two fraudsters caught my attention, especially when they began working with you."

Hart detected an urgency in the fellow's tone as he continued.

"Whatever you have cooking with them, leave it. Pull out. I've been tracking several deals that these scoundrels have been working. The deals are starting to crumble now. When I finish this story, it's gonna be big, and you'll be the hero. The way I see it, you're gonna get nailed too, but you can cut your losses if you pull out now and help us. There're twenty other companies that will fall before you."

"I have no proof of bad dealing," Hart argued, starting to feel annoyed with the reporter's persistence. "I can't walk away. I have a contract—"

"I'll bring you proof. I'll drop by in an hour and show you what I've got. Don't do anything till I get there. 'K? Don't contact them."

True to his word, Ned Roberts arrived in Hart's office an hour later, with a companion he introduced as Sofie Walker, and a file folder filled with news clippings, notes, and photographs that clearly supported his theory.

Roberts was heavier and taller than Hart, middle-aged with thinning, sandy-coloured hair. Sofie was young and attractive, with blue eyes and a blonde, shoulder-length coiffure.

"So, why me?" Hart asked. "Have you alerted the others?"

"Yeah, but none of them would listen. Now, they're falling like dominoes. It's not too late for you to cut your losses and walk away though."

"But this can't be right," Hart protested.

"I know it all sounds far-fetched, but it's true," Sofie argued. "We have been tracking these guys for a while now. I do the sleuthing. Ned does the office work. When we have enough information, Ned starts to write."

"If you're willing to help," Ned said, "I think we can catch them red-handed. Whaddayathink? Will you work with us?"

"*Us*? You keep saying *us*. You and Sofie?"

"Yes, and no. We took our pitch to the RCMP last week," Ned clarified. "They said that, if we could convince someone to step forward, they'd investigate further."

Ned and Sofie grinned at Hart.

"You're *it*, man," the reporter said. "You're the guy we need. Far enough down the line that you won't be suspected, but in far enough to be hurt badly if you don't react. So, whaddayathink?"

Reluctantly, Hart agreed to work with Ned and Sofie and the RCMP. Eventually, the two Irish men appeared in court and justice was served. Hart's losses had been few, limited to the cost of developing the project over a two-year period. Because Lange Machinery never delivered its share of the investment, it saved millions of dollars.

In the process, Hart, Ned, and Sofie became fast friends and Hart came to rely on their insights before agreeing to take on any future partners.

CHAPTER THIRTY-FIVE

S oon after they were settled in Calgary, Ursula realized that life in a small Canadian city would never be as thrilling as in a German hub like Bayreuth. She determined that, if she could not have the career of her choice, she could at least have fun. Her drive for entertainment kept her out most evenings.

We've been married for almost seven years. Hart is rarely home, always chasing farmers and tradeshows. When he's here, he's too tired to take me out. Hart is dull and boring. Calgary is dull, boring and routine. I need a little spice to liven things up!

Ursula preferred an evening at the theatre, an opera or the symphony, but if none was available, she went clubbing. After a few months of partying, she noticed that the single friends she had made on the night club circuit often left in pairs. She began to contemplate the possibility for herself.

The following week, while Hart was travelling, she flirted with every fellow on the dance floor, until finally she identified someone interesting. Her first tryst ended in a sleazy motel, and the guy left without paying the bill. *That will never happen to me again,* she promised, and from that time onward, she took them home. *Hart's rarely there. He'll never know.*

On the rare occasion that Hart was home, Ursula telephoned to let him know that she was bringing home someone interesting. Hart waited for her and chatted with her guests. However, on the third occasion, he told her that he had an important meeting early in the morning, and that she would have to entertain her guest on her own. Ursula interpreted her husband's suggestion to suit her own needs.

When Hart awoke the next morning, Ursula was not in their bed and, as he passed the guest room on his way to the shower, the normally open door was closed. His belly coiled in a knot when he realized that his wife was sleeping with her over-night guest. Telltale evidence was visible everywhere— discarded clothing and empty liquor bottles in the living room and unwashed dishes and pots all over the kitchen.

Soon, Ursula stopped sleeping in their bed and took over the spare room.

"You snore too much," she complained when he asked her why she slept in the other room. "I can't sleep!"

He knew snoring was not the issue. He pleaded with her to return to their bed. She refused, saying that she liked having her own space.

At first, Hart was too overwhelmed with work to dwell on the matter, but soon his emotions began interfering with his concentration and he was forced to pay attention.

⚜

"Sofie," Hart said, when she answered her telephone, "I need your help. Ursula has developed a habit of bringing home stray men. Before I can confront her, I need evidence. She's very careful and secretive."

"You want me to watch her for a while," Sofie said matter-of-factly.

"Ja," he replied. "I suspect her behaviour is a little less discrete when I'm on the road. I doubt you'll have difficulty finding proof."

"When are you next away," Sofie asked.

"As a matter of fact, I'm leaving early tomorrow morning."

"Leave it with me then," Sofie assured him. "I should have something for you when you get back."

Ursula watched the money roll into Lange Machinery with each successful sale. She complained to Hart that the advertising orders and organization of deliveries were taking too much of her time.

"I don't have a chance to follow my own dreams," she complained.

"What do you mean?" Hart asked. "The money is rolling in. We're both paid well for the work we're doing. What more could you want?"

"Hmm, let me think," she said, face-tiously, one arm crossed over her chest, supporting the elbow of the other while it tapped a pink fingernail against off-white teeth. "How about a business of my own, where I can sell my own ideas to my own clients?"

"Are you saying you don't want to work for Lange anymore?" he asked.

"I'm just saying that I'd like to find other clients with more interesting products to market. Something that suits my sensibilities. And that, by the way, is not cows! I've had it up to here," she said, saluting from her eyebrows, "with cows, and how much they piss and shit, and how it can all be converted into fertilizer, and recycled into clean drinking water." She returned to her drafting board, continuing to rant. "I gave up everything to come to Canada with you! I had a great job, a future doing what I loved, an opportunity for advancement, and a

355

chance to make a lot of money. Instead, here I am working as your office gofer! Go for this, Ursula, go for that—", she said, scrunching her face at him.

"What do you want to do, then?" he asked, while he tried to determine what her needs were. *If I've learned anything, it is to pay attention when someone grumbles. Good often comes of it: new ideas, new designs, new possibilities.*

"I want you to hire someone to do the office work, so I can be free to pursue other interests."

"Hire someone?"

"Yes! Quit repeating what I'm saying," Ursula shouted impatiently.

"I'm not!" He saw the anger in her eyes, and he tried again. "Sorry, Ursula, my mind is racing to find a solution that will help you achieve your goals."

She folded her arms and glared at him.

"Thinking out loud here," he said, his mind racing. "We have a budget from Germany that we have to work within. If we hire someone to work in the office, that means we take home less pay. Are you prepared to take a cut in pay? Can you stay home more often and spend less time in nightclubs? We'll have to sacrifice something."

"So, you're blaming the shortage on me?" Ursula shouted. "What about you? What will you sacrifice? Your precious skiing?"

"If I must, I can cut back on skiing," he answered calmly. "I'll need to train the new hire, after all, that will take time. Besides, I don't go skiing often, only in the winter, and always with you. You're the one who's out clubbing most nights, whether I'm home or not, and you're always bringing home strange men that you meet in these places. It's not right, Ursula!"

There. I've said it. I've finally had the opportunity to challenge her habit of bringing home stray men and flaunting her trysts in my face. The photos that Sofie gave me are conclusive. It's embarrassing and painful to have to greet her stay-overs politely every morning. If it doesn't end soon, I'm going to explode, and violence is not my nature. Hell! The most rebellious thing I've ever done involved Manfred and a skeleton.

⚜

"Hart!" Ursula demanded. "Are you listening to me?"

"I am."

"I can pay my own way. I don't need an income from Lange. I can find my own clients and take care of my own expenses. You'll see. My income will far exceed yours, before you know it." Her words pounded through his wounded fog. "I don't need you, or Lange."

"Fine, I'll place an advertisement tomorrow," he acquiesced. "Where will you go?"

"Go?" she asked, incredulous at the question. "Why should I go? I see no reason to go anywhere. Everything I need is right here," she said, sneering at him. "I'll even pay you rent."

"Okay," he surrendered. "We'll work it out."

❖

A while later, after they had both cooled down, Hart approached Ursula again.

"Ursula? Should we start a family? Would you like to have children?" he asked tentatively.

"Are you crazy!" She glared at him, throwing her pencil onto the drafting table. "I'm no baby-making machine! Look at this figure!" she retorted, running her hands down the sides of her body. "I have no intention of ruining my looks for children. Besides, you're not fit to be a father! If I wanted children—the key word being, *if*—I'd find a more suitable man. One who stays home and excites me. One in whom I have confidence. Not you." She curled her lip and wrinkled her nose in disgust, picked up her pencil, and returned to her work, clearly dismissing further conversation.

"What about these men?" Hart demanded, fed up with trying to be polite.

"What men?"

"The guys you bring home with you. The ones you entertain in the spare room."

"Who told you that?" Ursula asked with a hint of defensiveness. "If someone told you that, they're lying!" She picked up her pencil again and tapped it on the table. "Now, leave me alone, I'm trying to concentrate."

CHAPTER THIRTY-SIX

That night Hart went to bed early. Soon after, Ursula left for the evening. He lay in the dark, one hand sandwiched between his pillow and his head, his head resting in its palm. *What a mess! How did this happen? Ursula is slipping away from me and, no matter what I say or do, I can't seem to pull her back.* He looked at the clock on the night table. The illuminated hands told him it was still early morning in Germany. *Perhaps I can catch Vati before he leaves for the office.* Sitting upright, he swung his feet to the floor, and reached for the telephone.

Hart explained his circumstances to his father as best he could without a clearer understanding of his wife's behaviour, other than the photographs that Sofie had taken as evidence to his suspicions.

"I've been puzzling through every-thing, trying to understand how we reached this point, and hoping that some-how we'd work it out," he said. "But when we visited Sofie and her family over the Christmas holiday, Ursula was so offen-sive toward her that her husband asked us to leave. 'Come back any time,' he said, 'but not with her.' On a parting note, he strongly recommended that I find a new wife. Needless to say, I've been struggling ever since. But, now ... with the photos that Sofie's provided ..."

"Have you talked about children?" Paul asked.

"Yes, I raised that as a possibility. Let's just say that the suggestion wasn't well received," Hart said, sadly.

"Well," Paul said, "as I see it, you have three choices—if you think you've done all you can to salvage your relationship."

"You can close the office, so both of you can return to Germany—see what happens when you get here. You can divorce Ursula

362

and stay there, or you can divorce her and come home. I doubt any of those are particularly pleasing."

"No, they're not." Hart's words were contemplative. "Hearing them said aloud, though, makes me realize that there is really only one option. I'm sorry to disappoint you and Mutti, but I think the answer is divorce. I was hoping for a long marriage like all the Langes before me." He sighed deeply. "I have always tried to be a good person, to treat people fairly, and with respect—as I would want them to treat me."

"Hart—"

"You and grandfather," Hart pressed on, "taught us to be good soldiers. Although I've never spent time in the military, I know what it means to be a good leader, to inspire a team of people to work together for success. Ursula is headstrong and not the least bit interested in working as a team. She has a low opinion of her own parents and I suppose her childhood experiences are driving her."

"Not all Langes have had epic marriages, son," Paul said. "And you shouldn't let the thought get you down. Your mother and I would rather that you were happy and productive, than feel trapped in a miserable marriage. Perhaps, second time lucky?"

"Thanks for your support, Vati. I'll speak to a lawyer in the next few days."

Hart hung up the telephone with purpose. He tugged on a bathrobe and bounced down the stairs to the kitchen, feeling lighter than he had in months. Relieved that he had his parents' support, he retrieved a pen and paper and began listing steps that needed to be accomplished in order to ensure a smooth divorce.

Lots to consider—impact on business, connections, reputation, schedules, an assistant to hire, a new office to find.

An hour later, Hart returned to his bed. His sleep was so sound that he did not even hear Ursula return with her two playmates.

364

At sunrise, ice drops pattered on the bedroom window, waking him to a new day of purpose and planning. He rose, showered, made coffee to take with him, and left through the garage, ignoring Ursula's mess in the kitchen and the snoring body on the sofa. He surprised himself as he backed his Mercedes-Benz onto the street. He was humming and could not remember the last time he had done so.

When Hart reached the office, he checked his watch. It was still too early to call his business solicitor to ask for a referral to a family lawyer. In the meantime, he reviewed some plans he had been working on for one of the Hutterite colonies and made another list. The new list became a job description for the assistant he would hire. *Need to call an agency.* A second list described the attributes of the office space he would require. Humming, he headed to the coffee counter and made himself another coffee. *Need a real estate agent, too.*

Returning to his desk, he checked his watch again, picked up the telephone, and began dialing. One call led to another and as each call ended in success and action, he updated the lists he had on his desk. By the time Ursula arrived, after noon, Hart's new life was organized and underway. The only thing remaining was to tell Ursula.

"You're what!" she exclaimed when he raised the matter of the divorce. "You can't do that!"

Hart watched her face, her eyes moving rapidly, her mouth gaping and closing. *For once, she's speechless!* He chuckled at her responses, feeling empowered, no longer abused.

"I can, and I will," he said, with confidence. "You'll need to move out of the house. The company owns it and you no longer work for the company." He watched her process this information. "You're fired, by the way."

Her eyes bulged, and her even breathing changed to shallow panting. A purple hue began to shade her face.

"You can have this space, if you want it. I'm moving my office. I've given the landlord thirty days' notice. If you want to stay here, you'll need to negotiate a new lease." Hart rose from his chair, grabbed his coat and briefcase, and headed for the door.

"Where are you going?" Ursula demanded. "Don't you dare walk out that door. We need to talk this through. You're being ridiculous. Get back here!"

Hart opened the door to the parking lot and looked back over his shoulder at Ursula.

"No, Ursula. There's nothing to talk about. We're done." He closed the door gently behind him and smiled. A new day had dawned.

The divorce went smoothly, once Hart realized that Ursula could be paid to go away. He packed up his office and moved to a new location at the end of the month. Finally, free of Ursula, he turned his focus to the promotion of Lange Machinery and Mikel & Co. throughout North America, determined to fulfill the plan that he had created with his father in 1977.

PART V

CROSSED PATHS

HART AND MIRIAM

CHAPTER THIRTY-SEVEN

As was often his escape, Hart took a skiing holiday in the Rocky Mountains. Each time he raced down a mountainside, with crystallized snow shushing under his skis, he felt free, light, strong. The weight of his oppressive marriage and divorce forgotten, he would reach the bottom of a ski hill, his head clear, creative juices and determination flowing again.

On one such occasion, after a morning of skiing under clear blue, cloudless skies and blinding sun, unexpected clouds had encumbered the mountaintop, strewing about a blinding blizzard that closed the

371

ski hills. Hart decided to join a group of friends for some après ski conviviality in a ski-in ski-out pub at the foot of the mountain. Hart's friends frequented the pub, but he had never been there, preferring a homey pub near to his lodgings. They stowed their skis in the racks outside and made the awkward march up to the door in their bulky boots.

Inside, the piercing collection of patrons' voices accosted his ears. The constant squeak of ski pants rubbing and ski boots clunking on the grated floor underlined the din of boisterous conversations as patrons came and went.

Hart spied vacant chairs in front of the smooth stone hearth.

"Let's sit near the fire," he said, as they mustered inside the door, slush dripping from their boots.

"The sign says we have to remove our boots and check them, if we want to sit by the hearth," one of his companions remarked.

"I'm okay with that," Hart said, already unbuckling his boots. "My feet are freezing."

The others grumbled similar responses, agreeing with Hart's suggestion. The promise of the fire was too inviting. They checked their boots and padded stocking-foot to the vacant chairs.

Most removed their ski jackets and gear and piled them near the hearth. Hart found an empty armchair, dragged it toward the fire, and put his feet up on the ledge to thaw them.

"I'm parched," one of the women said.

"Hey, honey! Over here!" one of the men hollered, flagging the waitress as she passed.

"With you in a minute," she waved as she headed toward the bar to place an order.

Moments later, the waitress returned.

"Sorry, folks. Busy, today," she said, slightly breathless. Smiling, she retrieved a pencil that had been lodged in her coiled hair, prepared to take their orders.

"It's always busy on weekends, Miriam!" one of the women said, laughing.

Hart noticed that the regular patrons seemed to know the staff by name, and the one called Miriam appeared to be a favourite. *Clearly, she's fast, efficient, organized, and pleasant. That must be the draw.*

Miriam took a headcount as she worked her way through the group, taking orders of hamburgers, fries, salads, cold beer, and hot chocolate. She stopped in front of the fire, next to Hart's chair.

"Can I get you something?"

Anticipating her question, Hart turned from his companion to order.

"I'll have a beer and the sausage plate, with fries." Then he looked at her, the sound of her voice taking time to permeate his frozen brain. "That's an interesting accent."

"Ja. Yours isn't so common, either."

They laughed together.

"Dutch," she offered.

"German," he answered.

"Hey! Come on, Hart. Small talk, later. We're tired, thirsty, and hungry. Miriam, can ya get a move on, honey?"

She winced.

She doesn't like being called honey, Hart noted, and found himself wondering what endearment might be pleasing to her. She smiled at his rude companion and excused herself to place the order. *Interesting eyes, like melted dark chocolate.*

Hart bided his time, waiting for the crowd to lessen. When the bar quieted and his friends had peeled away for the evening, he stayed behind. Miriam exited the kitchen, empty-handed, and took a wet rag from behind the bar. Hart caught her eye and smiled. She changed directions and walked toward him.

"You're all alone—not joining your friends?" she asked, one hand on her hip.

"Ja. I will later."

"Coffee? Another drink?"

She pulled out her notepad to take his order.

"No thanks," he cocked his head to look at her more clearly. "I think I've had enough for now. I should pace myself. I've been invited to a party, after dinner."

"I'll bring your bill, then." She put the notepad back in her pocket and stuck her pencil in a knot of her hair. It reminded him of a Geisha, the way it penetrated the coil of hair on the crown of her head. "You're the last of my customers. I can sign out and go home."

"Thanks," he said, holding her gaze. "Say, I'm wondering whether you'd like to come to the party?" When she hesitated, Hart expected her to decline.

He's German. Mama and Oma would die, if they heard I went out with a German!

"I'm afraid I can't. I have to get home to my kids."

He kept her chatting long enough for her to disclose that she was a single mother with two young children, a boy and a girl, and that she worked during the week, while they were in school.

"I live in the town at the foot of the mountain," she said.

"Perhaps another time, then?"

"I don't know," she replied. "Juggling my schedule is challenging. Why don't you give me your number and I'll call if I happen to find I can meet up with you."

He seems intriguing. Maybe I shouldn't be so quick to bow to the prejudices of old women. What do I care anyway! Mama and Oma will never know I went out with a German.

Within the hour, Hart returned to his motel room. He was working his way through an order of take-out Chinese food, and contemplating a hot shower, when his telephone rang.

"Hart, it's Miriam ... from the pub," she added, as if concerned that he may have forgotten her name. "Is your invitation to the party tonight still open?"

"Of course," he replied, eagerly.

"I've arranged for my friend to look after the children," she said. "I can go with you after all."

"Great! I was just about to take a shower. Give me your address and I'll pick you up in, say, forty-five minutes." *Pushing, pushing.* "Does that timing work, or am I rushing you?" His heart beat in his throat, anxious to please.

"Make it an hour, and I'll be ready," she said, laughing.

Hart tucked the address in his wallet when the call ended and padded into the bathroom for his shower. Minutes later, he wiped the steam from the mirror and made faces at himself trying to decide whether a second shave was required. He decided to err on the side of good impressions, finishing with a slap of refreshing aftershave.

Since his divorce he had dated other women, but only casually. None of them were particularly interesting, nor were they interested in a long-term relationship. Fun and sex were what they wanted:

no strings attached. He did not mind the fun, but he was not the kind of guy to jump into bed with every available woman. Sexually transmitted diseases were a dime a dozen and that was a path he preferred to avoid. Despite his usual concerns, he found Miriam intriguing and wanted to know more about her.

Hart opened his tote bag, searching for clean underwear, and a movement, reflected in the closet mirror, distracted him. He straightened and examined himself from head to toe. His hair was blue-black and shiny, like his father's hair once was. No signs of grey, yet. He had the military stature of his father, but he was fine boned and smaller, the influence of his mother's genes.

He ran his fingers through his hair, turned sideways and admired his still flat belly and strong legs—a skier's body. He slapped his belly with the palm of his hand, flashed a white-toothed smile at himself, and finished dressing.

The face of the travel clock on the night table told him that he was running late. He fastened his watch, stuffed his feet into his snow boots, and grabbed his jacket and car keys. The door to his room banged shut behind him as he hastened toward his old Mercedes-Benz.

He had bought the silver 450SL shortly after he and Ursula had moved to Canada. Ursula preferred the big North American cars, thinking they implied status and wealth. She dressed to impress and chose her vehicles the same way she shopped for clothes. Hart preferred a classic look and a reliable vehicle. He would have preferred a convertible but mounting a ski rack on a soft top was not practical. That was his only compromise. He had always driven a Mercedes and saw no need to change just because he lived in Canada.

The drive to Miriam's apartment was short. He arrived at the appointed time—precisely. She was ready and waiting at the front door of the cedar-sided apartment building.

Hart enjoyed the party, made more fun because of Miriam's companionship. She added spice to the predictability of his friends. She even danced with him, the way he preferred—the European way. He did not like the modern form of dance—standing in front of a partner, waving arms in the air and gyrating. It was impersonal. He liked to hold a woman in his arms and lead her around the dance floor—a linoleum kitchen floor, in that instance—all of eight feet square. *At least, I can hold her. And I like it!*

He introduced her to many of his friends, most of whom she knew as customers at the pub. They welcomed her and teased her about escaping the pub for a few hours and the dangers of hanging out with Hart.

"Ah!" Hart exclaimed, "there's Sofie." He led Miriam deep into the crowd and introduced her to their host.

"Miriam," Sofie replied, "I'm glad you've come." She smiled sincerely. "I bet you know the majority of my guests." Sofie's eyes swept the crowd as if searching for someone. "Yup. I can't identify anyone here that would not have met you at the pub. At least, tonight, you're not serving and will have an opportunity to get to know some of them better. That is, if Hart lets you ..." She winked at Hart.

"Nope, not a chance," Hart said, taking Miriam's arm gently. "Let's dance before Sofie tells you how despicable I am!"

"You seem to be close to Sofie," Miriam whispered in Hart's ear as he shuffled around the kitchen, keeping time with the beat of the music. "Have you known her long?"

"We met a few years ago," Hart replied. "She helped with a difficult business problem. Since then, we've worked together a few times. She's a loyal friend and keeps me out of trouble." Hart gazed into Miriam's dark brown eyes, his twinkling. "Most of the time!"

Miriam took care to observe the relationship between Hart and Sofie. She needed to identify any threats. She made a note to ask the cards later. She insisted that Hart deliver her to her apartment before midnight, so she would have time in the morning to send her children off to school and not be late for work. He asked her if she would have dinner with him the following evening and she accepted.

"A late dinner?" she asked, "so I can have the children settled before I leave."

He agreed and waited while she ran up to her apartment to ask her friend to babysit.

Miriam knew her roommate, Kristina, would be available. They had discussed the possibility earlier. Instead, she used the time to ask the tarot cards whether it was worthwhile for her to see Hart again. She should proceed with caution, they told her. Hart had mentioned his recent divorce, and how it had affected him. *I'd best heed the cards' warning.*

She appeared several minutes later at the building entrance and waved *yes*. He acknowledged with his own wave, waiting while she turned and dashed from view.

Miriam returned to her apartment and said goodnight to Kristina. She hummed through a shower, towelled herself off and went to the kitchen, tying the belt of her terry cloth bathrobe. She sat at the chrome-trimmed kitchen table and spread the tarot cards once again. The large-faced clock on the wall indicated that she had time to ask more questions. While a relationship with Hart could end her financial woes, they told her, it could also threaten her independence. Overall, he was someone worth marrying, and he would be a great companion and lover, the cards assured her. They also encouraged her to open her heart and allow love into her life. *Ha! Love! When was the last time I felt loved by a man?*

CHAPTER THIRTY-EIGHT

On the long drive back to Calgary, Hart felt disappointment that his vacation had passed so quickly. But for important business commitments, he would have stayed at the resort longer.

Miriam had introduced him to her children, Pauline and Jacob, on the second evening before they left for dinner. On the third evening, he had brought a gift for each of them, and on the fourth evening—the last day of his vacation—he had taken them all out for dinner.

During their last meal together, he took the time to watch mother and children interact. *Clearly, she cares for her children. She's attentive and kind. The children seem to love her. She seems different from any other woman I've met.*

As soon as he arrived at his home in Calgary he unloaded his car, stowed his skis to dry, poured himself a brandy, and called Miriam. She had just put the children to bed, she was tired, and, yes, she missed him. Hart sighed. *Things are looking up!*

✥

When time permitted, Hart made a long weekend and returned to the mountains to ski, hoping that he would be invited to spend time with Miriam and her children. Toward Christmas, he invited her to bring the children to spend the school break with him.

"I have a big house. They'd have lots of space and a Christmas tree," he promised.

He bought gifts and food. She brought the children, and they helped him decorate the tree. *This is how a real family should feel—happy! And I like it.*

"You'd make a great father," Miriam blurted one evening, after the children had been tucked into bed.

They were sitting at either end of an old grey sofa that still looked reasonably new. The softness of the cushions belied its age, made it cozy. Miriam sat with her legs extended the length of the sofa, her feet in Hart's lap.

"Why do you say that?" he sipped his brandy from a water glass and placed the glass on the end table. He took a foot in one hand and began massaging the sole with his other.

"I watch the way you talk to the children," she said. "They like you. You listen to them." She wiggled her toes and smiled at him. "Oooh! That feels good."

"I've never spent much time with children, but I have friends with kids. I seldom see them, but when I do, I always get along with them."

"Yet you have none of your own. You and your ex-wife, you never wanted children?" She held up her other foot to his busy hands.

"I did. She didn't. She didn't think I'd make a good father for her children. Truthfully, I think she abhorred the thought of children. Rather than admit it, she blamed me." He stopped massaging, feeling a stab of sadness with the haunting of Ursula's cutting words.

"I can't imagine anyone saying that to you. How hurtful!" Miriam wiggled her toes, bringing Hart's focus back to her.

"Well, she never minced her words, I'll say that for Ursula." He wrapped his hands gently around a slender foot and began kneading again.

"I think she was cruel." Miriam set her wine glass on the end table and drew her feet under her. "*Bad father* is the last phrase that I'd use to describe you," she said as she rose from the sofa, stepping closer to Hart and turning to face him. She lowered herself onto the sofa, placing one knee on either side of Hart's thighs. She wrapped her arms loosely around his neck, bringing her face level to his. Peering into his charcoal eyes, she purred wine-scented words. "I'm feeling very warm in some interesting places. Don't you think it's time you made love to me?" She pushed his shirt collar out of the way and nuzzled his neck.

Hart's hands found her thighs. He slowly slid them over her bottom to her waist. Miriam placed sensual kisses on each eye, then each cheek. She used her tongue to part his lips and inhaled his brandied breath. His hands crept under her knitted pullover, cool on her warm skin. Their kisses lingered long and searching, tongue over tongue, fluids blending.

His heart beat wildly in response to Miriam's attentions. She squirmed on his lap. At long last, Hart grasped her firmly about the waist and moved her gently away from him. She held herself suspended, still kneeling over him, her dark chocolate eyes large and inviting.

"Is something wrong?" she asked, her words softly panted.

"No. No! Not at all!" he said, chuckling. "I just think we could do better … somewhere else."

"Oh!" Miriam unfolded herself and stood up.

Hart stood awkwardly, shot back the last of his brandy, and took her hand.

"O-o-oh!" she said again, smiling, as she spied an indication of his desire.

"Are you sure?" he asked.

"Uh-huh." Her willingness reflected in her eyes. She licked her lips slowly, eyes on him, as if watching for his response.

Hart turned toward the stairs leading to the second floor and his bedroom, the room across the hall from the one he had assigned to her. At the doorway, he turned to her again.

"Are you sure?"

"I am."

Trusting chocolate eyes gazed into his. He led her into the room and closed the door quietly behind them.

Making love to a man came easy to Miriam. After all, she had learned from the best. Not everyone had a grandmother and mother who had worked in the Red-Light District of Amsterdam. She had overheard her mother and Astrid, her mother's roommate, often talking about their work and their clients and had applied what she had learned to her relationship with Rask. Miriam knew many ways to please a man, to service him, to make him beg for more. Her relationship with Rask was evidence of her abilities. Her charm and seduction of Hart was so subtle that he was blind to her deliberate intentions.

Early the next morning, Miriam awoke to predawn chirping. She rolled effortlessly out of Hart's bed, picked up her discarded clothing, and clutching them modestly to her nakedness, cracked the bedroom door for her exit. Closing it behind her, she stepped across the hall into the guest room and closed the door. Humming to herself, she extracted a deck of tarot cards from her travel bag and sat cross-legged on the bed. She was aware of the pungent stickiness on her inner thighs, as she leaned across her legs and dealt the cards on the bed, asked questions, and read answers.

Satisfied with the reading, she returned the cards to her bag, folded her clothes, and slid between the cool sheets. She stretched, enjoying the cover sheet's caress against her nakedness, wiggled her toes, and fell back to sleep, her lips forming a devious cat-like grin.

A few hours later, a gentle knock on the door woke her again.

"Mom?"

Hart and Miriam continued their long-distance relationship. Time and business trips dictated who would do the travelling. Sometimes, she would leave the children with Kristina for a weekend, and they would go out for a late dinner, to the theatre, or to a night club.

When the children were with them, Miriam could sense that he was watching her and made every effort to appear to be a doting mother. She could tell that he suspected nothing. He simply appeared to be happy.

Often, they would just stay in and enjoy their own companionship. As she intended, soon he declared his love for her.

CHAPTER THIRTY-NINE

One weekend in April, Miriam drove to Calgary, alone. Hart met her at the curb, where she parked her old Corolla, and retrieved her bag from the back seat. They walked to the door of the white split-level, his arm around her shoulders.

Miriam looked up at him, a sweet smile playing across her glossed, pink lips. Her heavy, chestnut hair, usually wound in a knot on the top of her head, cascaded past her shoulders, like that of a young girl. Her scent was light, and exciting.

"How beautiful you are today," Hart said. "You seem to be glowing. Radiant. I don't know. I can't think of the word. You look ... different." He closed the door and set her bag on a stair, leading up to the next floor.

"Really?" she stepped into his arms, snaking hers around his neck.

He placed his hands on her waist, drawing her closer. *She feels as though she's gained weight. I'm sure I read somewhere that women gain weight when they're happy.* She tipped her head back to better see him, her hair swinging in its freedom, and smiled.

"I know," he said, pleased with himself. "You look like you have the world's best secret."

Miriam stiffened. Her eyes studied his face and her smile disappeared.

"Well, actually, I do have a secret." Her smile gradually returned.

"Going to share?"

"Yes. Let's sit first." She led him to the old sofa, sat down, and patted a spot next to her. He sat beside her, curious, a knot of foreboding tightening his belly.

She held his hand between hers, and hung her head, a curtain of dark hair hiding her face. He felt her inhale deeply, as if bracing herself.

❖

Miriam lifted her head slowly and gazed into his eyes. Tears filled her eyes and rolled down her cheeks. She tried to look both demure and alluring at the same time.

"If I told you that you will be a father in the fall, would you be happy?" she asked, exhaling slowly. The question hung between them for a long moment. "Or upset?" Through glossy vision, she watched the movement of his eyes and his face. She watched as curiosity formed, vanished with realization, then transformed to joy.

"You're pregnant!" he blurted. "Really?"

She nodded.

"I can't believe it! Really?"

She nodded again.

Hart scooped her into his arms, kissed her passionately, lifted her onto his lap, and rocked her. He set her gently onto the sofa, jumped up, and began pacing.

"What is it?" Miriam asked, worried.

He scratched his head.

"Ha!" he said, as if deep in thought. Putting the fingers of his right hand to his lips in contemplation, he grabbed his right elbow with his left hand.

"Ha," he said again.

"Hart, what is it?" Miriam repeated, anxious to know his thoughts. "Are you angry?"

"What? No!" His head snapped toward her and he stopped pacing to stand directly in front of her. "No," he said again, gently kneeling beside her. "I ... am ... speechless." He reached for her shoulders, drawing her near, and kissed her on the forehead. "I have wanted a child for so long, and after Ursula, well, I never thought it possible." He released her and resumed his pacing.

"It is indeed possible! And, if you're half as good at parenting as you are at procreating," Miriam teased, "then you will be the most a-maz-ing father!" Miriam laughed, ending Hart's pacing. In that moment, she knew from the expression on his face that her control over him was absolute.

⚜

"I-I don't know what to do!" Hart said, puzzled. "We should get married!" He stepped in circles scratching the top of his head, not knowing where to go, or what to do. "Yes, of course! We should get married. Now!" Hart laughed, delighted that he had a plan of action. "And, you and the children will live here. I will take care of all of you!" Spikes of dark hair stood on his pate when he stopped scratching and smacked the palms of his hands to his forehead. "I need to tell my parents." He turned in circles again.

"Hang on, Daddy," Miriam said, seductively, "one step at a time. Bre-e-eathe. And stop pacing, please. You're making me dizzy." She rose from the sofa, obviously delighted that Hart was pleased with the news. "I need a drink," she said, padding into the kitchen. "We can discuss the rest over dinner. That is, if you're going to feed me. Mmm ... something smells yummy out here."

⚜

Miriam and Hart were wed by a marriage commissioner early in May. The Devonian Gardens, located in the centre of Calgary's business core, proved to be a perfect setting— lush gardens, small birds flitting about as if outdoors, all within a downtown greenhouse that protected them against the unpredictable spring elements. A chilly wind blew off the mountains that day, and they were glad for the humid warmth of the Gardens' embrace.

The affair was attended by a few close friends, including Sofie Walker and her husband, and, of course, Pauline and Jacob. No extended family. Hers lived in the Netherlands. His lived in Germany. An intimate reception was held at their favourite restaurant, a few blocks from the Gardens.

Hart could not have been happier. He finally had his longed-for family, a beautiful wife and his own child snug and growing in her belly. Miriam appeared happy to play the beautiful bride, drawing energy from being the centre of attention.

Hart took a few days off work, and the

small family drove back to the mountains to collect their things from the apartment shared with Kristina and her children. Miriam had little that she valued: all of her furnishings were second hand. They sold or gave away most items and, in the end, they were able to fit their personal items into a van that Hart had rented for the occasion.

A few weeks later, a parcel marked *Special Delivery* arrived at the house. It was addressed to *Herr und Frau G.M. Lange*.

"What is it?" Miriam asked when Hart held the specially wrapped package out to her.

"I don't know? Let's open it. It's addressed to both of us."

He cleared a space on the dining room table, pushing aside school books, socks, and a baseball cap, and set down the parcel. Together, they peeled away the brown paper wrapping, revealing a sturdy white box and a card-sized envelope. While Miriam opened the envelope and removed a card, Hart slit the Cellophane tape that held the box closed. The flaps popped free, revealing Styrofoam packing inside.

"We should read the card first," Miriam said, placing her hand on Hart's arm to delay his progress.

He snuggled close to her and caressed her growing belly as she opened the card.

"It's in German," she said, impatiently passing the card to Hart. He took it and read the translation aloud.

Dear Hart and Miriam,

We are so happy to hear of your marriage and of the coming child.

We hope you will be able to spend time with us during the Christmas break.

In the meantime, we are sending a small gift, so you will always find your way home.

With love,

Mutti and Vati

"Oh, how exciting!" Miriam looked at Hart. "Will we go? To Germany?" *Anything to get away from this boredom. I can't breathe!*

Hart hugged her to him.

"If all is well with you and our little one," he said, again caressing her swelling belly with his free hand, "I see no reason not to." He kissed the top of her head and released her, returning to the parcel.

He fingered his way into the box, pushing through the Styrofoam, until he found a smaller box, wrapped in blue tissue paper. Miriam tore through the tissue, revealing another, white box. She looked at Hart, confused. Once again Hart sliced through the tape and tugged at the covering until the bottom of the box fell away. He spread the white tissue packing, and gasped. A smile lit his face, and his eyes gleamed with joy.

"What is it?" Miriam asked again, starring at the crest. *What an odd wedding gift. How is that supposed to be exciting?*

"From its newness, I'd say that it is a copy of the Lange family crest," he told her as he lifted it reverently from its nest, kissed it, and handed it to her. "Let me tell you the story of the crest," he offered. "It may take some time. Come and sit. I'll rub your feet."

CHAPTER FORTY

From time to time, and more rarely than not, Miriam sent a note or a greeting card. Each one conveyed a similar message—she was happy and successful and would not be returning to Amsterdam. In other words, interference from her family was not welcome.

One frosty morning in the fall of 1986, Mina spied an envelope with Miriam's familiar handwriting tucked within the collection of her daily mail. Setting the pile of mail aside, she selected the envelope from Canada and tore along the seam. Miriam's correspondence was always brief and often terse. While she craved news of her grandchildren, Mina remained wary of Miriam's next hurtful remark. She tugged the folded note from the envelope and read,

"Mama.

Life is good here, as always. I got married a few months ago. My husband is Gerhard Michael Lange. We call him Hart. He's German. I don't care what you say about Germans or the war. You have another grandson—Matthew Paul Lange.

Hoping to move to Europe soon. Maybe Germany.

Don't bother with Oma's name interpretations. I don't care.

Pauline and Jacob are fine.

Miriam"

Mina reached for the phone.

"This is Punita Hendrik."

"Mama, how are you feeling today?" As she spoke, Mina eyed the Hermle mantle clock, subconsciously noting the time: 10:03.

"I've been better," Punita answered. "I miss Eamon terribly. My life is so empty without him. Time ticks by painfully slowly. I can't believe he's been gone for a year."

"I miss Willem too, Mama," Mina replied, "and I understand how you feel. At least when Eamon died of cancer, we had time to say good-bye, but Willem's death is a shock. He just had a check-up three weeks ago and the doctor pronounced him healthy and sound. Who would have thought he'd drop dead of a heart attack in the middle of his morning run!" Mina wiped a tear from her eye.

⚜

"How's your head, Mama?" Mina asked, as if to change the topic to one less painful.

"Oh. I still have headaches from time to time and my vision isn't as good as it was, but the doctor told me that that is just the way it will be. The stroke could have killed me and maybe one day another will. In the meantime, I'll manage."

"Mama, please. Come and live with me. I'll take care of you."

"I know. But ... I feel a need to stay here alone, just a little longer." Punita sighed, reaching to caress an emerald earring. "Enough of my distressing news," she said, hearing the tremble in her throat, a condition that had appeared since she had suffered the stroke. "Have you anything positive to talk about?"

"Indeed. I do have some news that might brighten your day." Mina read the letter.

"Just like Miriam. No real details," said Punita, chuckling. "Wait! What did you say is the name of her husband?"

"Hart Lange."

"No. His full name."

"Gerhard Michael La—"

"Gerhard Lange. That name sounds familiar ... Let me think." Punita tapped her fingernail on her front tooth while her memory reached into the past. Moments of silence filled the phone line. "I have it!" she exclaimed.

"Do you recall the story I told you? How Konstantin helped Mama and me flee from Germany during the War? How Herr Lange helped us find out about my father?"

"Of course."

"My mother and I met a Gerhard Lange on Konstantin's ship. He and his son—Paul,

I believe—brought some food and sausage to be transported to Amsterdam. Oh, my! The sausage—it was Schmidt sausage! But that's another memory ..." Punita rubbed her lip. "Very handsome men as I recall. They stood tall and straight like soldiers. I wonder whether Miriam's new husband is related."

"I'll ask," Mina said, "but I doubt that Miriam will tell us much. I suppose we should send a wedding gift and something for the new child."

"Of course. I'll write a little note too. About the baby's name. It is a good name as is his father's. Gerhard Michael means courageous, strong, proud and righteous. A moment longer, my dear."

Punita reached for her tattered tarot cards, shuffled them, then placed them across the table.

"The cards tell me that Hart has the spirit of a soldier. And Matthew Paul ..." She dealt more cards. "Matthew Paul means a small gift, which I'm certain he is. The cards tell me that he will have an unusual life. Much turmoil. But, he too has the spirit of a soldier and he will overcome his challenges to find happiness and fulfillment ... in time. There it is again, the reference to soldiers! Let me finish this reading." Punita spread more cards and ran her finger over them. "Hart is a man of the earth. He is firmly rooted in his life and family. Miriam is like water. She will wash over him and around him, and I doubt that he will ever find a way to ground her—to hold onto her."

"Mama—"

"Now, about the soldiers," Punita continued. "You'll recall my worry when I've mentioned German soldiers appearing in my past readings—"

"Yes, but—"

"Mina, this is it!" Punita exclaimed. "The time has come. The cards have been speaking of men with the bearing of German soldiers for a long time now, and I've been dreadfully afraid. The German occupation of Amsterdam still haunts me. But now I see

407

that I need not have fretted. Herr Lange and his son were soldiers, but they were not like the ones who occupied Amsterdam. Konstantin told me how they struggled during the war too. If Hart is a son of the Lange family, then Mama's prophecy is fulfilled. I can die in peace!"

"Mama, I appreciate what the cards say, but I don't think Miriam will care."

"She won't want to hear about the Lange family," Punita agreed, "but she need not. She's never known about my readings. She should know about the names, though. I will write anyway. Miriam can do with my thoughts as she pleases. But she knows … the cards don't lie."

Punita felt a sense of peace settling in her soul.

CHAPTER FORTY-ONE

A minibus was required to shuttle the Canadian contingent of the Lange family from Bayreuth's Bindlacher Berg Airport to the home of Paul and Ilse-Renata.

Paul watched from the doorway as the entire brood spilled out from the taxi, curious to finally lay eyes on the newest members of the family. Ilse-Renata stood next to him, clinging to his arm with anticipation.

The children, Pauline and Jacob, were old enough to tug their own luggage up the steps. Hart dragged two bigger cases. Miriam followed hesitantly, carrying their three-month old son, Matthew.

Hart introduced the older children first, then stood the cases out of the way and ushered Miriam forward to introduce her next. Ilse-Renata stepped toward her, gathering her in welcoming arms and cooing over Matthew.

"Please, call me Ilse," she said, remembering the English she had learned when she helped her sons with their homework. She stepped aside when Paul placed his hand on her shoulder as a reminder that he was awaiting his turn.

"Vati, this is my wife, Miriam, and your grandson, Matthew Paul." Hart stood proudly by his wife's side.

Paul offered his hand in welcome. When Miriam placed her hand in his, she looked up, smiling coquettishly. *Hmm, she looks like she's trying to impress me.* The deception set off warning bells in his head. He had seen enough during World War II to make him wonder what she was up to. *Melted dark chocolate … I know those eyes. I've seen them before.*

"Welcome, daughter. Please come in out of the cold." Paul's English was more fluid than his wife's. It had become a common language for business communication since the war. He raised his arms, crooking one behind her, the other shepherding her into the tiled foyer.

Turning back to the doorway, he took the large case that Hart had lifted over the threshold and moved it into the room. Hart smiled at his father but remained standing on the doorstep. Spontaneously, he raised his hand and placed it on the family crest.

"I'm home, Vati!" he whispered.

The two men smiled, the gesture reconnecting them. Ceremony complete, Hart picked up the second case and lifted it over the threshold, inhaling with pleasure.

"Mmm. Smells like home."

A flurry of activity followed, settling children and luggage to assigned rooms—a pleasant distraction for Miriam. Once that task was complete, they all gathered together in the sitting room, where Ilse served coffee and fresh Stollen. Pauline and Jacob had no interest in the Stollen. Bits of icing sugar plumed on their clothes, the coffee table, and the carpet when they picked out the dried fruit. Their behaviour mortified Miriam, who was trying desperately

411

to impress Hart's parents. Before they left Canada, the tarot cards had advised her to proceed with caution. She could not afford a misstep.

"They're not hungry, really. They ate a lot on the plane," Miriam apologized, trying to minimize the damage caused by her children.

"Miriam, dear, leave that," Ilse said calmly. "Cook will see to it when she clears the room."

Hart translated his mother's response.

"I think they're tired, too," Miriam replied, realizing that if she and her children were to fit in, they would have to learn more of the German language than Hart had taught them before the trip.

She fidgeted. She was uncomfortable and embarrassed, and she worried that she was being tested, even judged. She was not accustomed to such casual opulence. It exceeded anything that her parents had ever had. It was clear to her that Hart was financially secure, but the house in Calgary showed no sign of such wealth. Exhaustion overtook her, and she felt desperate to have time with the cards.

"Come on, you two," she said, addressing Pauline and Jacob. "You'll feel better after a nap."

"A nap!" the petulant children chimed, unravelling themselves from their cushion seats on the floor.

Miriam handed Matthew to Hart before heading up the broad oak staircase to the second floor with Pauline and Jacob in tow.

Miriam had been edgy and irritable for days leading up to their trip. Hart relaxed when she left, welcoming the quiet time with his parents, as well as the opportunity to share his son with them. With Miriam and the older children gone, Paul and Ilse became more animated, fussing over Matthew and taking turns to cuddle him.

"Son," Paul began cautiously, "what do you know about Miriam?"

"What do you mean, Vati?"

413

"Nothing offensive, I assure you," Paul said, attempting to calm any concern Hart might have in response to the question. "Your mother and I are just curious. You are living so far away. We don't see what happens each day of your life, nor do we need to." He raised his hand to still Hart.

"Before you married Ursula," Ilse finished Paul's thought, "we had time to run a background check. You married Miriam so quickly that we had no time to do so."

"Ah! Yes, I suppose from your perspective that provokes concern," Hart responded. Matthew had fallen asleep in his arms. He adjusted the blanket and continued. "I agree that a background check may be helpful, but it doesn't tell all," Hart said, nodding. "Ursula changed after we moved to Canada, and the background check could not have foretold what would happen. She became money-hungry. She needed money to play and she wanted to play. She played a lot." He gazed at Matthew before continuing. "She worked hard

414

all day. I'll give her that. But then she'd play hard at night. It was bad enough that she went out every night to clubs and parties, but when she started to bring her conquests home, rubbing her trysts in my face ..." Hart spit the last words from his mouth. Matthew squirmed in his arms. "I tried to reason with her. Suggested that we start a family. I had hoped that children would help settle her. She told me, in no uncertain terms ..." He paused, collecting his emotions. "She told me that she would never have a child with me. That I would never be a good father."

Ilse gasped. Paul had heard the story before.

"God knows. I tried everything to keep our marriage together. But I couldn't live with that last hurtful comment. Something inside me broke. Shattered."

"Oh, mein Herz." Ilse made a move toward him, but Hart held up his hand, tears issuing freely from his eyes. "I'm so sorry."

"It's all right, Mutti. In the past." He made a small smile, as if trying to convince them all, and continued. "So, we divorced. I focussed on business, travelled, did some playing of my own." He shrugged, as if to downplay previous events. "The first snowfall of last year, some friends and I went to the mountains to ski, and I met Miriam. We visited back and forth for several months."

"And then she announced she was pregnant," Paul finished the story. "Is it possible that the child was fathered by someone else? Clearly, the other two children have different fathers."

"Paul!" Ilse interrupted her husband's observations and moved to sit beside Hart on the settee. "How can you ask such things? Just look at this child." She reached to pull the blanket back from Matthew's face. Exposure to the cool air caused him to stir. "He's a true Lange, regardless of the parentage of the other two!"

"I apologize to both of you if you find my words offensive," Paul persisted. "But it must be said. There is too much at risk, here."

"I understand your concern, Vati, and I am certain that Matthew is mine. I made subtle enquiries beforehand. Miriam was not involved with anyone else when I met her."

"Still, there is something about her," Paul said. "I feel that I've met her before." *There's something about those eyes.* He crossed his arms, raising one hand to rub a finger over his lower lip. "If you don't mind," he continued, "I'd like to request a background check."

"I don't mind, Vati. If it will bring you both comfort. I doubt, however, that you'll find anything newsworthy."

Matthew began to squirm in earnest.

"I think he's hungry and needs a change," Ilse said reaching for the baby. "I'll take him up to his mother."

"Let's go into the study," Paul said. "We can continue our discussion over a glass of brandy. I want to hear how business is going in Canada."

Paul led the way, closing the door behind Hart, and pouring out two glasses of brandy. The room was darkening quickly in the late winter afternoon, and Hart walked from lamp to lamp switching them on. Father and son each folded into old leather armchairs and reviewed the Canadian venture. As the topic ran its course, Paul smoothly changed the subject.

"Son, how would you like to come home?"

"Return to Bayreuth?" Hart sat straighter in his chair.

"Yes. You've been in Canada for ten years, now. We know the business can work. Come home. We'd like to watch our grandchild—grandchildren," he corrected with a smile and a nod of his glass, "grow up. Be part of their lives." He cocked an eyebrow. "What do you think?"

"I'd like that very much, Vati. I miss my family. I miss Bayreuth, and its old beauty and the history here."

"Consider it done, then. When you return to Canada, start wrapping things up."

⚜

During the next several days, Hart often marvelled that that Christmas holiday was the best he had had in his life and could not imagine a way to better the occasion, unless they were living in Bayreuth.

Every day, he bundled up his family and chauffeured them around Bayreuth, sharing its ancient history, its surprises, and Lange Christmas traditions. After ten days of non-stop excitement, Miriam asked whether they could stay in and do nothing for a day.

"The baby is fussing and not nursing well, and Pauline and Jacob need some quiet time," she complained. "They are being spoiled. I feel like I'm losing control of them."

"I have a lot to learn, don't I?" Hart responded. "I've been trying so hard to share with you in just a few short weeks all of the things that I took a lifetime to know and appreciate."

419

"I can see that," Miriam conceded, "and we love you for it. You are a prince for trying, and for understanding."

"Let's take today off then," Hart said, seeking to mitigate any misgivings. "Say, why don't you call your mother? You haven't talked to her since we arrived. Ask her whether she's able to come for a visit. She could spend *Silvester*—actually the whole of the New Year break—with us."

"I'll ask, but I don't think she will."

Later, Miriam advised him that her mother would not be visiting.

"You spoke with her already?" Hart asked. "That's odd, I didn't hear you make the call."

"You were indisposed, darling." She smiled coquettishly. "You probably couldn't hear. Besides, it was a short call. Mother was too busy to chat."

CHAPTER FORTY-TWO

The next morning, Hart's family was well into their breakfast when he entered the dining room.

"Anyone interested in a surprise?" he asked with secretive suspense. His eyes twinkled with mischief.

"Me, me!" Pauline and Jacob exclaimed.

"A surprise?" Miriam asked with suspicion.

"When you said that your mother was too busy to come here for New Year's Eve, I asked Vati whether we could borrow the company car for a few days." Hart began to unravel his surprise. "I thought we could drive to Am-ster-dam for a few days. Who wants to go to Amsterdam to visit Oma?"

"Me, me!" Pauline and Jacob shouted again. Miriam's mouth gaped and a scowl shadowed her face.

"Amsterdam?" she hissed.

"You two run upstairs and pack an overnight bag," Hart said, ushering the children out of the room. "Mommy and I need to work out the details."

"Hart, how could you do that without talking to me about it first?"

"I thought you'd be happy!" Hart replied, taken aback by his wife's protest. He poured himself a cup of coffee and sat next to her. "You're always saying how you miss Amsterdam and your mother, and you're worried about your grandmother's health."

"A little notice would have been nice," she said, juggling Matthew on her lap while she attempted to butter a roll.

"I'm sorry," he apologized, reaching to spread the butter for her. "I was afraid that you'd say it was rude for us to leave Mutti and Vati, but when I raised the possibility with them, they encouraged it." He placed a roll on his own plate and passed her a cheese slice. The room was quiet as Hart buttered his own roll and layered it with sausage and cheese.

"I hope you know what you're doing," Miriam said flatly, watching Hart munch on the roll. "I'd better call Mama and tell her we're coming," she said.

"You do that," Hart agreed. "I'll be up as soon as I finish here to help you throw some stuff together. We should be away within the hour, if at all possible."

"Here. You take Matthew," Miriam said rolling her son into Hart's arm. "I can work faster with two hands." *I need time with the cards. Amsterdam is not a place I expected to be going. I need to prepare myself.*

The drive from Bayreuth to Amsterdam ate through the entire day, but the children occupied themselves with games they had brought for entertainment on the plane, and Matthew slept most of the time. When they arrived at the foot of the stairs that led up to the townhouse with the blue door, it was early evening.

"Come in! Come in!" Mina welcomed them. "It's too chilly to waste time on the landing."

"Hart, this is my mother, Mina," Miriam said matter-of-factly, once the five of them were inside the door, "and this is Matthew."

Pauline and Jacob kicked off their shoes and hung their coats on the hooks inside the door. "Where will we sleep, Oma?"

"Upstairs, in your old room," Mina replied. "Pauline, do you remember where it is?"

"Yes, Oma," Pauline said, dragging the overnight bag up the stairs. "Come on, Jacob, I'll show you. You probably don't remember."

"Do too," Jacob said doubtfully.

"I'll just finish preparing the food for the table," Mina said, gesticulating for Hart's benefit.

"I'm going up to make sure the children get organized and washed up," Miriam said to Hart. "You take Matthew and entertain him in the parlour. Mama is going to get food ready for the table."

⚜

424

A moment later, the two women were gone. Hart walked into the parlour, noticing the orderliness of a room without children. As he lowered himself into an old green sofa, he was startled to realize that he and Matthew were not alone.

"Oh! Hello," he said to the small woman cocooned in a wing chair. "I'm Hart, and this is Matthew." He held Matthew up for the woman to see. The woman's eyes grew wide with pleasure.

"You are Miriam's new husband," she said, her dark brown eyes clear and bright. "I'm Miriam's grandmother, Punita."

"You speak German!" Hart replied with surprise.

"I speak many languages, but not so well any more. When I was young, my German was perfect." Hart felt the woman's scrutiny. "You remind me of someone I met long ago. They were German soldiers, at least one was. The father, he was tall with dark hair and black eyes. His son, Paul, was too young to be a soldier then, but my cousin

Konstantin told me that he became a soldier in the last war." She sighed. "They were kind for German soldiers, not like the ones who came here. Gerhard Lange helped us find my father. He was taken by the Brown Shirts and died in Dachau—"

"I'm sorry for your loss," Hart set his sleeping son on the sofa beside him. "You mentioned Gerhard Lange, and his son Paul," he said, shifting toward the edge of the sofa. "Paul Lange is my father!"

"I thought so. I wanted it to be so. The cards have been telling me that you would come." She held out her hand to him. "You must tell him how grateful I am for what his father did for Mama and me."

"I will," Hart said, dumbfounded by Punita's story. "I had no idea …" Matthew awoke and began to fuss. Hart lifted him onto his lap.

"You wouldn't have a way of knowing, unless your father told you, and why would he? My story is in the past. Miriam knows nothing of it."

"Dinner in ten minutes," Mina said. She flitted into the dining room with condiments for the meal and disappeared into the kitchen as quickly as she had appeared.

"May I hold him," Punita said, gesturing toward the baby.

"Of course!" Hart set Matthew on the lap of his great-grandmother.

Matthew gazed at Punita with curiosity, then gave her a toothless grin, his eyes crinkling in the corners.

"You are a beautiful boy," she said, catching her finger under his chin. "Such dark eyes for one so young." She looked at Hart. "Your eyes are the colour of charcoal, like your father's, as I recall. He was a handsome man and must be still. You resemble him, but you are not so tall."

"My mother is small," Hart replied. "I picked up a few of her genes too."

"Of course," Punita said, "but eye colour isn't usually obvious until a child is at least six months old, and you ..." She turned her attention to Matthew again. "You are

427

only, what, three months old?" Matthew grinned at her attention, drooling down the front of his shirt. "The only time I've ever seen an infant with dark eyes at this age is when their heritage is African or Asian. My heritage is Indian. I suspect that his eyes will have our eye colour. Like melted dark chocolate, my husband always said." Punita frowned as she spoke the last words.

"Mina," she hollered toward the kitchen. "Mina, you must come quickly."

"Mama, what it is? Are you all right," Mina asked hastening into the parlour.

"Yes, my dear, but you must hear this." Her free hand reached for her daughter's. "I wasn't accurate when I said the prophecy had been fulfilled. Matthew is the prophecy!" she whispered earnestly. "He has the genes of the German soldier, and I am almost certain that he will have our dark brown eyes! I fear for this child!"

Hart listened to the exchange between Punita and Mina, finding the conversation difficult to grasp, until Punita shared an abridged version. *This is weird. What is going on? All of a sudden, they both seem worried.*

"Prophecy?" he asked. "I don't understand."

"Dinner is almost ready," Mina said in a hushed voice. "May we continue this conversation later? Perhaps when Miriam is putting the children to bed?"

"Of course," Hart said, confused and curious.

"Mina," Punita implored, her voice equally quiet. "A blessing ... please. You do it. In German, for his father ..."

"All right," Mina said, hesitantly. Her hand rose to clasp the large emerald hanging from her neck. "Welcome, little Matthew. May your burdens be light, your sorrows few, and your joy abundant."

"Amen to that. Thank you, my dear," Punita sighed. She kissed the top of Matthew's head and returned the child to his father. "If you'll excuse me, I must consult the cards."

"Be quick," Mina whispered. "Dinner is almost ready."

"Excuse me, Hart," Punita said, leaving him alone with his son. "I'll find out what's taking Miriam so long too."

I'm beginning to wonder whether Miriam has been slow coming down deliberately. Something weird is going on, Hart thought. *Hopefully, it will all be clear after our discussion later.*

CHAPTER FORTY-THREE

The remainder of their Christmas holiday was a blur, ending with a flight back to Calgary in early January. Hart never found the time to have a conversation with Miriam about his unusual introduction to her family, because of subsequent conversations he had with his father.

On the morning of New Year's Eve, Hart found himself alone with his father enjoying a cup of coffee in the study. Before Hart sat down, he closed the study door.

"Vati, do you recall meeting two dark-haired women—mother and daughter—when you were young, around sixteen?

"I've met many dark-haired women, Hart," Paul replied, chuckling. "Can you be more specific?"

"You would have met them on a ship. I think the captain's name was Russian. Kon—"

"Konstantin! Konstantin Anker!" Paul grinned. "I remember him. He and his brother imported Schmidt sausages into the Netherlands before the war. We dealt with another fellow after the war—Willem, Willem van Bosch. He died unexpectedly," Paul mused. "Heart attack during his morning run, I believe."

"Vati, the women!"

"Ah, yes, the two dark-haired women. On Konstantin's ship." Paul scrubbed his knuckle along his unshaven cheek. "As a matter of fact, I do," he said. "Both of them were very beautiful. But that was a long time ago. Why are you asking?"

"Turns out," Hart said, "that the young girl is Miriam's grandmother!"

"Ha! Eyes like melted dark chocolate!" Paul exclaimed. "I knew I'd seen those eyes before!"

"Tell me what you remember."

Hart watched his father's face light up as he seemed to recall his encounter with Rosalee and Punita Kota. Giving him time to collect his thoughts, Hart rose from his chair, set his cup of cold coffee on a tray next to the brandy decanter and resumed his seat across from his father.

When Paul spoke again, he told Hart about the odd encounter on the ship, and how his father had encouraged their hasty departure when the two women arrived.

"I didn't know then, of course, but they were running from the Brown Shirts. Hitler had already started rounding up people he deemed enemies of the state, including criminals, homosexuals, Jews, Romani, and any folks without legal citizenship papers. Father presumed that the Kotas were Romani and doubted whether they had papers. Konstantin told him that Herr Kota was his cousin and that he had to help get them to Amsterdam. Herr Kota was separated from them and ended up in Dachau. When Father reached Dachau, he learned that Herr Kota had died of typhus." Paul closed his eyes and hung his head. "Those were bad times. He hated

433

having to break that news to his friend, Alexi Puchinski. He too had ties to Konstantin. The three were cousins. We never knew what happened to any of them," he said with a heavy sigh.

"I think I can give you a little more information," Hart said, feeling his father's sadness. "I met Miriam's grandmother Punita and Punita's daughter, Mina—Miriam's mother. I had a long conversation with them the evening that we arrived." Hart stared at a spot on the ceiling as he recalled the conversation. "It was a very curious conversation in the end."

Hart shared the information imparted by Punita and Mina, about the sea voyage to Amsterdam and the interesting life they had lived. When he finished, he allowed Paul to digest the tale before asking his father a question he had been deferring.

"Vati," he asked, summoning the courage, "is there anything else that you remember from that time, perhaps even earlier. Something about a prophecy?"

Paul sat back in his chair, amazed at his son's question. The cup he still held in his hand rattled. Hart took the dishes from his father and set them on the tray.

"As a matter of fact, I do. It is something that has haunted me my entire life." Paul shook his head in awe. "The first time I met Rosalee, Punita's mother, was at the Liegnitz fall fair of 1928. I was just a boy. Mutti and I wanted to have our fortunes read. And Rosalee was the fortuneteller. I remember everything about it, the smell, the light, her voice. She told me that I came from a powerful lineage, that I would be an inspiring leader and a hero, if I survived danger, death, and horror. She warned me to take great care, or I would die." He scrubbed his cheek again before continuing. "It's because of her that I always took great care to be aware of my surroundings, all through the war. It kept me safe and brought me home … alive."

"Did she tell you anything else," Hart asked.

"She didn't tell me anything specific,"
435

Paul replied. "But, I recall her saying 'eyes like melted dark chocolate' and when I asked what she meant, she said that those eyes would play a significant role in the future of my family. Then she warned me to be careful and ended the reading."

Hart frowned, trying to fathom his father's tale.

"Why are you asking?" Paul asked a few minutes later, slowly unraveling himself from the chair. "More coffee?"

Hart nodded and accepted the steaming cup his father offered.

"Punita told me what Rosalee saw in that reading. Sit and I'll tell you about the prophecy that she says has haunted her life since that day too."

At the end of the morning's revelations, both men were exhausted from the adrenalin that coursed through their veins as they shared the story of three remarkable women and discussed the prophecy—their prophecy—that seemed to have fallen on Matthew's tiny shoulders.

"It's all very unusual," Paul said, "to be sure. And if I were another man, I would dismiss this prophecy business. But I'm not another man, and on reflection, I can see that what Rosalee predicted has come to pass. If Punita is worried about Matthew's future, then we must pay attention." He sat straighter in his chair and rubbed the dent on his forehead, a dent that resulted when a sniper's bullet hit his helmet with a glancing blow. *It hasn't pained me in years, but this talk of war and the past has brought it back. I hope the nightmares don't follow.* "Have you said anything to Miriam about the things we've discussed this morning?"

"No, not yet," Hart replied, "I wanted to talk with you first."

During the return flight to Calgary, after everyone had eaten and the children were sleeping, Hart reached over to Miriam and took her hand.

"What's on your mind, my prince?" she teased.

The baby slept in her arms. She took a deep breath and willed herself to relax, closing her eyes for a moment.

"Tired?" he asked.

"A little," she said, smiling drowsily. "When you add children to travel, the whole process is quite tiring. Add an infant and ..."

"Want to talk, or sleep?" Hart wondered.

"I have a few more minutes before I pass out. What's on your mind?"

"Vati and I have had some long conversations over the past few weeks," he began. He hesitated, as if searching for the right words. "He'd like us to come home. He thinks we've accomplished what we set out to do when I moved to Canada ten years ago, and he wants me to take over the factory operations." His words hung for five heartbeats before he went on. "He's going to look for a house for us. I can wrap up the business and shift it to Bayreuth. There's no need to stay in Calgary. And," he paused, again, "we'll be closer to your family. What do you think?"

"Oh!" Her head snapped off his shoulder, so she could look at him. "I'll want to hear more about the logistics, and it means taking the children out of school mid-term, but I suppose it can be done." Her face took on a dreamy look, her eyes glazing while she imagined a life in Germany—Europe at her doorstep, once again. "It sounds rather exciting, actually." Nodding her head, contemplatively, she turned toward him. "Okay." She returned her head to his shoulder and closed her eyes. "We'll all need to work on our German before we move, though."

Hart agreed and stroked her crown. Her hair fell forward curtaining from his view her look of satisfaction and accomplishment. *The tarot cards are correct, again! I just wish they'd stop warning me to be careful. It's very clear to me that the strength of the Lange family is formidable.*

⚜

Preparation for the return to Bayreuth took longer than anticipated. Hart had commitments—travel, trade shows, pump installations, and so on. The business wind-up took time.

While they waited and prepared, Hart insisted that they spend at least one hour every day learning to read and write German.

"You can study while I'm away. By the time we return to Germany, you should all be able to carry on a conversation in German, and at least have some fundamental writing skills before you two," he looked at Pauline and Jacob, "start school."

In the meantime, Miriam expressed disgust that she was unable to recover her figure after Matthew's birth. Her doctor advised that it could take a year or two, depending on her lifestyle. Miriam was impatient and insisted that she should have surgery to remove the fat and flab caused by multiple pregnancies. *He's got the money. Why not?*

"I want to look good when we return to Europe," she told Hart, explaining that surgery would be something she could have to fill her time while they waited for Hart to close the business. *I want to look sexy in a bathing suit, and tight pants. I want to turn heads again!*

Two weeks before their departure, just as Miriam was tucking the children into bed for the evening, the telephone rang.

"I'll get it," Hart said, reaching for a nearby handset. "Lange."

"Hart, it's Ursula," the voice announced.

"Ursula," Hart replied with caution in his voice. "I haven't heard from you in over two years. What do you want?"

"I'm in a bit of difficulty, and only you can help," she said.

"Me? How? What have you done?"

"It's more ... what have you done. You divorced me."

"And not without reason," Hart snapped.

"That's beside the point," she interrupted. "My father is coming to stay with me for a month."

"So?"

"He doesn't know that we're divorced. I don't want him to know. I want to prove to him that I became successful, no thanks to him."

"And to prove that you are successful, you need a loving husband standing by your side?"

"Well ... yes."

"Ursula," Hart replied, starting to chuckle. "Do you hear yourself? Do you know how ridiculous you sound?"

"I do," she answered, desperation seeping into her voice, "but you don't need to do anything. Just hang around for a month, then you can go off and do whatever you do every day."

"Ursula, not only is your request ridiculous, it's impossible."

"Why?"

"Because I'm married. I have children. I can't just leave my family for a month!"

"Married! Children! But how—"

"It was easy," he replied, trying to

442

contain his laughter. "Maybe you should ask one of your lovers to act as a husband for the month."

"No! It needs to be you. Tata's seen photos of us together!"

"Sorry, Ursula," Hart smirked. "You're out of luck. I'm taking my family home to Bayreuth in two weeks. I won't be here." He cleared his throat. "So, even if I wanted to help, which I don't, I can't 'cause I won't be here. You need to grow up and take responsibility for yourself."

"But, I—"

"Good-bye, Ursula!" Hart replaced the handset, still chuckling.

"Who was that?" Miriam asked as she descended the stairs to the living room.

"You won't believe it, but I have to tell you anyway. Come into the kitchen with me. I'll tell you as I clean up the dirty dishes."

All things considered, it was the end of June before the Lange family was packed and ready to leave Calgary. In early July, their

443

household goods were shipped, leaving them free for their flight to Germany.

By the time the children and luggage were organized and loaded into a taxi on their last day in Canada, it was past noon. The morning of their departure date expired in a blur, and they arrived at the Calgary International Airport with barely time to spare.

Ilse stood alone at the door to the Lange home when the taxi arrived. Before any of the Canadian family reached the doorstep, however, Paul appeared by her side, and together they welcomed Hart's family, once again.

"Perfect timing, son," he said, embracing Hart in a bear hug. "I just got off the phone with the estate agent. He has a house for you to look at. I told him I'd call him in a few days so he can arrange a viewing for you."

"Why don't we arrange a viewing for tomorrow?" Hart asked. "Miriam, are you up for a tour tomorrow?"

"That would be fine," she replied, her Dutch accent making the German words she spoke thick on her tongue. "The sooner we have a place of our own, the better. We don't want to impose on your parents or wear out our welcome here." *The sooner we're out of here the better! Their scrutiny is intimidating.*

"Nonsense," Ilse assured her. "This is your home, too. You are always welcome here."

"I'll call the agent back now," Paul said, "so he can make arrangements."

Paul excused himself and headed for the study. Hart and a gardener carried the luggage upstairs, while Ilse fussed over Matthew and the other children.

"You must be exhausted, Miriam dear," Ilse said, "and the cases are already in your rooms. Shall I look after Matthew while you organize things?"

Miriam handed Matthew to his grandmother and led the other two children up the broad oak staircase.

"Coffee or a nap?" Ilse's question followed them up the stairs.

Miriam stopped and lowered her gaze toward Ilse who stood at the bottom of the stairs.

"Small refreshments would be welcome. Then we can nap. What do you think?" she asked, turning to the children, who both answered at once.

"Soda!" Pauline said.

"Cake!" Jacob said.

"Ilse, thank you, we'll be down in about twenty minutes."

Ilse took Matthew into the kitchen to arrange for coffee and cake in the parlour, chatting amicably with Matthew who was pleased to show her his new teeth.

CHAPTER FORTY-FOUR

The following day, the agent called early for Miriam, Hart, and Paul, and drove them around Bayreuth, giving them a sense of the city—mostly for Miriam's benefit—and showing them a few homes. In the end, they purchased a four-storey townhouse, not far from the Roter Main River in the Linde Forest and enrolled the older children in school.

Having arrived at the beginning of the national summer vacation and knowing that it would be some time before their household goods arrived, Hart and Miriam agreed to accompany Paul and Ilse to the family summer-house in Croatia.

Pauline and Jacob enjoyed the vacation, passing the days swimming in the ocean. On occasion, Ilse packed a lunch and Paul took everyone out on their largest yacht, where they would spend the day exploring hidden coves and new beaches. Sometimes, they dropped anchor and dove off the bow.

Miriam was concerned about the damage that the salt water could do to her coloured hair. The salt content in the air alone was enough to break off clumps of treated hair and she was forced to wear a scarf or a hat all the time. She obsessed about her trim body and decided that an all-over tan was a preferred alternative. While the others swam, she spread a blanket on the bow of the yacht, slathered herself with sun screen, and slept through the oppressive heat.

Miriam found the daily routine within the compound monotonous. Whenever the opportunity arose, she wandered off to visit the neighbours, or take a walk along the seawall, leaving her son in the care of his father and grandparents. Without continuity of care, Matthew became listless.

Hart worried about Matthew's lack of interest and lethargy. He refused to eat or play. When he discovered his son lying

448

on a cot on the veranda, unattended, and Miriam gone, Hart called upon his parents for assistance.

"I'm taking Matthew to the hospital. Something's wrong. I don't know where Miriam is. I need help."

Paul drove Hart and Matthew to the hospital, leaving the older children with Ilse. At the hospital, the attending physician diagnosed that Matthew was dehydrated. He was treated and released, with a warning to Hart and Paul to ensure that the child drank more liquids.

"Too many people caring for him, but no continuity of care," Hart muttered on the drive home. "Miriam is usually more attentive, but she seems distracted lately. I wonder where she's wandered off to."

As they drove through the small village on return to the summer-house, Paul pointed toward a café.

"There she is."

"With whom?" Hart asked, leaning toward the windshield for a better view.

"Looks like locals. She certainly seems to be enjoying herself," Paul commented in a judgmental tone. "I'd keep my eye on her, son, if I were you. Do you want me to stop?"

"No. I think we need to focus on Matthew and get him home first. I'll deal with Miriam later," Hart replied. "Besides, I wouldn't want to risk a spectacle. This town is too small."

Sometime later, Miriam sauntered into the compound, humming to herself and swinging her sandals in her hand. Sunlight cast shafts of brightness when it caught the facets of her diamond engagement ring. Seeing her return, Hart jogged to her side and escorted her into their apartment.

"We need to talk," he said, his hand firmly on her elbow.

His grip snapped her out of her reverie.

"About what?" she asked defensively, yanking her arm free of his hold.

He told her about the emergency trip to

the hospital, and about Paul's observations on the return.

"Your parents are a couple of busybodies. They should mind their own business!" she snapped. Immediately after, as if regretting her carelessness, she apologized.

"Hart, I didn't mean that," she said petulantly. "I'm tired. I need a nap."

She rested an open palm on his chest and sensuously licked her lips.

"I've been naughty, and I'm sending myself to my room for a time-out." She giggled, trying to break the tension between them.

"How is Matthew, by the way?" she asked over her shoulder, as she headed toward the bedroom. "Has he recovered?"

"He's fine ..." Hart started to say.

The remainder of his explanation ended when she closed the door on his words.

Taken aback by her sudden departure from the conversation, Hart opened the door and followed her into the bedroom.

"Miriam, are you not happy? Is something wrong between us?"

A knot that had been forming in his belly since the rushed trip to the hospital tightened. *I lost Ursula. I can't be losing Miriam too!*

Miriam's demeanour shifted abruptly. Her defensive countenance changed to sultry. She wrapped her arms around Hart's neck and cooed on wine vapours.

"Of course not, my prince, we are perfectly fine."

She kissed him passionately, licking his lips, her tongue invading, searching and finding his. Her hands lowered and she moved against him with sexual suggestion. Hart tasted the residue of wine on her lips. Her hands fondled him and he felt himself stir.

Matthew is safe, asleep in his crib. I suppose it'll be okay for me to accept her overture as an apology. He lifted her toward the bed. *Maybe I'm worrying unnecessarily. Miriam just needed time for herself,* he thought, as he untied the straps of her sun top.

When they returned to Bayreuth, the container of goods had not arrived, but local businesses were opening again. The national vacation was ending.

Hart arranged to report to the office each day with Paul, and again immersed himself in business operations. He felt energized and ready to explore new ideas at Mikel & Co. In the meantime, Miriam busied herself looking after the three children, and shopping for school supplies with Ilse.

At long last, the household goods arrived, and the family set to work organizing their new home so that work, school, and play ran smoothly. The Lange crest was installed above the door lintel, so every family member could find their way home. Pauline and Jacob insisted that a stool be set by the door, so they could climb onto it and reach the crest with their own hands.

✛

Two weeks into September, Paul knocked on the jamb of Hart's open door.

"Got a minute?" he asked, stepping into the tidy office furnished with a sleek desk and matching chairs and cabinets—all created by Hart before he left for Canada.

Hart waved his hand to invite his father to sit in one of his padded, orange guest chairs.

Paul sat, but did not appear to relax. He dangled a file folder between his knees.

"I've received the background check on Miriam," he said, eyes on Hart's face. "I'm afraid it's not a glowing report."

Hart's face went blank.

"As is obvious by her children, she has had several relationships, one marriage, and some abortions. Her mother was married to a wealthy merchant, and her grandmother was married to a doctor. Both men died a while back."

"Nothing new," Hart said. "I know that."

"Did she tell you that both her mother and grandmother worked in the Red-Light District, prior to their marriages?"

Hart shook his head.

"Do I really need to know that?"

"Perhaps not, but there is some concern about other men and ..."

"Enough, Vati. I don't want to hear it. I know she has a past. I don't need to know everything about it. If ever the day comes ... and it won't ... that there is trouble, you can tell me then." Hart held up his hand. "I love my wife. She is a good woman, and we have a happy home. That is all that matters to me."

Paul inhaled deeply.

"As you wish," he said on the exhale. "But don't say I didn't warn you. If you took the time to read the file, you'd know what to watch for."

He held the file out to Hart. Hart held up his right hand, palm forward.

"No, Vati. I don't want the file. Please, take it away with you. I don't want to

455

know anything that could cast doubt on my marriage."

"Very well," Paul said. "I'll keep it locked in my office cabinet. If ever you change your mind ..."

"I won't," Hart said firmly. "Thanks, anyway."

Paul left Hart's office and returned to his own where he locked the file safely out of the path of curious eyes. *I truly hope, for Hart's sake, that he never needs this information.* He locked the cabinet and put the key in his pocket.

CHAPTER FORTY-FIVE

For Hart, life was idyllic. He had the family for which he had always longed. He had a purpose in the factory, with licence to be creative. He worked with his father on new ideas for farm and general use. They vacationed every summer on warm beaches, enjoying their yachts and time together.

In the winter, they took ski vacations in the Harz Mountains or the Alps. He taught his family to ski. Matthew was the only one who thrived. He was a natural athlete, and followed his father down the bunny hills, laughing with pleasure each time he reached the bottom without falling.

Miriam often reminisced about the mountains in Canada, and how she missed working for a living. Hart assured her that they had a great life in Bayreuth and reminded her that she had a full-time job looking after their home and family. She had no need to seek employment elsewhere.

One afternoon, Hart and Miriam sat relaxing on the deck of a mountain restaurant, enjoying a hot chocolate before setting out again. The three children had been signed up for ski lessons and would be occupied until dinner time.

"Remember the Rockies?" she asked. "When we met. The job I had in the pub."

"Ja, but you don't need to work. You can enjoy life now. You are my princess!"

"And you are my prince. You rescued me from a dismal life, and I am grateful." She raised her hand to shield her eyes from the bright sun as she continued. "It's just that ... well ... I've always taken care of myself. And, I guess ... I'm just conditioned to be doing something ... more."

"What would you like to do?" he asked. "Go back to school? Take some courses ... about things that interest you? Maybe do some volunteer work? You don't need to work for an income."

"No!" her response was a little too quick. The force of it startled Hart.

Miriam searched in her backpack for her sunglasses, giving herself time to settle. *Hart treats me like a child and minimizes my desires! I could just scream! This life is making me crazy.*

"No, I don't want to go to school," Miriam said again, struggling to keep emotion out of her voice. "I've done that. I just need to find a way to keep busy. Matthew will be in kindergarten before we know it. Then what will I do?"

She made a desperate face and shrugged, leaving the question to dangle between them.

"Aw, come on," Hart replied, "it can't be that bad. Matthew won't start kindergarten until August. You have four months to think about it. We'll take our beach vacation in July."

She frowned, folding her arms.

"Once the children return to school, you'll be free to do whatever you like," Hart suggested cheerily, reaching across the table and taking her hand in his. "Take some time and think about what you'd really like to do."

"Okay," she said petulantly, removing her hand and picking up her mug. "Yuck. My chocolate is cold."

"Mine too. Ready to ski again?"

Miriam rose from her chair, with reluctance. She loved life in the mountains, and winter and snow, but she realized that she no longer enjoyed skiing, especially with Hart. He was a great skier and his skill made her feel incompetent. The pretense of enjoying it made her anxious. *What if he realizes that I hate it? I need some time with the cards. Maybe I can feign illness and return to our room early.*

"Yup. Let's go," she said, turning and walking away from him in the duck-walk fashion of skiers in ski boots, shrugging into her backpack.

He followed, doing the same.

❖

Throughout the following months, Miriam

was constantly distracted by her boredom and thoughts of what she could do to change her situation. The tarot cards were clear. If she followed the path dictated by them, she would find happiness. As the time for summer vacation approached, her thoughts finally gelled. She had a plan and began to implement it.

Preparation activities for, and during, their beach vacation helped distract her, kept her calm. When she focussed on her plan, she managed to appear happy and positive.

It was not until the return drive home to Bayreuth that her anxiety returned. While the children slept, huddled together in the back seat of the Mercedes sedan, Hart kept his eyes focussed on the road, and she steeled herself to carry out her plan.

"How's your search progressing?" Hart asked, startling Miriam out of her reverie.

"Hm?" She let him think she had not heard him while she conjured up a response.

"How's your search progressing?" he repeated. "Have you decided on an interest that you'd like to pursue? You haven't said

461

anything since our ski trip." He reached across the front seat and squeezed her hand. "Matthew starts kindergarten on Monday. If we lived in Canada, you'd have another two years to think about it, 'cause kids don't start kindergarten until they're five. Putting him in kindergarten at three should give you lots of free time to pursue your interests."

He's never asked before. Why now? Does he suspect something?

"Have you any ideas for what you will do with the extra time?" Hart persisted.

"I think so."

Miriam left the conversation dangling.

"Care to share?" he asked.

"Not yet, darling," she responded sweetly, patting his hand. "You'd better keep your eyes on the road. We can talk of this later."

"You're right. I should watch the road. We'll be home sooner if I do."

He moved the sedan into the fast lane and accelerated.

CHAPTER FORTY-SIX

Early on Monday morning, Hart kissed Miriam goodbye. He stroked her cheek as she confirmed that she would drop the children at school and take Matthew to his first day of nursery school.

"You're so beautiful," he said. "If I didn't know you were almost forty, I'd think you were twenty." Hart was anxious to get to the office, following his long absence, but worried about Miriam's frame of mind. Before she closed the front door behind him, he returned, took her in his arms and kissed her passionately.

"Whew!" she said, catching her breath. "What was that for?"

"Simp— ... I love you. I had a great vacation, as always. You and the children are everything to me and I feel rejuvenated. Ready for anything!" He looked into her dark chocolate eyes and caressed her cheek again. "I'll see you after work." As an after-thought, he added, "I hope you've found what you're looking for."

"What do you mean?" she asked, holding her face still.

"I hope you've found something to keep you busy, something that you will enjoy. Maybe you'll tell me about it this evening?"

"Of course," she said.

He turned and ran youthfully up the steps to the car park.

⚜

After his departure, Miriam returned to the kitchen and dealt the tarot cards again, looking for certainty that her plan would not fail. An hour later, a moving van rolled into the car park and four burly young men joined their supervisor at the door of the Lange residence. Before the supervisor could ring the bell, Miriam, dark hair knotted at her nape, opened the door.

"Shhh," she motioned with her red painted fingertip pressed against her lips. "My children are still asleep."

She opened the door wider and ushered them in.

"Please pack the lower floors first. That will give me time to wake the children and get them ready."

She gave instructions for the packing and excused herself. Upstairs, she manoeuvred the suitcases to the hallway and opened them. Instead of putting the children's clothing away after she had laundered them on the weekend, she had discreetly repacked them. Only a few items remained in the drawers and closets. She quietly moved through Matthew's room, taking anything he would not need for travel, put them in his suitcase, and zipped it up.

One by one, she woke each of the older children and asked them to do the same with their things. When asked why, she shushed them and said she would explain later.

"Not again," Pauline grumbled sleepily.

Miriam silenced her with a slap to her cheek.

"Just do it!" Miriam demanded. "Help your brother. I'm going up to finish my own packing."

Pauline rubbed her stinging cheek as she shook her brother awake and explained their mother's instructions. Grumbling, Jacob threw back the covers and scooted to the bathroom.

Fearing Miriam's wrath, brother and sister quickly packed their portable possessions into suitcases and prepared for a day of travel. Just as Miriam descended from above, they were dragging their cases into the hallway.

"Go down to the kitchen and have something to eat. Don't make a mess." She glared at them to ensure they were listening. "When you're done, organize some snacks for the car. I need to talk to the mover."

While Pauline and Jacob ate, three of the men methodically moved furniture out of the house, up the stairs to the car park, and into the white moving van. *'Fast movers! Anywhere!'* read the advertisement plastered on either side, next to a photograph of two of the men, arms crossed, biceps flexed.

The other two men moved from room to room, stuffing smaller items into boxes and labelling them. Miriam found the supervisor and told him that the upper floors were ready to be packed. Batting her eyes at him, she dangled her car keys and asked him to arrange for the suitcases to be put in her car. He took them, promising to do so.

With the men and the children working like bees, she buzzed up the stairs to Matthew's room. *Time to get him ready.*

"Mommy?" Miriam turned to look at her older son who was standing in the bedroom doorway. "Where are we going this time? Back to Pete's?"

"No, of course not. That's too far." She buttoned Matthew's shirt, and stuffed his feet into his pant legs. "We're going to see your grandmother." Smug that her plan was in progress, she tied Matthew's shoes and patted his bottom. "Go with Jacob and have some cereal. We're going on a long car ride." Miriam ushered both boys out of the bedroom and surveyed it one last time, satisfying herself that it was ready for the packers.

With the moving van loaded, the men drove off, directions in hand. Miriam locked the front doors and ushered the children up the stairs to her car.

"Good morning, Frau Lange." Frau Stein's voice halted Miriam's rush. "What is this? You are moving? I thought today it is back to school for the children."

"Frau Stein," Miriam replied, quickly recovering from the old woman's interruption. "How good it is to see you." She smiled the same sweet smile she had used on the supervisor. "It is all very last minute. My husband has taken a position with a manufacturer in Hastings, England. Family difficulties, you see …" Miriam shrugged. "Oh well, these things happen." She fished in her pocket, drew out her car keys and glanced at her watch. "Gosh, look at the time! We must be off, if we're going to keep to our timeline." She gave a small wave to Frau Stein before taking the stairs to the car park two at a time.

One more stop, she mentally ran through her checklist, *and we're gone.* A short time later, Miriam left the children in the car and disappeared into the Sparkasse Bank.

"I'll be twenty minutes," she told them. "Stay out of trouble."

CHAPTER FORTY-SEVEN

Hart had a productive day, catching up on correspondence, ensuring that the cast iron ovens were up to melting temperature, and seeing to the start of new productions. Some of the staff would not return from vacation for another week. As it was still quiet in the office, he made an executive decision. He would leave early and surprise Miriam.

When he arrived home, Miriam's car was missing from her parking spot. *She's gone to pick up the children.* He put his key in the door lock and turned the latch until he heard the click of release. The house had a different sound when the children and Miriam were away. As he pushed the door open and stepped onto the landing, he looked up at the Lange crest and rested his hand on it.

"I'm home," he said.

He unlocked the inside door and stepped into the quiet house, sensing that it was not just quiet. It echoed with emptiness. Stunned, he walked into the kitchen, his footsteps reverberating off the uncovered walls, and opened the cupboards. *Empty. The table and chairs are gone. The coffee machine, the kettle ...* As the situation slowly penetrated his consciousness, he moved more quickly, first into the dining room, then the living room. *Empty. Everything is gone.* He ran up the stairs to the first landing. *The children's bedrooms are empty.* Up to the top floor, he raced, his heart pounding in his chest. But for his clothes and personal items, everything was gone.

He dialled the number of Miriam's car phone. *No answer.*

In disbelief, he telephoned his parents and spoke with Paul. Neither Paul nor Ilse had heard from Miriam. They knew nothing about the missing household items, nor the whereabouts of his family.

Hart tried Miriam's car phone again. Nothing.

He telephoned the school and spoke with the administrator, who advised that the children had not reported for school that morning. He telephoned the kindergarten. Matthew had not been dropped off, he heard the voice say.

Anxiety overwhelming him, Hart sat on a stair and hung his head in his hands. His knotted stomach burned with nausea, when his father's words of warning came back to haunt him.

"Think!" he disciplined his thoughts, pounding his fists into his temples. "What should I do next?"

A soft rap came from the front door. Hart looked up, hoping to see Miriam and hear her say that she had made a mistake. Instead, a neighbour pushed open the door.

"Herr Lange!" Frau Stein exclaimed, her kerchiefed-head bobbing in the doorway. "I'm surprised to see you here!" She stepped

472

uninvited into the hallway and closed the outer door behind her.

Hart unravelled from the step, blue-black hair spiked where his fingers had been. He stared at her, puzzled.

"What do you mean, Frau Stein? You're surprised to see me here?"

"I spoke with Frau Lange this morning," she said, stepping along the hallway. "I saw the moving van, you see. It arrived early, around 8:00. They were quick, those fellows. Like it read on the side of the van: *Fast movers! Anywhere!* They had everything out and loaded well before noon. As soon as the children and the luggage were in her car, Frau Lange drove off."

"Did she say where she was going?"

"You don't know?"

"I'm supposed to meet up with her, and …" Hart stammered, trying to find words. He looked at his shoes, chastising himself for the forthcoming fib. "I can't remember the meeting place. Stupid, huh?" He gave her a feeble grin, hoping his reply was sufficient.

"Oh! She didn't say anything about a meeting place, only that you were all moving to England. I thought that was curious." She waited for a response and he delivered.

"England? But why would they go to England?" He scrubbed his head. It hurt from thinking. "Frau Stein, I'm confused. Are you saying that my wife arranged for our things to be loaded into a moving van and that she's gone off to England?" His voice sounded shrill to his own ears.

"Well, yes. But she said that you would join her at the end of the week. Is that not so?" Frau Stein's plump facial expression suddenly quivered with the apparent realization that Hart knew nothing of his wife's departure.

"Why would I do that?" he asked himself aloud.

She placed a trembling hand on her heart.

"Oh, dear me."

Hart led Frau Stein to the stair where he had been sitting moments before.

"Frau Lange said you had taken a new position with a manufacturer in Hastings. She said you'd had a falling out with your father."

"A new position! A falling out with my father!" he yelled. "That's—that's—ludicrous!"

Frau Stein cowered at his volume.

Another rap sounded at the door. Paul pushed it open at the same moment as Hart bellowed at Frau Stein.

"What is it, son?" He walked briskly to Hart's side.

Hart repeated Frau Stein's story, still in disbelief.

"I don't understand ..." Hart exclaimed.

Paul interrupted, thanking Frau Stein and escorted her to the door. He asked if he could call on her later if he needed further information. She nodded excitedly and turned on her heel, her matronly body scooting along the pathway. She was reputed to be the neighbourhood gossip, Hart told him, and no doubt was anxious to share the scandal with her husband and the neighbours.

❖

Seeing his son's distress, Paul took command of the situation.

"Collect some things, Hart. You can't stay here. You'll come home with me."

"But ..." Hart began to protest. "What if they come back?"

Paul gave his son a disbelieving look.

"They won't! Go pack your things. I'm going to call Albrecht. He's Chief of Police now. I'll see if he has any ideas. We may have to come back later, but, in the meantime, we can work in comfort at home."

Hart ran upstairs, while Paul called his friend and asked for help.

❖

An hour later, the *Polizeipräsident* rang the doorbell and Cook showed him and two police officers into the study. Hart paced to and fro, with an untouched glass of brandy in his hand. He stopped abruptly and set his glass back on the brandy tray when

Polizeipräsident Fritz Albrecht stepped into the room.

Chief Albrecht introduced the two officers, Constable Feld and Constable Klein. Paul invited them to sit and offered each a glass of brandy. They declined. Instead, the constables withdrew notepads and pens, while Paul asked Hart to relay the story of his family's disappearance. After considerable discussion, the five men drove to Hart's house and he walked them through the way his afternoon had unfolded.

"Feld and Klein are two of our best investigators," Albrecht said. "Let them review this information and do their jobs. They'll get back to you as soon as they have news. Please keep them informed if you discover anything else."

"Notify all ports and borders, as soon as you get back to the station," he instructed the constables, as they prepared to leave. "I'll follow along shortly."

"Fritz," Paul extended his hand to his friend. "Thank you for responding so quickly. Anything your men can discover will be helpful and appreciated."

"As you say, my friend. One of us will call you as soon as we know something. Stay strong, son," he said directly to Hart. "We'll find them."

"Thank you, sir."

They stepped through the doors to the sidewalk, Hart locking each door behind him. *Why do I bother locking them? The house is empty!*

"Do you mind if we add the background check that we did a while back to our current file?" Albrecht asked.

"Of course. Please do so," Hart replied, looking at his father. "Perhaps, now is the time for me to review it as well."

"I'll give it to you in the morning," Paul replied.

⚜

Miriam soon caught up to the moving van, then trailed it the rest of the way. She stopped when they stopped and gave the children time to play away some of their

pent-up energy. Her children were familiar with long drives—from the mountains
to Calgary and back, and to and from the
European vacations—and were not too dis-
ruptive. The older children kept Matthew
amused and the time passed. It was late
when they finally crossed the border into
the Netherlands.

Freedom at last! Miriam celebrated
silently.

CHAPTER FORTY-EIGHT

Early the next morning, the telephone rang as Paul crossed the foyer on his way into the dining room. He snatched the handset from its cradle.

"Ja," he barked.

Then he listened. When he hung up the telephone, he carried on into the dining room. Hart and Ilse were already sitting at the table picking at the cheese and black bread on their plates, their coffee untouched and cold.

"Was that the police?" Ilse asked.

"Ja. Miriam's car and the moving van were spotted a few hours after midnight, crossing the border into the Netherlands." Paul lowered himself into a chair.

"Paul, darling, you've gone awfully pale," Ilse said rising to his aid. "Are you all right?"

"Yes, my dear," he waved her away,

rubbing his chest. "I've just had a start, that's all. I'll be fine in a minute."

"They're going to Amsterdam!" Hart jumped up from the table and headed for the hallway.

"Where are you going, Hart?" Paul moved to stop him, but remained seated, clutching at his chest.

"I have to get to Amsterdam. I know where she's going, now. Vati, drive me to the airport?"

"Paul! Did you take your medication this morning?" Ilse demanded.

"Huh?" Paul turned his gaze to his wife, forcing a smile, then closed his eyes. "No," he said quietly, "I guess I forgot in all this chaos."

Conveniently, the cook appeared at that moment, and Ilse asked her to fetch Paul's medication and a glass of water.

While she continued to fuss over Paul, Ilse also encouraged Hart to delay his departure at least until he had a shower and shave and put on some fresh clothes.

"Taking time to improve your appearance will only help the matter," she said.

Sheepishly, Hart acknowledged the merit of her suggestion.

Paul reminded him that, if Miriam crossed into the Netherlands at such a late hour, they would already be in Amsterdam, so there was no need for him to rush off. Hart agreed, and while he prepared to travel, Paul telephoned Fritz Albrecht to review their options.

By the time Hart was ready to leave, Paul had taken his medication, and recovered from the shock.

Hart parked the sporty rental car at the curb, locked it, and trotted up the front stairs of the townhouse with the blue door. He listened, heard nothing, and knocked. He wiped his sweaty hands on his black cotton trousers. The door cracked open an inch.

"Mina!" he blurted.

Mina put her finger to her lips to stop him.

"Go next door," she whispered pointing to her left, "to the yellow door. I'll meet you there in a minute."

Confused, Hart turned around and took the stairs to the street, then ascended the stairs to the yellow door. As he raised his fist to knock, the door popped open.

"Come in, Hart." Mina opened the door wide, ushering him into the living room. "I've been expecting you," she said. Her ability to speak German was not as fluid as her mother's, but Hart understood her. In her hand, she held a deck of tarot cards.

"Miriam! The children! Are they here?"

"They're next door. Both townhouses are mine, you'll recall. The three of us lived in the other one until Miriam went off to Canada, then my husband and I moved in here. Too many sad memories in the other one. Nothing was touched when we left. It was easy enough to tidy it up now for Miriam."

"You'll want coffee and something to eat after your flight," she said, ushering him into the parlour and indicating a maroon sofa near the window. "The coffee is on. We can sit here while it brews."

Hart hung his jacket on the hook inside the door and removed his shoes. He joined her on the sofa, wondering how she knew he had flown, then realized the obvious.

"Confused, angry, frustrated?" She looked at him. He nodded. "I read the cards after I settled Miriam and the children into their beds. It was a long drive for her, alone, with the children. You have questions. I will answer what I can, and then we will ask the cards." She held up the deck. "Ah! I hear the coffee is ready. Give me a few minutes to organize it. We can sit at the table," she said, leaving him to ponder his current dilemma.

As he waited, Hart contemplated his mother-in-law. He thought Mina and Punita were both interesting women, scary maybe given the prophecy, but interesting nonetheless. She had never visited them, despite his offering on the rare occasion when she called to speak with Miriam. She told him once that her home brought her a sense of security and comfort. Her husband, Willem, had died the year before Hart had met Miriam, and she had no desire to be anywhere else. She had experienced enough in her life, she had told him, and preferred the quiet of her own space. *Willem,* he thought, *Willem van Bosch. My gosh! Vati knew him too! He's the one who died of a heart attack while running. If it were any other time, I'd ask Mina about it.*

Hart turned his thoughts from Willem van Bosch and found himself thinking of the first time he had met Mina and her mother. That odd evening, as the two women told him the story of their life, and the strange prophecy involving Matthew, Mina had delivered a warning.

"You must work hard to keep my daughter's interest," she had said. "The moment she becomes bored, she will leave you."

"My granddaughter has the true soul of our people," Punita had added, "and will not sit still unless something holds her interest."

"Your people?" he had asked, trying to comprehend her meaning

"Yes," Punita had replied. "My mother's people were nomads until the war."

Now, Hart watched Mina set the table, efficiently organizing the china, napkins, and cake. He offered to help, but she declined, saying she preferred to do it herself. She thought it good exercise to think of others from time to time.

"I miss my husband," she mused, smiling fondly as she flitted about the table like a small bird, petite, fine boned. "We worked so well together—we were like bread and butter, cream and sugar. Mama said it was our destiny, and she was right. Mama was always right." She laid out some cloth napkins and placed spoons on them. "It's a pity you never had a chance to meet him. I think you two would have found each other good company. He was a successful businessman too. Shipping." Her hands stilled, and her

486

face became a vacant space for a moment. When she began moving again, she looked directly at him. "He died unexpectedly, not long after my stepfather passed. Mama and I remember them every year." She swiped tears from her cheeks. "Remembered. Now, the remembering is left to me."

She straightened the dishes and disappeared into the kitchen again. When she returned a moment later, she set slices of cake on the table and continued.

"I loved Mama so much. Did Miriam tell you that she died of a massive stroke last spring?"

"She did," Hart responded. "I'm sorry for your loss. It must have been devastating for you."

"It was quick, thank goodness. No suffering." Mina smoothed a wrinkle in the table cloth. "I had hoped that Miriam and I would have a similar relationship, but that will never be," she said sadly. "Mama warned me the day Miriam was born. She said that name meant rebellious and disobedient. I have marvelled many times since at the way a person's name can chart their life path. Over the years, others have warned me to beware of Miriam's deceptions, too. I was blinded by a mother's love for a long time, but now I see her for who she is. She is so unlike Mama and me. I suppose I'll never understand why."

Hart observed Mina as she fussed about the table. *Her eyes are like Miriam's—pools of dark chocolate—alert with cleverness, but something is different too. It's kindness. I've never seen kindness in Miriam's eyes. She's beautiful. I can see Miriam's resemblance, but, again, Mina has a softness and Miriam doesn't. Opposites, yet the same.*

"There!" Mina stood back from the table, hands on hips, assessing her presentation. "The table is ready. Please sit. I will get the coffee pot."

Hart rose from the sofa and walked with measured steps toward the table as Mina scooted in with the coffee pot and poured out two cups. The tarot cards rested near her plate. He sat where she pointed, focussing on the blue delft of the china dishes. His mind was both empty and full. He felt numb. The nutty aroma of the fresh coffee permeated his brain when he inhaled.

Mina perched on her chair and served him a piece of spice cake.

"Eat," she encouraged. "You'll feel better. And you will ask good questions."

He did not want coffee or cake. He wanted his wife and children. But he knew she was right, and that if he acted on impulse, he could lose everything. He took a small bite of the cake and sipped his coffee, trying to settle his churning stomach.

As they ate, Mina invited his questions and answered as best she could. She admitted that she had not been aware of Miriam's intentions until the previous weekend, and she had had to scurry to prepare the townhouse with the blue door.

Hart realized how little he knew of Miriam's past and her family and said as much to Mina. Mina encouraged him to focus on his primary concerns.

"My past will not affect your future," she said kindly, pushing dishes aside and dealing the cards. She invited him to ask questions, while she read the answers. "I am sorry, Hart," she said finally. "Miriam is going to make your life unbearable, and your relationship with your son impossible. To Miriam, you are as the earth, solid and unmoving."

"That's not true!" Hart objected, "I can change ..."

"Hart, Miriam is like water. Free flowing—always seeking something beyond her reach. You could try to change the future, but it's hard to do, especially when Miriam's involved." Mina shook her head as if in surrender. "Mama tried."

Hart sighed.

"I will encourage Miriam to return to you," Mina continued. "If she won't, accept her decision, and find a way to stay in your son's life. I will do what I can, but Miriam is strong-willed and determined. She is also independent and selfish. She will have her way." Mina pushed her chair from the table, neatly stacking the cards. "Now, I will go next door and see if they're awake. Be patient. I'll see what I can do."

Mina returned about twenty minutes later, carrying Matthew.

"They are all still sleeping. But this little treasure," she said, caressing Matthew's crown, "is hungry."

She encouraged Matthew to go to his father and disappeared into the kitchen to find food for the little boy. Hart sat on the sofa, entertaining Matthew. In his heart, he hoped that Miriam would come and see how wonderful they looked together, that he was a good father. He hoped that she would change her mind and return to Bayreuth with him. His stomach ached with unknowns.

CHAPTER FORTY-NINE

Moments later he heard heavy, rapid footfalls on the outside stairs and the unlatching of the yellow door.

"Mama, did you bring Matthew back with you?" Miriam asked, as she kicked off her shoes.

She froze, her hand still on the doorknob, staring at Hart's shoes. Her head jerked up when Matthew giggled.

Hart was stunned. The hatred that he saw etched on Miriam's face betrayed her efforts at keeping her composure. He felt as if he had been punched in the gut. The coffee and cake that he had recently consumed congealed into a hard lump. His chest constricted and breathing became difficult. Never in their time together had he seen such a look.

"Miriam!" he said, as he stood to greet her. "My darling, what—?"

Miriam snatched Matthew from the sofa, holding him so tightly that the child screeched in protest. She backed away from Hart.

"Why are you here?" she demanded.

Hart struggled to find words.

"Mama," she yelled to the kitchen. "Why is he here?"

Mina came running from the kitchen, sending words of assurance ahead of her, trying to calm her daughter.

"Miriam, you had to know that Hart would come looking for you. He loves you, and you have his child."

"Children," Hart corrected, looking from one mother to the other.

"Yes, of course," Mina acknowledged, "children."

Miriam glared at Hart and sneered.

"You are cleverer than I thought. I expected you to run off to England, that I'd be gone before you'd find me here."

Confusion and clarity played across Hart's face as his thoughts raced to catch

493

up with the truth of her remark. Hart reached for Matthew, and she turned away.

"No!" she shrieked, alarming Matthew. The boy began to cry.

"Mama, take Matthew into the kitchen and shut the door. Now!" She handed Matthew to Mina and turned back to Hart.

"Miriam, I don't understand," Hart pleaded. "Why are you doing this?"

"Simply put. I'm bored. You bore me. I can't stand to look at you. I—" Hart reached toward her. "No! Don't touch me!" She stepped back, raising her hands to ward him off.

"But Miriam, what have I done ...?"

"Shut up!" she cut him off. "Get out!" Miriam pointed toward the door. "Get out now, or you will never see Matthew again."

"But, what about us?" Hart pleaded again. "Tell me what to do. We can fix whatever ..."

"No!" she cut him off again. Daggers of anger shot from her eyes, her face contorted with rage. "There is no *us*," she screamed. "We. Are. Over. Now leave!"

She jammed her finger at the door again, willing Hart to obey her command. Hart heard the finality of her words. He dragged himself to the door and put on his shoes and coat.

"Can I at least speak to my son first?"

"Mama!" Miriam yelled to the kitchen. The door cracked open. "Bring Matthew."

Mina came into the room, carrying Matthew. Matthew's hand, mucky with biscuit crumbs, clung to the emerald that hung above Mina's breast. Tears rested on his cheeks.

"Say goodbye to your son. And leave."

"Miriam, I don't understand any of this," Hart said, as he walked toward Mina, arms outstretched to take Matthew. Mina moved her supporting arm toward Hart, shifting Matthew's weight. A dry sob escaped through the mashed crumbs on Matthew's lips.

"No!" Miriam screeched again.

Matthew's bottom lip quivered in fear. Tears filled his eyes and he reached for Hart.

"Daddy, take me wiff you," Matthew cried, reaching small arms toward his father.

"Mama, you hold onto him," Miriam hissed. "Say goodbye, Hart, and ... get ... out!"

Hart stepped toward Mina to embrace his son. Matthew sobbed again and clung to Hart's neck. Mucky bits of biscuit stuck to Hart's collar.

"Daddy, Daddy," he sniffled.

Mina held Matthew loosely to allow the embrace but pulled back when Matthew tried to climb to his father. She looked at Hart, her eyes endorsing his pain.

"I'm so sorry," she whispered, gathering Matthew to her, tears filling her eyes.

"Go!" Miriam held the door open for him.

"Miriam, please," he implored once more as he passed her.

She shoved him free of the door and slammed it shut. He heard the latch lock with certainty. Hart took each step down to the street, feeling gravity pulling at his leaded feet. When he dropped into the driver's seat, he folded his arms on the steering wheel, lowered his head, and wept.

CHAPTER FIFTY

Hart returned to Bayreuth, broken-hearted, his dream of a happy family pulverized. Paul met him at the airport and he reported his experience.

"You might want to have a look at this," Paul said, handing him the file that he had kept under lock and key for several years.

As Paul drove, Hart scanned the documents. He felt his chest constrict and struggled to catch his breath.

"Speak to a lawyer tomorrow," Paul said. "The sooner you take control, the sooner you'll have Matthew back. I'm afraid the other two children will be lost to us."

They were approaching a Sparkasse Bank. Hart pointed toward it.

"Will you stop at the bank, Vati? I'm low on cash." Paul pulled over and waited.

Hart disappeared into the Bank only to emerge a few minutes later. Approaching his father's sedan, he threw his hands in the air with a gesture of frustration. Paul lowered the passenger window and leaned toward it.

"What is it?"

"Vati, you'd better come in." Hart hesitated. "She's cleaned out my accounts."

When they were married, Hart had created two accounts in their joint names—one for household expenses, and the other for savings. Every year at the end of August, he deposited a sum into the savings account, and Miriam transferred funds, as needed, into the other account to pay various household and other expenses. Before leaving Bayreuth, Miriam had closed both accounts using the same story she had given Frau Stein—that they were moving to England. The teller checked the bank's electronic records. The bank draft for the balance—a sum of over 85,000 Deutsche Marks—had been cashed that morning, in Amsterdam.

Hart confirmed that the closure of the two accounts was appropriate, opened two new accounts for his own use, and moved funds from his investment portfolio. He and Paul left the bank, angry at being duped.

"I strongly recommend you divorce the witch as soon as possible," Paul growled, as they slid into the car.

"Vati!" Hart was stunned at his father's vehemence. "She has to live. She'll need the money to look after the children."

"And set herself up somewhere else ... I'm sorry, Hart, but you must accept that she is gone. Miriam has finally shown her true colours."

Paul steered the car into traffic and headed for home. Minutes later, he turned off the street and drove his car into the garage. He switched off the ignition and turned to his son.

"I tried to warn you three years ago that she would be trouble. And now you must accept the truth of it."

"Yes, Vati. I admit it. Your sources were correct. And the warnings of Miriam's mother have come true, too." Hart stepped out of the car and looked over at his father, each man closing a car door simultaneously. "What was I to do? Matthew was just three months old! She is the mother of my child. I had to trust her."

Paul nodded sympathetically.

"She was so different this morning," Hart said, his words burdened with despair, "and she was very clear. Our marriage is over. There is no point dwelling on that. I will call Konrad Schneider tomorrow and ask him to commence the divorce proceedings. But I am far more worried about Matthew, and how to get him back. She can't take him away from us. She just can't."

Ilse hustled from the kitchen to meet them, anxious for their news. Paul led them to the study and poured them each a glass of brandy.

"Hart, get the door, will you? I know Cook is the only one around, but I'm more comfortable with it closed. Old habits ..." he said shrugging bashfully.

Hart took two glasses of brandy from his father and gave one to his mother, before he sat beside her on the settee. She snuggled close to him and took his hand. The comforting smell of sauerkraut and sausage tickled his sinuses and he inhaled deeply.

"Tell me. You came home empty-handed. I presume you have no good news," Ilse said.

Hart repeated his story, including the discovery at the bank, and the conclusions he and Paul had reached on the drive home. Ilse's tears flowed, unchecked, as she listened.

"What if we never see Matthew again?" she moaned.

⚜

The following morning, Hart met with his friend, Konrad Schneider. After graduating from the private school in Marburg, Konrad and Penn Tresler had attended university and studied law. Penn found employment with a government agency, while Konrad established a family law practice.

"This will take time," Konrad said, after listening to Hart's story. "Family law is complicated, and slow, and you're not just filing for a divorce, we have custody to contemplate too. Lots of hoops to jump through. In addition, we have to file similar documents in the Dutch court, in accordance with Dutch law."

"Are you saying you can't help me?" Hart asked, flustered by Konrad's explanation.

"Not at all! I'm on this, Hart. I would be remiss, though, if I didn't caution you to be patient." Konrad waited until Hart's eyes met his. "It will just take time," he said, "and there's little possibility of expediting the process. The simplest divorce can take six months, but I'm hoping two issues might expedite our work."

Hart fought himself for calm and waited for his friend to speak again.

"Now, what's important," Konrad said, "is proof. We have to give the court a reason to grant you custody, rather than Miriam. As I see it, Miriam took Matthew away from the family home and across an international border without your agreement. She also emptied your bank accounts without prior discussion and stripped your home of all assets. Is that correct?"

Hart nodded.

"I want to investigate whether we have a criminal element that could weigh to our advantage. Thinking out loud ... if we can prove a spousal kidnapping, and/or theft, we might advance our cause and the timing. I need you to think on this. Did Miriam give any sign that she planned to take everything and run?"

"I don't th—"

"Don't answer now. Go home and review her behaviour, her actions. Anything that, at the time, seemed odd. Anything that might now give us evidence of a premeditated act. If you come up with anything, let me know right away. In the meantime, I'll have a law student begin the research, and I'll start drafting documents. I'll call you as soon as I have something to review." Konrad escorted Hart from his office, giving him a final thought of encouragement. "Be patient, my friend, and remember, in order to out-fox a fox, we not only have to think like one, we have to be more astute about it."

Frustrated by delay, Hart returned to work and tried to focus on something else. In the meantime, papers were drawn and filed in the German courts for the divorce, and for custody of Matthew, and supporting documents were prepared in Amsterdam in anticipation of orders that favoured Hart. As Konrad had cautioned, Hart found the process protracted, in spite of his friend's assurance that the actions were fast-tracked.

In late June, Konrad telephoned Hart.

"Good news, the court has granted you a divorce and custody of Matthew. I've just sent documents by courier to our lawyer in Amsterdam. They'll be filed tomorrow with the documents he's prepared. He says, with luck, we should have a decision by early June."

Three months later, Konrad telephoned again.

"The Dutch courts deferred to the conclusions of the German courts and upheld the findings. Your divorce is recognized in the Netherlands, and you have legal custody under both courts of law. How soon can you get there?"

Two days later, an entourage including Hart, his Dutch lawyer, and several police officers arrived at the blue door, unannounced. Chaos followed. Miriam protested the custody arrangement and refused to co-operate. She demanded that they all leave and was furious when one of the officers advised her that they were obligated to enforce the custody order. Another officer restrained her, while she squirmed to get away, screaming obscenities and threatening all of them.

"Madame," the restraining officer said, in a calm and equally threatening voice, "I suggest you be quiet, now. Otherwise, we'll have to take you to the station."

Miriam's anger flared, but she stilled, like a cobra about to strike, her breathing heavy.

Mina, who had been sitting on the sofa reading a book to Matthew before the men arrived, sat quietly holding her grandson on her lap. Tears trickled from her eyes. Hart knelt before Matthew. Confused and frightened, Matthew tucked his face into his grandmother's chest when he saw the police uniforms, clutching the emerald that always sat above her breast as if it would bring him comfort. Hart hesitated for a moment, seeing Mina's silent plea glistening in her eyes.

"I'm sorry," he whispered, scooping Matthew from her lap, his eyes black with anger meant for Miriam. Mina sat motionless and closed her eyes.

"Daddy, Daddy. Where you bin? I miss you," Matthew asked in a small voice. "Why Mommy yelling at policeman?"

Hart rumpled his son's blue-black hair and gave him a reassuring smile. He realized that his son's questions were spoken in an odd mixture of English, German, and Dutch.

"I don't know, son. Shush now. Say byebye to Mommy."

Hart walked to the door, Matthew in his arms, and grabbed a jacket from the coat hook. Matthew looked over his shoulder and smiled at his mother.

"Bye-bye, Mommy. I go home now." Matthew waved to his mother as they passed.

Hart skipped down the stairs and slid into the back seat of the squad car. He continued to hold Matthew in his lap as he helped him into his jacket. Then he nuzzled Matthew and held him close, told him he loved him, and confirmed that they were indeed going home.

Seething with anger, Miriam slammed the door behind the police officers, threw the court documents on the floor and stomped on them. She walked to the window, yanked the lace curtains apart, and watched the cruiser drive away, carrying her ex-husband and her youngest child.

When she could no longer see the car, Miriam dropped the curtain and marched to the dining room. She grabbed Mina's tarot cards from the side table and began shuffling the deck.

"We'll see who wins this round," she muttered.

Mina continued to sit on the sofa, her head bowed in silence.

With Matthew now in his custody, Hart arranged to refurnish the house and moved back into it. Because Matthew had been in Amsterdam for his fourth birthday, Hart and his parents held a small birthday party to celebrate.

"Yay!" Matthew cheered, "More cake and presents!"

Hart enrolled Matthew into kindergarten, and took great care to shuttle his son to and from the school himself. He left a strict instruction that under no circumstance was Matthew to be released to anyone except himself, or his parents.

Life became a new normal for Matthew and Hart. Occasionally, during the first few weeks, Matthew asked for his mother and siblings, and then he asked no more.

CHAPTER FIFTY-ONE

As the months passed, Hart found himself pressured by friends to find female companionship. He entertained the idea and dated occasionally, but he did not feel a need to have a woman in his life permanently. He did not trust them, or himself. His two ex-wives had certainly proven his folly; however, he did wonder whether Matthew might benefit from a mother's influence.

In time, Konrad introduced Hart to a young woman who had lived in East Germany until the dismantling of the Berlin Wall began in 1990. As soon as she could, Leni Fischer had moved to Bayreuth, looking for work and a new, unrestricted life. She had found employment working in a dress shop managed by Konrad's wife, and the two women had become fast friends.

Hart admired the young woman for her strength and courage and invited her to dinner more than once. Jaded by his relationships with Miriam and Ursula, though, he promised himself that he would investigate her background before he made any serious overture toward her. *She makes me feel alive again, and I like it!*

In the fall of 1991, Hart finally introduced Leni to his family. They were celebrating Matthew's fifth birthday. Everyone, including Matthew, was charmed by Leni. Her effervescent personality drew people to her, the Lange family included.

The next morning, Paul told Hart that he planned to call his friend, Fritz Albrecht, to ask him to run a background check on Leni. He wanted to know who this woman was before his son made another grievous mistake. Hart concurred.

✤

Within the week, Constable Klein appeared at the office to deliver a folder of information with the compliments of the Police Chief.

"The lady's own reputation is unblemished," Klein told Paul and Hart. "Both her father and former husband have the colourful pasts."

Leni's father, Felix Fischer, had been forced into the Wehrmacht in 1941 at the age of fifteen. He had served on the Russian front and had been taken prisoner in 1945. As with many other Russian "guests", he was sent to a camp in Siberia. During the five years he was imprisoned, he had attempted to escape three times. He had been recaptured after his first two attempts but succeeded on his third try.

In 1950, Herr Fischer had walked home from Siberia to Poessneck, where his family continued to live. By that time, the city was within East Germany's territory. When he had arrived home, he was twenty-four and weighed thirty-eight kilograms. Not being dressed for extreme winter weather when he had escaped,

Herr Fischer's fingers and toes had frozen during his long trek. Two of his toes had to be amputated, and he lost the sense of feeling in three of his fingers.

"Herr Fischer," Klein told them, "eventually became a partner in a mill that owned a patent for the design and construction of lightweight wooden boxes. The unique design kept the mill in business, long after other mills had been closed by the Communist government. He married and had three daughters. Leni, the youngest, was born in 1964." He paused to review his notes. "In her youth, Leni enjoyed all forms of dance, and spent many hours learning the finesse of ballroom dancing. She met her former husband, Reinhold Bauer, in the dance studio. Bauer, a spy for the Stasi, had been tasked with marrying Leni and using the family relationship to extract intelligence about her father. Bauer appeared on the scene as a college student, with an interest in ballroom dancing. He wooed Leni doggedly. She finally agreed to marry him in 1987 and, because she was employed, she supported him through his studies until their divorce six months later."

"A spy!" Paul exclaimed.

"Yes sir," Klein replied. "In the meantime, Bauer reported to the Stasi that Herr Fischer was not a member of a communist party and spoke anti-communist rhetoric in his home. As punishment for his anti-communist beliefs, the East German government seized ownership of Herr Fischer's company. Disheartened, Herr Fischer died in 1989, soon after the Berlin Wall was torn down."

Paul thanked the constable for the report and escorted him out of the building. In his absence, Hart scoured the file, concluding that the summary given by the constable reflected the printed information. When he said as much to Paul, Paul locked the file in his fireproof cabinet. After further enquiry, Hart was elated to hear that his father felt a similar confidence in Leni.

"Third time lucky, I hope," Hart jested, sheepishly, when he told Paul that he planned to ask Leni to marry him.

The following weekend, Hart arranged for Matthew to stay with his grandparents and suggested to Leni that they go somewhere fun. Early Saturday morning, they hopped into his Mercedes, and he guided the vehicle south on the *Autobahn*.

"Where are we going," Leni asked.

"It's a surprise!" Hart replied with a mischievous twinkle in his eye.

Leni often told him that she had felt like Cinderella ever since they had met. She felt their relationship was magical, compared to her childhood in East Germany, where even the simplest luxuries were too expensive for her family.

Four hours later, when Hart turned his Mercedes into the parking lot of Neuschwanstein Castle in the village of Hohenschwangau, in southern Bavaria, Leni began to cry.

"Why are you crying," Hart asked, confused and concerned. He released his seat belt and turned to embrace her. "I thought you'd be happy."

"I am happy," she assured him through her sobs. "I don't know why I'm crying!" She swept her arm across the picturesque vista before her. "It's Cinderella's castle after all!"

Hart exited the vehicle and walked around to the passenger side. He opened Leni's door and extended his hand to her.

"Come," he said.

Leni unfastened her seat belt, collected her handbag, and accepted his hand.

"Are we really going in?" she asked.

"Sure! Why not?"

"I've dreamed of this castle since I was a small girl. I can't believe we're here!"

As they walked toward the castle gates, Leni stopped abruptly.

"What is it?" Hart asked, worrying that he had been too impulsive with his decision to drive to Hohenschwangau.

"I can't go in," she said. "My dream will be spoiled."

"Aw, come on," Hart said. "It's just an old castle."

"No," Leni said, standing firm. "I can't. It's my dream. I just can't."

Hart stared at her in disbelief.

"Are you certain?" he asked.

Leni nodded, tears still seeping from the corners of her eyes, eyes that glistened with happiness and stretched her smile wide.

"Okay," Hart said. "Then we'll just stand here and enjoy the view." He wrapped his arm around her shoulders and snuggled her close.

"Thank you," Leni whispered, holding his free hand firmly.

After several minutes, Hart stepped into her line of vision, obstructing Leni's view of the castle. When she turned her focus to him questioningly, Hart dropped to his right knee.

"Leni Fischer, will you marry me?" he asked.

Leni stood in wonder for many moments, then responded. "Yes, please."

Paul and Ilse hosted a small wedding in their home in the middle of November 1991, not so unlike their own wedding in 1945. Matthew too was excited to be part of the wedding.

"Now I have a nice mommy, not a mean one who likes to hit people and yells all the time!" Matthew declared during the wedding feast.

"Konrad will want this information for his file," Hart whispered sotto voce to the stunned wedding party. "I'll make further enquiries."

"Me and my daddy married my mommy last Saturday!" Matthew proudly informed staff at the kindergarten the following Monday morning.

Silvester celebrations were made extra special, when Leni chose the moment that the fireworks began exploding in the night sky to tell Hart that she carried his child. Hart was ecstatic to know that Matthew

519

would have a sibling. Paul and Ilse were pleased to hear that the family would expand again.

Hart twirled Leni in circles, her legs flying out behind her, giggling at his joy. He finally set her on her feet and held her firm when, dizzy from the twirling, her knees buckled. He kissed her passionately, not caring who noticed.

"Yay!" Matthew clapped his hands in glee. "A baby sister! I want a baby sister! Hurrah for the Lange family!" he shouted, hopping about under the brilliance and boom of New Year's Eve fireworks.

In January, Hart suggested that Leni consider working fewer hours, so she could take care of herself as the fetus matured. Leni agreed, counter-suggesting that she could use the time to focus on Matthew, taking him to and from school, solidifying her relationship with him, keeping him safe. He was already calling her Mommy, and she wanted to be his mommy in every possible sense.

✣

One morning in February, Leni walked Matthew into the school, then drove to a medical appointment. It was the end of her first trimester and she was scheduled for an ultrasound. The doctor told her it would be a routine procedure to document the development of the fetus.

Hart met her at the clinic and they were both delighted to see their child for the first time. They made a follow-up appointment in March for another ultrasound, during which, they were told, the sex of the new child should be visible. Although the sex of the child was not important to them, they were curious, nonetheless.

Hart kissed Leni soundly before tucking her into the Cabriolet that he had bought for her the week after they were married. She lowered the window and they chatted briefly, sharing the excitement of the new child. She put the car in gear and rolled onto the street, waving goodbye through the open window.

Hart inhaled deeply, enjoying the satisfaction and happiness he felt. Folding himself into his own sedan, he drove back to the office, effervescent with joy.

PART VI

SHATTERED DREAMS

CHAPTER FIFTY-TWO

Miriam was angry with herself. She had believed that the England ploy would distract Hart and keep him out of her way until she made her next move. She had been too slow and now it was too late. Matthew was gone, and so was her expected stream of income.

Stuck in Amsterdam until she could figure out how to get Matthew back, she bowed to Mina's suggestion that the older children be registered in the nearby school. *More time to think and plan.*

Miriam did not like the idea that Pauline was about to enroll in the same high school she had been forced to attend when she and her mother had moved into the blue-doored townhouse. *Oh, well, not here for long.*

Every day, Miriam consulted the tarot cards and constructed a plan to recover Matthew. Her confidence grew. The cards confirmed that, by biding her time, she would regain what she had lost. They also predicted travel to a distant place, and a new home, a safe home, with an abundance of wealth. Timing is everything, the cards told her.

By early February 1992, Miriam's plan was fully developed. She only waited for the cards to tell her when it should be implemented. Then the day arrived.

CHAPTER FIFTY-THREE

Late in the afternoon, on the day of her first ultrasound, Leni parked her Cabriolet outside the school and waited for Matthew. She was ten minutes early, but she liked to be early so she could park near the door. She cracked the window, so she could hear the bell marking the end of his day. As the bell rang, she left the car and walked toward the steps leading into the school.

The doors burst open, allowing thigh-high children to escape another day of learning. The cacophony of young voices filled the school yard. Leni smiled, watching for the small face that would call her name as soon as he spotted her.

"Mommy!" Matthew hollered with excitement, half running, half waddling, trying to pull his backpack on over his jacket.

"Matthew!" Leni waved her arm wildly.

A moment later, she was forced to take a step backward to absorb the impact of a five-year old wrapping his arms around her thighs. She rumpled his hair, laughing with him, bending her knees to bring her face level with his.

"How was your day, *mein Schatz*? Good?"

She helped him straighten his jacket and backpack.

"Uh-huh. Look! I drew a picture of us."

He held up a colourful drawing of stick people.

"That's Daddy. That's me," he pointed, "and that's you and our baby!"

Pleased with his drawing, he indicated a very small stick person that he had placed sideways, across Leni's stick belly.

"Matthew, this is so wonderful. Are you excited about the new baby?"

She stood again and took his hand, leading him down the staircase.

"Oh, yes, Mommy. I told everybody in

class today that it's already three months old!" He looked up at her. His small earnest face was framed in blue-black hair, long black lashes accentuating his charcoal eyes.

"Is it all there?" he asked, placing a small hand on her belly.

"It is. I have a photo at home. You can stick it on the fridge when we get there if you like."

"Yay! Okay!" he skipped off the last step.

"Want to hold onto your drawing so I can drive?"

"No, Mommy. It's for you." He stopped. "Put it in your pocket. And don't lose it!"

Leni folded the drawing carefully and put it in her handbag, instead.

"So it will stay crisp and safe," she told him.

Small children from kindergarten and first-grade filled the sidewalk with bodies and voices that encumbered their walk to the car. Leni did not notice the older boy sauntering down the street or a red compact car wending its way toward them. Matthew did. He stopped again.

"Mommy," he said, tugging on her hand. She bent to hear his words. "I know that boy."

He pointed.

"You do? How could you know him?" She looked up. He was only metres away.

"I think. I think he's my broth—" Matthew's words ended when the boy lunged.

The boy shoved Leni out of the way and grabbed Matthew roughly. With his little brother tucked under his arm, the older boy turned around and ran.

The red compact car had slowed, two car lengths behind Leni's sports car, but continued to roll forward. The driver reached behind her and unlatched the right rear door as the older boy neared it. Realizing what was happening, Leni ran in front of her Cabriolet and into the street, screaming for help and waving her arms trying to stop the advancing vehicle.

"My son! They're taking my son!" Leni screamed.

Somewhere in her subconscious, Leni heard the silence, saw parents stop and grab their children, but she kept moving. She heard Matthew's small voice shrieking as the older boy stuffed him into the red car.

"Ma—mee! Ma—mee!"

The little boy fought back. He kicked his legs and flailed his arms making it difficult for him to be stuffed into the car. Finally, the car door slammed shut, and the driver accelerated with purpose.

Leni felt the impact of the car's fender, felt the bones in her right calf snap. She felt the impact of her right hip on the hood when she rolled up and into the path of the forward-moving vehicle. She felt her neck jerk and her head smash into the hood as her legs rolled up the windshield, her body sliding, and then she felt no more.

⚜

Miriam had purchased a small, used automobile. She was not keen about the colour, but it was what she could afford. She hoped no one would remember that it was bright red. She kept Jacob out of school for the week, telling the administrator that he was ill. Her daughter, Pauline, was old enough to stay at home alone, and she made the girl promise not to tell her grandmother where she had gone.

"Try to avoid Oma if you can," she encouraged. "If she knows nothing, she won't ask questions."

"But ... where are you and Jacob going?" Pauline asked.

"I'm not going to tell you. That way, if anyone asks, you won't have to lie. We should be back in three days." Miriam grabbed her bag and car keys and called up the stairs, "Jacob, hurry up. We have to go."

Jacob came bounding down the stairs with his backpack stuffed with school books and clean underwear.

"Ready, Mom."

He stepped into his sneakers, grabbed his coat, and followed her down the front stairs of the townhouse.

Pauline watched through the lace-covered window as her mother drove the red compact down the street and out of view.

Miriam explained the plan to Jacob during the drive to Bayreuth.

"Try not to be obvious," she reminded him repeatedly. "We don't want anyone to realize who we are."

Jacob was nervous, but they had discussed and reviewed the plan until he knew it by heart. During the long drive and the overnight stay in a cheap inn, Miriam was adamant that he should have a clear understanding of what he had to do, especially if something went wrong. They had spent the earlier part of the day driving around the area where she knew the kindergarten was located, checking the most efficient way out of Bayreuth and onto the Autobahn.

"Well," she turned to Jacob as they approached the school, "this is it! Are you ready?"

"I think so," he said, wiping his sweaty hands on his faded blue jeans.

His heart raced. *Don't screw this up. She'll kill you, if you do.*

Miriam did not stop. She took the corner hard and slammed her foot on the brake pedal.

"Out! Now! Go!" she yelled.

Jacob had his hand on the door handle. He pulled the lever and jumped out as the car continued to roll forward. He stumbled briefly, but found his balance, then walked briskly down the sidewalk, his hands stuffed in his jacket pockets, head down, hoping that his dark skin would not be obvious in the mostly-white community. He reached behind his head and flipped up his hood, keeping sight of the car in his peripheral vision.

Jacob heard the school bell and quickened his pace, skirting around human obstacles. The doors of the school burst open and he spied Matthew running into the arms of a pretty young woman, wearing tight white pants and a white quilted jacket. The woman bent to speak with him. Jacob slowed his pace.

Miriam had warned him to let Matthew reach the curb, so he would not have too far to run. Jacob kept awareness of the car over his left shoulder and watched Matthew and the woman progress toward the sidewalk. He had not expected so many parents and small children. He quickened his pace again and deliberately walked into the young woman, bumping free her grip on Matthew. He swung around, hoisting Matthew under one arm, like he had seen North American football players do when they were running the ball for a touchdown. Matthew's small legs kicked in protest behind him. Jacob darted back to the car, not feeling at all like a football player.

Matthew kicked and screamed. He was stronger than Jacob had anticipated, and he had to use force to stuff his brother into the car before he could slam the door shut.

Miriam turned her head quickly, seeing Jacob struggling to sit up upright. Matthew sat crumpled on the floor.

"Ma-mee!" Matthew screamed again, beating his little fists against Jacob's leg.

Miriam turned her eyes to the road in front of her, both hands clutching the steering wheel.

"Mommy's here, sweetheart," she cooed, accelerating the vehicle forward.

Jacob bent forward and wrapped his hands around Matthew's middle. As he raised Matthew to sit beside him on the seat, he felt the impact and heard the pretty woman dressed in white scream. Matthew fell against him, momentarily knocking the wind out of both of them. Jacob had just enough time to see the woman fly over the hood of the car and crash into the windshield before Matthew blocked his view.

"Ma-mee!" Matthew screamed again.

"Shut him up! Now!" Miriam snapped.

Miriam turned hard at the next corner, braking only enough to take the curve, and accelerated again. Buildings blurred as the car sped past. Jacob had no time to watch. He struggled to get Matthew into a seat-belt so his little brother would be safe.

Miriam, swerving in and out of traffic, yelling over her shoulder.

"Stay down, both of you. I'm turning into traffic now and I don't want either of you to be seen."

Horns blasted at her erratic driving, but the sound diminished as the car sped onward.

Jacob wrapped his arms around Matthew, so he could not be seen from the street, and steadied his own body against the swaying movement of the weaving vehicle. He whispered reassuring words in Matthew's ear, trying to stop his sobbing. They remained curled together for some time, while Miriam negotiated through traffic.

"You can sit up now," she said sometime later, her voice flat.

They were on the Autobahn and Bayreuth was a half-hour behind them.

Jacob sat up, shifting Matthew into a more comfortable position, and held him securely. Matthew had sobbed himself to sleep.

"Watch for the police. If you see any police cars, duck out of sight again."

"Did you kill the lady?" Jacob asked.

"What lady?"

"Mom, you know. The lady in white. You drove right into her! Did you kill her?"

"There was no lady in white, Jacob. You must be imagining things. Now, shut up! I'm driving."

Jacob slumped into the seat again and closed his eyes. He wanted to throw up but knew his mother would not react well if he asked her to stop. He swallowed several times and inhaled deeply, until the urge passed.

"We need to keep driving until dark," Miriam said. "I'll pull over later and sleep for a bit. I want to be over the border and home by morning."

Jacob ignored his mother. He was happy to have his little brother with him, but he felt horrible for having to grab him. *I don't understand why she doesn't just talk to Hart about Matthew. Why did we have to do this? Mom doesn't think of others, only herself. I hate to see the pain she causes others, especially Oma. Now someone could be dead because of her.*

Jacob knew that what they had done was wrong. Fear gripped his belly and prickled the back of his neck.

CHAPTER FIFTY-FOUR

The intercom on Hart's desk squawked.

"Excuse me, Herr Lange. The Police Chief is on the line. He said it's important."

"Thanks, Helga," Hart said, reaching for the handset on his desk. "Lange."

"Herr Lange, Fritz Albrecht speaking," the Police Chief said urgently. "You need to get to Klinikum Bayreuth immediately. Your wife was hit by a car, and I'm told her condition is critical."

"What about my son?" Hart asked, rising from his chair and reaching for his car keys.

"So far as I know," Albrecht said, "he wasn't injured. The information I have at the moment isn't very detailed, nor is it reassuring. As I understand it, though, your son was grabbed by a dark-skinned boy and stuffed into a car. Your wife ran in front of the car trying to stop it."

Hart's mind spun with speculation, but for every question posed, Albrecht had no answer. He could only stress the urgency of Hart getting to the hospital.

"But my son!"

"I have men at the scene and they're interviewing witnesses. As soon as we have more information, you'll be the first to hear it."

Hart grabbed his keys and raced to his car, calling over his shoulder that Helga should consider him gone for the day.

As he sped along the Autobahn to the hospital turn-off in Bayreuth, he called his parents on the car phone and told them what little he knew.

Constable Klein was waiting for him at the entrance to the hospital.

"Herr Lange, your wife is in surgery. It will be a while."

Hart stopped in mid-stride, recognizing the constable.

"Can you tell me what happened? Where my son is!"

"I have some information, but not a full picture yet. Witnesses are still being interviewed." He extended his arm toward the admitting desk. "Perhaps you'd like to report to the staff that you're here, first. Then I'll tell you what I know."

The constable walked alongside Hart to the admitting desk and waited while Hart identified himself to the clerk. The clerk offered to page Hart as soon as she had word that Leni was out of surgery. In the meantime, Hart followed Constable Klein to a quiet waiting area where he started to impart the details of the incident.

"Albrecht already told me most of that," Hart said, holding up his hand to stop the constable. "This is all too much to fathom. Why would anyone kidnap my son?" As the words tumbled out of his mouth, he stopped. "Wait! Woman with dark hair and dark-skinned boy? They'll be headed north," he said. "You've just described my ex-wife and her son Jacob." Hart reached into his pocket and extracted his wallet.

From a slot within, he removed a slip of paper, which he handed to the officer. "This is her address in Amsterdam."

Constable Klein scribbled in his notebook and returned the paper to Hart.

"Police and ambulance were called, immediately. Frau Lange was treated curbside, then transported here. I'll leave it to the doctor to report on her condition." He paused again. "I'm deeply sorry, sir."

"I'll worry about my wife, constable," Hart retorted. "You find my son and bring him home!"

"Attention, please," a female voice squawked over the intercom, interrupting the hush of the waiting room. "Herr Hart Lange is asked to pick up one of the information phones."

Hart heard his name and went in search of a telephone.

"Your wife is out of surgery," he was advised, and given directions to a ward where he could speak to the attending surgeon.

Hart, walking smartly toward the ward, called his father and reported the information shared by the constable. He also speculated that Miriam was involved.

"Leni is out of surgery and I'm about to meet with the surgeon." He ended the call as he approached the nursing station, marking a tall man in hospital scrubs as the likely surgeon.

"Herr Lange?" the surgeon extended his hand, introducing himself and inviting Hart to a quiet corner for a private conversation.

"Frau Lange is in room 121B, just there." The doctor pointed to a room near the nursing station. "She is resting now and will likely sleep for some hours. We repaired the break in her right leg—both the fibula and the tibia. She has swelling in her spine, so we've stabilized it for now and will continue to monitor for damage. She has a concussion and some brain swelling. Her head hit the pavement quite hard. She's lucky she didn't land face first. It would have been worse. Lots of cuts and bruises, but they'll heal." He paused, as if searching for words.

Hart had been standing with his hands folded in front of him, head lowered, trying to grasp the doctor's words and control his emotions. He raised his head when the doctor paused.

"May I see her now?"

"Yes, of course ... but, there's one more thing you need to know."

Hart waited.

"Your wife was pregnant."

"Yes, three months." Hart's words halted as he absorbed the surgeon's statement. "Was?"

"I'm sorry for your loss, sir," the doctor continued, shaking his head. "The fetus aborted naturally. Given the force of impact ... well ... she didn't stand a chance."

Tears flowed unrestricted from Hart's long-lashed eyes, and a wave of nausea washed over him. "I don't feel well," Hart said.

The doctor was quick to grab Hart when his knees buckled.

"A chair here, please!" the doctor barked toward the nursing station.

An orderly, pushing a cart nearby, grabbed a chair and held it steady while the doctor lowered Hart onto it. Hart covered his face, rolling his head from side to side.

"No," he moaned, feeling a twisted fist in his gut. "No. Not again. This can't be. That witch has taken both of my children."

The doctor crouched beside Hart, watching his distress and not understanding his last remark.

"Sir, are you and your wife having difficulties?" he asked.

Hart looked up at the doctor, dumbfounded by the question. Clearing his thoughts, he answered.

"No. No! Of course not. I'm referring to my ex-wife. She's the devil incarnate. She kidnapped my son, and now ..." Hart waved his hand toward Leni's room. "Oh God! My wife! My children!"

The sound of rapid footsteps echoed down the hallway, growing louder with each step.

"Hart!" his father called.

"How's Leni?" Ilse asked, reaching for Hart's hand.

The surgeon helped Hart to his feet and led the three of them to a quiet sitting area.

"I must return to the OR. I have another surgery," he said. "I'll leave instructions at the nursing station. When you're ready, you can speak to the nurse assigned to Frau Lange's care."

Paul thanked the surgeon while Ilse comforted Hart. When Hart finally had control of his emotions, he told them about the kidnapping and relayed Leni's medical details. Together, they sat quietly, mourning the loss of Hart's unborn child and fearing for Matthew and Leni.

Leni's healing was natural, but slow. The swelling of her brain and spine eventually subsided with no immediate indication of long-term complications. The bones in her right leg knitted well. Eventually she regained her strength and the limp disappeared.

What could not heal easily was her psychological loss. She blamed herself for Matthew's disappearance, and mourned the death of her unborn child. Hart tried to encourage her, to give her strength, but he, too, felt an emptiness in his soul and mourned for both of his children. He claimed blame for putting Leni in a vulnerable position.

Hart framed the ultrasound print and a photo of Matthew taken during the kindergarten Christmas concert, and kept them on the desk in his office. Leni would not have them in the house. Guilt gnawed at her constantly. She was anxious and began smoking, hoping it would help. She quarrelled with Hart over the smallest of matters, straining their fragile relationship.

CHAPTER FIFTY-FIVE

M onths passed and the search for Matthew continued.

Hart reached out to his former classmate Penn Tresler. Penn had studied law with Konrad Schneider but chose to apply his talents another way. Instead, he worked in the Lyon office of the International Criminal Police Organization. After hearing Hart's story, Penn promised to do all he could to ensure INTERPOL's help.

The townhouses in Amsterdam were monitored. School registers were checked constantly. Airports and train stations were alerted. The Lange family waited.

In the meantime, the investigation launched by the Bavarian State Police resulted in criminal charges being made against Miriam, *in absentia*, for the abduction of Matthew, attempted murder of Leni, and the murder of Leni's fetus. If Miriam tried to enter Germany again, she would be arrested and tried for her crimes, but, she had no reason to return. She had custody of Matthew.

Hart contacted everyone he knew in North America and any connection he had ever made in any other location—including his old schoolmates—asking for help. No one had information for him, but all promised to watch for Miriam and the children. Those who could offered to contact their own connections too. Paul also made telephone calls.

The wait continued.

In October of that year, Hart and Leni were sharing Sunday dinner with his parents. As Cook placed a bowl of boiled potatoes on the table, the telephone rang. She excused herself to answer it and returned moments later.

"Herr Lange," she said to Paul, "a woman is asking for you. She says her name is Miriam."

Hart jumped up from the table and was about to push past Paul when Paul placed a hand firmly on his arm.

"Wait. We'll take the call in the study, on the speaker phone."

Leni perched on the settee, and Hart sat opposite his father at the desk, the telephone resting between them. Ilse sat next to Leni and took her hand.

"Who is this?" Paul challenged the caller.

"Paul, don't toy with me. Surely, you remember my voice. I have Matthew." The steely voice sounded calculating and empty.

"Prove it." Paul demanded.

They sat and listened to muted voices.

"She must have her hand over the speaker," he whispered. They all leaned toward the telephone.

"Say hi to *Opi*, sweetheart," the voice crooned.

"Opi! Opi, is that you? I miss you, Opi! Where's Daddy?" Matthew shouted, before his words were cut off abruptly. Muted voices followed.

JERENA TOBIASEN

"Matthew! Let me talk to Matthew!" Paul demanded, again.

"Listen. I proved it. That's all you get, for now."

"Miriam, for God's sake, what are you doing?" Hart interrupted.

"Oh! So, the puppet speaks!" she crooned again. "Shut up, Hart! Be a good boy, will you? I'm speaking to your father."

Leni and Ilse covered their mouths to stifle their gasps.

"What do you want?" Paul demanded.

"What do you think I want?" Miriam's voice was snide, provoking. "Money, of course. It costs money to care for your grandson."

"Ha! Now the viper speaks," Paul said, his voice dripping with sarcasm. "How much do you want Miriam? Another 100,000 Deutsche Marks? 200,000?" He raised his hand to Hart, halting any further interruption.

"Well," she said, her shrug palpable, "200,000 would be a good start."

"And ... what? I just give you the money?" Paul paused. "What about Matthew?"

"What about Matthew?" she mimicked Paul's question.

"When do we see him?"

"Ah! That's the best part," her voice was as sticky as maple syrup. "You don't! A child belongs with his mother. And you are going to pay me to take care of him."

"And if I don't?" Paul shot the words back at her.

"If you don't," Miriam's voice was threatening, "you will never see your grandson again."

"Vati!" Hart hissed.

"Ah, the puppet is worried. Poor puppet," she said, mocking Hart.

Paul coiled himself slowly, like a snake preparing to attack its prey. He inhaled deeply and released his response.

"The amount you ask is irrelevant. No amount will motivate you to return Matthew to us. I know your type." Standing, Paul shouted his rage at the telephone. "I will not allow you to use my grandson as a pawn. If you want money, return him to us!"

He punched the end button, terminating the call, and collapsed into his chair clutching his chest.

The four adults sat speechless.

Miriam never called again.

CHAPTER FIFTY-SIX

In the spring of 1993, Penn Tresler telephoned Hart.

"I think we have something. I just heard from the Dutch police chief that a child matching Matthew's description was registered in a school in Amsterdam, and he's been seen in the company of a woman matching your former wife's description. If the boy is Matthew, he's registered under an alias."

Hart rose slowly from his office chair.

"Are you able to fly to Amsterdam tomorrow? The police will meet you at the airport and take you to him." Hart assured him that he would be on the first flight the following morning.

"Expect to be there for a few days," Penn reminded him.

"If the boy is Matthew, arrangements will be made for you to appear in court and apply for custody. Take all of your papers—divorce, custody, passport, everything."

Hart thanked Penn for the information and replaced the receiver on its cradle. He snatched up a pen and began making a list of people to call. First, Konrad Schneider.

"Do you have all of your documents?" Konrad asked.

"Yes," Hart replied. "I should meet with the Dutch attorney."

"Absolutely! The last thing you want to do is appear in a foreign court without legal counsel. I'll take care of it," Konrad offered. "Let me know when you've booked your flight. I'll arrange for you to be met at the arrival gate."

They chatted a few minutes longer, then Hart hung up and called his travel agent.

"Book the hotel for a week," he said. "I don't know how long my business will take. If I need more time, I can take care of the extension myself."

As Konrad promised, Hart was met at the airport by his lawyer and a member of the City of Amsterdam Police Department. While the officer drove them into the city, his lawyer explained the court process.

"The officer will drop me back at my office, then take you directly to the school. There's no point taking any further action if the child isn't Matthew. The officer will stay with you until a representative from the Child Care and Protection Board arrives at the school. The rep will guide you from there." He handed his business card to Hart. "Call me when you're settled in your hotel. We'll need to talk about next steps."

Hart and the officer spoke with the school matron who confirmed that a boy matching Matthew's description had been enrolled at the school in January. The name given on registration was different though. The matron led Hart and the officer along a corridor that ran the length of the school and stopped near the second to last door.

She asked the men to wait, while she stepped forward and knocked lightly on the door's glass insert. A woman, the teacher, cracked open the door. In hushed tones, the matron asked that she send the new boy out. The teacher turned into the room, summoned the new boy to the door, and ushered him out to the matron's care. The boy stepped out of the room, and the teacher closed the door behind him.

"Yes, Madame?" he asked, looking up at the matron. He had not noticed the two men standing in the shadows.

Hart stepped forward into the light and lowered himself to a squat. Matthew recognized him and ran into his arms, almost toppling them both.

"Daddy! Daddy! You found me! I knew you would."

He buried his face in Hart's neck and sobbed, repeating a mantra of "Daddy, Daddy."

By the time they returned to the matron's office, a representative from the Child Care and Protection Board had arrived. He confirmed that the earliest court date he could arrange was the day after tomorrow.

"I want to keep my son with me at the hotel," Hart said. "I don't want him returning to that woman. She'll run again, and we'll never find her."

"Don't let them take me away, Daddy. Mommy's mean to me. She beats Pauline and Jacob. Daddy, I'm afraid!" Matthew clung to Hart.

The officer agreed to escort Hart and Matthew to the Board office for a further discussion and gave the matron his business card. The representative also gave her his card and an envelope containing a copy of the order for the custody hearing.

"Please deliver these to the boy's mother when she arrives to collect her son today. If you encounter any difficulties, telephone the officer."

Miriam sat outside the school, waiting in the red compact for Matthew to exit through the main door. She watched as other children from his class exited and headed for home, but Matthew was not among them.

Growing anxious, she collected her handbag, locked the car, and headed into the
school. She stopped at the administration
office and asked the secretary why Matthew had been detained.

The secretary excused herself and
knocked on the matron's door to announce
that Miriam had arrived. When she
returned, she ushered Miriam into the
matron's office, where she was invited to
sit in an old wooden guest chair. Miriam's
anxiety rose.

"Where's my son?" she demanded.
"What have you done with him?"

The matron calmly explained why her
son had been removed by the authorities
and that he was temporarily in the custody
of his father, pending a court appearance in
two days' time.

"How dare you!" Miriam shrieked, jumping to her feet and hunching over the matron's
desk, her face glowing crimson with anger. "I
trusted my son's care to you, and you let that
devil take him! How dare you!"

The matron tried to calm Miriam, without success. In the end, she managed to convince Miriam to accept the court documents and the police officer's business card and escorted her out of the school.

The matron returned to her office, shut the door and sat in the chair behind her desk, waiting for her shaking to subside. She had encountered difficult individuals in the past, but none had been as threatening as Miriam. The matron sincerely feared for her safety and reported as much to the police officer when she called him a few minutes later.

⚜

Miriam returned to her car, jerked open the door, and threw her handbag into the passenger seat. She started the car and sped toward home. At intersections, she sped up and honked to other drivers to get out of her way. When she reached the townhouse, she parked the car and stomped up the stairs. Slamming the blue door behind her, she picked up the telephone and pounded the officer's number into the handset.

Her voice was low and threatening when the officer answered. But he was ready for her. He let her rant for several minutes, then took control of the call as soon as she took a breath. He was polite but curt, told her to contact a lawyer and that she was expected in court in two days. Miriam threw the telephone across the room when the officer hung up abruptly. It smashed against the parlour wall, leaving fragments of plastic embedded in the plaster and a pile of broken bits on the floor.

Breathing heavily, she searched through her handbag for her telephone book and stomped into the kitchen to use another telephone to call her lawyer.

Hate and fury oozed out of Miriam's pores as she punched the lawyer's number into a second handset. *Hart will pay for this, big time!*

CHAPTER FIFTY-SEVEN

That evening Hart telephoned his lawyer to inform him that the boy was indeed Matthew, and that he had temporary custody until the court hearing in two days' time.

"The evidence is certainly in your favour," the lawyer told him the following day. "Your documents are in order. You have every legal right to the custody of your son."

As the lawyer reviewed what Hart might expect during the proceedings and how he could best impress the court, a young woman knocked on the boardroom door and waved at the lawyer from the hallway through a large, paned window. The lawyer beckoned her in.

"I just got off the phone with the Child Care representative," she said. "We have a problem." She looked at the two men and swallowed hard.

"Where's my son?" Hart demanded.

"He's safe," she said smiling. "He's keeping two of the secretaries entertained." The smile disappeared abruptly.

"This morning, I checked the case list for tomorrow. At the time, any one of the judges listed would have been agreeable to hear Meneer Lange's case tomorrow." She took a deep breath before continuing. "The rep said that an amendment was made to the list an hour ago. The judge now slated to hear the case is Dinah Meijers!"

"Oh no!" the lawyer said, pushing back into his chair. "This is not good news."

"Why?" Hart asked. "What's wrong."

"We will have to prepare a whole new approach for our argument tomorrow," the lawyer said. He removed his tortoiseshell bifocals and rubbed his eyes. "This woman— Dinah Meijers—is a relative of Eduard Meijers, the founding father of the new Dutch civil code. She knows the law well."

"But that's not the issue, sir," the young woman interrupted.

"You're right," the lawyer replied, placing his glasses on his nose again. "It is much worse than that—Judge Meijers was interred in a German concentration camp during the occupation. If the Allies hadn't arrived when they did, she would have been transferred to Auschwitz. I don't know all the details, but, from what I understand, the rest of her family was sent ahead of her. They never returned."

"So … she has a dislike for Germans?" Hart asked.

"Unfortunately, yes."

"Then let's get to work," Hart demanded. "I promised that I'd take my son home, and, by the grace of God and Judge Meijers, I'm going to do it!"

The courtroom was not ornate, nor were its furnishings. Judge Meijers sat behind a framed desk, built of light oak, mounted on a dais. Two long tables, the tops made of the same oak, were placed in front of the dais, one on the left, and the other on the right. Miriam and her lawyer sat at one table. Hart and his lawyers sat at the other. Behind them, in a row of chairs, sat the matron of the school, the police officer, a representative from the Child Care and Protection Board, and Mina.

Matthew was in the custody of another Board representative. Together, they waited in an adjacent room. A police officer stood guard outside the room to ensure Matthew's safety.

The courtroom was quiet. If anyone spoke, it was in whispers. They waited while the judge reviewed her notes or asked an occasional question for clarity. Parties to the case were given an opportunity to speak to the issues, the primary issue being the custody of Matthew and who was best suited for it.

Hart's lawyer remained confident that the argument was in his client's favour. He had all of the necessary papers, including the custody papers granted in Germany. He had evidence of Miriam's criminal behaviour and the charges made by the Bavarian State Police, as well as testimony from various authorities as to Miriam's instability and sinister behaviour. Aside from Miriam, Mina was the only person who spoke in Miriam's favour, saying only that she was a good mother.

As the proceedings continued and the judge began to speak, Hart looked across the room at Miriam. She had been talking with her lawyer and glared at him over the lawyer's shoulder, eyes like daggers. An all-knowing smirk gleamed in her dark brown eyes.

Hart returned his focus to the judge's words, smarting from Miriam's obvious hatred.

"How much longer?" Hart hissed at his lawyer. He glanced at his lawyer, then the judge, then the clock on the far wall.

The judge agreed that Hart had a legitimate and well-documented claim. She also acknowledged the criminal charges made against Miriam. When she rested her eyes on Hart, however, her words were sharp, annoyed.

"Meneer Lange, you appear to be in a hurry," she said, peering at him over her glasses. "We won't keep you much longer. Before I deliver my findings, however, I must say that your lack of presence in your young son's life is negligent. You have contributed no supervision, love, guidance, or financial support for almost eighteen months. Your behaviour is reprehensible!"

Except for Miriam and her counsel, the others in the courtroom gasped.

"Because of your lack of parental interest, I grant full custody to Mevrouw Lange," she announced.

Hart jumped to his feet, aghast.

"Meneer Lange, have you something to say?" the judge asked.

Hart's lawyer jumped to his feet, shoving Hart into a chair.

"No, Madame. With respect, please excuse the interruption, and continue with your findings," the lawyer urged.

"Thank you. I trust you can manage your client's behaviour for a moment longer?" She glared at the lawyer.

"Yes, Madame."

"Then let us finish," the judge said. "I have dinner plans." She glared at Hart. "I have decided to grant Meneer Lange conditional visitation privileges of one hour per month, and these visitations must be under the supervision of a representative from the Child Care and Protection Board. If your involvement in your son's life improves, Meneer Lange, the Court will consider increasing your visitation rights at a future date." She straightened the paper on which she had been writing, and signed it with a flourish, indicating to the court clerk that the matter had ended.

Hart stared at the judge in disbelief, watching as she handed the paper to the court clerk. It was then that he noticed the judge's exposed forearm, made possible only because the sleeve on her gown caught on the edge of her desk. The numbered tattoo on the underside of her forearm confirmed all he needed to know. She had experienced the brunt of Hitler's torture, and for that he and his son would suffer.

Hart was granted a five-minute visit with Matthew before his son was to be released to Miriam. He sat in the chair next to his son, who had been drawing a picture with crayons provided by the Board representative.

"Look, Daddy! I drew a picture of me and you."

Matthew held up a drawing of two stick people, identical except for size, each with a curved red line indicating a large smile.

"Can we go home, now? I miss Mommy. Is the baby ready?"

A knife of anguish sliced through Hart's belly. He had avoided speaking of the miscarriage to Matthew. He did not want to have to explain what happened, worrying that it would upset his son. Words were lost to him. He grabbed Matthew from the chair and hoisted him onto his own lap, hugging him violently, kissing his child's head and face, tears in his own eyes. Matthew squawked at his abrupt confinement.

"Matthew, the judge says you must stay here." He choked, trying to help his son understand why he would leave without him. "I can come and visit you."

"No, Daddy! I want to go home!" Matthew twisted to wrap his arms around Hart's neck. He sobbed hysterically into Hart's chest. "Don't make me stay here. I'm scared! Take me with you! Please, Daddy. I'll be good."

Matthew's words cut Hart to the quick. He peeled his son's arms from his neck and held his hands gently. "Matthew," he said, raising a hand to smooth Matthew's rumpled hair, "we have to do what the judge says." Hart hugged his son to his chest, trying to control the flow of his son's tears and stifle his own sobs.

"Why?" Matthew whimpered. "I want to go with you, Daddy."

Over Matthew's head, Hart looked to the Board representative. Tears flowed freely down her cheeks.

"I'm so sorry, sir," she mouthed, raising a tissue to mop her face.

A soft knock sounded on the door and they both looked up, watching it crack open. The form of the same Board representative who had been in the courtroom filled the void, as he widened the opening.

"Sir, it's time."

He pushed the door again, revealing that Miriam stood just behind him. Her tight-fitting brown wool suit hugged her curves. On her feet, she wore shiny stiletto heels. Complimenting her trim outfit was the gloat on her face.

Matthew turned his head at the sound of the male voice, in time to see Miriam step into the door frame.

"No!" he screamed hysterically, twisting back to Hart. He wrapped his arms around Hart's neck, restricting Hart's ability to breathe.

572

Hart stood, loosening Matthew's grip, but continued to hold the boy in his arms. Matthew tightened his arms again and wrapped his legs around Hart's waist.

"No, Daddy!" he pleaded. "No!"

The representative stepped toward Hart with his arms outstretched.

"Come along, Matthew. It's time to go home with your mommy."

He extracted Matthew from Hart's arms and stood him on the floor, guiding him toward Miriam.

"She's not my mommy. I don't want her. I want my daddy and my new mommy."

Matthew twisted free and ran back to Hart, wrapping his arms around Hart's thighs.

"Matthew!" Miriam snapped. "Stop your nonsense and get over here, right now."

She stamped her foot and pointed at a spot on the floor where she expected Matthew to stand.

Matthew buried his face between his father's legs, tightening his grip around Hart's thighs, and rolled his head, no. The man bent to Matthew's level and gently pried Matthew's fingers free, once again directing him to Miriam. Miriam lunged into the room and clamped her fingers into Matthew's shoulder.

"Ow! You're hurting me! Daddy save me!" Matthew implored, trying to wriggle out of her grasp.

Hart tried to intervene. Miriam pushed him into the wall with her free hand.

"Out of my way, loser!" she snapped.

"No! Daddy! Help me, please!"

"Stop!" Miriam demanded, shaking Matthew's shoulder. Taking a firm hold of her son's hand, she jerked him to her side and stomped along the corridor. Mina scurried beside her.

"*Auf wiedersehen*, puppet!" she sneered over her shoulder.

Her words bounced off the walls of the corridor. The spiked heels of her shoes clacked on the white marble floor.

Matthew's continued pleas for rescue finally disappeared when Miriam turned the corner and stepped into an elevator.

"Da-dee!" Matthew's muffled plea dissolved behind the closed doors.

When the elevator doors closed, Miriam turned to Matthew and slapped his tear-drenched face. She bent from her waist, so her face was in line with his and hissed.

"Shut. Up. Now!"

Matthew defied her.

"I hate you! I want my Da—" Miriam raised her hand to strike him again. Matthew moaned and lowered his head, hiccupping and sniffling.

Mina searched in her handbag for a tissue and stooped to Matthew's level. She dried his tears and wiped his nose, trying to assure him that everything would be all right.

"Shush, now," she said, running the back of her fingers lovingly down his tear-stained cheek. "Shush."

✠

Hart collapsed into his chair again, exhausted and deflated. The Board representatives apologized for the decision of the court and excused themselves, leaving Hart alone to regain his composure. His lawyer, who had waited outside during the custody transfer, stepped into the room.

"Meneer Lange, you have our sincere condolences. I've heard of Judge Meijers' decisions before, but I have never witnessed one first-hand. Her decision is unfathomable and reprehensible." He sat in a chair opposite and waited.

"If the judicial system appoints people like her," Hart said, steeling himself with anger, "how can anyone ever expect a fair decision?" He jammed his finger through his hair leaving blue black spikes behind. "How could that happen? If I didn't know better, I'd say that Miriam somehow paid her lawyer to move the case to Judge Meijers' court!"

"We have our suspicions too," the lawyer said, nodding toward his colleague who remained standing in the doorway. "We plan to investigate further."

"In the meantime, we recommend that you appeal the decision," the woman said, stepping into the room. "If we find enough evidence of wrong doing—"

"Just get on with it!" Hart barked. "Do you have any idea how challenging it's going to be for me to be here for a one-hour visitation, once a month! That's preposterous!"

"We will start the paper work tomorrow. In the meantime, I strongly recommend that you make every effort to meet the judge's requirements."

CHAPTER FIFTY-EIGHT

Miriam was infuriated that she had to ensure Matthew's presence once a month for his visit with Hart. In fact, she resented Hart's involvement in her son's life at all. She accepted, however, that so long as she was financially bound to Amsterdam, she had to make the effort. Failure to meet the terms of the court order could cost her custody, and loss of custody would mean loss of future income. The Lange family would pay up eventually, of that she was certain.

In the meantime, she was glad for her free accommodation and Pauline's allowance from Rask, but her savings were almost spent. *My lawyer charged a hefty premium for arranging to have the custody dispute heard before the Jewish judge, but it was worth every guilder! I'll just have to find a part-time job to supplement what I have, until it's time to leave for Canada,* she thought. *Everything will work out fine. The cards don't lie.*

For several months, Hart made the arduous three-day journey to and from Amsterdam for the one-hour visit with his son. *It's not just the timing that's difficult*, he worried. *The parting at the end is the worst part.* Each time, Matthew clung to his legs, repeating his heart-breaking plea and begging to return to Bayreuth. *How are we to endure this torture? Konrad needs to light a fire under the Dutch lawyer. We can't take this much longer!*

During the first visit, Hart gave Matthew a Steiff teddy bear, suggesting that, when Matthew was sad, he could talk to the bear and share his secrets. Matthew hugged the bear and promised to take good care of it. On subsequent visits, he always brought the teddy bear with him.

In the late summer, Hart arrived early for his visit, laden with birthday gifts. Matthew would turn seven in a few days. He waited excitedly in the room assigned for their visit and chatted with the case worker. As the clock ticked into the visitation time, the case worker checked her watch.

"Oh, they're late!" She excused herself to enquire. "There's no answer on the home telephone number. They must be delayed in traffic."

When the hour passed and Matthew had not arrived, Hart returned to his hotel room with the woman's promise that she would call as soon as more information was available. Late in the afternoon, the woman called to say that Mina had finally answered Miriam's telephone. "She said that Miriam and the children were gone, and had no idea where they went, nor a return date. In fact, in her words, she said 'consider them gone forever', then she began weeping."

Hart returned to Bayreuth, ill with worry and loss. Trying to find Matthew became his primary focus. But for his family's support, he would have become an automaton. They grounded him and encouraged his search. Paul re-engaged his connections—official channels and otherwise. Hart called Penn seeking his advice. Then he called Sofie and asked her to watch for his son.

CHAPTER FIFTY-NINE

Miriam would rather be anywhere other than Canada. She loved the thrill of Europe, but, she knew she was safer in the small mountain town. She was familiar with the people and could count on one hand the few she dared to trust.

When she finally had the money to leave Amsterdam, she bought four airline tickets to Calgary and packed their belongings. When she told her mother that she was never coming back, her mother begged her not to go.

"Miriam, please don't go," Mina begged. "Think of your children!"

"Mama, you know this won't work," she argued. "You and I are complete opposites. We can't live in the same city, let alone the same house!" She wandered through the bedrooms ripping clothing out of cupboards and drawers and slamming them into suitcases. "I can't breathe in Amsterdam. I'm bored, and it's irksome that I have to obey a stupid court order just to have custody of Matthew! He's my child for God's sake! Besides, no one will bother us in Canada. No one will even know we're there ... unless you tell them." She glared at her mother to ensure silence.

She phoned Pete Dense from the Calgary airport to let him know she was back, and he immediately issued an invitation for her to stay with him. *Pete is always a sure thing.* Then she piled her family and luggage into a cab and headed for a used car lot where she bought another cheap Corolla for the long drive into the Rocky Mountains. Several hours later, she parked the old Corolla at the curb outside the white house with the green door. In response to her knock, the door flew open, and she found herself smothered in a bear hug.

"Miriam, you're really back!" He stood aside, letting her into the hallway. "I can't believe it. I was quite surprised to get your call."

Miriam pushed the door closed and sidled up to Pete.

"What? No hello-kiss?" she asked.

Pete smiled and bent his knees, lowering himself to her height. A carpenter by trade, he had injured his back in a fall from a roof the previous year. *His age is starting to show.*

Miriam snaked her arms around his neck and pressed her body against him. He kissed her, with obvious yearning.

"God, I've missed you," his husky voice told her.

She gave him her sweetest smile. *Good old reliable Pete.*

Pete's hands lowered to cup her bottom. He pressed her closer, into his groin, and she felt his welcoming intentions. Miriam lowered her hands to Pete's shoulders and gently pushed him away.

"Slow down, Petey," she protested. "The children are in the car. I need to get them settled, and me showered, before I can be greeted by you properly."

✣

"Okay. Let me help you," Pete said, stepping back and letting the moment of passion pass.

He opened the door and led the way back to the Corolla. The children had fallen asleep during the drive from Calgary and were starting to stir in the cooling vehicle. Pete opened one of the doors.

"Hi Pete," Pauline and Jacob chimed. Matthew had never met him and snuggled closer to his sister.

"It's okay, Matthew," Miriam said. "Pete's an old friend of Mommy's. We're going to stay here for a while." She looked at Pete. "We are, aren't we, Pete?"

Pete smiled warmly at Pauline, reaching across to tousle her fuzzy brown hair.

"Of course. Hey, Jake. Come and help."

"Pauline!" Miriam barked. "Get Matthew out of the car and go inside. See that the two of you get washed and into bed."

Matthew's sister grumbled at their mother's command and climbed out of the car, hauling Matthew and his teddy bear with him.

Pete surveyed his four guests. He could never say no to Miriam. He was addicted to her. She made him feel alive.

CHAPTER SIXTY

On the same day, in the early spring of 1994, Hart received three pieces of good news. The first was a telephone call from his friend Sofie Walker. Sofie called to say that she had been skiing in the mountains—their favourite spot, she reminded Hart—and that she had seen Miriam. Miriam was waiting tables in the same pub where Hart had first met her.

"As soon as I realized that she was back, I headed back to my car and waited until she got off work," she told Hart. "I knew her shift would end soon, and I recalled that she likes to be home before the children get out of school."

"Did you find out where she's living," Hart asked.

"You bet! I followed her to a white house with a green door and a picket fence. When I saw her use a key to let herself in, I turned my car around and waited a few houses away. I wanted to be certain that the kids were with her. Sure enough, about twenty minutes later a mob of school kids started filtering down the street. Miriam's kids were easy to spot. The two older ones are so opposite in colouring, and then there's Matthew. My gosh! He's a miniature image of you!"

"Thank God!" Hart sighed heavily. "They looked safe and healthy to you?"

"From what I could see," Sofie assured him. "Say, isn't that the house where that Pete guy lives? I remember thinking he suited his name when I heard that she was involved with him."

"Pete Dense?"

"Yeah! Pete Dense," Sofie repeated the name, chuckling as she emphasized the surname. "Anyway, what do you want to do next?"

"Do you know any lawyers that can help me get custody of Matthew?"

"I do, as a matter of fact," Sofie replied. "The application will have to be filed in

British Columbia, since Miriam is living here. I've worked with a fellow in Vancouver several times. He's good. Let me talk to him and find out what's required."

As soon as the call ended, Hart left his office. His excitement at the news buoyed him on his drive home. He never imagined that his joy would be tripled.

He and Leni had made a home in the house that he had bought when Miriam was his wife. He had repainted it before he and Matthew had moved back in, then he had refurnished it as needed. When Leni had moved in, she had been quite vocal about the sparse furnishings. The only room that had reflected any sign of a loving home was Matthew's. Some of the rooms had remained empty.

Hart had given Leni free rein to furnish the house, to make a home for them, and she had. Leni had a creative nature, and she decorated it with many of her own designs, making it unique. Her enthusiasm inspired Hart and he added a few designs of his own, including built-in cabinetry in the dining room.

Hart paused at the main entrance and placed his hand on the Lange crest. He was home, and one day, Matthew would be too. He would think about that tomorrow. Tonight, he and Leni would celebrate.

Opening the second door, he inhaled the aroma of one of his favourite dishes. *Stroganoff!* He hung his coat in the closet, exchanged his street shoes for slippers, and wandered into the kitchen. Lifting pot lids, he released steam and the heady aroma of what was to come, confirming his earlier suspicions.

"Caught you!" Leni startled him.

He jumped in the process of replacing a lid and it clanged noisily.

"You're home early," she said, kissing him hello and nuzzling his neck.

He hugged her, inhaling again. This time, his senses filled with the fragrance of a woman, fresh from the shower and lightly scented.

"I can't decide which aroma I prefer in the moment. The stroganoff ... or ... you." He grabbed her and swung her around him. She held onto him, giggling.

"My goodness! You're in a happy mood. I haven't seen you this playful in a very long time." She looked intently at his face as he lowered her to the floor. His smile stretched from ear to ear.

"I've had some wonderful news," he said, taking a bottle of beer from the fridge, and removing the cap. With his free hand, he took hers and led her into the living room. He sank into a black leather sofa and patted the seat beside him. She sat and curled into him.

"What wonderful news might that be?" she flirted coquettishly at him.

"Sofie Walker called me a while ago. I wanted to share her news with you, so I left the office early." As he sipped his beer, he relayed Sofie's discovery and talked briefly of what that might mean for them.

A bell dinged in the kitchen.

"I have to get that," Leni said, unraveling from the sofa. "Dinner will be ready in twenty minutes. You have time for a shower, if you like."

"I'd like that very much," he said, rising to follow her. "Care to join me?"

"Ha!" she laughed. "Dinner would burn. Besides, I just had one."

A brief tussle ensued as they battled over whether Leni would re-shower. In the end, Hart went up on his own, while Leni finished cooking the last-minute vegetables and dumplings.

When Leni hollered up to let him know dinner was ready, Hart bounded down the stairs, still excited about the news of Matthew. He was pleased to see that Leni had set the dining table with particular care. She had even put a vase of flowers in the centre and a lit candle on either side. Steam rose from the bowls of Stroganoff, boiled potatoes, steamed vegetables, and dumplings.

"Flowers?" he asked. "Candlelight? My favourite meal?" Hart looked at Leni, his eyes shining. "What's going on? If I'd told you the news about Matthew first, I'd understand the celebration, but, you had this all organized before I came home." He pulled out her chair and, once she was seated, he sat at the corner next to her.

"You're not the only one with news," she said coyly, trying to hold back her smile, trying to look innocent. She held out her hand toward him. "Here, will you dish out the potatoes, please?"

Still looking at Leni, he reached for the spoon in her hand.

"What kind of spoon is—?" He looked at what he held in his hand—a very small spoon, not big enough to hold more than a tiny mouthful. He looked at Leni. Her smile grew larger as she watched realization dawn on his face. He slid off his chair, onto his knees beside her. She turned toward him. Hart took Leni's hands again and looked up into her face. Her lovely round face, with wisps of dark hair framing her like the angel she was to him.

"A baby?" he asked, his voice barely audible.

"Yes, in the fall."

He wrapped his arms around her waist and laid his head in her lap.

"Life can be so cruel," he said. "But sometimes, just sometimes, it can be very wonderful!"

"Oh, by the way," Leni added, "I've quit smoking!" She tugged his hands and encouraged him to return to his chair.

"That is good news, indeed," he said. As he rose, he leaned into her and kissed her forehead. "I love you," he said, and held her hand for a long moment, blinking away the tears that welled in his eyes.

"I know."

CHAPTER SIXTY-ONE

On September 28, 1994, Julia Katharina made a quiet entry into the hearts of the Lange family. But for her gender, she was the image of generations of Langes before her: dark hair, dark almond-shaped eyes. Her face was round and her lips bow-shaped. *Cherubic* was the word people used most to describe her.

When her parents introduced her to her grandparents a few hours later, Paul interrupted the celebration.

"I have something," he said, reaching into a bulging pocket. From it he removed two small blue velvet boxes. "I have been remiss in carrying out a task that my father set upon me the day he died. I take full responsibility for the delay and apologize." He bowed slightly to show his sincerity. "On his death bed, my father gave me the ring that has always been given to the oldest son. This," he held up his left hand, "is a very old ring." These, however ..." He held out his hand. "... are new. I have one for you, Hart, and the other is for Julia." He handed one box to Hart and the other to Leni.

"Father wanted every Lange to have a copy of the ring, not just the first-born son. I have another one for Matthew, when the day comes that he is returned to us. And Joseph and Emma will receive theirs shortly."

Hart removed the ring from the box and slipped it on his finger.

"Thank you, Vati. This means a lot!"

A few days later, the telephone rang, startling Hart out of a deep sleep. Hart looked at the illuminated face of the clock on the night table as he reached for the handset. *3:30 a.m. Who—?*

"Lange," he answered.

"Daddy?" the voice whispered. Hart sat bolt upright, swinging his feet off the bed.

"Matthew? Is that—?" Before he could finish his question, a dial tone buzzed in his ear. *Matthew!*

"What is it?" Leni asked in a sleepy mumble, rolling over to face Hart. She lifted herself onto her elbow. When she opened her eyes and saw his face, she repeated her question. "Hart, what is it? Who is calling so early?"

"I think it was Matthew," he said, grabbing his bathrobe and shrugging into it as he walked out of the bedroom.

"Wait for me," Leni said, shrugging into her own bathrobe. She followed him down the stairs and into the kitchen. "Sit!" she commanded, turning on the light and taking up a can of coffee. She looked at Hart as he sat at the table and hung his head in his hands. "You don't look well."

"Something's not right. My chest hurts. I can't breathe," he complained.

"Hart!" Leni cried, seeing her husband slump in the chair, moaning.

She dropped the coffee can on the counter and grabbed the telephone. Coffee grounds spilled from the rolling can into the sink and onto the floor. Kneeling by her husband's side, Leni keyed in the emergency number and reported the circumstances. The dispatcher requested an ambulance and gave Leni instructions for making Hart comfortable until medical help arrived.

As soon as the ambulance peeled away from the parking lot, Leni called Ilse and arranged to drop Julia with her in-laws on the way to the hospital. Then she raced up the stairs, showered and dressed, and threw together a bag of the things that Julia would need for the day. When she had packed everything into her sports car, she ran back upstairs to collect their daughter. Leni wrapped the baby in a blanket and locked up the house. As she tucked Julia in her car seat, the little girl grunted once, and went back to sleep.

❖

"Daddy?" Matthew whispered, his hand cupped around the receiver. He tried to keep his voice quiet. He thought he was alone in the house and had already dialled the long-distance number when he heard his mother come through the kitchen door.

"Matthew?" she called up the stairs to him. "Matthew, come down and do your homework."

Matthew realized that he had no time to speak with his father and disconnected the line. He stuffed the handset under his pillow and fell to the floor as Miriam barged into his room.

"Why aren't you doing your homework? You know the rules." She stood in the doorway with her hands on her hips.

"I can't find my pencil," he said, standing up again. He walked past her out into the hallway. "I guess I don't need it for reading."

He went ahead of her down the stairs, took his school book, and curled into an armchair. He opened the book and pretended to read so his mother would leave him alone. His heart was still beating fast. *Daddy! I spoke to Daddy! I hate it here. I want to go home. I want to be with people who love me.*

Two days later Hart was released from the hospital. After a battery of tests, the doctor told him that he had angina and gave him strict instructions for ongoing care and management.

"I'll make sure he follows your recommendations, doctor," Leni stated. "We have two children who need their father!" She glared at Hart as she said the last.

A few hours later, Hart glanced at his watch, then placed a telephone call to Sofie. *She should be out of bed by now.* When Sofie answered, Hart brought her up to date telling her about Matthew's early morning call, and his own hospital visit.

"What's the status of the custody application," he asked.

"It's going well," she replied. "As a matter of fact, I suspect it's time for you to pay a visit. Can you travel?"

"I can," he said, "I have clearance from my doctor."

"Good, then let me talk to the lawyer. I'll call you later with a plan."

CHAPTER SIXTY-TWO

Miriam loaded soiled lunch dishes onto a tray and briskly scrubbed the table, readying it for the next customers. When she turned to remove the dirty plates, she stopped abruptly.

"Hello, Miriam," Sofie said, her smile genuine. "I haven't seen you in a long time."

"What do you want," Miriam snapped, feeling panic swirl in her belly. *I've been careless. She found me.*

"Nothing today, thanks," Sofie replied, reaching into a satchel that hung from her shoulder. "I just stopped by to give you this." She withdrew a thick envelope and handed it to Miriam.

When Miriam stepped back, refusing to take the envelope, Sofie set it on top of the dirty dishes.

"Consider yourself served, Miriam. You are to appear in Family Court in Vancouver, next month. You might want to get yourself a lawyer. You're in for a fight." Sofie turned on her heel and left the restaurant without looking back.

Miriam dropped the tray on the table with a loud clatter. Ignoring the gawking customers, she ripped open the envelope and scanned through the pages.

"What's going on, Miriam?" the manager of the restaurant asked. "You look like you've seen a ghost."

"Perhaps I have," she replied. "I need to leave. Now!" She ripped off her apron, dropped it on top of the tray, and stormed out to her car.

Miriam stabbed the key into the ignition of her old Corolla and twisted. The engine growled but failed to start. She pounded the steering wheel in frustration and tried twice more. When the motor sputtered to life, she released the clutch, stomped on the gas and cranked the steering wheel. She pulled out of the parking lot, onto the mountain highway, forced to push the gas pedal to the floor as a lumber truck barrelled toward her, horn blaring.

That was stupid, Miriam. Calm down. You need to think this through. Court in Vancouver, in a month. You don't even have money to hire a lawyer!

When Miriam arrived home, she reread the court documents thoroughly. *I'll have to draft the counterclaim myself. I can't afford a lawyer. And where exactly am I supposed to stay in Vancouver. Breathe! Maybe Pete will lend me some money. He likes Matthew. I'll ask. I should have the car checked too if I'm going to be driving through the mountains in winter conditions.*

❖

"What are you going to do?" Pete asked that evening as he leaned against his kitchen counter listening to Miriam's rant.

"I need to file a counterclaim," Miriam replied. Hands on her hips, she tapped a foot. "I'm not going to let him take Matthew!" Miriam forced herself to stillness, then she sashayed toward Pete.

"Petey, will you lend me some money?" Her lips formed a pout as she placed her hand on his chest and looked at him through long, dark lashes.

"How much?"

"A few thousand."

"A few thousand!" he exclaimed. "Miriam, do you truly believe that I have that kind of money? It's almost winter. I won't have work for the next six months, for gosh sakes. What little I have saved goes toward the mortgage, food, and other expenses while I'm out of work."

Miriam drew back in response to his rejection.

"I'm sorry," he said, shaking his head. "I can lend you the money—*l e n d*—to pay the cost of filing the counterclaim, but you have to pay it back. That's all I can spare."

"That's better than nothing," she said. "I'll take it!"

Late that night, Miriam telephoned her mother.

"Did you tell Hart where I am?" she demanded, when her mother answered.

"Miriam!" Mina's quiet morning shattered. "Of course not. What's wrong?"

"I need you to send me some money," she said.

"Why? What's happened?" Mina's thoughts raced to catch up with Miriam's lack of propriety. "How are you? Are the children all right?"

"We're fine," Miriam replied curtly. "Hart found us. He's filed for custody and I have to appear in court next month—in Vancouver! I need five thousand guilders to fight him. How soon can you send money?"

"Five thou—I don't have it," Mina said. "I receive a monthly allowance from Willem's investments, but not enough to send you that much money. I'd have to apply to have a greater sum advanced, and that could take months." The line was quiet while neither of them spoke. "Miriam, I'm sorry, I can send you a small amount, but—"

"Fine. Send what you can," Miriam snapped.

"Miriam?"

"What!"

"Dear, have you ever stopped to think that perhaps Matthew might be better off with his father? Your expenses—"

Miriam refused to hear another word from her mother and slammed the receiver into its cradle.

She departed for Vancouver early on a crisp November morning. Snowbanks lined the highway, remnants of a blizzard cleared by snowplows following a recent storm. By mid-morning, enough light filtered through the overcast sky for her to see that another blizzard would start soon. *Great! Old snow tires, a faulty clutch and a temperamental starter—what more could I ask for? Oh yeah, a blizzard! If I survive this drive, I hope there's enough luck left over to make Hart go away.*

By the end of the day, she was glad that she had left a day early. Once the snow started falling, she was forced to tuck in behind a semi-trailer so she could drive in its ruts. When it pulled into a truck stop for the night, she was forced to do the same. She followed the driver into the coffee shop and struck up a conversation with him. He invited her to have dinner with him and paid for her meal.

"Are you heading out on the road, again?" he asked as they walked toward their vehicles.

"No, I'll wait until daylight. When will you leave?"

"I'm going to get some shut-eye now," he replied, watching the snow falling in the glow of a street lamp. "This snow is supposed to turn to rain before daylight. As soon as it starts, I'll move out. Too risky for me to stay longer."

"If you think of it ..." Miriam smiled at him, batting her long lashes, "... would you mind knocking on the window of my car? I'd like to follow you again."

"You're going to sleep in that thing?" the driver asked, incredulous.

"Yup."

"You'll freeze!" The driver scrubbed his chin whiskers, deep in thought. "I wouldn't normally say this ... but, uh, you're welcome to join me in the cab. It's a little cozy, but it's warm."

"If you're sure you don't mind," Miriam said, allowing a smile to curve her lips upward.

CHAPTER SIXTY-THREE

Miriam arrived at the Court House two hours before the custody hearing was to commence, parked her car in the parkade, and retrieved her overnight bag from the trunk. From her pocket, she extracted a slip of paper with the address of a YWCA. The truck driver told her that, for a small fee, she would be allowed into the locker room to shower and clean up. Fortunately, the building was near the court house and she was showered, dressed, and sitting in the court room with ten minutes to spare.

Miriam glanced nervously around the court room, trying to identify the role of each person, and wondering where Hart was. A moment later, she heard familiar laughter and turned to see a handsome middle-aged gentleman enter the court room, still grinning, followed by Hart and Sofie Walker and seconds later, Paul

Lange. The lawyer genuflected before the court and led his clients toward chairs indicated by the bailiff.

Miriam sat alone on her side of the room, eyes bulged at the sight of Paul. Paul caught her look of astonishment and flashed her a confident smile.

When the judge entered, the lawyer and his party rose in deference. Miriam bounced out of her seat in response to the judge's scowl and stood rigid until Hart's lawyer began to sit.

The judge explained that the proceedings were in aid of a custody application arising pursuant to an order issued by the German court. He invited Hart's lawyer to address the reasons why custody should be granted to Mr. Lange, considering that the custody order was granted several years before. The lawyer explained to the court how his client's right to custody had been thwarted by the unscrupulous actions of the defendant, citing a list of dishonest and criminal events.

Miriam stared at her hands, folded over the court documents that rested on the table in front of her. The anger pulsing in her ears made it difficult to hear the lawyer's words. Occasionally, she took up her pencil and scribbled a rebuttal. By the time the lawyer thanked the judge for listening to his client's claim, and resumed his seat, Miriam's purple countenance betrayed the fury she fought to contain. When the judge addressed her, she jumped to her feet.

"Everything he says is a lie!" she shouted. "He's trying to take my son from me! He pays me nothing. Do you know how expensive it is to house and feed a child?" She pounded her fist on the table, trying to slow her heavy breathing. "He is never, ever going to take my child! Do you hear me!"

The judge peered over the bench, without saying a word. When it appeared that Miriam would be quiet for a moment, he leaned forward. "Ms. van Bosch, this court will not allow an outburst from anyone. If you continue your behaviour, I will have the bailiff remove you from the room. Do you understand?"

Miriam nodded.

"I have read your rebuttal, and I find nothing to support the decision made by the Dutch court, or to otherwise support your claim for custody. In fact, I find your actions reprehensible."

Miriam vibrated with frustration and anger but held her tongue.

"Mr. Lange's solicitor has produced a thorough history of the matter, and the testimony of two highly regarded witnesses." He gazed toward Paul and Sofie and nodded. "Aside from the counterclaim that you have filed, Ms. van Bosch, have you any other information that would help me decide this matter in your favour?"

"Matthew is my child! He has no right!" She glared at Hart.

"Mr. Lange has every right, and as far as I am aware, you have little, if any." The judge examined pages of paper spread across his desk, running his finger along the information. "Where is the child?" he asked. "He's not in the court room, and I don't see the address where he's housed."

"And I won't tell you!" Miriam snapped. "You're not getting him! If Hart wants to see him, he can pay!"

As the judge motioned the bailiff toward Miriam, she noticed movement out the corner of her eye and saw Sofie lean toward Hart's lawyer, passing him a slip of paper.

"Your Honour, may I be heard," the lawyer interrupted, as he rose to his feet.

The judge nodded.

"I have the address here." He approached the bench and placed the paper in the judge's hand.

"Very well," the judge said. He wrote the address on one of his pages, then he placed his pen on the desk and peered at the parties before him. "I have considered the information presented here today and have determined that the custody order issued by the German court is a valid and true document. Therefore, this court will uphold the findings of the German court and consider the most recent findings of the Dutch court out of order, and void." He picked up his pen and signed the papers with a flourish. "Mr. Lange, I suggest that you find your son immediately, and take him home." A moment later, the judge rapped his gavel, marking the end of the hearing.

Miriam grabbed her purse and the court documents and turned to leave the court room.

"Miriam," Hart said, walking toward her. "I—"

"Get out of my way," she said, shoving him into Paul.

In the hallway, her spiked heels clacked on the marble tiles, as her angry steps carried her out of the building and back to her car. She stabbed her key into the ignition, and the engine growled. *Damn!* She twisted

JERENA TOBIASEN

the key again, and the motor roared. *I have to get home before they do! I have a long drive ahead of me, but by the time I get there, I'll have a plan!* She pushed her way through rush hour traffic, honking at slow drivers to move out of the way, and being honked at by drivers cut off by her aggressiveness. On the highway an hour later, she checked her gas tank, glad that she had filled up at the truck stop. Travel through the mountains slowed to a crawl as she drove through another snow storm. *I should tuck in behind another semi. I should have put new snow tires on the car last month. The tread is worn and it's sliding too much. Oh well, I won't need them for much longer. Warm climate, here we come!*

⚜

On the doorstep of the court house, Hart shook hands with the lawyer and thanked him for his efforts.

"What will you do now?" the lawyer asked, looking at his wrist watch. "It's too late to drive into the mountains tonight."

"I've rented a plane," Sofie said. "A private car will pick us up in a few minutes. We'll stop by the hotel and pick up luggage, then head directly to the airport. It's rush hour now, so it could take us forty-five minutes to get on the plane. Then, it's a ninety-minute flight to Cranbrook, plus a ninety-minute drive to my holiday cottage. Plus, the time change. We should arrive before nine, provided we don't encounter any snow storms." She turned her attention to Hart and Paul. "I'll leave it to you to decide whether you want to wait until morning to collect Matthew."

"I know it will be late," Hart replied, "but I'm worried that Miriam may get there ahead of us if we wait until morning."

"Good thought," the lawyer said. "When I get back to the office, I'll contact the RCMP and let them know you're coming."

"Thanks," Sofie said, giving him a business card. "Call me if you have anything to report."

The lawyer raised his arm to flag a cab. As one pulled alongside the curb, the private car slowed to a stop behind it.

"Good luck!" the lawyer said as he closed the cab door.

PART VII

PROPHECY MET

CHAPTER SIXTY-FOUR

Two and a half hours later, Sofie and her guests climbed into another hired vehicle that took them to her cottage. As the men dozed in the back, Sofie made some phone calls to ensure that Matthew's pick-up would go smoothly. At the cottage, she retrieved some frozen food from the deep freeze and popped it in the microwave.

"Be right back," she said. "I'm going to change. Food should be ready in a few minutes. We can have a quick bite, then head for the RCMP detachment."

"I'd rather skip the food and just go," Hart said, glancing at his wristwatch.

"Son, it's been a long day," Paul said, his hand resting on Hart's arm. "If you don't mind, I would like a few minutes to eat something. Maybe freshen up."

"All right," Hart said, seeing the tiredness in his father that he felt in himself. "You sit, Vati. I'll set out some dishes."

As the microwave dinged, Sofie walked into the kitchen and deftly removed the container. She ladled a hot stew into three bowls, placed a basket of rolls on the table and offered to make coffee.

"The detachment isn't far," Sofie said, as they piled into her SUV fifteen minutes later, "nor is the house."

In less than an hour, Sofie's black SUV pulled up in front of the white house with the green door. Two RCMP officers in a Ford Interceptor pulled in behind her.

"Wait here," Sofie said. "Let the officers handle this." She exited the car and followed the officers up to the door but remained in the shadow.

In response to their knock, the porch light popped on and Pete opened the door. The officers explained the purpose of their visit.

"Where's Miriam?" Pete asked.

"Somewhere along the highway, I imagine," Sofie suggested. "We flew."

"You haven't heard from her?" an officer asked. Pete shook his head.

"I've heard that there's another blizzard over the Rogers Pass," the other officer said. "If she's smart, she will have pulled over till morning."

"Knowing Miriam," Pete said, "I doubt it."

⚜

While they watched the conversation unfold on the porch, Hart and Paul exited the vehicle and stretched.

"It's been a long day," Hart said to his father.

"And a lot of sitting!" Paul replied. "So, this is where you used to come skiing. Where you met her?"

"Ja."

In the next moment, Sofie and the officers disappeared into the house, leaving the two men waiting by the car.

"It's chilly up here," Paul said, flapping

his arms, watching his breath frost over and dissipate. "Refreshing!"

A few minutes later, the green door burst open and Matthew flew through the gate.

"Daddy!" Matthew exclaimed, jumping into his father's arms. "You didn't forget me! You found me!"

"Forget you!" Hart said, twirling his son in a circle and hugging him fiercely. "Never! It just took a while to find you." He set Matthew on the sidewalk and tousled his hair.

"Opi!" Matthew exclaimed again and ran to his grandfather. "You didn't forget me either!"

"Never," Paul replied. "You're a Lange, and a Lange is never left behind."

Twenty minutes later, three generations of Langes sat in Sofie's living room enjoying a family reunion. Sofie's quiet humming drifted in from the kitchen where she was tidying up dinner dishes left in haste earlier. An almost-full moon filled the picture window, reflecting its glow off freshly fallen snow, and illuminating the room as if it were daytime.

"If you don't mind, son," Paul said, "I think I'll turn in. It's been a very long three days."

"Could you wait a few minutes longer, Vati," Hart asked. "There's something I'd like to do, and I'd like you to be part of it."

"Of course." Paul rose from the armchair in which he had been trying not to doze and walked across the room as he stretched.

At that moment, Sofie appeared in the doorway.

"I'm off to bed, folks," she said. "See you in the morning."

"Good night," the three Langes chimed.

"Matthew," Hart said, scooping his son onto his lap. "Are you happy to be going back to Germany with Opi and me?"

"Oh yes!" Matthew exclaimed. "I can't believe you found me! I prayed every day that you would come and rescue me from that horrible witch." Anger flared in his dark brown eyes. "She is so mean, Daddy. I wish

Pauline and Jacob could come with us. Can I phone them in the morning and ask?"

"You certainly can!" Hart replied, "but don't be surprised if they decline. They're older than you, and they may have other ideas."

"Okay," Matthew said frowning. "But, I can still ask."

"Certainly," Hart replied. "Now, I have a surprise for you."

"A surprise! You always bring me surprises. Wonderful surprises!"

Hart laughed and tousled his son's ebony hair, then reached into the pocket of his trousers.

"This is for you," he said, handing a small, blue velvet box to his son. "Vati, would you like to explain?"

"Indeed!" Paul sat in a chair opposite Hart and Matthew and told the story of the Lange family crest.

"Like the one above the door?" Matthew asked, opening the small blue box.

"You remember?" Paul exclaimed.

"I could never forget, Opi."

※

Matthew extracted the ring, noting the rings on the left hands of his father and grandfather. He placed his on the same finger of his left hand, then held it up to show his elders. The weight of the crest caused the ring to turn, and the crest fell to the underside of his hand. Hart chuckled.

"I guess we'll have to have it sized when we get home," Hart said. "In the meantime, I think I can fix it in the morning so you can wear it, if you like, but you might be wiser to leave it in the box so you don't lose it."

"I don't want to lose it," Matthew said, removing the ring from his finger and placing it in the box.

"Good boy!" Paul said. "Now, can we all go to bed?"

"Can I sleep with you, Daddy?"

"I think we can bend the rules this one time," Hart said. "Come on, let's go. Sofie's already sound asleep, so be quiet."

CHAPTER SIXTY-FIVE

By the time she had passed Hope and turned north on Highway 5, Miriam's fury had settled into a simmering anger. *Hart is not going to get Matthew. I will win. I just need to get home before them. We'll be gone before they can get there.* She pushed the speed limit at every opportunity, but one snow squall after another hampered her progress. The roads were either too slippery or too snow-covered to even travel at the posted speed limit. *If this snow is slowing me down, they'll be stuck too. But I know the roads. I'll beat them.* Once she reached the Coquihalla summit, she had to reduce her speed again and follow in the treads of semi-trailer trucks. She stopped briefly in Kamloops for gas and a snack, then pressed on. Near the summit of Rogers Pass, she encountered a snowfall so heavy that she could no longer see treads on the road in front of her and realized only then that the last truck she had been following had disappeared. *He probably pulled over at Revelstoke and I failed to notice,* she muttered. *Fool! I have no choice now. I'll have to pull off and wait for the snow ploughs. If Mama had loaned me the money, I'd have good snow tires and could keep going. This is all her fault!*

Miriam yanked an old blanket from the trunk, which she kept for emergencies. *Not that there are many emergencies,* she thought, sniffing at the blanket and wrinkling her nose in response to the smell of mildew. She crawled into the back seat of her car and wrapped her coat around her, before adding the blanket as an extra layer of warmth. She was exhausted and immediately fell into fitful slumber, not noticing that the snow ceased falling a mere fifteen minutes later. She slept until her shivering woke her up. Groggily, she rubbed the frost from the back window and, for a brief moment, marvelled at the clear, quiet night and the almost-full moon.

She exited the back seat to survey her surroundings. The road was barely visible and the snow too deep for her to go further without the ploughs. She opened the driver's door and started the ignition. Leaving it running to warm up the car and clear the windows, she trudged toward some nearby bushes to relieve herself, glad that she had changed into winter clothes during the Kamloops stop. *I'd better get the car in a better position so I don't get trapped behind a pile of snow when the ploughs show up.*

Having no choice, Miriam followed the slow-moving ploughs until she reached Golden and turned south onto Highway 95. She stopped at an all-night café to buy a coffee and climbed back into her car. *The roads look better along this stretch. I should be able to make up some time. It's not even sunrise yet. I just need to be home before Matthew leaves for school.*

As Miriam pulled out of the café parking lot onto the service road, accelerating without hesitation, the horn of an oncoming tractor-trailer blasted. She knew she had cut him off, but she had no time to think about the niceties of driving. When she heard screeching brakes and a thud, she glanced once in her rear-view mirror and saw the fruits of her impatience. The rig that had swerved to avoid hitting her vehicle had collided with a white pick-up truck. She kept going. *I'm almost home. Nothing's going to stop me now!*

Miriam gripped the steering wheel to hold the car steady when it swerved on the icy service road, then accelerated beyond the speed limit as she merged onto the highway. The vehicle fish-tailed around curves and she was forced to release the accelerator to take them cleanly. *This is crazy! The cards never revealed any of these events.* Eventually, the road flattened out and straightened as it followed the course of the rushing Columbia River. She relaxed. *Now I can make up some time. The road will be easy for a whi—*

From a small side road on Miriam's left, a blue sedan with frosted windows pulled out onto the highway, directly in her path. She slammed on the brakes and the car spun full circle as it continued to careen along the highway. Her vehicle slid sideways for several yards, finally coming to rest across the lane. She felt her heart racing. *Great! Just what I need. So close to home and someone runs me off the road! Idiot!!* She straightened the car into the lane and accelerated again, wiping her sweating hands off on her thighs as she did so. Moments later, she approached the blue sedan and pounded her hand on the horn, holding the blast as she passed it, and cut her return to the lane short, sending the sedan into a skid off the road.

"That'll teach you!" she screamed. "Idiot!"

She felt the pounding of her heart lessen, but the adrenalin rush spurred her on.

Near the beginning of Spillimacheen, she heard a clunking noise coming from the front wheels and had difficulty controlling the car's direction.

"Not now! I don't have time for this!"

Damn you, Pete, if you had given me the money I needed, I could have winterized the car and had snow tires put on before I left. Just wait till I get back. You'll get an earful. I wouldn't be sliding all over Hell's half acre if I had winter tires, and I'd be home by now.

Eventually, the highway climbed higher than the river and the snow-white land in between. The height of the frosted trees that edged the highway was deceiving because of a sheer drop-off. She glanced at the clock on the dashboard frozen forever at 3:15.

"Damn!" With one hand on the wheel, she shoved up her sleeve to expose her wrist-watch. The car wandered across the lane when she took her eyes off the road, but she quickly straightened it out. Her watch read 6:05. "I'm going to make it before Matthew leaves."

In the moment of relief that followed her realization, Miriam began to finalize the escape plan that she had been formulating since she left Vancouver. Anxiety drove her onward—the need to arrive before Matthew could leave for school, the need to gather their belongings and head for Calgary before anyone could stop her. Then her anxiety gave way to rage and resentment as she focussed on the reasons she needed to leave.

"Hart! You're a fool!" She shouted out loud in the speeding car. "You think you can best me, but you can't." Her mind raced with burning emotion. Her focus on the road wavered.

As she neared the turn-off to Bugaboo Provincial Park, she heard the clunking sound again, bringing her attention back to the road conditions and her surroundings. Her hands clasped the steering wheel tightly, her knuckles whitening. Her elbows locked as she struggled to maintain control. The road curved to the left, but, as she tried to turn the steering wheel, the car continued in a straight line, racing off the highway toward the metal barrier. She clamped her jaw tight as panic seized her.

Time seemed to slow. Miriam saw the metal barrier split in two, unable to absorb the pressure of the projectile that entombed her. And then she saw nothing but tree tops and false dawn.

As the car dropped into the trees below, Miriam saw her fate rushing up to meet her—a fate that the cards had overlooked. She screamed with realization.

CHAPTER SIXTY-SIX

The next morning, Sofie made waffles topped with whipped cream and strawberries to celebrate Matthew's return. As they munched through their breakfast, they talked about the return home.

"We're going to spend a few days in Vancouver," Hart said. "Rain isn't the best weather for a tourist, but Vati and Matthew have never seen the city and who knows when we'll return."

"Soon, I hope!" Sofie replied, sitting taller in her chair and giving them an encouraging smile. "Or at least Calgary, or here. You know you're welcome any time."

"Ja, I know," Hart said, "but, aside from rescuing Matthew, Canada doesn't really hold a lot of good memories for me."

"Maybe a tour of Vancouver will change your mind," Sofie replied.

In that moment the doorbell chimed,

and a loud rap pounded on the front door of the cottage.

"I wonder who that could be," Sofie said, looking at her watch. As she walked down the hallway, she called back over her shoulder, "The plane leaves at two. We should think about getting ready for the drive to the airport."

"Mrs. Walker?" an RCMP officer asked as Sofie opened the door.

"Yes."

"May we come in?" The officer gestured to his colleague.

"Of course," Sofie replied, taking a step back and inviting the officers into the hallway.

"Is Hart Lange still with you?"

"He is. We're just finishing breakfast. Please come through to the kitchen."

"We don't want to interrupt your meal," a second officer said.

"Nonsense," Sofie insisted. "Please come through."

By the time the officers reached the kitchen, most of the breakfast had been cleared away, and Hart was wiping the table. He greeted the officers and invited them to sit.

"Did I hear you ask for me?" Hart said.

"Yes sir." The first officer spoke again. "We've just come from the home of Peter Dense, and he suggested that we could find you and Matthew here."

"Are we short on paper work?" Sofie asked.

"No," the second officer replied. "We have some unfortunate news." The officer looked at Matthew, then settled his gaze on Hart. "Perhaps, Mrs. Walker, you might like to take Matthew—"

"No!" Matthew declared, sidling toward Hart. "I'm staying with my Daddy."

Hart indicated that the officer should continue, then sat in one of the chairs and pulled Matthew to him.

"We received a report a while ago from one of the highway patrols. They were called out just after sunrise. A truck driver said he watched a car skid through a turn and go off the highway near the Bugaboo turnoff. He stopped his rig in the nearby rest stop, but there was nothing he could do to help. The car was lodged in the trees. By the time emergency services arrived and extracted the driver, she was in rough shape."

"She?" Hart asked.

"Yes," the first officer confirmed. "The driver was Miriam van Bosch."

"Mein *Gott*," Paul muttered. "Will she be all right?"

"No, sir," the second officer continued. "She died en route to the hospital. She was pretty banged up. The medic said she died of head injuries."

Hart hugged Matthew tightly, but the boy pushed away.

"Daddy, is my old mommy dead?"

"Yes, son, she is."

"That's okay. She was bad."

Hart hugged Matthew to him again, rubbing his back for comfort.

639

"What will happen to Miriam's remains?" Paul asked.

"It looks like a straightforward case," the first officer replied. "The body will be released as soon as the coroner signs the death certificate."

Sofie offered the officers a coffee before they took their leave, but they declined.

"There is one more thing," the first officer said as he rose from the table. "She was conscious for a brief time during transport and asked that a message be passed along. We told the other children already, but Matthew, you might like to hear too. She said 'tell my children I'm sorry'."

"Mommy didn't know how to say sorry," Matthew cried. "She was always right!" Matthew turned his face into Hart's shoulder and sobbed.

"I'll walk you out," Sofie said, quietly leading the officers toward the front door.

"I'd like to make funeral arrangements," Paul said after the officers departed. "She was the boy's mother after all."

"Thank you, Vati," Hart replied. "I agree. I'll call Mina. She should be here too." He looked at his watch. "If I call now, I might just catch her before she goes to bed. Excuse me. Matthew, you stay with Opi."

✿

"Don't worry," Hart told Mina a short time later. "I'll make the arrangements and call you back. You just be at the airport in time for the flight."

"May I bring a friend?" Mina asked.

"Of course," Hart replied. "Let me grab a paper and you can give me details."

Next, he telephoned Leni and told her what had happened.

"Don't come," he said. "Vati and I will manage. Perhaps you could check on Mutti for us. Tell her that we'll be delayed. Let Helga know too. I'll call you in a few days and let you know when the funeral can be held, and when we'll be home."

✿

Mina telephoned her friend to tell her about Miriam and invited her to attend the funeral. While she awaited Hart's return call, she wandered through the townhouse with the yellow door, making a list of items she would need for winter weather in the Canadian Rockies.

Miriam spoke of the beauty and wildness of those mountains so often. Perhaps she loved it because her spirit was the same.

She tugged a suitcase from a cupboard on the lower floor and dragged it up the stairs. *What will become of her children?*

⚜

Sofie met Mina at the Vancouver International Airport and, using a lot of hand gestures and an English-Dutch dictionary, conveyed her from the Vancouver arrival gate to a private hangar near the South Terminal. As they approached the hangar, Mina looked around, eager to spot her former roommate.

"Astrid!" she exclaimed, when she spied her friend. She dropped her suitcase and ran into Astrid's arms. Together, they embraced and wept.

Sofie hesitated for a few minutes, giving the two women time to collect themselves, then ushered them toward the awaiting Learjet 75.

CHAPTER SIXTY-SEVEN

A few days later, Miriam's mother and children stood over the frozen ground that would soon enfold Miriam's casket. Although the gathering was sombre, Hart realized that no one shed a tear. When they met in Sofie's cottage for hot drinks and remembrance afterward, Jacob spoke with bitterness.

"I hate her, and I'm glad she's gone," he declared. "We wouldn't be in this mess if she hadn't left you, Hart. She made me grab Matthew from the school." Tears trickled from his eyes. "I'm sorry, Hart. Is your wife all right?"

Hart hugged Jacob and assured him that Leni was well. He said nothing about the child she lost, feeling a fleeting heaviness in his heart.

"I won't miss her either," Pauline said. "Pete has been more of a parent to us than she ever could be. Pete's house is the only place that really feels like home for Jacob and me." She stepped into Pete's arms and sighed as he hugged her.

"Well," Matthew said, "she was our mother, and even if we didn't love her, we should wish her a happy time in heaven. Shouldn't we, Daddy?"

"That's a generous thought, son," Hart said, placing his hand on his son's shoulder. Matthew shrugged.

"She was mean, though. She hit Jacob all the time, and one time she punched Pauline right in the tummy." Matthew smiled at his siblings. "If it wasn't for Jacob and Pauline, she would have hurt me lots. They protected me." Matthew looked at his grandmother and Astrid. "Was mommy always mean?"

Mina gasped, covering her mouth with a handkerchief, unable to restrain a sob.

"No, child," Astrid replied in her lyrical voice. "Your mother was a beautiful young girl, full of life, full of curiosity. Then, one day, she changed and we never understood

645

why." Astrid gazed at Mina. "Did you ever discover why she changed?"

"Nee." Mina shook her head as she replied in Dutch, her voice barely audible.

⚜

Mina stood alone near a large paned window with a view of the mountain top, hugging a coffee mug to her breast.

"Now I know how Mama felt," she said as Astrid walked up beside her. Although each woman was multilingual, Dutch was the only language they shared.

"What do you mean, dear?" Astrid said, rubbing her friend's arm with concern.

"Mama said she was afraid to let anyone love her. She thought that everyone around her died because of her. That's not true, of course, but that's how I feel."

"What's that," Paul asked, joining the two women. "Did I hear you speak of your mother? Punita?"

"Yes," Mina replied, switching to German, as she stepped away from Astrid. "I was just reminding Astrid how reluctant Mama was to marry Dr. Hendrik, my step-father." She smiled warmly, thinking of her mother and the doctor. The fingers of her free hand wrapped around the emerald that hung from her neck. "The good doctor asked her to marry him two weeks after I was born, and every year after on my birthday. She always declined. She was afraid if she told him that she loved him, he would die. She had loved her parents and my father deeply, and they died. It sounds odd, I know, but that was her belief."

"But she married him anyway?"

"It took a lot of convincing," Mina said, offering a small smile, "but yes."

"And now you feel the same way," Paul said. "Is that it?

"Yes." Mina smiled meekly, her teary brown eyes meeting his.

"You have eyes the colour of melted dark chocolate," he said, his memory reaching into the past. "Like your grandmother's and your mother's."

A tear escaped and trickled down Mina's cheek. Paul wrapped a comforting arm around her shoulders. When her sobbing stopped, Mina translated their conversation for Astrid.

"I think I'll help Sofie in the kitchen," Astrid said, excusing herself. "I can't follow German. You can fill me in later." She made a slight bow to Paul and headed for the kitchen.

"Pauline and Jacob will remain here with Pete," Mina noted, "and Matthew will go home with you and Hart. And my beautiful, wild daughter will remain in these mountains, frozen here forever." She clasped the emerald necklace again. "And I will return to my empty townhouse and await the day that I will be reunited with my family."

"Mina, you're not alone," Hart said, crossing the living room to stand beside his father. "I heard what you said, and it's not true. You are a part of our family as much as Matthew is. You are his grandmother.

648

You are the voice of the legacy that your family leaves Matthew, just as my father is. You will never be alone. Never!"

"What are you three talking about?" Matthew asked.

Paul stooped and lifted his grandson to the height of his elders and looked into the same brown eyes as his grandmother.

"Mina," Paul said, "fate decided long ago that you and I would be family, and no matter what events have tried to thwart that connection, the evidence is quite clear." He set Matthew on the floor and tousled his blue-black hair. "This boy is clearly a Lange. His bearing and his colouring will tell you that. But he also has the dark brown eyes that look like melted chocolate, the eyes that your grandmother long ago prophesied would be important in my life."

Mina reached for the left hands of Paul and Hart. Holding them before her, she examined the hands closely.

"I've never noticed this ring before, Hart," she said. "It is something new, yes?"

649

"Yes and no," Paul said, and briefly told her the story of the Lange crest.

"I have one too!" Matthew said, pulling the blue velvet box from his pocket. "It's too big right now, so I'm keeping it safe." He opened the box and withdrew the ring. Placing it on his finger, he plopped his left hand on top of the two hands that Mina still held.

Mina sighed and smiled, as she released their hands.

"Then I have a story to tell you too." She lifted the emerald and held it in the palm of her hand. "This stone has been handed down for centuries to the first daughter of every woman in my family. Until Pauline was born, the first daughter of every third generation was named Punita. Pauline should have had that name. Mama said that when Miriam chose to name her baby Pauline, she broke the tradition, changed the path of our destiny."

"May I touch it?" Matthew asked.

"Certainly, sweet boy." Mina leaned

forward and Matthew reached to hold the stone in his hand.

"Wow!" he exclaimed. "It's alive! I can feel it's heart beating!"

Mina cocked her head sideways and smiled.

"Then the path has indeed changed," she said. "Not everyone feels a pulse when they hold the stone. It appears that the stone has chosen you. When the time comes, you will wear it as many before you have, and one day you will pass it to the next one who feels the heartbeat, as you call it."

The three adults stood shoulder-to-shoulder encircling Matthew, embracing him in their love and legacy. Mina looked into the dark eyes of the men who chose to welcome her into their family. She placed one hand on Matthew's crown and grasped the emerald once again.

"This is Rosalee's prophecy!" she declared. "From this day onward, we three must nurture Matthew to ensure that he fulfills his destiny."

651

Paul and Hart each gently placed a left hand atop Matthew's crown. Matthew twisted beneath the weight of the three hands. His chocolate brown eyes shone up at them full of love and delight.

"We will," the two men replied.

NOTE TO READERS

Thank you for reading *The Destiny*, Book III of the Prophesy Saga. I hope you enjoyed the adventure as much as I did.

Other readers find reviews helpful for locating books they prefer to read. All reviews are appreciated.

Don't forget to visit my website: jerenatobiasen.ca, to read about my other works and inspirations.

ABOUT THE AUTHOR

"The thrum of city life runs through my veins, and I draw energy and inspiration from my west coast lifestyle. I've had stories swimming in my head my entire life, and when I returned to the west coast, those stories surfaced with a determination to be heard."

Jerena Tobiasen grew up on the Canadian prairies (Calgary, Alberta and Winnipeg, Manitoba). In the early '80s, she returned *home* to Vancouver, British Columbia, the city in which she was born.

Although Jerena has occasionally written short stories and poems since her return to Vancouver, it was not until 2016 dawned, that she began writing her first full-length manuscript, which was set primarily in Germany during World War I and World War II. When that draft was complete, she travelled to Europe and traced the steps taken by the story's primary characters. Then, she rewrote that manuscript, embellishing it with experiences and observations. The manuscript evolved into three volumes, the first of which tracks a family of German soldiers through two world wars *(The Crest)*. The second volume tracks a family of Roma who are forced to flee Germany during the early years of Adolf Hitler's round-up of undesirables *(The Emerald)*. The third volume reveals what can happen when the paths of two very different families collide *(The Destiny)*. Together, these volumes became the saga *The Prophecy*.